BANANA KING

NGÔO TSÍN-SUĪ

Also by Wang-tai Lee

Syu Bang-Sing (2021, Taiwan Interminds)

Gao Sai Zhe Yi Jia (2018, Mirror Fiction)

Harima-maru (2016, Yuanshen Press)

Du Jiao Ren Wang Guo (2015, Chun-Hui Books)

BANANA KING

NGÔO TSÍN-SUī

a novel

WANG-TAI LEE

TRANSLATED *by* TIMOTHY SMITH

Shadelandhouse
MODERN PRESS

Lexington, Kentucky

Banana King Ngôo Tsín-suī
a novel

English translation
First edition 2024
Literature from Taiwan Hakka
Translated by Timothy Smith
Translation copyright © Hakka Affairs Council, 2024
All rights reserved and controlled by Hakka Affairs Council
English translation completed with the support of the Hakka Affairs Council.

All rights reserved/Original title:《蕉王吳振瑞》
Originally published in Taiwan by Mirror Fiction Inc.
Copyright © Wang-tai Lee, 2020

English translation printed and manufactured in the United States of America.
Published in the United States of America by:
Shadelandhouse Modern Press, LLC
Lexington, Kentucky
smpbooks.com
Shadelandhouse, Shadelandhouse Modern Press, and the colophon
are trademarks of Shadelandhouse Modern Press, LLC.

ISBN: 978-1-945049-44-6 (paperback)
Library of Congress Control Number (applied for)
Cover and book design: iota book
Cover images used under license from stock.adobe.com.

*To all those Taiwanese who were born and grew up under Japanese colonial rule
and, after the change to the Chinese Nationalist Party's one-party rule,
endeavored to submit, or endeavored to not submit,
but who all continued to re-study and re-adapt until the end of their lives.*

CONTENTS

INTRODUCTION

The full name of our "Hakka Literature" is "Taiwanese Hakka Literature." We use Taiwan as a regional category for Hakka literature because Hakka people live in places all over the world, especially in Southeast Asia. In addition to having the same Hakka language, and culture, Hakka people from different countries and regions, all identify with different nations and therefore could never produce the same kind of Hakka literature. Aside from the history, culture, and life of the Hakka people in Taiwan, the essential elements for the production of Hakka literature in Taiwan are also inseparable from the history, natural environment, and realities of Taiwan.

Because the use of Hakka language has continued to decline over the past two hundred years, the number of "invisible" Hakka who are not able to speak the language has increased. The Hakka population only accounts for about one-sixth of the current population of Taiwan. The ancestors of most Taiwanese Hakka were farmers who immigrated from Fujian and Guangdong provinces during the Qing Dynasty in the early eighteenth century, and most of them continued to farm the fields and mountain slopes in Taiwan. Not only was the process of emigrating across the sea full of hardship, blood and tears, establishing a presence in the history of Taiwan was also extremely difficult. Depicting these difficulties became the special mission of Hakka writers, as well as a unique literary nutrient in their work. In order to record the history of their ancestors' emigration, their pioneering labor opening up the fields, as well as their cultural background as immigrants, Hakka writers have produced literature in all genres, and this is part of the uniqueness of Taiwanese Hakka literature.

By far, the majority of Hakka ancestors who immigrated to Taiwan were illiterate, but they still expressed the process of crossing the sea to Taiwan, and the dangers, difficulties, setbacks and disappointments that they encountered in the early days of emigration in their oral traditions. Those who listened to the famous *Dutai (Crossing to Taiwan) Elegy* know that the pathfinders who first made the crossing told tales of how "in Taiwan money flows like running water." Yet those who followed them soon discovered that "Taiwan is a mountainous deathtrap" and "of the thousands of people who go there, none return." Although the ancestors felt deep resentment and anger about the immigration experience in which "for every ten who went, six died, three stayed and only one returned," three out of ten who stayed left behind songs that testify to that history.

This was the character of the ancestors who passed down these songs. Even if you didn't die and you couldn't go back, you just kept your head down and worked hard to survive. And so it was that the illiterate Hakka ancestors left behind ballads like the *"Camphor Refining Song"* and *"Ramie Making Song,"* describing their lives amid peril. In songs like *"The Song of Wu A-lai,"* they described tragic heroes who sacrificed their lives in ethnic conflicts, and they evoked their exploits in fighting rebellions in songs like the *"Jiang Shao-tzu Memorial Song."* These works of Taiwanese Hakka oral folk literature, collectively called *Chuan-tsai*, (Tales) are narrative poems with seven-character lines. Although they have a rhyme scheme, they are completely different from Chinese poems written by literati. Their tone and content are deeply colored by the hues of the lives of commoners, and most importantly, *Chuan-tsai* reflect the documentary quality of Hakka literature.

Beginning with the end of the nineteenth century, Taiwan was colonized by two foreign regimes for more than a hundred years. Taiwanese literature thus entered an era of colonial resistance. The "Taiwan New Literature Movement" launched in the 1920s was part of an anti-colonial alliance fighting shoulder to shoulder with the Taiwan social movement to seek national self-determination. Hakka writers Long Ying-tsung, Chang Wo-chun, Chiu Chun-jung, Lü He-ruo, and Wu Cho-liu were all part of this alliance and played important roles. Wu Cho-liu wrote his novel *The Orphan of Asia* at great risk during the final stages of the Second World War. This work recorded the anti-colonial thinking of Taiwanese intellectuals under Japanese rule and opened a new chapter in the history of the documentary tradition of Hakka literature.

After the war, Wu Cho-liu continued to use Japanese, which was banned by the new Chinese Nationalist Party regime. He wrote two novels, *Figs* and *Taiwan Forsythia*, which serve as a testament to history, and also continue the tradition of Hakka documentary literature. In the postwar era, Chao-cheng Chung wrote *Taiwanese Trilogy*, *The Mahebo Situation*, A *Loyal and Confident People—The Biography of Chiang Shao-tzu*, and *Raging Sea*. Chiao Lee wrote *Brotherhood of Tapani*, *Wintery Night Trilogy*, and *Grievance. 1947. Grievance.* Li-ho Chung never finished his *Song of Tawu Mountain*, but the immense documentary writing tradition constructed by all these works is undoubtedly the greatest contribution of Taiwanese Hakka literature to Taiwanese literature in general. From documenting individuals to documenting ethnic groups, and even documenting the nation, Hakka literature not only remains close to the history of Hakka ancestors' migration and settlement but is also intimately linked to the living culture of later Hakka groups.

The special documentary quality of Hakka literature has not only flourished among Hakka writers who write in other genres but has also become the greatest weapon of Taiwan's decolonial literature.

As Taiwan's Hakka literature enters the twenty-first century, it will produce another season of bountiful harvest. The Hakka Council has thus made a timely launch of "Translation and Overseas Promotion of Hakka Literary Works 2021-2023" which has seen the translation and publication of eight Hakka works:

1. *The Poetry of Kuei-hai Tseng*, 30 poems, published in Taiwan in Chinese, English and Spanish.

2. *The Poetry of Ching-fa Wu*, 30 poems, published in Taiwan in Chinese, English and Spanish.

3. *The Poetry of Fangge DuPan*, 30 poems, published in the United States in English.

4. *The Poetry of Fang-tzu Chang*, 43 poems, published in Ecuador in Spanish.

5. *Anthology of the Short Stories of Chiao Lee* (1) including "Record of Taimu Mountain" and eight other short stories. Published in Czechia in Czech.

6. *Anthology of the Short Stories of Chiao Lee* (2) including "Searching for

Ghosts" and eight other short stories. Published in Ecuador in Spanish.

7. Ching-fa Wu's novel, *Youth Trilogy*. Published in the United States in English.

8. Wang-tai Lee's novel, *Banana King, Ngôo Tsín-sui*. [Publication forthcoming in 2024] in the United States in English.

The eight published translations selected for the project are samples from the past century chosen in 2020s as we look back over the glorious panorama of Hakka literature in Taiwan. Among the authors of the four collections of poems, Fangge DuPan (1927-2016) was a leading poet in Taiwan's modern poetry circles. She began writing in Japanese, then transitioned seamlessly to Chinese and Hakka. Her poetry provides a perspective on the history of poetry in postwar Taiwan. It is also a testament to social changes in postwar Taiwan. Dialogue with political hegemony and the redemption of a devout Christian are the two main axes of DuPan's verse. During the February 28th Incident, relatives whom she admired were massacred for no reason by the military. Because of this, she felt resentment and hatred, and was even more perplexed by the evil of human nature. Deploying a gentle irony unique to female poets, she condemns the brutality and cruelty of the regime and is guided forward by the force of Christian love and inclusiveness. Fangge DuPan's poems are not only a model of Hakka female poets, but also an exotic flower in the garden of Taiwan's modern poetry.

Kuei-hai Tseng (1946-) is a doctor and a poet. Since the 1980s, he has expressed his concern for the people, things and environment around him with the caring heart of a doctor and an eye made meticulous, acute through medical training. The facets of his experience that have unfolded in the course of his life are the same facets developed in his poems. With the discernment of an intellectual he creates poems that view the human landscape through a microscopic lens, recording the suffering of the land, the lesions and scars of his people, as well as the imagination and sorrow of his nation. His documentary poems are a brief history of the heart and spirit of intellectuals in Taiwan over more than forty years.

Ching-fa Wu (1954–) served as the vice chairman of the Council for Cultural Construction of the Executive Yuan and has worked in the media industry for many years. In his youth, he mainly wrote fiction, and the poems selected and translated are all recent works. These poems recall and reflect on the poet's life when he was young, and revolve around confession made to the elders, the ebb and flow of family relations, and the criticism of society and current events at home and abroad. The poet records the awareness he has gained at the important turning points of his life. The perspective is personal and is oriented toward all aspects of the self, the family, and the nation.

Ching-fa Wu's *Youth Trilogy* is a collection of three novels: *Attic, Spring and Autumn Tea Room,* and *Autumn Chrysanthemums,* written after the author entered middle age. As the name suggests, it is a memoir of the author's youth when he was a middle school student. It depicts the lives of young people born in the Hakka mountain village of Meinong, in Kaohsiung County. They must travel to the city for their education and are driven by the fervent drive for academic success. Subjected to urban bias towards the rural areas, they also feel the disorientation of minority Hakka people who live amid Taiwan's Hoklo-majority society. All the while they are subject to the curiosity and temptations of youthful lust. Such a suite of youthful novels constitutes a history of personal growth, and it is also the youthful memoirs of the youth of the whole era.

Fang-tzu Chang (1964–) is a Hakka poetess who first made her appearance in the resurgence of Hakka writing in the 1990s. She is a rare Hakka poet with a Tapu accent from southern Chiayi County. Although verse written in Mandarin represent the majority of her poems, writing in the Hakka language is of profound significance to her creative project. She uses the Hakka language to write about family relations, stories of Hakka elders, the images and minutiae of life, Hakka history, their products, and customs and culinary culture. She is a new force in mother tongue Taiwanese literature who stands in the vanguard of Hakka language writing.

Chiao Lee (1934–) is a Hakka author of the postwar generation. He is one of the most important authors of *roman-fleuves* in Taiwanese literature. His *roman-fleuves* novels are among the most representative of documentary-style literature in Taiwan and among Hakka authors. Short stories were Chiao Lee's main form of expression in the first twenty years of his literary life. The works selected in two different translation collections are all from his early works. Chiao Lee was born in the poorest of mountain villages in Taiwan before the Second World War, and some of the earliest images imprinted on his mind were of starvation and death. He thus began with these impressions of the human condition as he explored the meaning of life and sought the way of liberation and redemption.

These became persistent themes in his short stories. His creative project is a history of his personal spiritual growth, and it can also be seen as a record of the development of contemporary rural intellectuals. Both translations include a number of stories from the White Terror period as that era made a deep impression on Chiao Lee and all Taiwanese of his generation. The other stories chosen count among Chiao Lee's novels concerning redemption. Chiao Lee's novels dealing with both these themes depict some of the most indelible memories of Taiwanese people.

Wang-tai Lee (1948–) worked for many years as a newspaper reporter and editor, and his novels are written with a unique focus on history, involving historical figures and events. In the past ten years he has completed three historical novels, with *Banana King Ngôo Tsín-suī* being the most recent. Ngôo Tsín-suī (Wu Chen-jui 1908–1993) was a real person. When he served as the chairman of the Qishan Green Fruit Cooperative Association, he successfully marketed Taiwanese bananas in Japan, accounting for 70 percent of the market there. At the same time, he fought hard against the Green Fruit Export Guild with its monopolistic practices and windfall profits, ensuring that the profits from banana exports were returned to the farmers. This led to an economic miracle in banana exporting, and banana farmers grew to venerate him as the "God of Bananas" or the "Banana King." In order to benefit his family, a bureaucrat of the Kuomintang (Chinese Nationalist Party) surnamed Li initiated the "banana exploitation case." He fabricated evidence against Ngôo, and the case eventually resulted in Ngôo being imprisoned in a black site jail. Subsequently, the Taiwanese banana export trade built up almost single-handedly by Ngôo was utterly decimated. Although the author only profiles the incident, it is sufficient to evoke traumatic memories for Taiwanese farmers. Wang-tai Lee's dedication to writing history represents a renewal or innovation in the tradition of Hakka documentary literature.

Ruijin Peng
Taiwanese literature researcher
March 28, 2023
translated by Terence Russell

FOREWORD

Banana King: Ngôo Tsín-suī by Wang-tai Lee is part of "Translation and Overseas Promotion of Hakka Literary Works 2021-2023," a major, multi-linguistic project sponsored by the Hakka Council of Taiwan. The project is designed to provide quality translations of literary works by Taiwanese Hakka writers to an international audience. *Banana King: Ngôo Tsín-suī* (hereafter *Banana King*) is a full-length historical novel that looks back on an important transitional era in Taiwan's history. As Professor Ruijin Peng notes in his preface to the series, one of the great contributions of Hakka authors has been in the area of historic and "great river novels" (M. *dahe xiaoshuo*/Fr. *roman-fleuve*). Such works make use of the freedom of fictionalized narrative to connect and find meaning in the events that have shaped Taiwan's history. *Banana King: Ngôo Tsín-suī,* the story of the rise and fall of one of the most important figures in the banana industry during the early years of Taiwan's economic miracle from the 1960s to the 1980s, is such a historic novel. Its author, Wang-tai Lee, who himself grew up in a family of banana producers, had a special interest in bringing the story of the "Banana King" to public attention, and he chose the historical novel—fictionalized narrative based upon factual events—because it enabled him more easily to give color and vitality to the real experiences of a heroic figure like Ngôo Tsín-suī (Wu Chen-jui).

For so much of its history, Taiwan has been a nation caught in the fissures of great power conflict, denied the basic right of self-determination, misunderstood, and betrayed. It is not a coincidence then that until recent times, the Taiwanese novel best known to the international community is Wu Cho-liu's *The Orphan of Asia* whose main protagonist struggles to find an identity for himself between the opposing cultural poles of Japan and China. After World War II and the end of Japanese control, many in Taiwan had hoped that they would be able to find their place as citizens of China, the nation where most found their ethnic roots. But the Chinese

Nationalist government that arrived to assume the administration of Taiwan after the departure of the Japanese treated Taiwan as a colony with an alien population, a different culture and different languages. When conflict inevitably arose with the native Taiwanese populace, the Nationalists imposed a brutal martial law regime and forced their Taiwanese subjects into political and cultural subservience. It was not until martial law was finally lifted in 1987 that the people of Taiwan found the freedom to be the agents of their own destiny and begin the process of defining who they are in the modern global context.

In *Banana King,* the main character, Ngôo Tsín-suī, grows up under Japanese colonial rule and is educated in Japanese. After the Japanese surrender in 1945, Ngôo hopes to establish a place for himself under the newly arrived Chinese Nationalist government. Unfortunately, despite considering himself to be ethically Chinese, Ngôo finds that the cultural divide with the mainland Chinese who dominate the Nationalist regime is even greater than that with the former Japanese occupiers. In this respect, he is representative of many Taiwanese of his generation, especially those with education and ambition.

Because of his personal experience working on his family's banana plantation, Wang-tai Lee is able to provide highly nuanced and moving insight into the challenges that Ngôo Tsín-suī faces as he works tirelessly to improve the lot of banana farmers and to build the banana trade between Taiwan and Japan into an important pillar of Taiwan's economy. We see Ngôo as a man of principle and determination, and his hard work, combined with excellent negotiation skills, is initially rewarded as bananas from Taiwan come to dominate the Japanese market. Ngôo's success also derives from the personal connections that he has cultivated both within the community of banana producers in Taiwan, and in the commercial agencies in Japan. His role as intermediary is further enhanced by his fluency in Japanese language and social manners on the one hand, and his understanding of local farmers and their Hoklo language, on the other.

However, the bureaucrats of Nationalist administration who have come from various locales around mainland China have very little sympathy for either Japan or native Taiwanese. The Japanese were their enemy during the eight years of the Sino-Japanese War, and they see the Taiwanese, who had been subjects of the Japanese empire for fifty years, including the war years, as more Japanese than Chinese. For that reason, Ngôo Tsín-suī with his linguistic and cultural skills, is viewed with considerable antipathy and disdain. Confronted with these negative perceptions, as well as with the endemic corruption of the Nationalist government, Ngôo and his ambition to bring prosperity to the local farmers of southern Taiwan, is doomed to failure. *Banana King* is thus a human tragedy and a political cautionary tale.

Based on information gained from interviews and document research, author Wang-tai Lee narrates his story as a biography of Ngôo Tsín-suī, adding certain fictional elements to simplify and dramatize the actual events. One of the most unique aspects of the novel is Lee's liberal use of Hoklo, Japanese, and even Hakka language to simulate more closely the actual linguistic environment of the story. In this way, he not only makes dialogue between characters more realistic, but he also uses language difference to highlight the struggles of native Taiwanese to adapt to successive colonial regimes with completely different cultural and linguistic demands. Of course, this strategy presents challenges for the reader, even if they are familiar with the languages in question, but Lee clearly feels that important narrative depth would be sacrificed if he wrote only in standard Mandarin.

The multilingual nature of *Banana King* presents even greater challenges for the translator. Standard Mandarin is already one of the most difficult languages to render faithfully into English, but here we are confronted with dialogue in Hoklo and Japanese as well, so the translator must deal with the thorny issue of how to convey this multilinguistic environment to the English language reader. There is no perfect solution to be found here, only a variety of imperfect ones. Fortunately, those working on behalf of the Hakka Council of Taiwan were able to acquire the rare services of Timothy Smith, a translator with fluency not only in Mandarin, but also in Hoklo and Japanese. For this project, Mr. Smith has deployed not only his panoply of language skills, but also his impressive arsenal of cutting-edge translation skills to bring Wang-tai Lee's moving historical narrative vividly to life for English language readers. This English version of *Banana King* thus stands as a major milestone in the project of employing literary works to open a window on Taiwan's fascinating history and culture to the world.

Terence Russell
University of Manitoba
March 2024

HIDDEN HISTORY, INJUSTICE IN TAIWAN, AND AN UNDERHANDED OPPRESSIVE GOVERNMENT

Ngôo Tsín-sūi (Wu Chen-jui) (吳振瑞) is a historical figure I'm very well acquainted with. Born in Kaohsiung's Ch'i-shan district, Wu attended elementary and middle school in Pingtung County before attending high school in Kaohsiung. In the 1960s I really began to hear his name popping up everywhere. It should be known that all the bananas from the Kaohsiung and Pingtung area were exported to Japan, and tales of the economic miracle that banana farmers experienced had long been passed down as a sort of oral tradition. Our own "Banana King," Ngôo Tsín-sūi, was a miracle within a miracle. The Vietnam War was raging off on distant shores. There were just a handful of American GIs that came to Taiwan for leave at the time. They went mostly over to the bars at Ch'i-Hsian Third Road over by the docks of Kaohsiung Harbor. Perhaps it was the unconventional style of foreigners, or perhaps American sentimentality served as an excuse for the opening up of the Chong-hsin Bridge Flea Market and the little shops and stalls along Ta-Kou-ting in the Yancheng neighborhood, that built up a sense of Kaohsiung as a port of mainly imports. When my friends and I were in middle-school, we read *Wen-hsing magazine* (文星雜誌), but the contemporary "Declaration of Formosan Self-salvation" that landed P'eng Ming-min (彭明敏) and two National Taiwan University students in hot water was of no concern for most people in the area. Postwar Taiwan seemed to have moved on after the KMT's brutal and barbaric martial suppression in the 228 uprisings. With U.S. Aid and a growing economy, Taiwan was moving into a new era. Apart from tales of the economic miracle that banana farmers were experiencing at the time in and around Kaohsiung and Pingtung, the boom led to situations where even remote locales in the area were generally living a life high off the hog—it looked like the plot of a novel set amid a bucolic countryside background. And no doubt about it, Ngôo was the highlight of the entire show.

The Chiang regime that came along with its Chinese Nationalist Party (Kuomintang (KMT)) after their defeat by the Chinese Communist Party (CCP) struck it lucky with the start of the Korean War on the horizon. They had already consolidated their single-handed control over Taiwan in the immediate postwar years, dominated by 228 and martial law and the White Terror. Along with their mutual defense treaty signed with America, the Chiangs and the KMT formed an anti-communist bloc all but guaranteeing the stability of the government. The blatant White Terror of the 1950s appeared to have stopped temporarily with the stabilization of the regime. And yet Chiang Kai-Shek, his wife Song Mei-Ling, and his oldest son Chiang Ching-kuo, formed a triangle of power. Chiang Kai-shek's power was being torn at by both his wife and his son in a power struggle that had flared up and made itself known from time to time. The 1964 incident with Peng Ming-min was suppressed; the Chiang family used the opening of special economic permissions to win over newly wealthy and burgeoning capitalists, and formed subservient financial groups and consortiums, turning them into a new cudgel to be used in their rule over Taiwan. The robust export of bananas to Japan was a source of pride for the Taiwanese agricultural sector, but the politics behind all of it were murky and perplexing.

Ngôo was at the helm, leading banana exports to Japan as Chairman of the Board of the Fruit Marketing Cooperative. At the time, Taiwan's international trade relations with Japan were incorporated as a part of the local economic system, to say nothing of the larger national economy, and were often wrapped up in the entanglements of party-state politicians. The legend of Ngôo Tsín-sūi as the Banana King and the Golden Bowl Affair was principally a result of the power struggle between Chiang senior, his wife, and his son.

Ngôo's legend highlights the 228 uprisings, the aftermath of the White Terror in the 1950s, the Chiang dynastic regime, and the KMT party-state's internal power struggles. This struggle actually hindered and hobbled the further economic blossoming of Taiwan's trade relationship with Japan, and it goes without saying that Taiwanese banana farmers suffered greatly from the undue hardship created by the Chiangs. For the Taiwan of today, which has no hope of ever recovering its lost agricultural heyday, we are brought back to a legend from a long-lost era. Only now is the story of Ngôo Tsín-sūi appearing, nearly fifty years after the fact.

A historical novel is much better at gaining interest from readers than a regular old history book with dates and timelines. Historical novels inevitably fictionalize some aspects of history and use a freely structured format to satisfy the cultural expectations of the general readership.

In Taiwan, where historical memory has been lost or [intentionally] obscured, our identity must begin with the recovery of memories. The "Taiwan Historical Novel Award" has been sponsored by the Taiwan Peace Foundation, and it was established with the goal of the recovery of memory in mind.

Lee's other novel, *The Harima-Maru,* takes as its plot the story of a Taiwanese man serving overseas in China in the Imperial Japanese Army and his return to Taiwan following the end of the Second World War. While this work of Lee's didn't garner him first place, it was however lauded as an excellent piece of writing alongside other finalists' works. *Banana King Ngôo Tsín-sūi* is likewise another of Lee's works to have vied for first place but was just shy of the mark, yet still earning much praise and critical acclaim.

Like myself, Wang-tai Lee also grew up in the Kaohsiung-Pingtung area in the same era I did and was in fact one of my coworkers during my short stint as a news reporter. He is very well read on and acquainted with the story of Ngôo Tsín-sūi. Lee had himself, in the 1960s, lived and breathed the banana export boom brought about by the "Banana King." In his journey as an author, Lee's training and experiences as a journalist has made him well-honed and are constantly in the back of his mind. By using the medium of the historical novel, which has its special qualities, the tragic history of Taiwanese people—where economics and politics are woven together to pierce through sorrow-filled history of the party-state regime controlled by the Chiang family, which marred the lives of many a Taiwanese family—can be portrayed. Historical novels are both histories and well-spun yarns, and they require the dual deployment of an eye for news stories and a mind for literature. Wang-tai Lee has navigated through Ngôo Tsín-sūi's life story, the export of bananas abroad, and the iron-fisted rule of the Chiang family and Taiwan's political struggles under them to give life to a living history of Taiwan as a post-war colony.

Lee has said in interviews that he used an autobiographical narrative to write this novel. His own childhood was spent growing up on a banana plantation. Lee's own father was an association representative while Ngôo was serving as the director of the Green Fruits Association, and Lee brings particular savvy and background knowledge to the figures and characters in the book through his own experience and memories of helping to grow banana trees and of how this crop improved the overall economy. In one scene in 1963, where a Pingtung student's association is formed in Taipei, he reveals the indifference and coldness shown towards Ngôo's imprisonment. We're brought through to a stage where different persons of import are being presented with awards on a panel. The novel's setting begins in the Japanese Colonial Era. It then takes a turn through the early postwar years, then on to the martial law era under the KMT-controlled party-state, to the late 80s after Taiwan's democratization where we see the narrator as a journalist going on a travel-tour trip to Tokyo where the tour-guide makes a brief stop in a decrepit alleyway where Ngôo resided. We're brought back to a narration of Lee's experiences and his thoughts while he was growing up. We see Ngôo's behavior mirroring that of the tenacity and strength of a Taiwanese water buffalo; the high spirited, hopeful air of the times; the experience of the downfall; and the spectral shell of exile to a land across the sea. Lee's historical novel then ties in the disastrous power struggles of the Chiang family, Taiwanese elites and the phenomena of the postwar economy, politics, and cultural groups all mixed together.

The prewar colonization of Taiwan by Japan and the postwar colonization by the KMT provided special historical constructs for Taiwan that furnish the Taiwanese people's history with all sorts of stories and tales, sowing a truly never-ending, ever-fertile ground for the writing of Taiwanese historical novels. Taiwanese people's historical consciousness must be awakened and deepened through such works.

From The *Harima-Maru* to *Banana King Ngôo Tsín-sūi*, Wang-tai Lee's journey into historical novel writing continues to etch out milestones in Taiwan's historical landscape.

Min-yong Lee
Poet and winner of Taiwan's 2007 National Award for Arts
March 2020

PREFACE

I was just twelve or thirteen years old back then. I must have been in the first or second grade of junior high school when my family all of a sudden became a banana-farmer family. That year, my father decided to turn two productive rice paddies into banana tree fields, but it didn't end there. He also went off in search of land to work on contract. This too wasn't enough. He wanted our land to become a "banana shipment de-pot." Banana farmers at the time sent all their produce to collection areas run by the Green Fruits Association. Once the produce was all weighed, the produce shipments were stamped with a trademark and the money would flow back about a month and a half later. Those farmers who were in urgent need of money could bring their order stamps to our house and cash in. The villagers could also come to our house first to take out loans and buy up unharvested bananas at a discount from farmers scattered all around the district, and then, after the bananas were harvested, they would bring the order stamps back to pay off their loans at a discount.

At that time, we used to refer to our house as a simple "banana farmer bank" in our small village, but I shouldn't use such an imposing name in reference to it or make it out to be more important than it actually was.

In our household when we kids came home from school, and especially on the weekends, we were all forced by our fathers to go out to our banana fields to hoe weeds. Back in those days there was no such thing as Roundup or herbicides or weeding machines. The only tools a farmer had at their disposal in the war against the weeds was typically a hoe, or other garden tools, perhaps a scythe. We had to do hoeing and weeding under a brutal sun, and we had no real respite, even after an afternoon thunderstorm. We had monthly tests or end-of-term exams at school, but none of that compared to the importance of caring for the banana trees our families were growing.

Those who've done actual farm work will know exactly what I'm talking about. Weeds are a scourge whose growth will always outpace each downward swing of a garden hoe. Southern Taiwan is an extremely humid environment and our family's banana farm was rather large-scale. And so, all my years as a teenager were spent as a soldier in the constant war against the weeds. My dreams as a child, both realistic and fantasy, were mostly destroyed with each strike of the hoe or shovel and slash of a scythe.

In spite of all the above, banana farming allowed my family to prosper. Vivid images of the excitement on my father's face and his overflowing enthusiasm linger in my mind's eye to this day. I also received a lot of encouragement when I was younger. Two or three days every week, we would be woken up by my father at just after three in the morning to go out to the fields. My father would grope in the dark while cutting down all the bananas he could get his hands on and my mother and I were responsible for moving them out of the field, bunch by gigantic bunch. We would carry a bunch on either end of our shoulder poles and walk along the narrow footpaths along the field embankments, then cross over a small footbridge until we reached the side of the main road running by our house. We'd gently place our burdensome harvests on cotton quilts laid down in advance. I'd carry one load after another, usually until the first rays of sunlight spread out over the horizon, then continue until the sky was completely illuminated, before we'd quickly walk back home. Then, I'd scarf down my breakfast and rush off to school. Back during the harvest time, I'd constantly be marked down as tardy, and it was mostly for this reason.

I remember once complaining to my father, asking him why we always had to get up in the middle of the night to rush around in the fields collecting banana bunches. He responded, saying that there was always a crush of shipping trucks and people early in the morning at the collection depot and if we wanted to avoid long line-ups, we had to go early. We had no choice but to pick bunches of bananas early in the morning.

Back in that era (the 1960s), every male child in a farmer's family was expected to help out with the farm work. It just went without saying. Nobody complained, and they didn't even know that they should have complained; that it was some form of abuse or anything of the sort either, and in any case, nobody would have known who to throw a lawsuit at for it.

Growing up as a child on a banana farm, I later gradually came to realize that I was growing up in an unprecedented "golden age of bananas." The Kaohsiung Green Fruits Distribution Association bought up bananas at a very advantageous price every season, and it was on the up-and-up. It was also from the mouth of an elder that I heard of the executive chairman named Ngôo Tsín-sūi (Wu Chen-jui). My father would later be elected as a representative for the Association, multiple times even, and serving under Ngôo was a major source of pride for him.

Back in those days, Taiwanese agriculture was still largely a poor man's industry where it was hard to escape poverty. It was Ngôo who allowed for all of us people of lowly and humble origins to make a name for ourselves and get some real cash in our pockets.

Ngôo of course wouldn't have known it at the time he was in charge, but I was a participant in the "golden age of bananas" that he created.

The moment I had finished the first draft of this book, I lifted myself up from my writing desk and walked about the room for a bit. I thought to myself, having just finished typing out the last words in the story, that this book of mine was an account of all those years spent as a youth toiling with my family in the banana fields.

When I was a young adult, I worked for a while for a newspaper. Once, due to good fortune, I ran into Ngôo in the small Japanese-style *ryokan* inn in a back alley in a busy district of Tokyo when on vacation in the 1980s, and I was able to do a long interview him. It was so long in fact that the two of us, one young and one old, talked about his life on and off for the better part of three days and three nights. At the time, he was already in his twilight years and the appearance and demeanor that I imagined this "Banana King" to have had disappeared. But when we talked about bananas, his face lit up and he spoke with great animation about the singular fruit he came to market so successfully. I told him of my own experiences with banana plots and farms when I was growing up, and he told me in detail about what he was most proud of in his long life. To use a metaphor, my experience was merely one single banana, his was a whole bushel; a bushel of gigantic, long bananas; a bunch of dreams—ones that had ripened to fruition, and those that were utterly squashed and bruised.

And so, it is... This book is more or less a narration of all the different twists and turns in Ngôo Tsín-sūi's life, though the greater part of the narration is from my own mind, the overall tale is all true.

And yet this is a novel after all. It's not an absolute historical timeline or a biography. There are some fictitious characters I developed for the plot to better illuminate certain important characters and their roles in the era. Using such characters makes it easier to write about history, and it's far easier to remember it all that way.

Sometimes I think myself very fortunate. The express train that was Japan had already left Taiwan's station. It had already sounded its steam whistle a long, long time before I arrived on the scene, but its rumbling sound still lingered. The Chinese train had already pulled into the station, so to speak, and it was busy offloading passengers and goods. The image of a train platform in this station arises in my mind, and on this platform there are many scenes of sad partings and joyful reunions, and this story of Ngôo Tsín-sūi and his like is just one of them.

People from my generation were taken from rags to riches, from exploitation and hardship to joy and pleasure. It used to be that our hands were blackened with the ink from iron plate printing, but now everything is copied and printed in a single mouse-click. Before, when martial law was strictly enforced, everyone was forced to give obeisance to the state. Today, those stodgy chants of *wan-sui* ("long live—") from the martial law era have been replaced with the vivacious debates and lively voices of a healthy multiparty democracy. It is not every generation that gets the chance to experience these sorts of changes. Those who have undergone such experiences are fortunate. Those peoples' experiences have helped me to effortlessly record all these stories of heroic local people, who, facing the foreign rulers who once dominated us, lived lives filled with bone-splitting pain and sorrow and largely paid for it with blood and tears.

In trying to keep with the spirit of the languages used in Taiwan in each time period in the novel, I've transcribed much of the dialogue using Taiwanese Hoklo instead of Mandarin Chinese. However, I didn't select a standardized version of character transcription. At some points in the dialogues, I've intentionally written the speech in a half-Taiwanese Hoklo, half-Mandarin script, or only used phonetic characters to represent some words so that those who may not understand Taiwanese Hoklo may be able to read this work.

Finally, I would like to thank several of my friends who gave me invaluable help during the creation of this novel: Mr. Su Tien-chen, who is an old farmer friend of mine. I sometimes call him the *Ox Professor* as I often sought his wisdom about beasts of burden when writing this book. Ms. Lin Chun-mei is another person I'd like to thank. She was one of the few people pushing for the redress of Ngôo's tarnished record. She provided voluminous, precious historic records and materials for this work. Yet another person I'd like to thank is Mr. Huang Hsu whose work, *The Legend of the Golden Banana*, was something I paged through quite often. I'd also like to thank Lin Tsuei-yi the current Tokyo correspondent for *The Liberty Times*. When I was in need of Japanese expressions for the book, it was often her help that I sought out. To Professor Chao-wen Yu, the director of the Department of Chinese Language and Literature at Pingtung University, I owe a great thanks for proofreading the Taiwanese Hoklo/Mandarin Chinese version of this book and for providing invaluable pointers and ideas. I would also like to give a special, heartfelt thanks to the editors of *Mirror Fiction* and to my wife, Lee Chin-chu. Through their careful readings of my drafts, they helped me immensely by frequently pointing out my omissions.

Wang-tai Lee
October 2019
Pingtung, Taiwan

BANANA KING

Ngôo Tsín-suī

PROLOGUE

THE SETTING OF THE STAGE

The curtain is pulled open—
Electricity is suddenly cut from the solemn stage,
The microphone falls silent.
All because of Ngôo Tsín-sūi.

Act Two of the play begins—
We see an old banana farmer from Taiwan,
Facing a narrow Tokyo alley, making deep bows,
And it's all for Ngôo Tsín-sūi.

1.

It's late August 1973. A typhoon has just passed over Taiwan. In the morning aftermath, the gusty afterwinds are still blowing lightly along the avenues and boulevards. A young journalist has just waltzed into the Wang-K'ai Hotel and Conference Center, which sits directly facing the Taipei Train Station. He makes his way up to the third floor of the hotel. The main event in the grand hall has already begun. The mayor of Taipei, Chang Feng-hsu, is giving a speech. The mayor looks down and reads his draft of the event program. A second later, he looks at the guests sitting in front of the stage. His Mandarin has an accented inflection, and he speaks in breaks and pauses. The reporter has long before been acquainted with the mayor's mannerisms and speaking habits. Luckily, the mayor wrapped up his remarks pretty quickly. He returns to his seat on the stage over to the left side. The flower poking out from his left lapel pocket droops over.

The journalist is standing over to the front left of the hall in front of the stage. An usher invites him to take a seat elsewhere. The journalist continues to stand, a smile on his face. He's staring fixedly as the distinguished guests on and off the stage take group photos.

This is the founding conference for the Pingtung County Hometown Association in Taipei. Tsai Hsiu-hsiung, a member of the prep team staff, is a good friend of the journalist. The two shoot the breeze and talk about trivial stuff for a bit.

"Hey, A-Tshiânn-á, you're late!"

"*Pháinn-sè! Pháinn-sè!* (Sorry, sorry!) The conference only just started. I already had a copy of Mayor Chang's remarks."

The two friends' conversation ended at this brief exchange. The master of ceremonies (MC) was just starting to introduce the luminaries and distinguished guests of honor. "The first of our distinguished honorees is Mr. Sung Bing-tang, an outstanding graduate of Waseda University in

Tokyo, Japan, who is currently serving in his capacity as the school director of the Hwa-Chiang Girls' Middle School in Wanhwa."

"Next, we have Dr. Hsu Pang-hsing,[1] a renowned Pingtung physician and the director of the Hsu Outpatient Clinic."

"Mr. Tai Yen-hui here is a gifted Pingtung native, currently serving as the vice-head of the Judicial Yuan."

"Mr. Liou Chien-shan is our representative in the provincial government and a consultant for the Examination Yuan."

"Mr. Wu Wen-hua is an industrialist from Chu-tien and the chairman of Wan Ja Shan Foods."

With every introduction, the honorees would either stand up, nod their head, or make a short bow, receiving applause from the audience.

The rambling off of honoree names continued. Next up, the MC introduced Ms. Lin Chu-ing, an associate professor at Chung-Hsing University. Then there was Mr. Lin Cheng-tzu, an experimental researcher. Then, when the MC finished calling out, "Mr. Tsai Hsi-k'un, a well-respected lawyer from our Pingtung," A-Tshiânn spied Tsai Hsiu-hsiung giving a nod to a young man off to the side of the stage. Right then, the microphone suddenly went dead. Only those standing next to the stage and those in the first row could hear anything. The introductory words that A-Tshiânn could faintly make out were, "Mr. Wu Chen-jui (Ngôo Tsín-sūi), a native of T'ou-Chien-Hsi, the former chairman of the board of the Kaohsiung Green Fruits Export Association." Nobody applauded because hardly anyone could hear the MC's voice. A-Tshiânn couldn't see anyone named Ngôo standing up to receive his accolades either.

After the MC finished calling out Tsín-sūi's name and introduction, the microphone, like a person holding their breath for several seconds, suddenly sputtered and screeched back to life. Everyone could now hear clearly as the MC continued calling out the remaining names and their respective kudos: "Chung Tuh-chun, presiding head of the high court; Mr. Tsai Chieh-sheng, the chairman of the Hotel Roma."[2]

After that, A-Tshiânn didn't bother remembering the names of the other honorees. The name Ngôo Tsín-sūi and his accidental encounter with here him made A-Tshiânn's think of his childhood at home. He remembered

---

1. Hsu Pang-hsing was also the head of the Taichung Chung-shan Medical School. He would later return to Pingtung to further educational opportunities for Pingtung locals. He was the founder of both Meiho Middle School and Meiho University, and a promoter of the Meiho baseball team. He was a cofounder of Kaohsiung Medical University.
2. Tsai Chieh-sheng is the father of Taiwan's current President, Tsai Ing-Wen (2016–2024).

his father often pulling a pile of newspaper clippings out from a drawer. The contents were all news stories about the "Banana Maggot and the Golden Bowl Scandal." His father often read these articles and scoffed at the content, saying "It's all horseshit." This figure, Ngôo Tsín-sūi, was truly a magnanimous hero who fought hard for banana farmers in Pingtung County. The legal case against him was a massive injustice. "He was our benefactor," A-Tshiânn's father would often remark. "You and your brothers and sisters were all able to attend universities in Taipei, and it's all thanks to growing bananas."

The microphone boomed loud and clear. The convener for the prep team, Wu Chin-lin, was making up a preparations report. A-Tshiânn complained to Tsai Hsiu-Hsiung standing beside him, "Why did you do that? Was that really necessary? Ngôo's already served his time. The case has long been over. He's a bona fide Banana King. How could you possibly treat him like he's nothing but dirt?"

"You're not allowed to write a news story about what just happened. If you do, I'll be a dead man."

"I won't. I just can't believe you did that though."

"It was the organization's decision. Everyone's worked hard to make their way up to Taipei from Pingtung. If anyone in the audience knew that Ngôo was up on the stage, the whole place would have erupted in wild applause. It would have garnered tons of attention, including from the authorities. How would any of that be a good thing? The authorities wouldn't be happy with that."

A-Tshiânn cursed Hsiu-hsiung under his breath, "To hell with the organization... Those weak-kneed shits."

"Don't say that too loudly!"

"I'm asking you straight up, did you do it on your own or did they order you to do it?"

"It's what I thought the authorities would want."

"Ugh. There's no need to do that. I don't know why you're working yourself up into a panic."

"A-Tshiânn, the Banana King came here today. As long as we're all hunky-dory, then that's fine. We don't want to stir up trouble and cause quarrels, yeah?"

The MC kept going, and the microphone volume was loud and clear— there were no sudden drops in sound or static. Wu Chin-lin had finished his report. It looked like the hometown association was about to select its supervisor. A-Tshiânn scanned the room with widened eyes. He spotted a tall, lanky man in the fifth row with a slightly thin face. It looked like the man from the photos in his father's newspaper clippings. He was certain of it. The man was speaking with a slightly portly gentleman sitting right next to him. They were talking very excitedly, as if they were long-lost friends. Ngôo's expression looked lonely. Occasionally, his face oscillated between a look of indignation and a bitter smile from time to time.

A-Tshiânn thought of something. "If you felt that Wu Chen-jui was such a taboo person to the point that you cut the mic when his name was called, then wouldn't it have been better not to have invited him at all?"

"It was Hsu Pang-hsing who invited him and helped get his name on the list. He also paid for—"

"Oh, I see now. So that's who's sitting right next to him. The two of them are talking to each other right now."

"Right. The two of them. I heard he was a classmate of Wu's when they were in high school in Kaohsiung during the Japanese era."

"Oh, no kidding!" A-Tshiânn stared at Ngôo Tsín-sūi, looking at his every hand movement and shift of his legs, every expression as he conversed with Hsu. "So I unexpectedly bump into him today, the man my father has praised at least a million times." His eyes moved over to the journalist section where he saw some colleagues and acquaintances and thought to himself, "Probably none of the other journalists know the Banana King is here in this room today. Hah."

The microphone blared. Was that the default volume on the microphone? The MC was declaring nominations for the first board of supervisors. These must have been decided in the back room. A-Tshiânn listened closely, but he didn't hear Ngôo's name mentioned at all.

After the association's first meeting concluded, Tsín-sūi left by himself. He was standing on a street corner waiting for a stoplight to change color. The typhoon had only passed the day before. A slight, chill wind was blowing. Red changed to green, and a group of people hurriedly made their way across the wide road. He was the tallest person in the entire crowd making their way across. In the way he walked, there was clearly the demeanor of old age.

2.

Several years later, the Republic of China government finally lifted restrictions on free travel. It was pure coincidence that A-Tshiânn was also able to take a long holiday. He took his father with him to sign up for a group tour. Several of the older folks from the farm village he grew up in also caught wind of the news and signed up too. It was decided—they were all going to go on a vacation tour to Japan!

Many of the people on their charter bus were mostly grandmas and grandpas. The tour guide was a Taiwanese guy who had been living in Japan for a long time. A-Tshiânn sat next to his elderly father to keep him company and take care of him.

On that first day, the itinerary included a trip to the gardens and vicinity around the Meiji Shrine, the Ginza district, and Shinjuku. Right before dusk, as they were headed to a restaurant, the guide first called everyone together and told them, "Wait a second. We're about to go past an alleyway. There's a very famous Taiwanese man who resides there."

The guide was expecting he would see some of his charges' eyes light up and be barraged by a flurry of questions like, "Who are they? Who's the famous person that lives down that lane?" but the response was low-key, to say the least.

Many of the elderly tour guests didn't even bother lifting their tired eyelids or look in the direction he was pointing, so he just muttered to himself, "There's a man who moved here a while back, the Banana King, Ngôo Tsín-sūi."

There was still no clamor or noise from any of the passengers, but then the two people in the row behind A-Tshiânn piped up, "Oh!!!" and began hurriedly talking in hushed tones. Just then, A-Tshiânn's father lightly patted his son on the thigh. Both father and son gave each other a glance. The *ojisang*[3] sitting in the row in front of them turned around

---

3. *Ojisang*, from the Japanese, *ojîsan*, means "elderly man or grandfather." It is one of the remnants of Japanese language still used in everyday speech in Taiwan.

and exchanged a glance with A-Tshiânn's father, raising their chins in recognition of the name. The tour guide didn't pick up on this subtle commotion among his tour guests, however.

As dinner was wrapping up, five of the tour guests sat the tour guide down for a private chat to bargain with him. They begged him to take them back to the alleyway so they could catch a glimpse of Ngôo Tsín-sūi.

"Do you personally know him?" the tour guide asked incredulously.

"No, we don't. We want to go to his residence and just take a peek through the window is all," A-Tshiânn's father replied.

"His house isn't an ordinary home. It's a *kha-sau-king-á* (a brothel)."

"It's a *kha-sau-king-á*?!? And Ngôo Tsín-sūi actually lives there?!"

"That's correct. A group of *tsuán-tsiah-tsa-bóo* (prostitutes) also lives there." The guide replied.

"That's very strange!"

"It can't be true!"

During the free time following dinner, the tour guide led them outside. He was very familiar with all the roads and buildings in the area, so they reached it very quickly. It was an ordinary-looking, two-storied, Japanese-style wooden structure with a sign hanging by the door with the words "Sanyō Guesthouse" written on it.

Everyone in the tour group tiptoed, standing on either side of the two windows on the first floor of the house. There was a raised floor with tatami matting. There were stacks of lockers on both sides of the raised floor. A tall, thin, old man was busying himself over by a gigantic multiuse space heater next to the *genkan* foyer. If you were to look carefully, you'd see the man was cooking some noodles. He was using a gigantic pot. He was expending a lot of effort, stirring them. Was he cooking for everyone in the residence? It was already past nine o'clock when he was starting to cook a meal. It didn't look like there was anyone else in the room with him. Was he just cooking for himself?

Just as it seemed everyone was starting to get bored, four people came down the stairs carrying suitcases. It looked like they were two ordinary husband-and-wife couples who had come on vacation to Japan. The old man turned around and greeted the four of them. Ah! It is Chairman Ngôo! He was wearing a plain, old, white T-shirt. The trousers he was wearing were actually pajama pants, old and wrinkly.

The tour guide was at the side of his group, urging in a low voice, "In Japan, poking around and looking into people's houses is considered extremely rude. You've seen him. Let's go now!"

With the tour guide insisting that their behavior was extremely rude, A-Tshiânn's father took a step back from the window and he made a ninety-degree bow in the Japanese manner towards the inside of the house. Under the dimmed yellow streetlights, the shadow of his bow kind of resembled a banana tree being blown down by typhoon winds.

The tour guide was at his wits' end with impatience and had already walked halfway down the alley. Several older folks were following him. They huffed and puffed to catch up to him and asked frankly, "You said this house was a *kha-sau-king-á*.[4] Well, where are the women then? We didn't see any ladies of the night there."

"I've been by here many times before. There are three to five women who live here. This time of night, they're probably off making their rounds. They'll come back around twelve or so."

"So it's not a brothel. It's just a regular inn."

"Right, that's correct. I called it a *kha-sau-king-á* because I wanted to make it seem more interesting."

"So Ngôo Tshín-sūi was just making a bowl of noodles for those young women?"

"Probably, yeah. He might be making food for the other guests too." The tour guide paused for a minute and added, "I heard he's the manager of this *ryokan*. The owner is his niece."

"*Aiyee*. What a sorry sight to see a director such as the Banana King end up like this."

"It pains my heart greatly just seeing him like this."

The next day, their charter bus left Tokyo and they drove on to explore the Kansai Area, Kobe, and the Setō Inland Sea. They were going to spend three days and two nights then return to Tokyo. After that, they'd prepare to board their flight back to Taiwan.

On the last night, they had another night of free time to go and do whatever they wished. A-Tshiânn's father and five others once more pleaded with the tour guide to take them back to Ngôo Tsín-sūi's *ryokan*. The guide adamantly refused. A-Tshiânn's father tried making the pitch this way, "This time, we're not going to peep through their windows. We want to go and express our

---

4. *Kha-sau-king-á*. Euphemistic Taiwanese Hoklo term for "brothel," establishment for prostitution, and other pleasure quarters.

thanks and respect."

"We're all old farmers who were blessed by Chairman Ngôo's leadership. When we were farmers under his helm, we flourished and were finally able to earn some real money. It's because of him that we are able to go abroad and do tours like this now in our old age," another of the old men added.

"Take us back there, please!"

"Please. We're begging you!"

The tour guide couldn't resist their pleas, and with a flashlight in hand, once more led the way.

It seemed as if the lanterns and lights of the Sanyō Guesthouse were shining brighter than they had been the other night. Before they even got close to the *ryokan*, they could tell that there were several people inside the front room. That being the case, the group of old tourists made no rush to move towards the door. They stood over by the window looking in.

Ngôo Tsín-sūi was still dressed similarly to how he was a couple nights before—in a Taiwanese way—wearing a white Taiwanese-style T-shirt and pajama bottoms and sitting on the tatami matting. There were two women and a man sitting before Ngôo. The man's Western suit was perfectly pressed. The women's Western-style dresses were likewise well-suited to them too. The three of them were all very slim. Were they Wu's family members? Leaning in a bit more to hear, the old tourists overhead the conversation.

"*A-pa* (Dad), stop being so stubborn! What kind of a life are you living here? I want to cry every time I see you like this," a woman's voice said.

"Why don't you want to come to live with us in America? Is that honestly so bad? You're not giving us a chance to take care of you," the other female voice said.

"I can still take care of myself. I'm taking care of those women from Taiwan. This way, I still feel like I have something to live for," Ngôo said forcefully.

"You don't need to be taking care of them at your age—"

"Two of the ladies were taken in by the police yesterday evening. Fortunately, I was here to protect and take care of them."

A voice shaking with angry tears rang out through the house. "*A-pa*, you're making a mockery of us. We can help you—"

"What mockery? *Honnh*!"

"*A-pa*!"

"Enough. Stop talking about the matter. Your *A-pa* wants to stay here. There's no shame in that, and I'm not going to move to your house in

America. That's the end of it!"

"*A-pa*, you're being the most stubborn old grouch in the world!"

The tour guide realized that some Japanese people in the lane were starting to glance over as this clutch of old people were crammed together, standing by the windows, peeping in and listening in on the conversation emanating from the *ryokan*. Noticing some of these people watching his group, the tour guide started frantically pressing his charges to leave. When his tour group got to the head of the alley, A-Tshiânn noticed there were tears welling up in the corners of his father's eyes. A-Tshiânn didn't know what he could possibly say to make the situation better. But then his father shouted with raw emotion, "Nothing could ever be more gratifying than this trip to Japan. I'll never forget it!"

ONE

THE JAPANESE COLONIAL ERA

Ngôo Tsín-sūi was just a youth—
After graduating from Takao Secondary,
He worked in the fields, with an ox as his trusty sidekick.
Later, he joined an agricultural research station,
A love drama unfolds with two neighboring sisters,
A wonderful performance.

1.

With one foot in the murky, turbid water, Uncle A-Tsòng was already starting to wade into his rice paddy, his other foot still planted up on the embankment. He threw the loose end of the lead rope he was dragging the buffalo with onto the animal's back. He made a cruel attempt to throw a yoke over the neck of the newly purchased animal. But the animal kept holding its head up high, leaving A-Tsòng with no way to harness it. Angrily, he shouted out, "*Lâi! Lâi!* (Come on!)" and tried once more to harness the buffalo from the right side. But the beast suddenly threw its head to the left and glared back at A-Tsòng, showing him its sharp horns in the process. Uncle A-Tsòng tried twice more but to no avail. He grabbed a strip of bamboo and began whipping the buffalo hard along its back and hindquarters. *Thwap, thwap, thwap*, the bamboo strip came down again and again, but the buffalo just stood where it was, unyieldingly receiving each blow. Its nostrils were flared, and it puffed out several angry snorts.

Uncle A-Tsòng kept trying to beat it into submission until his own hands were sore. Then he tried the yoke again, this time from the left. But the buffalo lifted its head up to the left even more stubbornly, raising its horns up to shake off the yoke. A-Tsòng's head was dripping with sweat. The angry sun was fiercely beating down on the darkened skin of his dejectedly broken and livid grimace. The sun also shone on the fresh scarlet scars along the back of his buffalo. He started to curse, "F***. F*** you worthless buffalo. You're nothing but worthless!" He lifted up the strip of bamboo once more in an attempt to strike at the draft animal again, but then he glanced up and noticed that the bamboo was already beaten to shreds, so he flung it aside in a rage, and clenching his right hand into a fist, he threw a fierce punch at the animal's belly. The beast gave out an anguished *nyeeee—nuh.*

Just as he was preparing to throw a second punch, this time at the buffalo's ear, he heard the lad from the farm next door. That youth, skilled in plowing the terraces and paddies, Ngôo Tsín-sūi, shouted out to him, "Uncle A-Tsòng! Don't hit it again! Let me check the animal over!"

Already in a fit, Uncle A-Tsòng threw vitriol back at him, "You've only just finished your agricultural school, and you think you're already better than me. How would you know a damned thing? I don't believe it." He promptly squatted down on the embankment and took off his conical bamboo hat to reveal a hairline that had long ago receded and his high, glistening forehead, then used his hat as a fan, burning through much of his remaining post-rage energy to cool himself off *fwa, fwa, fwa, fwa*. "I've been plowing the fields my entire life and I've never come across such a stubborn buffalo as this one in all my life," he muttered to himself. His rage still hadn't dissipated, and his bottom lip was clamped over his top lip, his chin was slightly raised, and a long scowl had taken over his whole face.

Uncle A-Tsòng was neighbors with the Ngôo family, and he often saw his younger neighbor going down into the paddies to help out with the farming when he came home from school. A-Tsín-sūi, standing before him, was tall and thin. He had already graduated from high school and seemed to grow more handsome by the day, and so cultured and well mannered. By what measure could anyone say that A-Tsín-sūi was a farmer?! Looking at him now, also with his conical *dou-li* hat off, wiping his brow, A-Tsòng could see his sun-darkened face, ruddy and glistening beneath an oily sheen. He was winding up to belittle A-Tsín-sūi once more, but the lad stood next to the buffalo and began to lecture A-Tsòng, "A buffalo that's just changed hands will always act this way. It doesn't know its new master at all. It has no feelings towards you. Of course, it wouldn't want to plow fields! It's good enough that you managed to get it out to your field in the first place!" Tsín-sūi spat a big gob of spit into his palms and lightly massaged it into the wounded back and hindquarters of the whipped animal. Then he moved along to its front and looked the buffalo straight in the eye. As they stood gazing at each other, Tsín-sūi felt a sense of great familiarity, as if they had known each other for ages from some far-off place. He blinked and then looked back into the buffalo's eyes, this time scrutinizing it for a long time. The sense of familiarity remained. There were complex feelings of fortuitousness and gratitude in the buffalo's eyes. Shifting his gaze away from the beast, A-Tsín-sūi quipped, "Uncle A-Tsòng, where did you purchase this buffalo from? I feel like I've seen it before."

"You must be seeing an apparition. It was A-Li-Kang's buffalo from Su-Tsha over in Tâi-lâm (Tainan). You spring chicken, how could you have ever gone over to Su-Tsha?"

"Ah, is that so? It's true, I've never been over that way." Answering this way, Ngôo Tsín-sūi was aware of the ridicule and scorn in A-Tsòng's stinging words. He waded into the rice paddy and picked up the rope lead A-Tsòng had thrown in anger. With every soothing stroke of Tsín-sūi's hand, he managed to not only put the lead back on the buffalo but the yoke harness as well. At this, the buffalo willingly lowered its head for Tsín-sūi, allowing him to lightly put on the harness. Tsín-sūi felt both astonished and exhilarated. He quickly strapped on the tillage ropes and hooked them to the plowshare blade. With a very light tug on the rope lead, the animal naturally started taking strides. Its four quarters were muscly and had an orderly rhythm to each step taken. From the feeling in the pull of the rope lead, Tsín-sūi could tell the buffalo was perfectly willing to pull the plow for him. All these movements went remarkably smoothly.

This was A-Tsòng's field, on the edge of Thâu-tsîng-khe in Pîn-tong Prefecture. With every inch and every yard, it was just the right time to transplant rice crops in this field that was just filled and plowed. An inverted image of faraway Mount Tāi-bú and puffs of clouds reflected in the shallow waters of the paddy. The plowshare seemed to want to turn over the whole mountain peak and break a path of blue through the clouds. Ngôo Tsín-sūi felt a sense of lightness and ease, and A-Tsòng's voice had lost its mocking tone as he said, "You're driving this buffalo so well. Say, how about I sell it to you?"

A-Tsín-sūi responded with a long *waaaaa* sound. The beast stopped in its tracks, standing as still as a statue. Imposing and valiant looking, it continued to stand firm in the mud. A-Tsín-sūi cocked his head. "Our family already has a buffalo. We have no need to raise a second one."

"The one your family owns? That old thing? You should put it out to pasture and take this younger one. I'll sell it to you for cheap. It'll be worth it."

"How much exactly?"

"I'll give it to you for ninety-three yen and fifty *sen*."

Ngôo Tsín-sūi stayed silent and pensive.

A-Tsòng then suddenly lowered the price, "Eighty yen. I'll cut it down to eighty for you."

"I'll take the buffalo home first, and then I'll give you my answer about buying it tomorrow."

"If you're taking it home, then you're going to have to buy it. Why do you want to wait for tomorrow?"

"I want Uncle A-Huàn to give it a look over."

"OK, well, fair enough. At least then we can settle the matter. I'll give you two days then. I'm not going to worry myself to death over this buffalo."

"Well this is what typically happens when a buffalo gains a new master. You need to have a commanding presence."

"But don't forget. Sometimes A-Huàn is kind of quirky. What he says isn't any better than a bunch of cow farts. There's no substance to them. You just listen to him, but there's no need to believe everything he tells you."

Uncle A-Huàn lived in the next hamlet over. He was known far and wide as a master of oxen and buffalo, and he was a part-time bovine vet. When there was a festival, snake-oil salesmen would roll into town and set up a stage and do operatic performances for small change. There's a half-sung line from one of their operettas that goes like this: "This young cowherd before us... Thao-lam is to the south; Pak-sek-thau is to the north. Ga-tang is to the east and Sai-kang-a to the west. All in all, one hundred *li* between them, and he's nowhere to be found. Nobody knows an ox better than Uncle A-Huàn!"

When Tsín-sūi brought the buffalo to him, A-Huàn was just squatting down beneath a banyan tree, smoking a water pipe. He looked like he was asleep. The metal tube of the water pipe was hanging at a precarious angle from a corner of his mouth. He inhaled deeply, and a gurgling noise emanated from the base of the water pipe. When Tsín-sūi was a young lad, he often came over to Uncle A-Huàn's farmstead to play. Once when A-Huàn was taking an afternoon nap, Tsín-sūi secretly took a puff or two of the tobacco in the water pipe. It only took him one drag of the tobacco to leave him coughing and hacking, however. He was so struck by the stark taste that he nearly stopped breathing. This time, he didn't immediately wake his neighbor. The buffalo wasn't afraid of strangers either, and it stood stoutly like a strong god next to its new owner, Tsín-sūi, who was quiet and at ease. Uncle A-Huàn had aged considerably. He had many more wrinkles than other elders in the vicinity. All of a sudden, A-Huàn's nose wrinkled up, as if the animal's odor had startled him awake. With his eyes wide with astonishment, he asked Tsín-sūi, "Whose buffalo is this?"

A-Huàn's right eye was completely blind. The whole orb was a milky gray, and a discharge flowed from the corners.

"It's my buffalo, Uncle. It's Ngôo Tsín-sūi. Ngôo Tshiu-ing's eldest son. Do you remember me still?"

Uncle A-Huàn rose to his feet, not bothering to give Tsín-sūi any visual acknowledgment. Instead, he looked at the buffalo first. He carefully looked over the entire animal from head to hoof, no detail spared. Since he was completely blind in his right eye, he used his left eye much like a scientist squinting into a microscope. His footsteps were uneven as he staggered along. First, he looked at the buffalo from its front and head. He bent his body down to get a better look, feeling around the animal's front legs. Then A-Huàn moved on towards its stomach, then lowered his head to feel around the animal's belly for a bit. He lightly squeezed one of the udders. Next, he lifted up the buffalo's tail and ran his hand across the animal's loins and rear. It was very strange that the buffalo just let him do what he wanted and didn't try to resist. Finally, A-Huàn went along the buffalo's back from head to tail, feeling every vertebra, from neck to tailbone. Once more, he moved from the animal's back to its front, from time to time using both of his hands. He had a cool and collected attitude. His demeanor was a little like a pianist who was lost in the middle of a performance.

Uncle A-Huàn went about his inspection in this way for about twenty minutes, then he cocked his head and began to speak, "A-Suī-á, this is a first-rate cow you have here. It's a female. What was the price you paid for her?"

"Uncle A-Tsòng is practically forcing me to buy her. He says he wants eighty for her."

"That's not very expensive at all. You can afford her. She's worth at least one hundred actually. Snap her up. Don't give it a second thought!" A-Huàn pointed to the buffalo's hocks.

"Look right there and you'll see what I mean. When she's standing, her fetlocks are bent forward a bit. It's like she's preparing to step forward. This is a buffalo with sturdy legs."

"Do you know how old she is?"

"Wait a second while I look. I'll check her teeth." A-Huàn moved around to in front of the buffalo. He lightly tugged on the lead cord, raising up the buffalo's head. He opened up the beast's mouth and used the fingers of his left hand to pinch at the animal's tongue, then lightly pulled it and pressed it down. The ox had a healthy tongue the color of a pink spring peach. Using his right hand, A-Huàn stuck his hand into the animal's mouth and felt around the teeth on the left side and then moved his hand to the teeth on the right. Ngôo Tsín-sūi watched from the side, looking a bit tense. Finally, he piped up, "Uncle, careful or you might lose a finger if she chomps down."

"She won't. Have you never seen me hold down a cow's tongue before? If you hold it down, it won't bite down at all. Though, you can't press its tongue down with too much force or else it'll vomit." A-Huàn kept working at the teeth as he was explaining this all to Tsín-sūi. Soon after, he pulled his hands out and let go of the buffalo's head. He wiped the cow saliva on his trouser legs, not bothering to wash his hands.

"She's about four and a half years old. She's at a good, strong age to be pulling a plow. When you want to know the age of an ox, you first take a look at its eyes. The younger ones tend to have a spark of life in their eyes. Second, you want to take a look at their overall physique and their bone structure. Just a minute ago, when I was feeling all around its back vertebrae and all that, I had a good idea about how old she is. Lastly, and it's a much better indicator, is to check their teeth. It's very accurate. Since they're always chewing cud, their teeth will grind down the longer they've been living. If you can figure out how worn down their teeth are, you've got yourself a pretty good guess. It's different when it comes to horses and rabbits though. Often it's because they just eat grass—"

The buffalo made a oaaaannnnn noise just then. It shook its horns at them, and its tail swatted left and right. Uncle A-Huàn noticed this and gave the buffalo two soft pats on the back and swiftly changed the topic. "A-Sūi-á, your father came over to visit the day before yesterday. He sat with me for a very long while. He said you were pissed off at him, and he was pretty angry with you too. What's the reason for all the hullabaloo? One of the two of you is going to have to relent and give in—"

"Uncle A-Huàn, you might not know it, but the thing I'm angry about is that he kept me from going back to Taihoku to attend university there. I'm one of the best students in this area. I graduated in the top five of my class at Takao Secondary. I could have been guaranteed a scholarship to go to Taihoku. It meant I wouldn't have needed to take an entrance exam to get into a school. Did my father tell you any of this? For now, I've listened to him and done what he wanted me to do, which was to stay here and help out. I take the buffalo out to our rice paddy every day and get to work, and he's still angry with me?"

"Yep. That's right. I understand you. He's said, 'The eldest son stays at home,' and 'It's the duty of the eldest son to sacrifice for everyone else.' A-Sūi-á, your father is like heaven above, and there's no way to stand up against heaven."

A-Tsín-sūi wasn't keen on continuing this topic. He turned back to look at the buffalo and said, "Uncle, when I first saw this buffalo, it felt like there was a bond between us, like we'd known each other for a long time. This buffalo is quite peculiar! It was very unruly with A-Tsòng. It wouldn't budge a single step for him, but when I came up to her, she was completely obedient. I was able to drive the plow without any protest from her whatsoever."

"Oh, is that so? As a rule of thumb, when a buffalo changes hands to a new master, it'll definitely fly off the handle a bit. It'd be the same with just about anyone."

"Maybe it's because I've been trained."

"A-Tsòng's been plowing fields with buffalo for nearly half his life. I'd say he's not as wet behind the ears." Uncle A-Huàn was staring into the distance, and the profile of his head resembled a hen looking out at the sky. A twinkle came to his blinded right eye. "I'll think about what you've just told me and keep it in mind."

"Think about it? You'll know the answer just by thinking about it?"

"I'll let you in on a secret. I hardly ever talk with other people. I only ever talk about things related to buffalo. I've always had them on my mind. When I go to sleep in the early hours, I lie in bed silently. My entire body feels free, and then I have a *bāng-kah*[5]—a revelation that appears to me. And just like that, I'll know exactly everything about the problem and how to solve it."

Tsín-sūi thought about what Uncle A-Tsòng had told him earlier. He said, "All you have to do is just listen to Uncle A-Huàn. You don't have to believe any of what he says if you don't want to." And so, Tsín-sūi didn't bother to keep these words of the elderly villager in mind much. He interrupted A-Huàn. "Uncle, I wanted to get your guidance about this buffalo. How much do I owe you for the consultation?"

"Owe me what? Your father's such a good friend of mine. You've always played over here since you were knee high to a grasshopper. Why would I want you to give me any money?!"

"I want to. I need to." Tsín-sūi was fishing through his pockets for a five-yen bill and then shoved it into A-Huàn's hands. A-Huàn took a step back and tried to refuse, trying to pass the bill back.

After three refusals, the old man said, "If you're so keen on paying for it, then wait for me for a second. I'll find you some change." A-Huàn fished out a small wallet from a trouser pocket. Opening it carefully, his fingers were trembling slightly. He counted out two ten *sen* bills and said, "I'll give you one yen back. You can pay me four yen."

Just as Tsín-sūi was about to leave, he suddenly thought of something. In a deliberately deep voice, he said, "Just now, when you were talking about the buffalo, it started to make that calling sound. It was waving its head back and forth, and its tail was swaying. Take a look. You gave it two

---

5. 夢甲 *Bāng-kah*, in Hoklo means a kind of aspirational dream.

light pats on the back, and then you hurriedly changed the subject. I don't understand how to do any of this."

"This is what I do when trying to build trust with a buffalo. It's like communicating to them."

"You can talk with them?"

"More or less. There's never a one-hundred percent guarantee that they'll understand. It's not like talking with another human."

"Is that so?" He started again, "Later on, when I have some time, I'll come back here to study from you."

"Just come over whenever you wish. No need to be polite."

Tsín-sūi lifted the lead rope and was already preparing to walk away, when two people came out of A-Huàn's house. He recognized them as Uncle A-Huàn's son and daughter-in-law. They urgently called to A-Sūi.

"A-Sūi-á! Don't go yet, don't go! Come have dinner with us! You can head home after you've stuffed your face first."

"I can't, I have to go tutor one of my students. I have to be at their house by seven, sharp."

"What's 'tutoring'?"

"Does that mean you're going to somebody else's house to teach them to read?"

"What can they make by reading? Can they make any money?"

"Of course they can. I'm going to teach three different students—one for an hour each," Tsín-sūi replied emphatically.

"Oh well, you'd better hurry along then."

***

Tsín-sūi was able to sell off the old family buffalo rather quickly. It only got to spend a couple of hours with the new one. The new buffalo was so quick in its plowing pace, it was astounding. For example, when turning up the soil in a field, each owner has different commands for their oxen or buffalo. Tsín-sūi's was a *whaaa* that started out long and was given a slight pitch raise at the end. This was his command for a buffalo to halt. A short *shiewww* or *tuooo* was his command to spur the animal on quicker. A long *yeeew* was what he used to tell the buffalo to slow down. If he lightly tapped on one side of the animal's rear end using a cane, with a field embankment up ahead, he wanted the buffalo to make a turn. The buffalo would oblige by turning towards the direction it was tapped. Often, it would take two to three days for the beast to learn its new owner's commands. Yet this new buffalo of Tsín-sūi's took to the commands the very first time it went out into the field, almost without making a single mistake.

That day, he was standing on the flat bar of the plow while the ox was pulling. The width of the plow sled was about eight feet across. Plowing the semidried paddy field before transplanting the rice seedlings was the last step before letting further water flood into the field. The buffalo was pulling steady and strong, drawing horizontal harrows across the mud of the uneven ground, with little ripples of mud here and there. Tsín-sūi's legs shook slightly with each pull of the plow. He mused as the plow was pulling along, as if he were sailing on the sea with a smooth breeze and calm swells, standing at the stern, guiding with an oar rudder. Or at least that's what his feet felt like as he was surfing along the mud! It was fine weather for the day.

"Everywhere we've combed over, the dirt clods we've plowed have slowly turned to a fine silky silt. Each area with a stubborn bump has been flattened down with each cut of the plowshare. We'll give the field two more runs and then call it a day. This new buffalo is just fantastic! Studying and trying to get into university was never going to be as easy as plowing the fields. Was I always just destined to be a farmer forever?" As his heart was filled with lamentation and his head up in the clouds, one of his feet suddenly lost balance and he slipped right face down into the mud. He called out in a long *wwahhhhhhh*, and his buffalo came to a halt, allowing Tsín-sūi to get right back up onto the flat bar. He needed to shake the reins once more, but his buffalo just turned its head and gave him a look, opening its mouth and showing its teeth as if to grin and snicker at him, as if chiding him, "If we're going to plow the field, then let's plow. Stop going off into flights of fancy!"

After plowing the field over once more, he saw his mother trudging over from a ways off, bringing out a kettle filled to the brim with tea and some snacks. Tsín-sūi didn't stop. In just a couple more runs, he'd be finished with the plowing. He called out lightly with a *yeeeewwww*, and the buffalo continued making strides. One run after another, the animal's pace was very steady, and the plow path followed in its evenness.

Once the field was fully plowed, he bent over at the waist to wash his hands off in the water around him. He heard Uncle A-Tsòng had already made his way over and was yacking away to Tsín-sūi's mother.

"I gave this buffalo to Tsín-sūi. I just had to sell it to him. When I owned it, I still had to beat it just to get it to move. It was living such a miserable life."

"As soon as A-Sūi-á got his hands on it, it suddenly became a fantastic worker and it's doing a lot better," she replied.

"Speak of the devil, he sure is a smart fellow. Not letting him go off to university is such a shame. *Tsin-bô-tshái*."[6]

"*Aiyee*... His father wouldn't let him. He was so adamant that he stay."

"You should've stood up to your husband."

"I wouldn't dare to even if I had wanted to."

"I'll teach ya something. If you argue loud enough and add in some tears and loud sobs, men sometimes get scared and back down and away."

"So you're saying you want our family to start making a ruckus, *honnh*?"

One evening several days later, Tsín-sūi had just finished working out in the field and was on his way home. He looked over to see Uncle A-Huàn, who was slowly ambling his way over, supporting himself with a walking stick. A-Huàn hadn't even gotten up close before he started to ask Tsín-sūi the million-yen question, "Well, did you buy it?"

"I did. It's an amazing animal. It drives the plow superbly. Right now, the field doesn't need any more plowing. I set it free to go have a mud bath over in the pond."

"Come over here for a second. A-Sūi-á, I have something to tell ya. I had a *bāng-kah* (premonition or vision) the other day. It was truly something, I tell ya. Let's sit down, and I'll tell ya more about it."

"Ok, let's. Let me bring out the tea kettle first, and I'll serve you."

"I don't keep things to myself. It's the longest-lasting *bāng-kah* I've ever had. It happened over an entire week—"

"Well, out with it. What was your *bāng-kah* about?"

"There were three or four beauties with golden hair. Their bodies were so gorgeous. Oh they were such beauties, like goddesses. They were captured by a group of soldiers and locked up in a room. This metal door was bolted shut. It was a tall, gigantic building by the sea, all made of large stones. It looked like an official's residence of some sort. It was well past midnight, and a plains tribesman came along in the dark. He snuck in and opened the metal door and set the women free. He brought them to the water's edge and dragged along a small boat with oars. He rowed for a long time all the way out to this ship out far in the distance. When he rowed the boat up to the ship, it was already light out. There were different soldiers on this ship though. The bridges of their noses were very high, and

---

6. 真無彩 "Tsin-bô-tshái." Taiwanese Hoklo for "It's too bad," "It's pitiful/a pity," "What a shame," "It's a waste of time/work/talent," or "It's not worth it."

they were wearing such bizarre military uniforms. They busied themselves getting the women up aboard and onto the deck. If I looked carefully at the tribesman's face, his eyes looked golden. The oddly dressed fellows spoke with him in some weird language, saying, 'Thank you for saving our daughters. You'll come back as a buffalo in your next life. You'll be rewarded for your favor.'"

"What?" Tsín-sūi guffawed after hearing old A-Huàn spinning this yarn. "Uncle, you're so talented at spinning a yarn. I never know whether it was real or not, but you paint a pretty fantastic picture."

"I'm not trying to *uē-hóo-lān*.[7] It really happened in my *bāng-kah*."

"I've gotta ask you, who were the soldiers in your vision? Were they Japanese?"

"No. It was clear as night and day. They were soldiers from Thang-suann (China). They belonged to Kok-sing-ia—the king of Ian-phenn—and other figures vaunted in the temple paintings and street operas." Uncle A-Huàn stared at Tsín-sūi with his one good eye and started to drift off in thought. A second later, he started up again, "If I wanted to trick you with a big *hóo-lān*, I'd wait for you to come back to my house and slowly spin the tale. Why would I need to take the trouble to walk all the way out here to tell you!? It's not like I just sit around doing nothing after I eat my fill. I was afraid I'd forget all about my *bāng-kah* if I didn't tell someone right away."

"Uncle, that wasn't one of your *bāng-kah*. You were just dreaming in your sleep."

"No. It was clearly a *bāng-kah*. There's no doubt about it. It happens when I'm already wide awake. The sun was high in the sky. The rooster had already crowed. The birds were already in the tree boughs, tweeting and chirping away—"

"Uncle, you are just dreaming things up. And why am I so certain of that? Because you say a plains tribesman and four women can all speak one of the plains tribes' tongues. It would only have such sounds if you were dreaming in your sleep."

"I never said there were sounds. The ending of that *bāng-kah* had written letters and characters—romanized letters."

"Could you understand what the romanized words meant?"

"I wasn't guessing. From start to finish, I understood all of it."

"Uncle, when I was studying at the Takao Secondary School, I studied subjects such as physics and biology, with a scientific education—"

---

7. 畫虎爛 "Uē-hóo-lān." Taiwanese Hoklo. To tell a bullshit story in order to trick someone.

Mishearing what Tsín-sūi said, "Grain studies? What's grain studies? Was it sweet potatoes or daikon greens?"

"No, no, Uncle. Science isn't a kind of vegetable. It's not a grain either. Science is a perspective for solving problems. It means to continue asking questions—and keep asking them again—from the point that you don't know the answer until you do. Uncle, I'm sorry I'm being impolite with you today by asking you to repeat yourself over and over again."

"So what you mean to say is that you don't believe any of my *bāng-kah*?"

"Well...yes. I don't really believe in reincarnation or that sort of thing."

"Well, that's just too much of a shame for me then. I went out of my way to come here and tell you. What a waste of my time and effort—"

"I'm very sorry. It's quite rude of me. Come! Let's go back to your house. I'll bring around the oxcart and give you a ride back."

***

Taking advantage of the break in farm labor over the ensuing weeks, Tsín-sūi traveled to Takao to pay a visit to his alma mater.

He came on account of Uncle A-Huàn's tale. He'd heard slivers of tales about Kok-sing-ia and of the Dutch from his schoolteachers, but he didn't quite understand the whole matter. "I can't just let it go and not know the whole story. I'll go check it out. It's only worth it if I can study it thoroughly." This was an attitude that was instilled in him all the way from the commoners' school through Takao Secondary. What Uncle A-Huàn talked about was something nobody in Tsín-sūi's community would ever be able to teach him. There were no books in his village that he could peruse and consult. It hadn't even been a year since he had graduated. It'd be quicker if he just went back to the school to ask his *sensei* on the matter, he thought to himself.

Takao Secondary was the highest institution of secondary education for all of the Pîn-tong–Takao area. It was an elite center of education with a five-year program. Students of Japanese ethnicity accounted for 70 percent of the pupils. Local Taiwanese had to take battery after battery of tests just to be admitted. Everything was as Tsín-sūi had remembered it since graduation day. The school gate guard still remembered him and let him on through the gate. Tsín-sūi walked along the twenty-meter–long cement path, passing right by the administrative building. The first floor of the building had a high-ceilinged corridor and veranda. It was a refreshing feeling, stepping in from the hot sun. Tsín-sūi was well-acquainted with every window, door, path, nook, and cranny of the building. The headmaster's office was just up the stairs to the right from where he was, along the corridor. He was familiar with Headmaster Yoshikawa Yūkai, but he didn't feel any desire to pay the man a visit. He went up the stairs to the left. Kazuno *sensei*, who had taught history, had a corner space in the large office.

Kazuno *sensei* was actually a Taiwanese man whose family name was originally Kok. He himself was a graduate of the Tainan No. 2 Secondary School. He was only one of two Taiwanese instructors who taught at the prestigious school. He had very severe nearsightedness and his head was sunk low, reading student homework books. Tsín-sūi crept up to his side and respectfully addressed him. Kazuno *sensei* jolted up from his startle and scrambled to put on his glasses which had fallen off. "I got your letter the other day. I've been expecting you."

"It's been almost a year since I'd last seen you. How are you doing, *sensei*?"

"I'm fine. I'm doing alright. It looks like you've darkened a bit. Got a bit of sun, huh? You look a lot stronger now too!" He carefully looked Tsín-sūi over once more, then continued, "Please sit and have some tea. I'll take you over to the library afterwards."

The library was a room in a building over by the back gate of the campus, across the parade ground. Both teacher and former pupil went across the lawn, shoulder to shoulder. Tsín-sūi had a peculiar feeling about this place as he was walking across the field. Every day of the five years that he was a student here, he and his classmates lined up for morning assembly drills. By the time he was in his fifth year, he was the leader of his class cohort and he acted as their commander during military drill training. Every day, it was on this wide field when he would shout out commands. Countless times, he would lead his platoon in chanting, "May the martial fortunes of the Great Empire of Japan continue forever! *Banzai, Ban-banzai*!"

The two of them chatted in Japanese as they walked. At that time, the Kominka laws[8] were fully in effect. Japanese was the language of the literati and intellectuals, and polite society now. Yet every time Tsín-sūi would bring up the matter of Uncle A-Huàn, naturally, he would speak only in Taiwanese Hoklo. Not long after, when he talked about his *bāng-kah*, he would switch back to Japanese (as it was originally a Japanese word).

---

8. The Kominka laws were directed towards turning the Taiwanese people into Japanese imperial subjects. There was pressure to adopt Japanese language and customs to the exclusion of all local languages and customs.

He kept weaving a narration with both languages. When he had finished telling Kazuno *sensei* about the *bāng-kah*, his *sensei's* first reaction was surprise. "I didn't know there was anyone who knew about that period in history down in the sticks of Pîn-tong!"

"*Sensei*, are the dreams my uncle is talking about actual history? Does it match up with the historical reality?"

"It *is* true that the Dutch East India Company packed up and left after they were defeated by Kok-sing-ia. That much is true."

"But Uncle A-Huàn is completely illiterate. He's never read a book before in his life."

"Oh, is that so?" After expressing his surprise in Taiwanese Hoklo, he switched back to Japanese. "He probably heard it from some old fellow over in Tâi-lâm's old An-pîng district, listening to old tales."

"I know his family pretty well. Based on what I know, he doesn't have any relations in the old capital. Apart from going to the A-li-kang buffalo market, he's never set foot outside of our village or the hamlets in the surrounding area.

Just as they reached this part in their conversation, they arrived in front of the library doors. After entering the small space, they stood between two bookcases. Kazuno *sensei* whispered to Tsín-sūi in a hushed voice, "The *bāng-kah* in your uncle's story is just a snippet of that part of history. Since Kok-sing-ia's mother was a Japanese woman from northern Kyushu, the Japanese academic world has studied him in some depth. There are many works written about the pirate lord. I hope you'll be able to comprehend much of the major events and deeds of his life. I'm giving you two books on his life that you can borrow and take home."

"But I've already graduated. Can I still borrow them?"

"Just borrow them under my name. Send them back in the post when you're finished reading them."

Kazuno *sensei* took two small tomes off the shelf. Tsín-sūi stared down at them, looking over the titles. One of them was *The Siege of Fort Provintia*, and the other was *The Conclusion of the Tayou'an Negotiations*.

Kazuno *sensei* switched topics once they'd stepped back outside. "Wait a second. Don't you want to pay a visit to Headmaster Yoshikawa *sensei*?

"I'd rather not."

"You've already graduated. He's mentioned you several times at different events and occasions. He holds you in high esteem as a model student."

"Oh?" Tsín-sūi recoiled in disbelief. "My father was opposed to me going off to Taihoku to pursue further studies in a university. I had to give it up. When I came back, I pled with the headmaster to help me pursue tutoring or to give me some encouragement to disobey my father, but he flatly refused. He obviously didn't want to help me."

"Do you know why?"

"No, not at all."

"There were only five of you students who were given direct admission into universities. The sixth person was a Japanese student. I remember his name—Komura Takenobu. You are acquainted with him. When you gave up your placement acceptance, the headmaster was ecstatic because he could finally send a Japanese in your stead."

"I never knew that!"

"He is not in the wrong for doing so though. After all, you were the one who gave up your university placement." Upon hearing his teacher's words, Tsín-sūi felt a wave of prickly heat flash across his face.

Speak of the devil and he shall appear. Who else would it be but Headmaster Yoshikawa himself. He just happened to enter the administrative building corridor. He had just come down to the first floor when he noticed both Kazuno *sensei* and Tsín-sūi. He hadn't said anything. Tsín-sūi made eye contact and then quickly walked up to Headmaster Yoshikawa, making a deep bow. "Hello, Headmaster. It's wonderful to see you."

"Oh what's this? What occasion has led you to come back this day?" Headmaster Yoshikawa still had the same stern look he always had. His lips were tightly pressed together, the corners forming a constant frown, with two evident creases. His grimace tended to make people shrink back in fear.

"I had an issue I wanted to talk about with Kazuno *sensei* and to borrow two books."

"You didn't continue onto university. What are you doing these days?"

"Well, I'm embarrassed to say, but I'm engaged in farm work at the moment. There's no promising future in it."

"Why do you think there's no future in farming? Why be ashamed? Is it that you just don't wish to be a farmer, is that it?" Headmaster Yoshikawa replied rhetorically in an ever-sterner voice. Tsín-sūi didn't like the headmaster's condescending tone, but perhaps the headmaster had hit a little too close to home, so Tsín-sūi kept silent.

The headmaster continued, "'Agriculture is our mother, the nurturer of all industries / Those of means look down on it, in shame / Those who are strong and healthy and avoid engaging in it, are lazy and indolent.' This is, of course, from out of the third-year curriculum. Did you forget this poem so soon? Now then, can you tell me who was it that composed this piece?"

The maxim, written as a poem, was one that Tsín-sūi had had well-ingrained into him, but he decided not to answer the headmaster directly. He proudly, if not a little arrogantly, retorted, "Headmaster Yoshikawa, I'm not in the least bit looking down my nose at farm labor, if not ambitiously engaging in it. I'm engaging in it as a means of creating blessings and fortune for all farmers. I'm staying at home to work on the farm." In his heart of hearts, Tsín-sūi wasn't so sure what kind of career he wanted to be engaged in. He didn't have any dreams or aspirations to speak of either. He just felt like rebutting the headmaster in this way. He felt stung by the headmaster's reproach, hence his blurted-out response.

2.

Uncle A-Tsòng drove his oxcart urgently along, racing all the way down the road to Uncle A-Huàn's farmhouse. When he reached the entrance to Uncle A-Huàn's farmhouse, he turned in, then made a long, drawn-out call, "*Haiiiieee...chhhhaaaa.*" The buffalo immediately stopped in its tracks. A-Tsòng hopped down from the cart. Rushing into the house, he shouted at the top of his lungs, "Uncle A-Huàn! Where's Uncle A-Huàn!?"

A-Huàn's daughter-in-law was the first to answer, "What's the matter? What's wrong with your buffalo?"

"There's nothing wrong with it. It's A-Suī! Something's happened to Ngôo Tsín-suī!"

Uncle A-Huàn piped up from the kitchen table, standing deeper in the house. He called back loudly, "The buffalo A-Suī bought from you is healthy and strong. What could've possibly happened?"

"A-Suī-á was kicked out of the family home by his father. He told me to watch over the buffalo while he's not living there, but the beast holds a grudge against me. It won't budge an inch if I try to pull it along."

"*Aiyah*! How could A-Tshiu-ing do such a thing? His son, A-Suī is so hardworking. How could he possibly be dissatisfied with his eldest son?" Uncle A-Huàn said as he hurriedly shoveled the last of his food into his mouth. He then grabbed his walking stick and headed out the door.

After he climbed aboard A-Tsòng's oxcart, Uncle A-Huàn continued to prattle on about Tsín-suī's father. After going on for a while, he suddenly asked, "What do you mean, Tsín-suī's buffalo has it out for you?"

"I had beat her pretty severely when I was still the owner. When she looks at me with those big buffalo eyes, there's still hatred there."

"It won't hold a grudge. Buffalo don't remember cruelties for that long.

"A-Suī said that he already gave it a name—Mari."

"Mari? Is that a Japanese name or a Taiwanese name?"

"I dunno. It sounds Japanese, though are there any Japanese women around here with the name Mari?"

"Mari? Mari? I'm as old as the hills and I've never heard of anyone giving a buffalo a name! It's preposterous!" Uncle A-Huàn mumbled this several times more to himself. Before he knew it, they had arrived at Ngôo Tsín-suī's home. The buffalo was contentedly munching away at some hay in its pen. There was an oxcart parked next to the pen with twenty or thirty books piled up in it. "In all my life, I've never seen anyone put books in an oxcart!" he mumbled to himself once more.

Uncle A-Tsòng whispered an explanation into A-Huàn's ear, "Tsín-suī's moved into another person's house to become a live-in tutor. He asked me to take away the buffalo, the oxcart, and the books in the cart for him."

A-Tsòng was halfway through explaining to A-Huàn, when Tsín-suī's father came barreling out of the house. Uncle A-Huàn began by asking him candidly, "A-Tshiu-sai-á, hasn't Tsín-suī-á been such a good son to you by helping you take care of all the stuff with the house and farm? He's always out in the fields helping you. He's a good son you have, there. Why have you been so thick-skulled and cold-hearted that you'd kick him out?"

"Uncle A-Huàn, what do you know about any of this? Earlier this year, he said he wanted to move away and make his own way. I took him to the sugar mill company to try out working as a foreman clerk alongside an *ojīsan* over at the plantation in Tsong-Lan, who said he could get him an office job for eighty *sen* a day—"

A-Tsòng then cut in, "Just eighty *sen*?! You can find other jobs that pay a full day's wage of at least one yen."

"Don't you think I know that? But the thing is, this is the first time Tsín-suī's tried making his own way in life. He doesn't have any experience. What's more, having a titled position at the sugar mill is pretty good. Eighty *sen* a day is also pretty good pay."

"So, what the hell happened that you kicked out such a fine young man?"

"It happened like this: Tsín-suī led a group out to plant sugarcane and split them up over the work site. There was a lot of clay in the soil, so it was pretty hard work, so he went off to negotiate for better salary conditions since the workers were so miserable. They discussed two or three arrangements, but the higher-ups wouldn't allow it. He only just earned his secondary school diploma, and he threw away this opportunity. You think about that for a second. I tried pleading three, four times. I had tried so hard to get him this good job and then he quits over some stupid trifle. I was so angry, I was this close to wringing his sorry neck," Tshiu-sai gestured.

"A-Tshiu-sai-á, all you had to do was just kick him out for two or three days and blow off some steam, then take him back in. Ah... Look at that buffalo. Its spirit and life have all but drained from its eyes. It knows you chased Tsín-suī away."

"It's not something two or three days will fix. I want to teach that little bastard a good lesson and show him what it truly means to make one's own way in society. He can't just only consider those at the bottom. He needs to think about the company's position as well."

"Tshiu-sai-*hiann*, A-Suī is a good kid. I've seen him working the fields. He's always out there doing back-breaking work. He takes the lead whenever there's something to do. Take him back in. You've got a lot of work to do around the farm. You need him, no?" A-Tsòng added, "He's such a good worker. Ask him to come home. Call him home. There's nobody better at driving a buffalo and tilling a field than him."

***

Some distance away, Tsín-suī was in the middle of tutoring. His charge was Tông Tsuān-tik, a student currently enrolled in his second year of study at Takao Secondary.

When the tutoring was over, Tsín-suī didn't leave right away. He waited at the Tông family table for Tsuān-tik's older brother, Tsuān-tsong, to arrive. About twenty minutes later, Tsuān-tsong arrived home in a pedicab. Tsín-suī went out to meet him, saying meekly, "I've been kicked out of my home..."

"When did that happen?"

"Just this afternoon."

Tông Tsuān-tsong immediately called out to his little brother, "A-Tik-á, go make up the guest room, will you? Your *sensei*, Ngôo Tsín-suī is going to be staying with us, starting tonight."

"Which room?"

"The one he stayed in once a long time ago. That one." Tsuān-tsong barked out his order then turned back to face Tsín-suī, "So what was it about?"

Speaking in both Japanese and Taiwanese Hoklo, Tsín-suī got straight to the point and told Tsuān-tsong all about the affair at the Tsong-Lan sugar plantation belonging to the sugar mill. Tsuān-tik quickly ran out to hear what Tsín-suī had to say.

When Tsín-suī and Tsuān-tsong came to know each other, it began as a "tying of their fate with the Phênn-ôo'ers" (those from the Pescadores archipelago). It was on a winter night, just after Tsín-suī had gotten off from work at the sugar plantation. He got on his pedal bike and peddled off like the wind in order to make it to the other place where he was doing some tutoring—it was the Ôngs who ran a ceramics shop in the Kurogane-chō[9] district over in Pîn-tong town. Tutoring for this household normally started at seven in the evening, but there was no class scheduled for that night. After Tsín-suī had finished teaching his lessons with the family's young son the last time, Ông *thài-thài* especially mentioned that there was a group of relatives and friends from Phênn-ôo who were going to gather for dinner at her house. She took the opportunity to ask the *sensei* to come over for dinner as well. Ngôo Tsín-suī laid great store in being invited since Ông *thài-thài* was particularly kind and doting towards him. She never skimped on his tutoring fees and would often give him extra cash, even. Probably of more importance, though, was that the older of the Ông sisters, Giók-ìn, and he were quite smitten with each other. Often, they would chat for hours on end, so tutoring became just a secondary reason for going to her house. Spending time with Giók-ìn was more important to him than stuffy pages.

He was gasping for breath when he finally arrived at the Ông household. Ông *thài-thài* and her eldest sons were seated around the table in the living room, talking small talk. Ông Giók-ìn and her younger brother and sister were all moving back and forth from kitchen to table, helping to set the dishes out. Nearly all of the dishes on the menu for tonight were seafood dishes from Phênn-ôo (Penghu). Ông *thài-thài* noted Tsín-suī's arrival and called everyone to gather around the table. She raised her voice to introduce Tsín-suī:

"This young man here is the *sensei* to two of my children. His name is Ngôo Tsín-suī, from Thâu-tsîng-khe. Last year, he taught my younger daughter, Giók-bí, and now he's teaching her younger brother, Ông Than-á."

The guests from Phênn-ôo had a peculiar accent when they spoke in Hoklo. When they said the name of their island, they pronounced the "*phênn*" as "*phing*" and it was enunciated with a flat tone deep in the back of their throats. Tsín-suī knew now though that when Taiwanese from Phênn-ôo made their way over to the main island of Taiwan, they tried their hardest to speak with a Pîn-tong accent. But when it was just them under one roof, the authentic Phênn-ôo accent gushed out merrily, lapping like the ocean waves that surrounded their archipelago home.

---

9. 屏東市黑金町 "Heitō-machi Kurogane-chō." Japanese. The Kurogane block in Heitō City. A part of what is now the first section of Fengchia Road in Pingtung City.

There was a young man seated diagonally across from Tsín-suī. He looked somewhat mature and of some high stature and importance. He went ahead and directly introduced himself to Tsín-suī.

"My name is Tông Tsuān-tsong. I'm the technical engineer at the sugar company's Houbi sugar mill."

Tsín-suī's eyes lit up. "Oh! I also work for the sugar company. I'm the foreman over at the Tsong-Lan plantation."

"I heard Ông *thài-thài* saying that you graduated from Takao Secondary and that you were at the top of your class, that you were given open admission to a university." Tsuān-tsong kept switching into Japanese every now and then, "But your *tō-san* (father) wouldn't permit you to continue your studies. That's a terrible shame! I graduated from the forestry department of the Workmen's Training School in Taihoku."[10]

Tsín-suī responded to him using Japanese, "Ah, I'm sorry! How rude of me. It's quite something for any youth from Pîn-tong to be able to study in Taihoku at such a prestigious institution."

"I'm twenty-six this year. I was born in Meiji 37 (1904). Are you younger than me?"

"By about five years. I was born in Meiji 42 (1909). I'm twenty-one now," Tsín-suī answered.

Right then, an *ojīsan* (old man) sitting on Tsuān-tsong's other side said in a low whisper, "Oh I heard this Ngôo Tsín-suī is interested in the older young miss. It seems they've already entered into their courtship phase..." Though he was sitting right next to Tsuān-tsong, the older man was speaking in such a clear voice that it could be heard by several people around the table. Even Ông Giȯk-ìn, who was preparing tea and assorted sweets, could hear the old man. She turned her head to look back at him and teasingly scolded him.

"*A-pe* (Uncle), stop talking badly about me, *honnh.*"

"Strange, I'd say it's a good thing. What bad things did I say about you?"

Another of the guests jumped in, "Well, that's not where it ends, either. When he's done tutoring at other households, Ngôo-*san* always makes his way back here to speak sweet nothings to Giȯk-ìn. A lot of people have seen him doing so."

Ông *thài-thài* couldn't conceal the excitement on her face, saying, "Oh, the fishermen haven't finished weaving their nets. How can you talk about

---

10. The Taihoku Workmen's Training Institute would later be the Taipei Worker's Training School. Now it's a part of the Taipei Technical University.

catching fish? Come, come! Eat. Don't stop with your chopsticks. Drink up! Drink a little more. Don't hold back. There! There you go!"

But everyone understood the meaning behind her words and outward expression. Ông *thài-thài* had high hopes for this tutor. No wonder! Otherwise, why would this otherwise random young fellow even be invited to a dinner with a bunch of people hailing from Phênn-ôo if not to let them see her future Pîn-tong son-in-law?

Everyone at the table unconsciously gave Tsín-suī a glance or two. Surely, he was a top-notch guy! He had a presence about him. He was tall, the bridge of his nose was high, his ears were large, and his lips were the kind that spoke of strong emotions. In a place like Pîn-tong, you'd be hard pressed to find a better son-in-law, even if you took up a lantern and searched in the dark and went stumbling about to find one. Now, the people from Phênn-ôo looked at Ngôo Tsín-suī in a different way. Ông *thài-thài* knew everyone in town. Since her husband had passed away, she had no choice but to take over the family ceramics shop. It was then that she realized just how shrewd and insightful of a business owner she could be, doing even better for the store than her husband had. In just a few short years, her ceramics shop was doing far better than before. Nearly all the shops and restaurants around Kurogane-chō and Triangle Park were using her wares.

"If he marries the young Miss Ông, of course, he'll be inheriting this dowry in addition to a beauty of a bride," some of those sitting at the table were undoubtedly thinking to themselves.

In the intervening silence, Tsuān-tsong began to ask Tsín-suī a question, "Ngôo-*san*..."

"Call me Tsín-suī, please."

"Oh, OK then. Ah-Tsín-suī, do you happen to still have some free time in the evenings to do tutoring? I'd like to ask you to tutor my younger brother, A-Tik-á."

Tsín-suī hadn't yet had time to open his mouth to respond before Ông *thài-thài* pounced, despite the fact that she was still chewing on a bite of food. "Of course he does. He's free on *suiyōbi* (Wednesday) and *doyōbi* (Saturday), or at least that's what I know. A-Suī-á, did I remember correctly?" She didn't wait for Tsín-suī to respond and continued, "When my younger daughter, Giok-bí didn't pass her exams to get into any elite secondary school, I hired Tsín-suī here to help, and under his tutelage and guiding hand, she managed this year to get accepted into Taihoku No. 3 Girls' Secondary School. He's a spectacular tutor."

"What school is your brother currently attending?" Tsín-suī finally was able to get a word in.

"He's studying at Takao Secondary, in his first year. He's your *kōhai* (underclassman)."

"You're an older brother, why don't you give him some guidance?"

"My workplace isn't in Pîn-tong. It's a bit inconvenient for me. The other real reason is that we studied industrial subjects and learned how to ply business trade. Many of our courses were about physical techniques and know-how. I can't teach him any of the things he needs to learn at Takao Secondary."

"Well, OK then. It's settled. I'll tutor him. No problem."

"I'll stick to the rate Ông *thài-thài* pays you for tutoring, if that's OK."

Ông *thài-thài* once more interjected, "Yes, that sounds fine."

Afterwards, Ông *thài-thài* and her older son went around pouring a round of drinks for all around the table. She was very animated, talking about trivial, commonplace matters to do with the house, exchanging business news with several of the guests. The table overflowed with the warmth of Phênn-ôo-accented Hoklo. In the middle of the din, Tsuān-tsong and Tsín-suī quietly discussed different topics, switching to Japanese.

"You mentioned a bit ago that your business is more focused on industrial techniques training. So did you ever have to do military drill training?"

"Of course. We had to do it twice a week."

"We had to also, over at Takao Secondary."

"Do students from Taiwan get to take classes with the Japanese students over at Takao Secondary?"

"Yep, that's right."

Someone from the other side of the table piped up, "Hey you two young'uns. Speak in Hoklo."

Tsuān-tsong immediately switched back to Hoklo, "Was it worth studying in the same class with them, or no?"

"Of course, it was OK. Everyone had to play by the same rules. We all learned the same material. We Taiwanese aren't going to be outmatched by the Japanese."

"But my father said it might be better to keep Taiwanese and Japanese students separated," Tsuān-tsong unwittingly switched back into Japanese.

"Why? That would just create inequality and unfairness. It would only help the Japanese to discriminate against people from our island, no?"

"My father said that 'same school, same curriculum' only helps the Japanese to consolidate control and assimilate us. He'd rather that it be openly unfair and unequal and that our Han culture not be subsumed by the Japanese."

"I don't understand your father's thinking."

"He's got a more deep-set Han consciousness and identity than we do."

On the other side of the table, two *ojīsan* were speaking to each other in a hushed tone, "I'm hankering to tell those youngsters to stop speaking in Japanese."

"No need. It's useless trying to tell them again. It's all the youth ever speak these days—the 'national' language. There's nothing we can do about it."

Reaching this point in the conversation, they heard another *ojīsan* ask in Hoklo, "A-Tsuān-tsong, how come your father, A-Îng-*hiann* didn't come tonight?"

This interrupted Tsín-suī and Tsuān-tsong's conversation. He responded hurriedly, "My father is busy with some work at the Pingtung airport and couldn't make it out. He said I should give his regards to everyone."

"The next time we're all together, he absolutely must attend. We all miss him so much."

The evening feast continued until almost nine o'clock. As everyone was making their way out of the house, the Ông family came out to send off the guests and say goodnight. Tsín-suī and Tsuān-tsong kept talking up a storm.

Someone among the departing guests joked, "Even though you two spring chickens just met, you just keep cluck-cluck-clucking away."

"We're going home in the same direction," both youths retorted.

Just then, the younger of the Ông sisters, Giȯk-bí, came forward, "I'll send off Mr. Tông and *sensei*." Tsín-suī looked back and saw that her older sister, Giȯk-ìn, had already headed into the house to clear away the dishes and the table. He thought to himself, "It's Giȯk-ìn who takes responsibility for the care of her family!" He then walked up to Giȯk-bí and said softly, "Ah, the two of us still have a lot to talk about. Maybe you might want to head back to the house and help out your sister." As the words left Tsín-suī's lips, he paid no more attention to the younger Ông sister and walked shoulder to shoulder with Tsuān-tsong over towards the dark spot where his bicycle was parked.

Tsín-suī had just retrieved his bicycle when he noticed that Tsuān-tsong was getting into a pedicab. He was a bit shocked. "Oh, so he's actually a rich guy, huh? How could I ever compete with him?" he thought to himself.

He was about ready to hop on his own bicycle and ride on home when he heard Tsuān-tsong calling out from the pedicab, "Ah-Tsín-suī! Grab ahold of my cab and ride with me. Come over to my house and sit and chat for a bit, OK?"

He didn't know why, but he immediately shot back a "*Hó!* (OK!)" Then both of them rode side by side back to Tsuān-tsong's home. Tsín-suī noticed that the pedicab was a private one and that it was in peak condition, pedaled by a chauffeur. The cart went along smoothly, neither too fast nor too slow. It was almost silent as it moved along. As they were peddling along, depending on the road, sometimes they would be next to each other and at other times, one in front of the other. Once on the road, Tsín-suī didn't feel too inclined to pedal his heart out. He was afraid that his beaten-up bicycle, though not so old, would begin to make some frightening creaking noises.

Once at the Tông household, Tsín-suī finally looked up and was astonished. "*Wah!* Just what kind of house is this?!" It was a curious-looking, two-storied mansion built in a Western baroque style. At first glance from faraway, it almost looked like a church, but upon closer inspection, he realized it wasn't. In the surrounding darkness, he sensed that the walls were made of stone, the windows were small, and the gate massive. Tsuān-tsong stopped the pedicab in front of the main gate. The driver continued on and parked it off in a garage. Tsín-suī followed and parked his bicycle there, as well. Tsuān-tsong intentionally walked down to accompany Tsín-suī back up to the house.

There was a tall-ceilinged hall in the house. It was wide and airy. There were all sorts of furniture filling up every nook and cranny of the room. Tsín-suī opened his mouth to speak, "As soon as I walked in here, I felt that this must be some magnate's home—nothing like my family's house, a plain old farmhouse."

"My father is the owner of a rice shop and bakery. They make cakes and also contract out other businesses on the side. He's thought about starting up a factory."

"Your father's a pretty good man to have sent you off to a technical school."

"Perhaps, yes."

After the two of them sat down, they continued discussing the topics they hadn't exhausted back at the dinner party. Tsín-suī asked, "What do you feel that you learned from the Japanese when you were studying at the technical college?"

Tsuān-tsong paused while he brought a glass of water from the tea service, responding halfway back to his seat, "I learned one absolutely invaluable thing, and that was to 'be prepared.' When I was at the technical school, no matter what kind of homework it was, all sorts of tools—rulers, compasses, schematics, operators' manuals, and even short and long saws—if we weren't thoroughly prepared and knew our manuals like the backs of our hands, we'd be severely reprimanded and punished."

"Oh, I've had sort of a similar experience, though since you studied industrial subjects, you probably have a deeper appreciation of things."

"The Japanese are a bit fanatical when it comes to this point. No. Wait. What I ought to say is that they're a bit anxious. Our class was a mix of both Taiwanese and Japanese home islanders. I realized that our Japanese classmates maintained a sense of fear and anxiety. They were afraid of their work being seen as shoddy."

"And because of that, they've always produced excellent work?"

"Not just that, but overly, exceptionally well."

"We Taiwanese students were a bit more happy-go-lucky, and...sloppy. We were not as anxious."

That evening, the two youths talked about their schooling, work, agriculture, the differences between Japanese and Taiwanese peoples. When Tsín-suī suddenly realized that he should take his leave of his new friend, it was already past midnight. Tsuān-tsong persuaded him to stay the night and head back home in the morning. Tsín-suī adamantly protested that he couldn't, saying, "My father would tan my hide if I didn't." But Tsuān-tsong rationalized that it was safer to go back in the morning. This was the first time Tsín-suī stayed overnight at the Tông household.

Tonight was the second. Tsín-suī told the whole story from head to tail of how his father had kicked him out. "I'm afraid I won't be staying for just a single night this time. I might have to lay low here until my father cools down and his wrath subsides."

"Don't worry about the extent of your stay here. You can live here as long as you'd like."

After the guest room was all made up for him, Tsín-suī told Tsuān-tsong about the new buffalo he had just purchased, describing "A-Huàn's mystical 'ox-reading' abilities." Then he talked for a long time about Uncle A-Huàn's seemingly realistic *bāng-kah* vision and how he had gone back to his alma mater to search for some truth.

Tông Tsuān-tik, who was sitting off to the side, called out, "*sensei*, that's interesting! I never imaged that you did farming with a buffalo out in a field!"

Tsuān-tsong followed up, "A-Suī-á, since becoming an adult, I've always followed in my father's steps and worked in the rice shop. After that I went to the technical college. I never knew farming could be so interesting!"

Both the Tông brothers' responses seemed to stir up Tsín-suī's deep-seated feeling of self-effacement about how "staying home to work on the farm has no future." He took a deep breath, composed himself, and listened to Tsuān-tsong. "After today, I might not be coming home to Pîn-tong as often as I'd like. My father is gradually shifting his businesses to the port city of Takao. He's already told me to quit working for the sugar mill and to go on to Takao to help him out there."

That night, Tsín-suī tossed and turned in his sleep. He thought about how Tsuān-tsong and his father had a relationship like a fish does to water, and how he and his own father were always opposed to one another. He kept mulling it over until he just couldn't get back to sleep. He harbored a deep resentment towards his father over the past few years. Sometimes that resentment boiled over into pure hatred and loathing. Laying on this bed in the Tông household as he was, he rehashed the whole event of quitting the sugar mill job. Was it really so awful for him to have organized the workers in demanding a higher wage? Or was what his father said right? The afternoon Tsín-suī quit the mill and came home and his father found out, his father was implacable, and the two of them had a huge argument. Father and son shot broadsides of words back and forth at each other. His father pointed his index finger at him and cursed, "When you're a foreman, you have no choice but to stand on the side of the company. That's the right thing to do. You've f***ed everything up. You've refused to take responsibility for your actions, and you have the balls to dare raise your voice with me!"

Tsín-suī was still protesting when his father threw out his sternest rebuke of his son yet, "Get out of my house. Out! You're not allowed to come back! You're no son of mine!"

Tsín-suī was desperate to fall asleep. "Should you be sticking your neck out for the workers or for the company? Next morning at breakfast, I'll ask this question of Tsuān-tsong and see what he says." He turned over onto his side again. This question kept gnawing at his mind right until he finally fell asleep.

The following morning, Tsuān-tsong had already eaten and was preparing to fly out the front door when he stopped by the guest room to check in. Drowsy with half-awoken eyes, Tsín-suī jumped up to his feet in a dither. "*Tsin pháinn-sè* (I'm sorry), I could hardly sleep a wink last night..."

"Don't trouble yourself over it. I just came in to check in on you. You have a lot of pressing things to deal with today. I'm sorry for waking you."

"It's OK. It's about time I should be getting up."

"Since we're on the subject, A-Suī-á, I have a favor to ask of you. You're out of work, and your father's kicked you out of your house. There's a job over by the Pîn-tong airport that I have to wind up. I'd like to see if you're interested in helping me out with it." Tsuān-tsong looked at him with a cryptic look to his face and then continued, "It's building steel frames. You don't need to go do anything yourself, just represent me at on-site management and organize the labor and material needs is all."

"OK. Where's the jobsite location at the airport?"

"When you get there, just ask someone where Tông Îng's construction site is. Someone is bound to know."

"Yeah, but none of the workers will know who the heck I am. How will I manage?"

"You'll take the family pedicab there for the first day. They all know our chauffeur. You can order them around and all." As soon as he finished speaking, he turned around and left, having spoken this last sentence in Japanese.

About a half hour later, the pedicab was already waiting by the front gate. Tsín-suī rushed through washing up, combing his hair and eating before jumping into the pedicab. He got the feeling that farmers' families and business-owning families were quite different animals. As he got into the pedicab, he thought of the issue he had wanted to bring up with Tsuān-tsong.

"Mr. Driver, how did Tsuān-tsong-*hiann* get to work today?" Tsín-suī asked the driver.

"I took him to the train station, and then I came back to pick you up."

"Oh, *to-siā* (thank you)."

"The young master said to take you along the quickest and easiest road to get out to the airport. You'll have to ride your bicycle there tomorrow. You want to go there along the way I'm taking you."

"Oh yes, I'm thankful for Tsuān-tsong's attention to detail."

The pedicab was going along at a moderate pace. They first crossed over a truss bridge. Not long after they neared the peak, the cart slowed its pace. Tsín-suī noticed that the driver was giving it all he had, straining himself to go up the slope of the bridge. He felt like hopping down out of the pedicab and helping to push it, but he hesitated to do so. The pedicab was already over the hump and was going down the other side anyways. They went along a small street past the Ogawa-chō residential quarter and turned left when they hit the Kessei Workshop, where they could see the Ōda pharmacy and the Miyazoe Publishing Co. and then passed through the central market in Heitō City (Pîn-tong). They then went through a small alley heading north. Tsín-suī made a note of both sides of the entrance to the alley. On the left, there was a giant sign in red with the word "tavern" written on it. On the right, there was a sign in white with black lettering that said, "Fukuda Dentistry." Next, they kept straight and eventually the air felt cooler. Trees lining both sides of the road provided shade—banyans, camphors, and weeping willows. It was clean and tranquil all around. A variety of birds Tsín-suī didn't even know the names of were singing back and forth to each other from different trees, singing as if in a musical troupe. Occasionally, he would see Japanese men dressed in neat uniforms stepping out from residences hidden by the trees. Tsín-suī could sense the driver was picking up his pace. Not long after, he could hear a group of kids reciting lessons from a textbook. They looked up as the pedicab cycled by. It was a school. "Tax Bureau Elementary School" was written on the gate name placard. It was a school only for Japanese children, attached to their parents' workplace. Of course Tsín-suī knew that. The chauffeur began to speak, this time in Japanese.

"Up ahead...to the left...is a district office dormitory. Coming up in a bit is the barracks for the local army officers." All Tsín-suī could give in response was a simple "Oh." His heart was filled with emotion—despite having grown up his entire life in Pîn-tong, he'd never been to this district before. It was serene and refreshing. The air here had a sweet, clean tinge to it. He unconsciously took several deep breaths. He thought to himself that the Japanese had managed to turn this area into a little slice of heaven, and they were truly living in one by the looks of it.

He started to laugh at the absurdity of it all. How was it that he, having been chased out of home and family by his father should suddenly be sitting in a chauffeured pedicab, looking like a young lord? It was like he was some great character in a novel, hah! How pitiful though that his experience would only last for one day. He wouldn't have any such free ride tomorrow.

It was just four in the afternoon when he got back from the airport. Tsín-suī switched to his own bike from the Tông household and cycled hurriedly to reach Uncle A-Tsòng, but he discovered the buffalo wasn't at A-Tsòng's house.

"Yesterday, I went over to Uncle A-Huàn's and then went over to your house. Your father wouldn't let us take your buffalo. I took your oxcart with your books all piled up on it and hauled it over to A-Huàn's," A-Tsòng explained.

"Did you cover them up with anything?"

"Of course. I was afraid it would rain during the night or that there would be dew in the morning, so I covered them up twice. One layer was some old shirts and trousers I no longer wore. The second layer was a pile of some dried-up rice stalks."

"Thank you, thank you!"

"A-Suī-á, I need to tell you something. Your father was furious the last time I spoke with him. He was also threatening that if you were living just fine outside of his house, that you shouldn't bother thinking about going home any time soon. So you should wait for your father to ask you to come back. We'll see who can last the longest."

"Thanks for telling me. I'm going over to Uncle A-Huàn's for a short spell."

Tsín-suī hopped back up on his bicycle and thought to himself, "This A-Tsòng, he's not speaking like most other people! But what he says makes a lot of sense."

When Tsín-suī reached Uncle A-Huàn's house, he saw his oxcart and his books just as A-Tsòng had said. He parked his bicycle off to the side by the rice paddy embankment. A-Huàn's daughter-in-law came out just then and told Tsín-suī, "My father hired someone to watch after the buffalo. Your things are being stored over there. Everything's fine."

"Thank you, thank you! So I guess I should be taking my things now, then?"

"Sure, if you'd like."

Tsín-suī took off the rice stalks and clothing covering his books. He then lifted his bicycle up into the oxcart. The daughter-in-law came over to help him, asking him, "My father says you make money with these books. Is that true? How do you turn them into money?"

Tsín-suī was dumbstruck, then a slight smile creased along his face. "I told you last time, right? I teach others or help them study, and I get paid for it. That's how I make money with these books. That's what your father meant."

"Oh, I see."

Since Uncle A-Huàn wasn't home, Tsín-suī didn't linger for too long. Using both arms, he pulled that awfully heavy oxcart along, step by step. A-Huàn's daughter-in-law helped by pushing from behind for a couple paces, but Tsín-suī called out from the front, "You don't have to help. Thanks, though!"

The descending sun at half past five wasn't very strong, but it hadn't lost all its radiant power just yet. Its rays came at Tsín-suī from the west, hitting the left side of his face, casting a thin, lanky shadow on the ground. That shadow, as Tsín-suī was setting off from Uncle A-Huàn's home, seeped over to Tsín-suī's right side. The sun's rays weakened as they followed Tsín-suī as he walked forward. When he had finally made it back to Tsuān-tsong's mansion, the sky was fully dark. The lanterns of the luxurious manse were already lit, and Tsín-suī's shadow grew indistinct. The drops of sweat on his face glistened like beads of crystal.

3

The sun in southern Taiwan tends to "set behind the mountains" at about half past six. The last couple of days, the darkness had already crept on by the time Tsín-suī got off from work, riding his bicycle all the way from the airport, back to his family's house in the village of Thâu-tsîng-khe.

He was going back home just to visit Mari. He rode brazenly into the cow pen next to the grain storage shed. He reckoned his old man wouldn't want to bother coming out to see him or to ask him how he was. Mari relaxed as soon as she caught a glimpse of Tsín-suī. Her eyes lit up with joy at his return. This look of beaming joy was something only Tsín-suī could ever experience among any of his family members. After gazing at each other for a while, he would pat her on the head and stroke her face, then pat her on the belly. In doing so, he could tell whether or not his younger brothers were taking good care of her by letting her out to munch on grass whenever she desired.

Tsín-suī looked his buffalo over again. Surely, his whole family must have known he was out in the paddock, tending to Mari. Surely his mother wanted badly to come out and chat with him. Surely, his brothers and sisters were all dying to cry out to him, calling out, "Niiiiiiii-*san!*"

But it was all impossible. When his father's dour, ruby-red face, declared, "You aren't allowed to," that was most definitely the end of the matter. Everyone in the family had to suffer under their obedience to Tsín-suī's father.

It was only Tsín-suī's fourth youngest brother, Tsín-bú, who dared to disobey. "Why do we have to be this way? *A-Pa*, you've already taught him a lesson for long enough. One or two days would've been plenty. Why do you have to be this way!?"

"It hasn't been nearly long enough! Not by a long shot! One or two days of 'education' will never be enough for that good-for-nothing, ungrateful lout."

Tsín-suī looked at Mari. All he had to do was turn around and take two or three paces, and he would be back in his home. But the interior was pitch-black inside. All of the lanterns and candles had been extinguished. It was normally the end of dinnertime in the home, and everyone would be clearing up the bowls, chopsticks, and spoons and then wiping the table clean before going off one by one to bathe. Then his mother and father would pull the rattan chairs outside to cool off in the courtyard, and his younger siblings could begin to work on their homework. They should have had the lights and lanterns lit, so it must have been at his father's command that they weren't permitted to. He just knew his whole family was milling about inside going about their tasks in the darkness. "They're waiting until I leave, right?" As he was mulling this painfully in his mind, he went around every window and every door of the house looking in. He noticed a small kerosene lamp lit softly, over next to the Kitchen God's niche up on the right wall of the kitchen. It would definitely have been something his mother would absolutely have pitched a fit about with his father. She wouldn't let his father extinguish it, no? Tsín-suī tried as best as he could to voicelessly call out a single word, "*A-Bú* (Ma)," from outside the kitchen window, but then resolutely turned away and left in silence.

He straddled himself up onto his bicycle, lowered his face and began to pedal. He transferred all the anger and grief from his tattered heart into his leg and calf muscles, as he stomped down on the pedals as far as they'd go. He was pedaling so forcefully that the bicycle began to creak and groan from all the stress forces. He was about a hundred meters from the house when he heard a clear "*Niiii-sannnnn*" emanating from up ahead to the right. It was a shout he'd never tire of hearing. Tsín-suī raced over as fast as he could. It was his third youngest brother, Tsín-bûn, his second youngest sister, Kun-boo, and his youngest sister, Kun-tsín. The three of them were out there in the field, waiting for him.

Tsín-suī jumped off his bicycle, throwing it down, and he and his siblings crash-ran into each other. The younger siblings each called out again, "*Nii-san*," but then an awkward silence set in. They all stiffened like rigid corpses—none of them were sure what to say next. Prior to being kicked out, Tsín-suī's family treated him, being the eldest son, almost like a second father in character and manner. It was in this role of his that he had to put on fatherly airs and present himself just as their father did. Standing in deep silence, it was finally Tsín-suī who spoke first, "I went to the cow pen to check up on Mari today. Her belly is pretty full. Has she been let out to eat or has one of you been scything the grass to feed her in the pen?"

"Tsín-bu let her out to graze."

"And has he taken her down to the stream for a mud bath?"

"Yes, when he was bringing her back to the paddock. I know because I saw her body all muddy."

"Oh. Very good. You need to give her a mud bath every day. If Tsin-siann doesn't have time to do it, Tsín-bûn or Tsín-bu will have to do it. They can't be lazy about it."

"Yes, *Nii-san*."

"You should go back to the house now. Tell Mother that I'm doing well, everything's fine, and not to worry herself about me. I'm staying over at a business-owner friend's house. His name is Tông Tsuān-tsong."

"How do you know him?"

"I met him at Ông *thài-thài*'s house, where I tutor. I'll tell you more about him later, *honnh*. You should make your way back to the house now."

"Oh, *Nii-san*, this is a letter for you from mom that eldest sister wrote on mom's behalf. She gave it to me to give to you."

Tsín-suī took it in both hands, opened it, and saw that it was just two lines, written in Japanese.

> To A-Suī, whatever trials and troubles you face, I hope you won't give up. You should make your way to Taihoku and study and bravely pursue your dreams. This is your mother's truest intention for you.
>
> Written on her behalf by big younger sister,
>
> Kun-Giok.

He rushed through reading it and wanted to weep. His lips and cheeks were already quivering from the raw emotion, but he managed to stifle his feelings and steel himself. The eldest son couldn't cry in front of his younger siblings. They obeyed him and made their way back across the field to the house. He quickly hopped back on his bicycle and wailed in agony as he pedaled along. The sky was dark everywhere around him. Nobody would know it was him wailing out in the black.

It was an hour or two later that he was finally able to stifle his shouts and sobbing. The word his mother used, "*tsin-gi*" ("truest intention"). "Is that something I could faithfully do?" he thought to himself. Tsín-suī's father was king of the castle. What he said went. His mother would never speak her mind so strongly in his presence. "If I were to run away to Taihoku and take an exam to get into a university, I wouldn't have any issues—but my father on the other hand... Could it be that Mother's 'truest intention' is to give my father another slap in the face? Is my mother really so fierce and stalwart deep down inside?"

All of the Tông family's contracted work over near the airport was finished in a little over a week. As the work was winding down, when Tông Tsuān-tsong was having social engagements on the outside, he made it a point to pick Tsín-suī up and take him as his wingman. Sometimes they went out to a restaurant for a *nagashi* (float around), enjoying a delicious meal while listening to beauties sing and serenade. Sometimes they would go out to a bar where the lantern outside was red and the liquor inside green. In such places, the inside was as raucous as a herd of horses neighing and whinnying and a pack of dogs barking their heads off. The neophyte Tsín-suī, out of his element, watched and learned, marveling at how Tsuān-tsong seemed to schmooze his way with everyone, subdue his business targets, and Tsín-suī was secretly trying to learn this all from Tsuān-tsong.

"My father's quite set in his Han culture ways. He often tells me not to worry about going to bars. It's enough to know that 'alcohol can float boats, and it can also sink 'em.'" Tsuān-tsong had swiftly become his astute, learned guru in the arts of social etiquette.

"I don't understand the meaning behind these learned words of your oh-so-esteemed father."

"He means here that it's fine to go swimming, but you shouldn't allow yourself to sink or else you won't be able to claw onto anything to climb your way back up to the surface."

One night after another, the two friends made their way back home in the middle of the night, but the morning after, Tsuān-tsong still woke up a little after six in the morning and prepared to head off to work.

One afternoon, Tsín-suī was in the salon of the Tông household, deep in thought as he pored over a college textbook, when he heard someone's voice. It was an odd time, as those who had work were already on their way to start the day and those who were students were off to class. Who could it be that would come this early to pay a visit? He was thinking of craning his neck to take a peek and see who it was, when he heard Tsuān-tsong's voice call out, "A-Suī-á, you have a visitor. There's someone here to see you."

Tsín-suī hurried out, and upon first seeing him, it was someone wholly unknown to him. Tsuān-tsong gave an introduction using Japanese, "This here is one of my classmates from the industrial college, Chin Fo-sen. He's a full-time technician at the banana research lab run by the Takao Green Fruits Collective."

"And he's here for me?"

"That's right. He went right to my place of work to find me and asked me to accompany him and find you."

"How are you Chin-*san*? To what do I owe the pleasure?"

"I'm here at the behest of the lead technician of our field laboratory, Dr. Nakamura Jirō. He sent for you and asked if you would like to join our research team."

"I've never had anything to do with growing banana trees, and sad to say, I've never heard of your Dr. Nakamura. Why did you make a special trip to seek me out?"

"If you come with me, you'll see for yourself. I only just heard from Dr. Nakamura himself that you were a top student at Takao Secondary. As for exactly how he's heard of you, I have no clue."

"Where is your field laboratory research station located?"

"It's over in Lîn-lok, situated on a patch of 'reclaimed land' on the riverbed over there. It's about ten *li* (five kilometers) from downtown Heitō."

Tsín-suī and Tsuān-tsong glanced at each other. Tsuān-tsong could guess the doubts in Tsín-suī's look and said, "I think this is a good thing. Lîn-lok is east of the city, so you'll be heading east. You'll be heading in the direction the sun rises from. Maybe if you keep going, you'll also be heading in the direction of illustriousness." He felt his words were more of a fantasy and not so realistic, so he added "My colleague here, Fo-sen, lives over in Lîn-lok. He's a Hakka man. He can't really speak our Hoklo, but he's an honest man. You can trust him. You can breathe easy if you go with him."

"Go? Right now??"

"Oh, it's already late now. Bright and early tomorrow morning. I'll take you."

That evening, both Tsuān-tsong and Tsín-suī went out to the drinking quarter again. On the way back home, Tsuān-tsong was half-drunk, and he began speaking to Tsín-suī as if he were Tsín-suī's older brother. "Tomorrow, you're going to go to that banana field lab and you're...going to...meet that...*hic*...Dr. Nakamura guy. I'll say this once... In front of those Japanese...you need to be polite...*hic*...but don't let them...think that they can walk...all over you...or that you're a weakling—that you're...*hic*...worthless. Do you know...*hic*...what I mean?"

"I learned all of that when I was studying at Takao Secondary."

"You've never been to a banana plantation...*hic*...before. You just have to...*hic*...be more hard-working than others. Strive...*hic*...to study as much as you can...hic..., and then those Japanese won't look...*hic*...down on you."

"Right. I've already been preparing mentally for this."

"Oh, also...*hic*...if you have any ideas...*hic*..., you should buck up and express them...hic... The Japanese respect strong men who are capable... *hic*..., but they're not going to care...*hic*...about anyone who doesn't take responsibility...*hic*...or weaklings."

"Tsuān-tsong-*hiann*, I'm very grateful for your bits of advice here, but all it really means is that you didn't drink nearly enough!"

"Hahaha! *Shh*!"

***

Tsín-suī never knew there was a banana research field lab, let alone that it was located on an obscure patch of riverbed in the middle of Lîn-lŏk. It was new land reclaimed from an old riverbed. Not far away, the sound of running water gurgling and babbling could vaguely be heard. Tsín-suī kicked at the dirt under his foot, then he bent over and picked up a handful of soil, slowly kneading it between his fingers. The fertile black loam had a bit of sandy grit to it. Could bananas grow well in such soil? Or was it that they specifically chose this bit of reclaimed land to test out a new cultivar? He was deep in thought when a short, stocky, middle-aged man wearing a conical bamboo sun hat walked up toward them. Fo-sen said to Tsín-suī in a low voice, "This is Dr. Nakamura Jirō, the person in charge of the research lab."

Tsín-suī shook off the remaining clods of dirt on his hands, straightened up, and then made a deep bow towards the doctor. "*Man-hai* ([I am] your junior colleague), Ngôo Tsín-suī."

Dr. Nakamura's first words to him were, "Did you learn how to do farming after you graduated?"

"Nakamura-*san*, I've always done farming before, back at home. But I've never grown bananas."

"Come study with me. I have a handful of crack technicians here. Too many of you are from this island. Some of them speak in Hoklo, some in Hakka. You'll get the hang of things pretty soon."

"That's awfully kind of you. I am eternally grateful. Thank you."

"Regarding how your salary will be paid, Fo-sen will take you to see our accountant. As soon as you start, you'll be given an alternate's salary. Once you're fully on board, it'll change."

"Nakamura-*san*, I still haven't asked you but, was I recommended to you by Headmaster Yoshikawa over at Takao Secondary?"

"No, I'm not acquainted with Headmaster Yoshikawa. It was your *Tō-san*, Ngôo-*san* Tsín-sai who came and made the request."

"My father?" Tsín-suī was completely dumbstruck. "So it was my father," he muttered to himself.

His emotions welled up in his mind. For a while, he couldn't tell what he was so moved about, just that he felt moved. He wanted to both laugh and cry. He felt both a sense of fright and reverence and also gratitude.

"Just how exactly did my father know this technician?" Tsín-suī strove hard to connect the dots. "He's a graduate of Taiwan Normal School, and he was a common school instructor. He was once a worker for the Mitsui Resources Company. Oh! I've got it! He was once a volunteer appraiser for the Takao Green Fruits Collective! No wonder. That's where the connection comes in, and my father leveraged that connection so I could come here."

Tsín-suī turned his head and saw that Dr. Nakamura was already heading off on other business. Fo-sen was a little closer at hand, talking with some of the workers. Tsin-sui gazed all around him.

Banana trees were standing in row after neat row. Several of the rows had already grown tall. There were also a couple of rows that looked as if they'd just been planted. There were stalks of bamboo tied to each trunk, and placards with each cultivar name were stabbed into the ground in front of each patch. Tsín-suī went and crouched down to get a better look at the names written on the placards. They were written in Japanese-style Chinese characters: No. 1, No. 3, No. 5 varieties. Next to the numbers were some Japanese words he could not make heads or tails of. He deduced that they were likely specialized vocabulary related to botany or to pests or blights. There was a clean, cool, cross-breeze blowing. The sun overhead was beaming right into his eyes. Several of the taller banana trees whose trunks were yellow were already starting to show browned and withered layers peeling off. Some layers were still stuck to the younger, yellow trunks. Some seemed to resemble snakeskin, molting off into a pile. He reached out to lightly tear at a piece of the withered skin, and the slick, crystalline goo on the bolt upright, round trunk was exposed. The leaves grew out from the top of the round trunk, broad and lush green. They swayed up and down, left and right with the light breeze, giving the whole field of trees a look as if they were the wings on a fledgling bird aching to fly yet unable to do so.

So these are banana trees? It was only in recent years that farmers began to deliberately grow bananas in the Takao and Heitō area, though not too many just yet. One could sometimes spy a native banana tree in the front or back of some farmsteads, but there wasn't anything remarkable about that. This was the first time Tsín-suī had ever carefully looked over a whole banana tree. "This is a crop I'm unfamiliar with. I don't know about bananas, but of all places, this is where I've been assigned work. Is my father right about this?" Just as his mind was grappling with this doubt, the wind grew more blustery. The massive frond leaves rustled and slapped against each other. Amid this slightly disturbed air, Fo-sen appeared before him.

Fo-sen quickly took Tsín-suī over to complete his paperwork. His officially titled position at the field lab was "technical alternate." It just so happened that the research station was holding a committee meeting that day. It was a routine meeting. Tsín-suī was seated all the way in the very back, observing and taking notes. There was farming equipment of all sorts piled up on both sides of where he was sitting. There were three office tables standing behind the piles of farming implements, and on each of these tables were reams after reams of documents, notes, and reports. In this slightly rough-and-ready room, Tsín-suī noticed that there was a telephone, placed ever so grandly on the middle bureau.

Dr. Nakamura was sitting in front of the meeting table centered right in front of the first row. There was a display board easel upon which hung a diagram showing today's topic du jour: "The art of aeration and water conservancy/retention of soil."

Dr. Nakamura wasn't the only man to speak at the meeting. Other technicians frequently spoke up. Tsín-suī could sense that Dr. Nakamura wasn't as stern or uptight as the average Japanese manager was. Nobody had to raise their hands first before speaking. People were allowed to freely jump in to contribute. What was interesting about this was that when he was discussing a question with everyone, he randomly raised his head and pointed his finger at Tsín-suī, giving a simple introduction of the departments at the station, "Our research station is divided into three groups: soil research, pest and blight research, and cultivar research."

Tsín-suī continued listening. Dr. Nakamura came back again. He looked intently at Tsín-suī and, almost like a high-school band conductor, raised both hands and made a sweeping motion. Then he said, "Originally, bananas were only grown on this island up in Nantō. Nantō is in the middle of the central mountains of Taiwan, in a basin. The soil, air, and topography are quite suitable there for bananas. What we need to do here is promote the planting of banana trees in Takao and Heitō. As for whether this can be done or not, our research station bears great responsibility."

After this direct address to Tsín-suī, he switched back to the secondary topic under discussion, "The difference in soil qualities."

Tsín-suī was certain now that Dr. Nakamura was giving him a sort of precursor crash course before his work really began. He remembered the last time he held a job, over at the sugar mill, the mill's general manager had arranged for a professional worker to come in and teach the few new hires a crash course. Tsín-suī felt today was quite particular—and effective. His feelings were just now divided. Dr. Nakamura's eyes again swept over to him. He lightly lifted his chin and raised his hands up. "The most suitable soils for growing bananas are alluvial soil along flowing waters, sticky soil, sandy soil, and powdery sand. Therefore, Takao and Heitō are suitable for banana cultivation."

Tsín-suī anxiously gathered his thoughts, silently making a mental note of the specialized terms. Another technician carried on after Dr. Nakamura spoke, then yet another expressed a different viewpoint. After a round of animated discussion, the meeting quieted down and Dr. Nakamura made some concluding comments, "I haven't yet come to any firm conclusions for this problem. To sum up, everyone needs to acquaint themselves with the soil beneath their feet."

Tsín-suī felt the gathering's spirit of concentrated attention wash over him, and he was profoundly encouraged. He felt as if this discussion was more fruitful and valuable than the ones he had in high school. They were just a field research station for bananas in a derelict, impoverished village, in Lîn-lo̍k, but it was filled with passionate technicians who were there for the purpose of doing research on bananas as a cash crop.

Though sitting in the last row, observing, he became more and more excited by it all.

The last secondary item on the agenda for this special meeting was "The question of the density of the soil layers for banana tree roots in muddy conditions."

It was the first time Tsín-suī had ever heard of the problem of "subterranean draining." He otherwise never would have known that there is a wide network of water drainage under the ground we stand upon. Was Dr. Nakamura thinking of testing out a pioneering method for doing *kuàn-tshuah-pue-á*[11] (catching the channels of subterranean water) under the uncleared land? What method would they use to catch this water?

---

11. 灌抖杯仔 "Kuàn-tshuah-pue-á also called 灌杜猴 *"kuàn-tōo-kâu."* Taiwanese Hoklo. a kind of game where farm kids catch crickets.

Would it be like the way they used to catch crickets when they were kids? Many of the other technicians had opinions, to the point that people were coming up with ridiculous proposals and the discussion drifted all over the place. The final verdict was that they would form small groups and, using rounded hoes, dig along the likely subterranean routes, and when they dug up one area, they would place markers to indicate their findings.

Tsín-suĭ thought this method was quite frankly a bit stupid. He raised his hand to speak, and the whole room grew silent. It seemed strange that an alternate, who just showed up today, would speak about anything. Nakamura gave him a nod. Just as he had done as a schoolboy giving a report at the front of the class, Tsín-suĭ stood up and bowed, "Maybe I can go back to my family farm and bring our water buffalo over. Then we can use the plow to cut, row by row, and see where the pathways lay?"

The meeting rang with Japanese-style exclamations, "*Waaa*" and "*Heiii*."

Nobody responded, so Tsín-suĭ tried once more with a different tack, adding, "I have a lot of experience with plowing fields with a water buffalo. I've got a very strong animal that has a good rapport with me. I can make sure to cut into the field whenever you need it deep or shallow enough. I think I can help everyone complete this task very quickly."

Dr. Nakamura answered him, "Excellent. Let's try out your solution then. Our small team will be off to the side, assisting you. However, our research station is over ten *li* from your residence. How will you get the water buffalo here?"

"I'll take care of it, Dr. Nakamura."

Within a week, this new project at the research station was completed. Dr. Nakamura and their colleagues began to look at Tsín-suĭ with increased respect.

***

Since it was quite a way from the research station back to Heitō city, Tsín-suĭ quit the lion's share of his tutoring jobs, but he kept on his tutoring at the Tông and Ông households. One day when Tsín-suĭ was teaching over at the Ông household, he was casually chatting with Ông *thài-thài* and her eldest daughter, Giȯk-ìn. They were talking about his success at the banana research station. "A-Suĭ, you work yourself to death, tutoring night after night. Have you done the math to figure out how much more you make in a month of tutoring?" Ông *thài-thài* probed.

"I have. I was making fifty yen on average."

"So, since quitting most of your tutoring gigs, you've lost about forty yen a month. Are you able to support yourself with your work at the field station?"

"No, I can't. I'm just an alternate assistant. I don't even get thirty yen a month."

"Oh...so are you willing to do it? Is it worth it?"

"Yes, I'm willing."

"Well, good then. We should look at the advantages, not the shortcomings. I went to the Má-tsóo temple to *poaʰ-pue* (toss moon blocks). It indicated negative results for sugarcane and auspiciousness for bananas."

Giȯk-ìn chimed in then, "*A-Bú*, A-Suī doesn't believe in stuff like *poaʰ-pue!*"

"It doesn't hurt to try," her mother shot back. She waited until Tsín-suī left before warning again, "Afterwards, once you're married, don't let him get involved with sugarcane or sugar refining business."

"OK, I understand. You don't need to remind me."

4

I t was dusk, right around dinner time, when a certain young miss, who
looked to be around high-school age, came to the Tông household
and knocked rapidly on the door. Having come outside to answer the
door, Tsuān-tik recognized her as the younger of the two Ông daughters, Giȯk-bí.

"I'm here to find my *sensei*, Ngôo Tsín-suī."

"He no longer lives here. He's already moved back to his family home
at Thâu-tsîng-khe."

"When did he move?"

"Two weeks ago. If you have anything you'd like to tell him, I can do it
for you. He'll be back here the day after tomorrow to tutor me."

"Oh, that's not necessary, thank you."

"Oh... What about your *Nii-san*, Tsuān-tsong?" she asked shyly.

"He doesn't come back to Pîn-tong very much anymore. He spends a lot
more time with our father in Takao, nowadays."

"Oh, I see." As she was leaving, she suddenly instructed Tsuān-tik,
"Don't tell *sensei* that I came looking for him."

"Oh, OK."

Tsuān-tik kept to his word and never told Tsín-suī about the curious
visit from the second Ông daughter, Giȯk-bí. In truth, as soon as he shut
the door, he promptly forgot all about it.

That summer, Giȯk-bí was supposed to be getting ready to make
her trip up to Taihoku at the end of August to continue her advanced
studies at the famed No. 3 Girls' Secondary. However, she didn't even
bother to make any preparations at all. She had two suitcases that were
filled both slapdashedly and almost empty at that, just sitting there. Her
mother had washed and sun-dried her bed linens, but she never took
them to the train station to send them to Taihoku. Then the beginning of
September rolled by, and the first day of classes followed along not long

after. Gioʻk-bí said she wasn't feeling well and stayed in bed. Occasionally, she would get up, but she was lethargic and lazy, often throwing little fits, constantly muttering, "I don't have any desire to go back to school." She kept on in her pouty repose until the middle of September, when she got a registered letter in the post from the Taihoku No. 3 Girls' Secondary School, notifying her that she was being withdrawn from her studies.

Ông *thài-thài* was too flustered and discussed the matter with her eldest son, but he brushed off the whole situation nonchalantly. "If she doesn't want to go to school, then forget about it. Let her stay. It'll save you a couple yen anyway. I never even graduated from the common school, and I ended up staying home to help with the house and business. It's not like it matters if she moves up in her studies."

"That was your sacrifice for the family as the eldest son. Your duty was to help your dear mother raise your younger siblings. Your poor mother just can't let her little Gioʻk-bí throw away her studies like this. If you'd rather that she throws everything away, then all of your suffering and hardship would have been for naught. Ngôo Tsín-suī has been her tutor for all these years. All of his efforts will have been wasted too."

"I don't think of it as a wasted effort. If she doesn't go off to study, it just means we have an extra set of hands to help out around the house. Even better, we won't have to pay to keep on that apprentice, A-Hiông."

"Well, that just won't do. We need to find a way for her to finish her studies, and then there will be some hope for her. Right before your father left us behind, he told me that all of our children had to get an education beyond secondary school." She gave her son a stern glare as she said these words.

"Find the time to take your sister up to Taihoku. Beg the school director to take her back, won't you?"

"Mother, you know I don't have to time to do that. I can't help you. My hands are tied."

"So that's how it is, *honnh*? I'm going to find Ngôo Tsín-suī. She will listen to what her *sensei* has to say. I'll tell A-Suī-á to take her up to Taihoku and see what he can do."

"Well, OK then. Tsín-suī went to secondary school. He ought to know how to go toe to toe with the school."

"It's settled then. A-Hiông! Go fetch the pedicab! I need to get to Thâu-tsîng-khe!" Ông *thài-thài* yelled out across the shop.

"Doesn't Ngôo-*san* still live at Tông Tsuān-tsong's residence?" her eldest son asked.

"*Sensei* already moved back to Thâu-tsîng-khe a while ago," she called out suddenly in a loud voice from the kitchen. Her voice was filled with a fresh vigor.

The pedicab was already waiting by the front gate. Ông *thài-thài* waved her hand to call her eldest daughter, Giȯk-ìn, trying to be as discreet as possible. Seated in the pedicab, mother and daughter began to exchange ideas in a barely audible whisper. Ông *thài-thài* began, "I don't think it's her health that's keeping Giȯk-bí bedridden but that she secretly has a crush on Tsín-suī. When she heard me say that he would accompany her to Taihoku, she perked right on up and was flitting and darting all around the room just like a little sakura shrimp, happily swimming in a mountain stream."

"I've also gotten a similar impression. She really seems to have a crush on him."

"What else? I don't know if it's right of me to have asked Tsín-suī to take her up to Taihoku. I have a feeling that the situation is going to get more and more out of hand."

"It's what you decided on, Mother. I trust Tsín-suī will stay true to his feelings for me."

"Do you think he has any idea about what's going on?"

"He doesn't seem to have, no. I never specifically brought it up with him."

"Ah, OK. Your mother knows what she'll do."

Ông *thài-thài* and Giȯk-ìn helped to take the luggage down to Heitō station and send off both Tsín-suī and Giȯk-bí on the platform. Right before the train was about to depart, Ông *thài-thài* stuffed a fat wad of cash into Tsín-suī's coat pocket. As the train locomotive blew its whistle and steam began to burst from the wheel pistons, Giȯk-ìn let out a long, drawn-out sigh, and she walked back to the Ông residence alone and in silence. Not accompanying her daughter, Ông *thài-thài* immediately rushed like a racehorse over to the nearby Má-tsóo (Matsu) shrine. Amid the heavy clouds of incense smoke and people ambulating around from altar to altar, she stuck lit sticks of incense into the main brazier and knelt down on the supplication cushion in front of the visage of Má-tsóo. Immediately, she began mumbling off chants and mantras, pouring her heart out to the way-guiding Goddess to give her guidance about her younger daughter's school withdrawal letter and the daughter's love interest in the unsuspecting Tsín-suī, and imploring Má-tsóo to intercede and light her lantern to guide the way through the stormy, turbid waters of their lives.

Upon finishing her incantations and ritual prostrating, she rose up from the cushion and went over to the wall to draw out a numbered fortune stick. She shook one of the sticks out of the bamboo canister. It had a number that corresponded to a poem written on a paper sheet off in the cupboard near the canister:

A thousand mountain peaks are hard to pass, but passed they shall be;
The lonely bird, lost on its way, flies past its nest;
Within the abode, if the heart is virtuous and generous, it is as sharp as a sword;
The garments are not unbound, and this keeps impropriety at bay. No need to worry if the robes are loosened and belt undone.

Ông *thài-thài* could read the characters in the poem, but she couldn't make heads or tails of their true, intended meaning. She fetched a couple coins from her purse to drop into the "oil and incense donation" box and asked the temple keeper to enter into a séance trance and help unravel the riddle for her. But the explanation she got just confused her more: "Of the person for whom you're beseeching Má-tsóo's intercession and guiding hand, I'm not sure who this person is to you. Is this person tall in stature and in good health?"

"Yes, all of this is true!" Ông *thài-thài* shot back excitedly.

"So they will be able to 'cross over the thousand mountains.' This is a great boon. You don't have to worry yourself over it."

"And the second line?"

"The second line carries misfortune within fortune. Why would there be a bird attempting to fly away? Is that person going into a giant forest or someplace? I'm afraid that this line means something ominous will happen."

"What kind of thing???"

"The Guiding Lady doesn't say."

Ông *thài-thài* rose up from her seat by the keeper and went back to the altar to pray very earnestly, then tossed a couple more coins into the donation box. She went back to the temple keeper and peppered him again with questions, "And the third line? What about the third one?"

"Both the third and fourth lines are tied and thus read together. Are the person(s) you're beseeching Má-tsóo on behalf of two people?"

"Yes, they are."

"A man and a woman?"

Ông *thài-thài's* eyes suddenly lit up brighter than fireworks. She felt deep in her heart that Má-tsóo was going to guide her regarding the most pressing matter of all. Without hesitation, she replied sincerely, "Yes! Yes! That's right!"

In disbelief, the temple keeper said, "Why would a person with a good heart be carrying a sword on their person? Their heart is very generous, but the blade is sharp. That's what it means. There's no doubt about it."

The keeper gradually became more positive, and then he went back to expressing his doubts.

"This man is a person of outstanding moral character. The woman however... She has long, flowing hair. There's a phrase you hear in operas, 'The blade of wisdom cuts through the threads of emotion.' The phrase comes from a *kua-á-hì* stage performance. Have you ever heard of it before?"

"No. I'm afraid I seldom ever watch such performances."

"Well, I'll explain it for you. It goes like this: In this divination poem, both fortune and misfortune are interwoven together like braided streams crisscrossing each other down to the seashore, where they reach their ends. There are both winds and waves to slow their progress, and so the strands won't ever grow too large. You can return home and rest assured that they will return."

Being that the pronunciation for "he," "she," and "they" only differ by a hair, Ông *thài-thài* asked in disbelief, trying to get a confirmation, "Did you just say 'he' or 'they?'"

"Just then I was blindly trying to channel the Goddess to convey her meaning. Now that I've regained my consciousness, I can't remember if she said 'he' or 'they.'"

"Oh. Thank you. You've done your best. I'll be on my way now."

After she returned home, she told her eldest daughter all about the affair of the poem on the fortune-telling sticks. Giók-ìn kept her eyebrows firmly knitted. After a long while, she finally calmed down.

"Tsín-suí told me many times before that I shouldn't put any stock into *poah-pue* moon blocks or fortune-telling divination sticks."

"This time, the temple keeper became more indecent the more he explained, until it seemed completely dissolute."

"All the old man was doing was explaining the meaning of the characters in the poems for you, Mom. My *kanbun* (Japanese for 'Classical Chinese') *sensei* back at the Tainan Girls' Secondary could have done the same thing for you." Giók-ìn emphasized, "Next time, don't go pulling out a fortune stick for no good reason."

"OK! Fine!" Ông *thài-thài* responded in a fit.

Ông *thài-thài* had a habit of taking a little afternoon siesta. This day though, she kept tossing and turning. Half-asleep, she thought of a phone call that she should make right away. She got up and called Mr. Satō Kishin, a ceramics distributor in Taihoku. He was supposed to be Giok-bí's guarantor and guardian while she was studying at the Taihoku No. 3 Girls' Secondary School.[12]

"Satō-*san*, that younger daughter of mine, Giok-bí, has been a pain in the neck, causing all sorts of trouble. Only just now has she finally returned to school to report in. She's already received a letter from the school demanding she withdraw from her studies."

"So is she not coming up to Taihoku after all for her studies this term?"

"No, not that. I'm not going to give up on her. I begged her high-school tutor to accompany her on the train ride up to see if he couldn't help smooth things over."

"Well, he might not be able to redeem her chance of studying at the school. I'm not acquainted with the headmaster at the No. 3 Girls' Secondary School, but I've heard through the grapevine that he's as rigid as a piece of Kawasaki steel, unyielding and uncompromising."

"Well, regardless, if the school decides in the end to take her, I'd like you to remain her guarantor all the same, if it's alright by you."

"Sure. Of course it's fine by me! No problem."

"And also… Should Giok-bí and her *sensei* come to you seeking help, I'd like if you could spare no effort to help them."

"*Hai.* I'll do my best. The last time I made my way down to Heitō for work, I had heard that this *sensei* was slated to be your son-in-law, no?"

"Yes, that's right. I hope he won't go back on his word."

"No worries. There won't be any issues."

***

Tsín-suī took great pains to request leave from the field lab to take his charge, who had already received her withdrawal notice, all the way up to Taihoku to plead with them to take her back. He himself had no real right, not being related to Giok-bí, and his lack of Japanese blood flowing

---

12. The student guarantor system began in the Japanese colonial era, and it continued to be implemented after WWII had ended. Guarantors weren't needed after the ninth year of compulsory education.

through his veins and his lack of personal connections made it difficult to make a real case for her. It was far easier said than done! Once their train had pulled away from Heitō station, he was deep in his thoughts the whole way, collecting himself. Even in his breathing, he felt there was something in his chest blocking his breath, pressing down on him. By comparison, Giok-bí, sitting next to her *sensei*, seemed to be up in the clouds in incredibly high spirits. She was like a bird at sunrise, chirp-chirping at him the entire duration of the half-day–long train trip.

There wasn't a single moment when she wasn't prattling and chattering away.

Tsín-suí didn't respond to her even once.

When they reached the school, there wasn't anyone in the administrative office who could decide anything for them. It was all up to the headmaster.

Tsín-suí steeled himself to meet with the headmaster of the famed academy. The Japanese man sitting behind the bureau appeared at first glance to be friendlier than Headmaster Yoshikawa from Takao Secondary. However, as soon as his questioning commenced, Tsín-suí realized he had underestimated the man. This headmaster and Yoshikawa seemed to have been cut from the same cloth.

"Tell me right now just what relation you are to this pupil? Are you the head of her household or her guarantor?"

"I'm neither. I'm her home tutor. I've been expressly entrusted and tasked by her parent with bringing her here, all the way from Heitō."

"What is her excuse for not arriving and reporting to this institution at the specified time and attending to her studies when she should have?"

This is the precise question that Tsín-suí had racked his mind over for the entire seven- or eight-hour journey by train. In his experience of responding to Japanese instructors and Headmaster Yoshikawa in his time at Takao Secondary, the ideal would be to indicate something that was of practical meaning to the Japanese. His second ruse would be to make an excuse, high-flown and full of pretention. The third-best option would be to beg and grovel politely in a demure, quiet voice.

In that moment, even though he'd already made his calculations and reasoned out which tactic he'd use to respond with, his heart was still filled with trepidation.

"Well, it happened like this, sir: Ông Giok-bí's family ceramics business is an enterprise that sells its wares all across Taiwan island, not to mention the home islands.[13] She and her siblings are all needed during the summer breaks to lend a hand to the family business. Ông Giok-bí put all of her heart and effort into helping her family, from odd jobs to packing and shipping the wares. She's been busy both day and night. Around the end of August or the beginning of September, she was utterly exhausted and fell into a deep sleep. She slept for several days straight. After she recovered, she realized she had contravened the school guidelines. She felt lost and dejected, utterly devastated, and was afraid to be handed down her punishment. With fear on top of devastation, she kept hemming and hawing in her indecision, hesitating at what to do. And when she unexpectedly received the notice from her institution, what else could she possibly feel but out of sorts and out of options?"

As the words left Tsín-suí's lips, his brain felt sluggish and slow. He didn't have the rest of the story concocted and ready to go. He lifted his shamed face, and his eyes were met by those of the headmaster. The man's expression seemed to have softened from when they had first entered the office and taken their seats, if only slightly. Tsín-suí's courage grew again, and he continued, "Her mother is just a widowed *obāsan*. After her husband had departed from this world, she had to carry the weight of the entire family on her shoulders and provide for two sons and two daughters, one of whom sits here before you, and adamantly wanted to provide each of her children with the best education that they could possibly receive. Moreover, she often said, 'Without education, how could we make high-quality subjects; without high-quality subjects, how would we have a grand, exemplary empire?' Her mother knows her daughter, Ông Giok-bí, trusts her *sensei* and so she persuaded me to teach Giok-bí and exhorted me to bring her daughter to this esteemed institution and plead on her behalf for the withdrawal letter to be rescinded and for her to be allowed the chance to attend."

"Hahaha," the headmaster laughed sneeringly. "You spin a good tale, I'll give you that, but I know you're not being honest about several of the 'facts' in your tale. To put it frankly, there's several exaggerations or outright falsehoods in your performance, no?"

Tsín-suí was caught dead in his tracks, and he remained quiet as the seconds ticked on by, caught and unable to respond. The headmaster decided that he would answer his own question, "I think about half of

---

13. In that era, if a Taiwanese person referred to the *lāi-tē*, or the "inner lands," they were referring to the "home islands" or four main islands of Japan.

what you've told me is the truth—half-true, half-false. Am I incorrect in my deduction?"

"No, sir, you are mistaken. What I've told you is ninety percent the truth." He immediately corrected himself on such a brash and hasty answer, "It's ninety-nine percent the truth."

"It's likely that you embellished when you added in, 'If there's no good citizens, then how will we have a grand, exemplary empire?' An *obāsan* from the countryside wouldn't say such a thing, would she now?"

Tsín-suí's mind was like a balloon floating in the air, helpless without defense, aimlessly floating about, unsure how to respond appropriately to the headmaster. Just then, he heard the headmaster give his verdict.

"Fine. I agree to rescind the order to withdraw Ms. Ông Giók-bí here. She must complete her registration, dormitory, and class procedures today."

"*Hai*! Thank you very much, Mr. Headmaster-san." Tsín-suí stood up and gave a deep ninety-degree bow, stepped back two paces, then turned and left. From the corner of his eye, he noticed Giók-bí had not responded respectfully to the headmaster with a deep bow of her own but casually followed Tsín-suí out the door, with a bit of fanfare.

After they were out of the office, Tsín-suí turned to her and immediately rebuked her, "Just now, why did you not bow to show your respect and appreciation to your headmaster as I did?"

"Why should I have to? I just didn't want to."

"It doesn't matter if you wanted to or not. You have to show him your respect and appreciation for the grace he's given you."

"*Hai*. I know. You don't need to keep badgering me."

Right as the two of them finished this little exchange, a Japanese man with a short mustache quickly walked up to them. As soon as she caught sight of him, Giók-bí made a bow and greeted him.

"Satō-*san*."

He made a simple bow in return and extended a hand to Tsín-suí.

"Ngôo-*san* Tsín-suí, I presume? I'm Ms. Giók-bí's student guarantor, Satō Kishin. Her mother rang me up on the telephone. She was extremely out of sorts with worry. Have you already seen the headmaster?"

"Yes, we just did, as a matter of fact. He agreed to rescind the withdrawal notice and allow Giók-bí to continue her studies."

"*Wah*! Ah! What a feat!" Satō-*san* exclaimed as he shook Tsín-suí's hand again. He didn't let go of Tsín-suí's hand for some time. He set his keen merchant's eyes on Tsín-suí, sizing up his young Taiwanese counterpart, then opened up his satchel and fished out a carved name seal for stamping.

"Well, go quickly to register. I have to add my guarantorship seal to the documents again."

"Thank you, Satō-*san* for your consideration and for running all this way out here to the school. We should have come to your place to see you."

"Please. It's no problem at all. I've been doing business with Ms. Ông for several years now. We're already old friends."

Tsín-suī accompanied Giŏk-bí to get formally registered and to help her complete her dormitory residence forms. Feeling just peachy with how things had turned out, he had a light skip to his gait as he stepped foot out of the school's front gate.

Tsín-suī didn't expect Satō-*san* to be waiting for him right outside the school gate. The sky had already darkened by then, and Satō-*san* told him he'd like to treat him to dinner. For a Japanese man to be treating a Taiwanese person like this must have purely been due to the relationship Satō-*san* had with Ms. Ông, no?

Satō-*san* took Tsín-suī along, first cutting through a residential neighborhood. Japanese-style houses lined both sides of the street. They were all neatly arranged and maintained, prim and proper. Each of the houses had a front yard with a garden replete with all manner of flowers and trees. The entire neighborhood was spick and span. The lanterns and electric lights were already turned on or fires lit, glowing softly. It was time for supper in each and every one of these homes. The two men kept walking along. They caught sight of a street peddler calling out into the evening night air, hawking, "*Thau-hue* (Sweet bean curd)! *Ban-kau* (Rice cakes)! *Thau-hue! Ban-kau!*" The loud voice cut through the tranquil silence of the neighborhood. Tsín-suī began to ask Satō-*san* questions, "Do you know what it is that the *daidō shōjin* (street peddler) is selling?"

"Of course I do. I sometimes even buy what he sells."

They kept walking a short distance, and then they came upon the intersection of a small lane. There were people on the side roasting sweet potatoes, the aroma hard to resist, sweet and tempting. The people off to the side were calling out their wares in Japanese. "*Yaki-imo*! (Roast sweet potatoes!)" "*Yaki-imo!*" They kept calling out this way.

Satō-*san* took in a deep whiff of the drifting sweetness in the air and said, "This is my wife's absolute favorite thing to snack on."

"Do you not like to eat them yourself?"

"I like to cook it as tempura."

After they'd left this distinctly Japanese neighborhood, it wasn't long before they came upon the Inegawa Public Tavern. Satō-*san* took a happy and contented stride inside, into the *genkan* foyer. He was immediately hit with a flurry of enthusiastic greetings and light banter common in Japanese eateries. "He must have been a frequent patron," Tsín-suī thought. It was a surprising sight to see as Satō-*san* continued, ordering dishes from the proprietor in both Hoklo and Japanese.

Once Satō-*san* and Tsín-suī had finally sat down, he didn't see Satō-*san* ordering anything, but a serving boy came along with grilled meats, tempura, freshly cut sashimi, sushi, and other Japanese delicacies. Satō-*san* was the first to broach the topic of the Japanese headmaster.

"He's not the kind of man to easily change his mind so lightly. How exactly did you manage to win him over and get him to rescind the withdrawal notice?"

Tsín-suī then went all in, sparing no detail about the whole ordeal.

Satō-*san* continued asking questions, "So how did you know he would use that line of persuasion?"

"I learned quite a lot in my five years of secondary school at the Takao Secondary School, studying along both Japanese students and teachers alike, not to mention that severe, proud headmaster who presided over the place."

"Wow, haha! I admire you, Ngôo-*san*! Truly I do."

"You seem quite interested in this point, no, Satō-*san*?"

"It's because I work in marketing, you see. I'm always interested in how people can break through barriers and seal the deal." Surprisingly, Satō-*san* then switched to Hoklo, which was a little stiff, but quite understandable, "I wanted to take you out for dinner because I wanted to see just how you made the headmaster have a change of heart."

"Oh. Heh. Satō-*san*, you've learned how to speak like us islanders. You're not half bad at it, either."

"It's necessary for my business and more importantly, my wife herself is a Taiwanese."

"Oh, so that's the real reason!"

When they had eaten, Satō Kishin asked Tsín-suī, "When are you returning to Pîn-tong?"

"I'm taking the first train tomorrow morning."

"Oh, then I'll take you to the station. You can stay over in an inn nearby."

The two of them stepped into a pedicab in front of the restaurant, and the cab went along for quite some time before Satō-*san* pointed out the famous New Park to the left side of the cab.

"Oh, that's New Park over there."

Tsín-suī strained his eyes to make out anything in the pitch-black surrounding them, but he couldn't see clearly. He could only make out a bit of the night scenery in the slivers of moonlight and the light emanating out from private homes along the way. Satō-*san* was tour-guiding the entire way.

"We're heading north right now. Once we go from the First Chōme Block to the Fourth, we'll almost be there. My accountant often comes out here to take care of business. If we keep going straight, we'll hit the Kita-mon-chō. They call it the North Gate Ward because there's an old gate still standing there from the old city wall."

Tsín-suī looked anxiously out to the left, as if he were a parched man straining past mirages of oases in the middle of a desert. His eyes darted quickly to the right, fearing he'd miss something if he didn't look in time, as Satō-*san* kept calling out names and places. Tsín-suī didn't feel he could make out anything of the points of interest or even the shop signs.

The pedicab stopped in front of the doors of a certain Shin-ma Business Association. Satō led him into a quiet alleyway. There was a small inn at the end of the alley. It was run by a Japanese man, evidently. Satō-*san* helped Tsín-suī to get a discount for the night's stay. After everything had been taken care of, they said their goodbyes and Satō then promised him, "I'll make it a point to stop by and see you the next time I'm in Pîn-tong."

Once Satō Kishin had taken his leave, Tsín-suī decided he'd go alone for a nighttime stroll around the neighborhood. He stood in front of the doors to the Shin-ma Business Association. There were neither people nor lights illuminating the inside. He couldn't tell if it was owned by a Japanese or by a fellow islander. Since there was a store sign hanging over the door, in the daytime, there would be lots of well-dressed workers and managers coming and going. He headed south from the Shin-ma store for a little bit until he saw a place called Bijin-za (House of Beauties). Unlike Shin-ma, this place did have both lights and people. The lamplight made an amber backdrop. The shadows and silhouettes of the people motioning about inside seemed somewhat enticing. He knew exactly what kind of business went on inside the establishment's corridors.

He stayed his right hand from reaching into his pocket for his wallet. He kept moving along, and he spotted a two-story building. Kanan Banking Company, Ltd. was written on the outside. Across the street was a business with the name Takugōmei. He reckoned it was a company dealing with construction of some sort. Walking on, he passed by a woman's vocational school. He stood at the entrance to it for a moment, trying to think of what kinds of skills were likely being taught to the women pupils inside, apart from making Japanese clothing and cooking. Across from the school was a whole row of enterprises, the largest of which was the Mitsui & Co. Store, Taihoku branch. The store next to it, which was slightly smaller, was the Meiji Pharmaceuticals Co. Overseas Branch. He didn't know why, but he wanted to get a better look at how these businesses were run. He was thirsting for knowledge about how they conducted business. He could also sense a bit of absurdity at this welling up from within. He was as curious and enthralled as Uncle A-Huàn inspecting a new water buffalo.

Off to his front, some distance away, was the New Park, in utter darkness. He was afraid to walk through it. He turned right and there was another bank, the Kangyō Bank, right on the corner. Ten more paces down the road, and he saw the Chōshū Savings Bank. Tsín-suī couldn't loiter around for too long on the streets since he had to get up quite early to make his train, so he headed back towards his inn. Along the way, he once again ran across two more banks, the Taihoku branches of the Mitsuwa Bank and the Taihoku Credit Association. He suddenly realized this was the banking district for the city, what with passing by a string of five banks all crowded together within the same area.

Later that evening, after he'd returned to the inn and was lying on the tatami matting, he thought over this entire sojourn up to Taihoku. Everything was novel and strange to him. Satō Kishin had described his half-true, half-made-up story to the headmaster of the No. 3 Girls' Secondary School as a master class in marketing skills. Tsín-suī chuckled to himself as he mused about this point. What's more, all of the sights and sounds he had encountered while out on his night walking tour were fresh and a new experience for him. He was so excited that he could hardly sleep a wink for an hour, before finally dozing off. He had already left all the trouble of having to deal with the second Ông daughter and her school far, far behind him, as if he had walked out from a fog and into pure, all-knowing clarity.

He arose at the crack of dawn the next day. He was still in the middle of washing and brushing his teeth, when Satō Kishin and his Taiwanese wife frantically ran into the inn, searching for Tsín-suī. "Ông Giȯk-bí escaped from the dormitory last night! The school sent men to notify us today!" Tsín-suī stood in front of the washbasin, toothpaste foam still stuck to the corners of his mouth.

The Satōs took Tsín-suī out for breakfast, all the while rummaging and strategizing how they could manage the situation. The couple had decided on a plan. Mr. Satō would be responsible for asking the school where some of Giók-bí's best friends frequented. Tsín-suī would have to go find several of his own classmates who were either studying in secondary schools or medical school to help with the search. Tsín-suī would have to delay his return to Pîn-tong and move into the Satō household, which made it easier to keep in touch with everyone.

When they had reached the Satō residence, Tsín-suī was shocked at what he saw. He didn't think this Japanese man would have so much furniture inside that was Taiwanese in origin and style! The kitchen layout, especially the hutch where the dishes were kept, the tea table for performing a Taiwanese-style tea ceremony, the round dining table—nobody would have gotten the sense or feeling that a Japanese person resided in this house. Satō-*san* relished letting Tsín-suī take a tour of the house, showing off the two *âng-bin-tsng* redwood beds that could be found in any regular Taiwanese person's home, one made of redwood with exquisite floral reliefs and finishings. It was Satō-*san* and his wife's; the other was in the guest room, unadorned, without any carvings or decoration, though made from Taiwanese cypress, retaining its natural, honeyed sunburst color— and its pleasing aroma.

The two of them must have been highly successful at their business. It wasn't yet noon, and yet there were already several volunteers from Pîn-tong studying in Taihoku who went out to every street corner to look for Giók-bí. Some posted themselves at the train stations around the city, but by the time the sky had darkened, there was still no word on her whereabouts. After dinner, there still wasn't any news. Tsín-suī was beginning to panic to the point he felt his heart would jump out of his chest. They kept on painstakingly waiting till it was 9:30 p.m., when Giók-bí had finally placed a phone call to the Satō residence, saying that she was out of the school and that everything was fine. Tsín-suī demanded that she make her way to the Satō house. He didn't get a response before she slammed the phone receiver down hard. The whole lot of them waited until after ten, when Giók-bí finally showed up after taking her own sweet time.

Furiously, Tsín-suī began questioning her, "Why did you run away from school?"

"There's no reason why. I just don't want to study anymore, and this way is more final."

Tsín-suī and the Satōs were truly dumbstruck for a while, unable to respond to her. Little Miss Ông began speaking again, "I'm already a grown-up now. I want to get married. Yesterday when *sensei* brought me to school and was walking everywhere with me, my classmates all saw him. They said my boyfriend looked very handsome and sophisticated."

From the moment Tsín-suī's train had departed from Pîn-tong station, he had a slight inkling about what was going on, from her every word and movement, but it wasn't a sense that she'd never had a boyfriend and that she'd never experienced the secret joy of being the object of affection and desire. But rationally speaking, he had already come to the point where he would settle down for life with her older sister, Giok-ìn. Why would he ever want to be another person's love interest? What's more, Tsín-suī and Giok-bí were still technically teacher and student. If she just now spoke of her real intentions, it would be best if he adopted a severe attitude, but he couldn't bear to dash her feelings on the rocks of unrequited love. He'd have to intentionally play dumb, he thought, and wait till they had returned to Pîn-tong, when he would inform her mother and older sister and get them to help unravel this knot and let her down easy. What was most important at present was trying to figure out what to do about lodging for the night. Would they go out and stay at an inn again? It was already dark out. It would be safest to just stay at the Satō household. He wasn't afraid of Giok-bí attempting to escape at night again.

Satō-*san*, for his part, was thinking deeply about the situation, as well. This Ngôo Tsín-suī was the ideal, potential dashing prince on a white stallion son-in-law for the Ông family. Ông *thài-thài* had all but confirmed that in her phone call with him earlier. This time, with Tsín-suī bringing Giok-bí all the way up to Tâi-pak, the intent was obvious, no? Or so Satō Kishin had thought. Such as it was now, the girl was definitely not intent on resuming her studies. There wouldn't be any shame in having her married off at this point in time. Tonight, they were all still worried that Giok-bí might try to escape again. That would not be so easily explained to Ông *thài-thài*. Just as Satō-*san* was turning this problem over in his mind, Tsín-suī happened to turn his head towards him. He had a look in his eyes as if he had something serious that he wanted to consult with Satō-*san* about. Satō-*san* beat him to the punch and cut straight to the chase, "The two of you can just put up here for the night." As he finished speaking, he heaved Giok-bí's luggage up and was going to take both tutor and student to the guest room. Satō-*san* still had it in his mind to help spur things on earlier than expected.

Now it was Tsín-suī's turn to have a headache. He knew the Satō household only had one guest bedroom, and there was only the one bed, issuing a vague aroma of camphor. There were two large tatami mats on it. It was a novel thing for such a mixture of both Taiwanese and Japanese elements thrown together like this. There was a soft cotton quilt placed squarely and neatly on the tatami. How could there only be the one sheet!? Tsín-suī was just about to ask his hosts when the two of them gently reminded him, "It's already past October, and Taihoku tends to get very cold at night. You'll want to bundle up." They quickly added, "Unfortunately, we only have this one extra cotton quilt. We're sorry to have you make do with just this one."

Tsín-suī looked closely at them, but the Satōs didn't have any special expressions on their faces. It didn't look like they were playing games or had any ulterior motives. In contrast, Giok-bí's face was absolutely flushed red from blushing, but she didn't immediately say anything like, "I don't want to sleep in the same bed with him," or, "How's this going to work?" Tsín-suī scanned the room again and saw a very ordinary Taiwanese-style rattan chair. They were comfortable to sit in, but they were hell when trying to repose or lie back. Could he ever get to sleep sitting in one? As for sleeping on the floor, the flooring of the house was ordinary concrete, so it would be impossible to sleep on it without a cotton blanket.

So were they to be left there in a heap? It was almost eleven o'clock at night and there wasn't time to hesitate. It wasn't like he had much of a choice and could afford to put it off. Just then, he thought of all those times he saw theater troupes performing this one particular mini-drama at the temple. It was a scene from the *Romance of the Three Kingdoms*. Lord Guan-Yu was forced into an uncomfortable situation, and he had to spend a night in the same bed as the wife of Liu Bei, his sworn brother-in-arms. Lord Guan-Yu resolutely placed a sharp sword in between him and the lady and then they both slept soundly. The following verse was sung in accompaniment to this act: "*Sau-sau* (my brother's wife) is sleeping soundly, with a sword in between us, protecting her peace of mind, and aiding me in maintaining my virtue." Each verse that was sung was accompanied by the clarity-inducing crash of cymbals: *Dong!* *Dong!* *Dong!* Once the segment was finished, a *suona*, oboe, lute, and flute joined together in a furious refrain, signifying the end of the act.

This night though, Tsín-suī let Giok-bí go to sleep first. He gave her the quilt to use. He opened up the sliding door to the room, and the window. He didn't bother putting the mosquito netting down, nor bother taking off his coat, his trousers, or socks. He kept thinking to himself: "*Sau-sau* is sleeping soundly, with a sword in between us, protecting her peace of mind..." The entire night, he kept drifting in and out of sleep. The *dong!*

and the *bauwn!* and the *pa-tang!* of the lute strings and cymbals kept reverberating and swirling around in his mind.

The next morning, Satō Kishin waited until Tsín-suī had once more taken Giok-bí back to the No. 3 Girls' Secondary School before making his phone call down to Pîn-tong. He told Ông *thài-thài* everything that had happened, without missing a single detail. You could hear the anxiety in Ông *thài-thài*'s voice. She forgot that she was talking to Satō-*san* and thought it better to switch to Japanese, "Well, Satō-*san*, can you get that ungrateful defiant daughter on the phone right now?"

"Ngôo-*san* Tsín-suī already took her to the school again. He said he wanted to try again to stop the school from kicking her out again."

"The way things have unfolded, it's already too late. It'd be impossible."

"It's hard to say. This Ngôo-*san* fellow was able to convince the headmaster the last time."

Mrs. Satō took the phone from her husband and spoke into the receiver, asking Ông *thài-thài* "Ông-*san*, I have a question for you. Were you intending to pair Ngôo-*san* with your daughter, Giok-bí?"

"Heavens no! He's only for my eldest daughter, Giok-ìn. Why, what happened?"

"Oh no! I feel absolutely awful. Last night I woke up twice to check in on the two of them, him and Giok-bí... Nothing came about of it."

"What do you mean? What happened last night?"

"Nothing happened. Absolutely nothing. Please don't worry. It's just something I was thinking about and wanted to ask you."

"And you're telling me not to worry—"

"Both Satō-*san* and I had mistakenly thought that Giok-bí was who you were wanting to marry off to Ngôo-*san*... It just so happened that we only have one guest bedroom in our home, with just a single bed. We gave the bed to both of them to sleep in—in the same room, in the same bed..."

"How can you possibly say that absolutely nothing happened? How do you know that?"

"Nothing did. Nothing happened. I checked myself. That Ngôo-*san* is a true gentleman. When they went to sleep, he left both the door and the window open. He slept in his clothes all throughout the entire night."

"Well, that's fortunate... I'm so relieved..."

On the other side of city, Tsín-suī and Giok-bí tried their luck again but they were utterly refused by the No. 3 Girls' Secondary School and promptly kicked out on their rear ends. The headmaster wouldn't even give them the time of day—he had flat out refused to even see them. A new letter of expulsion was issued, this time with NEVER ADMIT stamped heavily in red on it.

Just as they were leaving the school entrance, Giȯk-bí tried pressing her luck, poking the bear in the process. She made a request, asking Tsín-suī, "*Sensei*, I don't want to go back to Pîn-tong. Please...let's run off to the home islands. Please?"

"Yeah, and go off and do what? What the hell do you want to do there?"

"The home islands are more developed. You could also apply to study at a university there."

"No. I can't... Absolutely not. I gave your mother my word. I have a duty to take you back home. Whatever you're planning on doing, you can wait until after you get back to Pîn-tong to figure it out and bring it up with your mother. Go beg her if you want."

"*Sensei*, you're...you're just so—"

"Enough! That's the end of the discussion. You're not going to dictate anything to me. Get your stuff packed, now! We're going back!"

5

Having delivered Giȯk-bí back to her family with no fuss, as soon as Tsín-suī arrived at the Ông household, he went around with eyes peeled, searching high and low... Why was Giȯk-ìn nowhere to be found? Surely, she should have come out to greet him by now, no? He went to her bedroom door and rapped on it lightly. He waited there a while but there was no answer. Ông *thài-thài* stealthily made her way over to his side. "A-Ìn-á is very upset at the moment. You should go home first. I'll coax her out when the time is right for you," she said in a low voice.

Filled with suspicion, Tsín-suī made his way back home and slept soundly the whole night. The next day, he went straight back to work and threw all his efforts back into the sweltering environment of the banana research station—burning under the blistering sun. A group of enthusiastic coworkers could help him ease his mind and shift his focus from the awkward emotions swirling around Giȯk-ìn and Giȯk-bí.

Another day passed and it was almost nightfall. He was in the bacteriology lab working with a petri dish when he caught a glimpse through the window of his father coming towards the research station for some reason. "Why was he coming all this way out here? Was he just here to make sure his son was actually doing his work diligently? Whether as a child or as an adult, in all my life, have I ever not been diligent, whether at school or going out into the field for farm work? But no matter what he was doing, this son of yours always hated it when elders were standing over his shoulder, monitoring him... Have you somehow forgot this?"

Thoughts were nagging at him. He didn't feel like going out to greet his father, and he quickly put his thoughts aside and continued with his tasks at hand. As Tsín-suī began to wrap up his work and call it a day, Dr. Nakamura came into the bacteriology unit with Tsín-suī's father in tow. Dr. Nakamura inquired about the progress of some of the work specimens from a couple of the workers assembled in the lab and then left after a short moment. Tsín-suï's father stayed behind, then walked up to Tsín-suï's side and said, "A-Suï, let's go back to the house together."

Father and son rode their bicycles along the road, with Tsín-suï's father sometimes riding in front and his son behind. Neither of them uttered a single word as they went along the dusty path. Tsín-suï hadn't talked with his father for nearly two or three years, other than being berated or when backtalking his father. It wasn't too long before they had left Lîn-lok. Right as they were about to make their turn onto the road headed towards the family home, his father pulled over to ride beside Tsín-suï and pointed to the left of the road. There was a schoolyard filled with a tall, dense forest. "This is Heh-Lok, one of the finest agricultural schools in all of Asia.[14] It'll be nice when you're able to attend."

Tsín-suï cocked his head to the side slightly and strained to gaze at that sliver of the school's campus through the dense growth. As they were riding down the road, all he could do was catch a quick glance of it. It was like he was a photographer using a camera, trying his hardest to capture a few good scenes, carefully looking for just the right shot before pressing down on the shutter button. He passed by this place every day as he went to and from work. He'd never paid any particular attention to it, and it surprised him that there were several rows of simple and tidy classrooms deep behind the lush, green groves. Just a bit further away in the distance, he could make out the light greens and emeralds of vegetation growing out in faraway patches, denoting rice fields and fruit orchards. It must have been a student-run farm. He thought back on the year he had graduated from the common school. His father had told him, "You're the oldest son. It's time for you to stay home and help out." Apart from that, his father's other pet phrase for nagging his son was to say, "Writing poems is useless compared to working out in a field." He had ordered his son to discontinue any further studies. As much as he didn't want to, Tsín-suï had to give up his studies for the time being. The next year, he had secretly gone off to take a school entrance exam. He already knew at that time that Heh-Lok was pretty easy to get into, and he didn't give it a second thought. He chose to go to Takao Secondary,

---

14. "Heinō" being the original Japanese name for what is now known as Heh-Lok. In the Japanese colonial era policy of "Industrial Japan and Agricultural Taiwan," there were many agricultural training schools like Heinō. Some of them include Ga-nō (now in Chiayi), Gi-nō (now in Yilan), as well as all sorts of training schools in various cities and townships across Taiwan. Some of them changed names after WWII to the "Tropical Agricultural Training Institute" of the "Feng-shan Tropical Fruits Research Institute."

where 70 percent of the students were ethnic Japanese. Islanders had to be the cream of the crop of the local elites and fiercely competed just to get their foot in the door.

"Father's probably forgotten all about how hard I worked to get to where I was. *Honnh*!" Tsín-suī mused.

He was brought out of his memories, when his father suddenly told him, "Dr. Nakamura used to be a *sensei* at this school. Did you know that?"

"Oh," Tsín-suī replied simply.

"Uncle A-Tsòng is a graduate of this school too."

"He sure doesn't look like it!"

"You don't give him enough credit. You can't just see him as some farmer, bumbling about in his field. He's got a lot of knowledge in that head of his. When your old man was working in the Green Fruits Collective, he was already working there for a while. He's much more experienced than I am."

"What!? I never thought so... No wonder..."

"No wonder what?"

"He often has different opinions from other people, but he often makes a good point."

"His mind's as sharp as the sharpest sickle."

That evening at dinner, his father made a big announcement at the dinner table, "Your old man went to A-Suī-á's research station today. I decided that I am going to rent that big piece of land over to the north of the station. It's more than three *kah* (2.39 acres). I want to plant bananas there." Tsín-suī's eyes lit up, but before he could reply, his father continued with his announcement, "The Japanese, regardless of whether they're here in Taiwan or off in the home islands, love to eat bananas from Taiwan. The Japanese government is preparing to import them into the home islands. They'll import as many as they can."

"This is something I'm already aware of. It can make us a lot of money," Tsín-suī replied.

"Three *kah* is quite a lot of land though. There's not enough of us in the family to work the fields," Tsín-suī's mother thought to herself. She was thinking of slamming the brakes on this conversation but didn't dare speak her mind.

"We'll need to hire some people. We need to start looking for some steady help."

"*Nii-san*'s workplace is nearby. He can go over and manage it pretty easily," Tsín-suī's second younger brother, Tsín-siann chimed in.

"Well, to be honest, aside from your older brother, the entire family needs to pitch in. When you're not in school, you'll all need to come and help out."

"Where will you find the seedlings for the trees, father? Have you fully thought this through?" Tsín-suī asked.

"I talked it through with Dr. Nakamura today. He said he'd help buy a portion of them for us and save the rest. We'll need to plant the rest of the trees ourselves and then cultivate more from the seeds of those trees."

"So later on, after we've succeeded in planting them, not only will we be able to sell bananas, but we can then sell the seedlings too."

"Heh, heh! A-suī-á's truly a genius! I didn't even think about selling the seedlings." The old man seldom praised his children. As soon as he heard the words, Tsín-suī unconsciously scooped a big helping of rice into his mouth.

Tsín-suī felt extremely excited as he ate his dinner. He knew the real reason why the Japanese wanted to set up the banana research labs. They were planning on building up Pîn-tong as a vast region filled with banana plantations. This was a top-level government policy. He prided himself on being able to throw some effort into this industry right then and striking the iron while it was hot. He also admired his father's ability to sniff out a business opportunity when it presented itself. Since he graduated from Takao Secondary, this was the first time he and his father had been on the same page. He felt that a good future was laid out ahead of them. It was a beautiful dream, all of it set out before him.

The next day, Tsín-suī was back doing his work in the bacteriology lab. He was about to finish up his work for the day, when a guest came by looking for him. It was Ông *thài-thài*. She had taken the pedicab out all this way and was waiting by the entrance to the field lab.

"A-Suī-á, ever since Giok-bí came back home from Taihoku, she hasn't been eating or drinking. She hardly speaks and it's already been three days! I'm afraid she's putting her life in danger!"

Tsín-suī stood there, absolutely stunned. He was left speechless. Ông *thài-thài* said, "Put your bicycle back and get into the pedicab with me. Come help me convince her to eat something. Giok-ìn-á says that only if you come can her sister's life be saved."

Tsín-suī let out a sigh. There was nothing else he could do but obey Ông *thài-thài*.

Once they were on the road back, she begged three or four times, asking the pedicab driver to hurry his pace, to the point that he was huffing and puffing like an ox. The only difference was that the chauffeur wasn't being led by a rope lead or being whipped on his back, suffering like an ox normally would.

When they reached the Ông household, Giok-ìn was already standing at the gate. She led Tsín-suī to her younger sister's bedchamber. A sallow, thin girl was lying on the bed. Her long hair was concealing half her face, her eyes looked like they had grown larger. It was because her face had become a lot thinner, and her eye sockets had sunk. She weakly called out to her beloved *sensei*. Tsín-suī's heart felt a twinge. He saw Giok-ìn blowing on a bowl of salty *muê-á* (rice porridge), trying to cool it off. She indicated to Tsín-suī that she wanted him to spoon-feed her sister. "It would be great if she would eat even just one bite of porridge. If she doesn't eat, we might have to force her... I'm sorry."

Tsín-suī made a sigh. All he could do was follow orders.

Next he took the bowl of *muê-á* and began softly trying to persuade Giok-bí. "Giok-bí, come. You haven't eaten at all. That's not OK. Come. Open your mouth just a bit. I'm going to feed you." He felt weird saying it. Strangely, she obediently opened her mouth and swallowed spoonful after spoonful of the porridge. In no time, the bowl was completely polished off. After she had finished eating, she drank a glass of water.

The Ông family all felt relieved at this.

After feeding her, he stole a look at Giok-ìn. He could sense very clearly a sadness filling Giok-ìn's face, making his own heart ache. Her own pain had begun to rise. She stood off to the side, aimlessly. He stood there dumbly, not knowing whether he should remain at Giok-bí's bedside or leave. The younger Ông son, whom Tsín-suī was tutoring, had come in. "*Sensei*, older sister cooked an entire pot of *muê-á*. Let's finish it off together. Let's go."

Tsín-suī's awkwardness finally dissipated, and he called out to Giok-ìn and Ông *thài-thài* to eat some of the porridge with them.

Giok-ìn kept her head lowered as she ate. Spoon after spoon went into her mouth. She took her time while eating, not speaking a word. Nobody knew what to say. Tsín-suī and the younger Ông Kia-iau both slurped down two bowls, and when they were done, A-Hiông called for the pedicab chauffeur. Ông *thài-thài* wanted Giok-ìn to send Tsín-suī off to the pedicab waiting outside. The two of them walked over to the side of the cab, and Tsín-suī lightly called out her name, "A-Ìn," and sought her hand in the dark. He touched it and lightly gripped it, but Giok-ìn only let her hand be held for a few seconds before she cast his hand aside.

"Agh," she cried out in an outburst, then quickly walked back into the house.

Tsín-suī sat in the pedicab. As it turned onto the road, his heart painfully jolted as they went along the gravel road.

He didn't tell anyone about this. He didn't sleep well that night, and before the sun had even risen, he had made his way out to the laboratory to bury himself in his work, hoping that he'd tire himself out or blunt the pain. But Giok-ìn's hurt and Giok-bí's annoyance wouldn't stop floating into his mind all the time. Dr. Nakamura tended to be the earliest to arrive and the last to leave. When he saw Tsín-suī already at the lab at such an ungodly hour, he at first didn't make a sound and stood off in the distance, watching him carefully digging up the seedlings from Area Five. Tsín-suī delicately excavated the roots and lifted the plant out of the soil, then he transplanted them to Area Two. This was the new experiment that their research committee had decided on in the meeting the previous day. Nakamura observed him for a long time, and then walked up to him. He just greeted him with a simple, "*Ohayō*," but didn't offer any praise, then kept on walking to the accountant's office, where he wrote a note for the accountant, "Promote assistant candidate Ngôo Tsín-suī to a regular technician position, and give him the full salary."

When Tsín-suī punched out of the office, the pedicab was parked outside the gate again. This time, Ông *thài-thài* wasn't sitting in it, but it was the same chauffeur. After he got into the cab, he told the chauffeur they didn't have to go as hurriedly as they had the previous day. They could go at a leisurely pace, yet the chauffeur seemed to have some secret understanding of something awful happening back at the Ông household. He ignored Tsín-suī's request, and pedaled as if his feet were on fire. They were speeding along so quickly that Tsín-suī had to lean back in the seat to keep from falling out. He watched as the sun sank into the west. The whole sky was a deep crimson. He thought of getting the chauffer to slow down a bit and began to make small-talk with him in a friendly tone, "Hey, *Nii-san*, the sun off in the west is so red, *honnh*? Have you seen it?"

The chauffeur shouted back at him, "I did, I noticed. It means there's going to be a typhoon coming soon."

"Oh yeah, that makes sense. It's gotten a lot hotter and muggier out."

"Whenever a typhoon hits, it always gets especially humid."

The two of them went back and forth, but the pedicab didn't slow down a bit. When they were going through the center of town, Tsín-suī then heard the chauffeur say, "The reason I'm rushing to get you to the Ông household is because Ông *thài-thài* will give me a *sio-huì* (tip)."

After stepping out from the cab, Tsín-suī went once more to Giok-bí's room to kneel by her bedside. Once again, Giok-ìn had prepared rice porridge as she had the last time. Tsín-suī used an even more gentle tone of voice to coax her to eat and fed her like a baby. He made sure she had eaten the whole bowl. As Giok-ìn took away the empty bowl, she was going to say something of her younger sister, but unexpectedly, her sister took a rattan switch out from under the covers and struck Tsín-suī on the back and shoulders as he was turned the other way. Each time she hit him, she hoarsely screamed at him, "Stupid ox! Stupid ox! You stupid ox!" Tsín-suī didn't bother to shield himself and let her strike him. A look of shocked perplexity hung from his face. Giok-bí struck him three times and tightly closed her eyes. Streams of tears flowed out, and she added two more sentences, "Who does the matchmaker want you to marry? Why don't you want to marry my sister?" After her tirade, she slumped back down, rolled over to face the wall and ignored everyone.

Tsín-suī took the beating in stride and had an inkling of the child's intentions. What was strange about it was the nonsense she was spewing. Giok-ìn was also a woman, and she was more knowing about what her sister was trying to say. This "accident" seemed to spur on a subconscious decision in Giok-ìn. She took the bowl away and said in an abnormally firm voice, "Go. Let's leave."

The pedicab was waiting outside the house-storefront. Tsín-suī was walking out with Giok-ìn at his heels. Just as he did the day before, he took Giok-ìn's hand, but this time she didn't push him away, nor did she cry. She just firmly talked down to him, "With the way you're running all around, you should take care of yourself. If you're truly tired, you'll know it when you're yearning for rest." She waited for Tsín-suī to get into the cab, and then she continued, "Tomorrow, I'll take care of it all. You just go home and rest. OK!" She turned and then went back into the house, where she discovered that Giok-bí had left her room and was standing at the threshold, watching them speak their goodbyes, hand in hand.

The pedicab wasn't waiting for him on the third day. Tsín-suī thought they probably didn't need him to help, and so he got onto his bicycle and rode back home, but when he got to the center of Heitō, he felt a bit off and went by the Ông household, only to see that things weren't good. The shop apprentice, A-Hiông told him, "I don't know where the younger miss got a hold of them, but she bought sleeping pills and tried to kill herself. She was sent to the hospital in an emergency." A-Hiông saw alarm growing on Tsín-suī's face, and continued, "Mister, you don't need to worry. She's not in any danger anymore. They've already taken care of her."

Tsín-suī clambered back onto his bicycle and sped off towards the hospital. People with serious illnesses were sent here, not for some trifling cold or some such nonsense. It was located by the triangular park across from the Taiwan Bank. The park was a full-on gossiping rumor mill. As soon as he parked his bicycle, he could hear others saying, "Oh, it was the second daughter from the ceramics shop, no doubt. I heard it was because she was kicked out of school—"

"That's not the reason why. I heard it was because she was trying to steal her brother-in-law, but the brother-in-law wouldn't requite her, and so she didn't want to live anymore."

"Both of you are wrong! The two sisters are vying after a *sensei*. The one who lost decided to eat some pesticide and kill herself."

Hearing these remarks, Tsín-suī lowered his face, turned around and walked away. He was worried that as the star of the show in this story, he'd be discovered in the hospital and it would only throw the rumor mill into full swing.

When he got home, he felt like his heart was going to explode. This constant emotional turmoil wasn't OK to be kept bottled up inside. Before dinner had been started, he popped into the kitchen to tell his mother about the situation. Before long, he was in tears. As they heard his sobs, his younger siblings all crowded around him, and even his father walked by. His father asked him to repeat the whole story from the beginning, "Tell us all the details. Don't leave anything unsaid."

Tsín-suī retold the whole story, and his youngest sister Kun-tsin sighed loudly, "I've seen a lot of *bāng-kah* fantasies, but none of them can ever compare to what *Nii-san* is describing."

The second-oldest daughter, Kun-boo, said, "I want Giok-ìn to be my *A-só* (older sister-in-law)."

Tsín-suī's fourth youngest brother, Tsín-bú chimed in, *Nii-san* ought to marry this Giok-ìn, and quickly."

The other siblings wanted to add their thoughts too, but then their father spoke, "Your old man will help you take care of it all. Don't worry. Just go to work tomorrow like you normally would, and your old man will set things right."

It was morning on the next day, and the sky was filled with dark clouds. The radio was announcing the imminent arrival of a typhoon, but all the workers went about their day as normal, and all the students went to school. Before the typhoon made landfall, the Ngôo patriarch ran over to the hospital where he discovered that the second Ông daughter had pulled through and would be discharged from the hospital that afternoon.

Around evening, the weather started to change. The wind picked up first, and then the rains started to pummel everything. The winds and rains then came together to create a terrifying scene. Rain was leaking in through the roof in several places, and they placed some face-washing basins and wooden buckets around to collect the water droplets. Occasionally, they heard the sound of straining and snapping tree branches outside the house. All the Ngôo household lay half-asleep, half-awake out of terror, but Tsín-suī hadn't returned from the laboratory at all that evening. After the sun rose, the winds died down, but the rain grew heavier. Father sent out Tsín-suī's second younger brother, Tsin-siann, to brave the rains and go to the village head's house to use the telephone. After calling, they found out that the banana lab was besieged by rising waters and nobody could get out. Everyone at the lab had stayed over the night.

After Mr. Ngôo knew his son hadn't left work, he put on a bamboo rain cape and a bamboo hat and went out barefoot into the rains, alone, from their home in Thâu-tsîng-khe. He went on foot, fording the rocky riverbed, slowly making his way into the city through the driving, pelting rains. He went as quickly as he could to the Ôngs ceramics shop. There weren't any customers on typhoon days, so as soon as he made his presence known, Ông *thài-thài* and her eldest son quickly came out from the back portion connecting to the house to greet him, inviting him in to sit down and have some tea. Giok-ìn stood behind the entrance to the back room, not daring to come forth from the shadows. Her heart was beating like a great, giant drum.

"Ông-*san*, *Góa tsin phainn-sè* (I'm so sorry to intrude), my son has given you so much trouble."

"*Bô, bô*, not at all. Tsín-suī-á has helped us so much." Ông *thài-thài* suddenly paused, her eyes all red. She lowered her gaze and continued in a near-whisper, "It's my younger daughter who's not here... My daughter just didn't know how to deal with her issues and she...and she...," Ông *thài-thài* choked up with tears, unable to finish the last string of words in the sentence.

"Ông-*san*, I've already asked about her. You've dealt with it the best you could. In fact, it's been too much for you. I just wish Tsín-suī had told me about these things much sooner." Mr. Ngôo stopped speaking for a second, saw that Ông *thài-thài* had calmed down, and then continued.

"I'm coming here today as a family member. Since the typhoon's here, I came as I am without either a matchmaker or betrothal, and I'm sorry to say I don't have any gifts prepared. I just came over as soon as I could. I'm sorry to have been so disrespectful in this regard. I'll settle up on that account at a later time."

The eyes of all the members of Ông household grew wide in excitement, and they couldn't think how to respond. Mr. Ngôo kept going, "I was thinking that A-Tsín-suī is still a young man, and if he had waited two or three more years, I wouldn't have worried... However, at this time and given everything that's happened, I'll have to tell him to hurry up and tie the knot to start a family. We could also use the extra help on our farm. A-Tsín-suī could also help you take care of your business."

"Ngôo-*san*, that's fantastic. I'm ecstatic to hear what you're saying...," a smile appeared on Ông *thài-thài*'s face. She started to softly ask, "Ngôo-*san*, so what you're saying is—" she stopped mid-sentence.

Mr. Ngôo knew where she was headed and cut right to the answer, "I'll manage A-Tsín-suī's marriage. I'd like to ask your eldest daughter, Giȯk-ìn, if she'd be willing to marry him. I hope you will help me to corral A-Tsín-suī."

"Yes, yes! That's all fantastic! I'm in full agreement."

"Since the typhoon's come today and it's not such an auspicious sign, I hope that the marriage will move along quickly, like a horse that's spurred on, galloping faster and faster."

"No problem. I was thinking, too, a while back that it would be best if they got married quickly."

Giȯk-ìn made her appearance just then, bearing a teapot with piping hot tea. She moved forward delicately, calling out to her father-in-law-to-be, "Hello, Ngôo-*san*, I am A-Ìn. Your tea has already cooled down too much. Let me help pour you a new cup."

Mr. Ngôo looked Giȯk-ìn up and down, "Oh, A-Ìn-á, *to-siā li*."

After pouring his cup, Giȯk-ìn then filled the cups of her mother and older brother.

Mr. Ngôo sat drinking his tea, "A-Tsín-suī didn't come back home last night. The waters have risen all around the research station he's working at. He'll be there for a while."

Giȯk-ìn responded, "That's right. This morning I phoned there, but I don't know if they have anything to eat over there."

"I'm not too worried about food. If the rain stops, the water will recede quickly."

Everyone switched to more mundane, lighter conversation topics, and then Mr. Ngô stood up to take his leave. Ông *thài-thài* waited at the door while he put on his bamboo rain cape and his bamboo hat. She herself had grabbed a paraffined parasol to accompany him on his way back out into the rains. Giȯk-ìn wanted to come out to see Mr. Ngô off, but her mother sent her away.

An elderly man wearing a rain cape and bamboo hat and a middle-aged woman holding an umbrella exchanged words in the downpour. The raindrops were falling like waterfalls from all around the rim of his hat, the brown fibers of the rain cape were beginning to darken more and more with every drop of rain seeping in. Small beads of water gradually grew into streams, and then one great stream ran down his back. The top of Ông *thài-thài*'s waxed-paper umbrella was pounded by a heavy tympany. With strands of water falling from all the sides, she looked as if she were standing in cylindrical shade of rain. She opened her mouth to speak, but she couldn't be too loud lest her daughter hear, "Ngô-san, have you ever considered marrying your son off to both my daughters? It's still considered fine in polite society for a man to take more than one woman as his wife—two, three even, wouldn't you say so?"

"I'd actually given it some thought the other night, but A-Tsín-suī isn't that kind of man. Our home is also not a very wealthy one. He's just a young buck who only just started to make his way in the world. If he were to take two wives at once, he'd become a laughingstock and the talk of the town."

Mr. Ngô started to take two steps forward into the rain, then he turned back and added something that had almost escaped his mind, "The most important thing is that I've asked him. A-Tsín-suī only has eyes for Giȯk-ìn."

"Of course! I understand well what you mean. *Aiyee*! There's nothing we can do about it. You have to make your way back home through this rain. I'll call the pedicab around to give you a ride back. Would that be fine with you, Ngô-*san*?"

"Oh, there's no need. I'm wearing my *mua-á*. It wouldn't be easy for me to get in and out of the pedicab."

Giȯk-ìn stood at the threshold, straining as hard as she could to hear what the two of them were up to, but the constant din of the rain was just too loud. At last, she faintly heard her mother mention calling for the pedicab, so she took an umbrella to walk out. She saw Mr. Ngô take a few steps, but her mother called out to stop him.

Her mother stood out in the rain, practically shouting over the din,

"There's another troubling matter I need to speak with you about. Would you be able to talk about it now or at another time?"

Mr. Ngôo stopped again and turned his head to speak, "*Tshiann kóng* (I'm listening)."

"We're a business-owning family. A-Ìn-á has no clue about going down into the fields to do heavy farm work. A-Ìn-á has no clue how hard it is to farm."

"Oh, don't worry about that, Ông-*san*. Rest assured. We're not going to put her out into the field to work. We'll cherish her as if she were a precious jewel."

***

A long distance away, in the Lîn-lok banana research station, eleven technicians, including Tsín-suí, were wearing their yellowish-brown rain capes and Japanese-style, oval-shaped plastic helmets. They were all standing in a neat row in the corridor in front of the office. It was pitch-black outside, and the winds were rising slightly, growing stronger by the minute. The leaves of the banana trees outside were swaying, against their will, left, right, left, right. The rain wasn't so heavy just yet—there were just a few large drops falling here and there. This seemed to be heaven's first warning sign to those at the research station, but Dr. Nakamura obviously ignored the portents, even thinking about challenging this warning. With that, he raised both his hands and, in a booming voice, said, "So there's wind and rain. It's a great opportunity for us to research our crops."

After he made his declaration, he began to divide up the labor. "Group One will go to Areas Three and Four and observe our latest dwarfed cultivars to see how they fare in the typhoon. As soon as it starts, you must record it all in great detail. Take special note of the resilience of the tree trunks and leaves and how the height of the bamboo stabilizing stakes affects their effectiveness."

"Group Two will be split into two smaller teams. Team One will be placed on higher ground, and Team Two will go to the lower-lying areas and observe the tree roots and how they change based on the conditions of the water levels. Remember, the root systems will change first by bloating, and then the color will gradually turn from yellow to pale. You'll need to overcome the rain and wind to make your notes."

"Group Three, you're coming with me."

As Dr. Nakamura barked his orders, the wind gradually strengthened and started to come in great howling gusts from the south. The banana leaves all around them were being blown in the same direction now, furiously leaning towards the north. The rain began to grow heavier, as dense as flying arrows penetrating into the earth.

"Right now, we must start our work immediately. Let's shout the second line of our lab motto together: 'In great winds and heavy rains, we shall not shirk; when the sky shakes and the earth rumbles, we shall not fall.'"

"The rains and winds were increasing, how are we going to record any of this?" That day, Tsín-suī's eyes were opened. He was in Group Three. Dr. Nakamura called him over to help him lift a camera out of a crate. It was so heavy that it took everyone in their group to get it out. It was packed in a wooden crate and took two men to lift it out, two people to position it, and two people to hold umbrellas over it. Dr. Nakamura said that it was the most advanced camera to date in Japan. It had a flash window that could illuminate and photograph subjects in the darkness. All around them, the sky and grounds were black as charcoal. Dr. Nakamura buried his face in the black bag of the camera body, extended his right arm, concentrating with such intensity, continuously gaging the distance, measuring the speed all throughout the torrential rain. The flash mechanism would light up just once in a long while, and then after it flashed, it was gone into dark nothingness without a trace. That camera could create "lightning" without the thunder that accompanies it.

Other technicians were working industriously at their research; they weren't given any cameras. Several of them were observing out in the middle of the rain, trying to shout out their reports over the howling winds. Another group on the veranda strained their ears to hear those reports, writing down the shouted notes, pen stroke by pen stroke, one entry after another.

Despite these trying conditions, the whole lot of them threw themselves into their work, continuing right until dusk, when they were startled to realize something shocking—the faraway creek was rising rapidly. The road out was cut off by chest-high waters. Each one of the men was forced to turn back in horror and rushed back to the research station to spend the night, searching for any dry rations to fill their stomachs.

That evening, Tsín-suī slept fitfully. He had so many sensations and thoughts running through his head. Banana trees were truly pampered, delicate plants. Their trunks couldn't resist the wind, and their roots couldn't handle being immersed for long. Today everyone had buried themselves in their work out in the rain and gritted their teeth, trying their best to carry out their work. Was all this being done just to record the frailty of these trees? A long time ago, Tsín-suī had once heard about another group of Japanese agricultural technicians who had spent tons of effort to cultivate hybrid "Penglai rice." Such rice could fill a grown man's stomach with just one cup. What was a banana compared to this? It was just a dumb piece of fruit, right? As he pondered this, his Japanese colleague sleeping over to his left began to snore. His colleague from Takao was sitting upright, vigorously scratching at an itch on his back that just wouldn't go away. It was wet and humid everywhere around them. In the moldy smell of a rainy day, combined with the briny stench of sweat, some of the men went straight to sleep and others were so bothered by it, they couldn't catch a single wink of shut-eye. Right here was a room full of crazed Japanese and Taiwanese agricultural technicians who couldn't be stopped by rains or winds, giving their all to improve everyone's lot through banana cultivation.

After the sun rose, the wind stopped howling, but the rains came down ever more violently. There was nothing to eat in the research station. Someone braved the rains to go out and pick some edible bracken. Someone dug up some half-rotten sweet potatoes, but none of this was nearly enough for the team.

"Aren't there fish in the river?"

Tsín-suī wasn't sure who had said it, but they were immediately met with a defeating remark, "The waters are rushing, it's turbid and murky; the fish are long gone."

Dr. Nakamura didn't dare to force any of his starving colleagues to go back out into the rains. He went himself to crouch down in the banana fields, not even bothering to wear rain galoshes. Tsín-suī heard that he was a rare breed of workaholic. Being moved by Dr. Nakamura's support and care for his subordinates, Tsín-suī followed him out into the field. The rains were coming down in such massive droves. The water only came up to his ankles. Tsín-suī praised his boss, "This station's drainage system is amazing."

"Yes, it truly is. It's partly to do with the accumulation of so much sediment over time and being raised up slightly higher. Otherwise, the waters would come in and flood everything," Dr. Nakamura responded.

Not long afterwards, Dr. Nakamura called out again, "*Wah*, Tsín-suī, look! When the Number One cultivars and Number Two cultivars are submerged, the shape of their floating roots is different, and even the color is different. It's obvious that these two types have a different water tolerance. Go back and get my notebook. I want to make a drawing."

"But it's raining so heavily, how on earth are you going to sketch them?"

"If you hold an umbrella for me, I can do it quickly."

Tsín-suī replied to him in the Japanese way, with a very heavy, "*Hai,*" and then he quickly added, "I'll go get everything prepared quickly."

The two of them got to work under the heavy rain. Once Dr. Nakamura had finished his rough sketches, someone in the office shouted out to them, "Nakamura-*san*, there's a telephone call for you!"

"Ask them if they're going to send any dry rations over, tell them how many people we have here. Tell them to send the food straight over," Dr. Nakamura shouted through the rain.

Another moment passed, and the other person shouted back, "They say that they're one of your old friends... They have a very pressing matter to discuss. They're asking you to answer the phone in person."

Dr. Nakamura carefully tucked away his notebook and, after going back into the office, took the telephone receiver. The first sentence he responded was, "Oh, he's here, he's just fine. He was just next to me out—"

Then Nakamura's expression and tone of voice changed. A string of surprised responses came out of him, "*O, sō-jya...* (Oh, I see...)." His eyes darted to Tsín-suī twice. All of the technicians and workers were in the room and moved closer out of curiosity, surrounding Dr. Nakamura and the telephone. "*O, sō-desu-jya.* (Oh, so that's the case)."

After the phone conversation had ended, he made a big announcement to everyone. "The phone call was from Ngôo Tsín-suī's father. He set a wedding date for our friend here. It will be this Saturday. Not including today, that's five days away. He's inviting the entire station to attend as guests."

The entire room erupted in cheers. Only Tsín-suī's facial expression was a little off. His lips were slightly parted, and he looked stupefied. He was mumbling, "I ought to go home now. Who knows when the water will recede from the front gate?" He was putting on his rain cape as he said the words.

Dr. Nakamura stepped in to block his way, "I just looked, and the water is higher and moving faster than it was yesterday. You absolutely mustn't go. Since your father's taking care of it all, just sit back and relax. It's all being taken care of by your family. When the water's lower tomorrow, we'll help you ford the river."

When Dr. Nakamura got to this point in the exchange, the others piped in, "Someone will prepare a rope long enough to cross-tie it to Tsín-suī's waist. We'll need to keep a good hold of the rope from over here to allow for him to swim or ford his way across and go back home. At least if he slips while crossing through the river, he won't be swept away by the currents, and we can pull him back in."

A very knowledgeable technician by the name of Khóo-*san* added, "I was here last year when it flooded. We also used this method to safely send over another man who had an emergency to take care of back at his home."

"We can't do this right away. We're definitely going to have to wait for the waters to lower a bit. Tsín-suï will just have to wait patiently," Dr. Nakamura added.

"But we've not had anything real to eat for the past two or three days. By the time the water's gone down, we'll all be in a hospital. How are we going to attend a wedding?"

"We're not going to starve. The wind has already died down. We just have to wait for the rains to lighten up and then the military will send out some soldiers to deliver us some relief food."

Tsín-suï started to look through the heaps of farm implements with his colleagues for a long coil of rope. He suddenly had an idea and quickly asked Dr. Nakamura, "Can I make a telephone call?"

Dr. Nakamura gave his assent, and Tsín-suï picked up the phone only to put it down.

"What's the matter?" someone asked.

Tsín-suï gave a bitter chuckle, "I just remembered that I don't have the telephone number of the village head."

"What do you want to call him for?"

"I want him to get my father on the telephone."

Not having made his call, he paced around near the phone. He seemed to look like a little mouse scurrying up and down the baskets in the office. He could hear his colleagues' conversations.

"Have you ever heard of a father planning a wedding? I've never heard of that, and the son who is to be the groom knew nothing of it. Who ever heard of such a thing! The groom's nervous as all can be."

"I'm thinking that his father must've been in a hurry to arrange it. The bride must have a big belly. If they don't get hitched early, the child will make its surprise appearance rather sooner than later."

The entire room was filled with chattering voices. A Japanese technician very solemnly asked, "There's one expression in your islander speech that I don't understand, pardon me, but '*toa-pak-too*' means 'pregnant,' right?"

"Yes, that's right. What else could it mean?"

"So, to go a little further in asking, why would the bride become pregnant for no rhyme or reason?"

Everyone cracked up at that. The Japanese technician was obviously faking his great seriousness. Even Dr. Nakamura, who was rather straitlaced, snickered at the exchange.

Afterwards, Hoklo and Japanese were intermixed, and everyone became more and more raunchy with their banter. Tsín-suī wanted it all to stop, but he wouldn't be able to explain what happened in just two or three words. He thought he'd be laughed at even more for the real reason. This was a man's world and everyone was starving. Just having them laughing and happy for a moment was enough.

The telephone rang amid all the ruckuses. Dr. Nakamura waved for Tsín-suī to answer it, "Heh heh."

The telephone call was for Tsín-suī in any case. Everyone listened with intense curiosity and could hear his first words, "Oh, A-Ìn-á, my father already told me he's arranging the marriage. Who is it?... Oh, what I mean is... is it you?... Oh, I see. Thank goodness... No, I was just afraid my father would completely misunderstand my intentions. I was afraid he would ask that I marry the wrong person... Oh, it's nothing. You should go start preparing... I'm doing fine here. Everything's OK... Yes. We've eaten... We won't starve... As soon as the waters have gone down and the rain has stopped, I'm going to be quick and try to make my way home."

All his colleagues listened with their breath held and their ears pricked up. When they finished listening, they began bombarding him with even more questions and made more small jokes at his expense.

"Hah, so this was what you were so concerned about! No wonder you were so worried... You mean to say there are a lot of potential brides out there... You were afraid your old man would pick the wrong one?"

"I'm still a bit curious, what kind of thing needs to be done five or six days before a wedding, when a typhoon is still raging on?"

"No, that can't be the reason... I think this is what happened...," someone mused.

Tsín-suī swept the anxiety off his face and cheered up. He decided he wouldn't let all this talk keep running on and on, so he made a big announcement. "My wedding is already decided for this Saturday. We'll hold it in the courtyard of my family home." He gave a deep bow after speaking, then continued, "Your humble brother in research respectfully invites everyone here to attend. I'll draw up a map for everyone in just a second."

Inside the room, all the workers huddled around and focused on Tsín-suī's marriage. Nobody was paying attention to how the rains were changing. The rains kept pounding down in heavy torrents. Heaven seemed to be tired. Sometimes the rain would ease up and come down flying like silk threads, thin and not like the giant wads that had fallen before. The rains had softened up for a spell. Dr. Nakamura first noticed it and then called out, "Ngôo Tsín-suī, you should go home now. There's some hope for you—the rains have died down a little."

"It's still raining."

"As long as it slows down a bit, the waters won't stay so high."

"I'll go out and check...," Chin Fo-sen offered up bravely.

A few minutes later, Fo-sen came back to the doors of the research station, completely soaked from head to toe. "The water level's definitely gone down a bit since yesterday when we wanted to go home."

Everyone got back to work. Not only did they need to tie a rope around Tsín-suī's waist, but they'd also need to tie it through a bicycle which would need to be tied to Tsín-suī's waist, as well. They'd also need to hook up his shoulders. The rope wasn't long enough. Tying another length to make it longer would mean it wasn't thick enough, they'd have to put together a thicker one. About seven or eight of the men scrambled about on this task for about an hour. They put on their bamboo rain capes and sedge hats and set out into the deluge together. They couldn't continue keeping their colleague from preparing for his wedding day. For the moment, they forgot all their hunger pangs.

As they got to the main gate of the research station, the waters were rushing swiftly, so they stopped. The yellowish turbid waters spread out before them. Sand and grit, large and small branches seemed to move as if alive, churning all over, bobbing and rolling violently in the flow. The many helping hands soon became many concerned voices.

"You don't need to rush it. Just go slowly as you place your footing firmly, OK?"

"Don't worry. We'll have a good grip on the rope. Just go slowly and you'll definitely be able to ford the river."

"We'll be there right on time Saturday for your wedding."

"I know I'm gonna be taking a good, long look at the bride's belly."

"If you get to a deep part and you can't keep going forward, don't try to force your way across. Come back and wait for a while, OK?"

Tsín-suī gave another bow in the group's direction, and he wanted to thank them again, but the words got caught in his throat. Both his hands gripped the bicycle handlebars. He strode, step by giant step into the waters without hesitation. The water gradually rose from his ankles up to his knees. As he kept toeing his way slowly into the torrent, the waters reached his waist.

Someone called out from behind him, "A-Suī-á, give the bicycle another wrap to increase your weight. The more you weigh, the harder it will be for bigger currents to sweep you away. A-Suī-á, *ganbare*![15] You can do it!"

Another pessimistic admonishment came again from behind, "A-Suī-á, if you get to a place you can't cross, don't try forcing your way. Just come back if that happens!"

Tsín-suī slowly continued to move forward, step by step. He felt that everything was fine. The water only came up to his waist. Just as he began to feel a little relaxed, he stepped into a deep pothole and felt a sharp pain on the sole of his foot. The water surged up from his waist all the way to his collarbone. This was where the pedicab had picked him up just a few days ago. He carefully felt around with the calloused soles of his feet for large rocks or boulders, roughly figuring out a more even path. The water level remained somewhere between his chest and his stomach. He didn't need to feel scared. He was quite familiar with the road he took to and from work. At least thinking in this way, he could try to embolden himself. He took a couple steps forward, but suddenly he felt something heavy float past him. It hit the bicycle tied beside him at high speed. He looked down— it was a corpse. The hairs stood up on the back of his neck. Thinking that it was a human body, he fixed his eyes on it just to make sure but realized it was just a dead pig. In the first few seconds after his realization, he thought about trying to free the dead animal from his bicycle frame and letting the waters take it away, but he had to keep both his hands on the handlebars, otherwise, he couldn't keep his balance in the rushing water.

"How can I get rid of it?" he thought to himself. Just then, the pig seemed to lift its head above the water as if swimming with a breaststroke, while at the same time giving out a wail. *Wah-sai*! It was unbelievable! It wasn't dead yet. It was still struggling to stay alive, battling the flood! The pig's head then slipped back under the water, and there was a *glug-a-lug* sound, as if water was flooding down its throat. The compassion in Tsín-suī's heart rose, "I'm so sorry, I can't spare a hand to save you. I'm sorry!" he said to the pig. Just as the words left his mouth, the pig's head bobbed up to the surface again, and there looked like there was a smile on its face. Its mouth was slightly open, allowing the turbid waters to gush in, and its eyes had glazed over. It was dead now.

Right then, Tsín-suī had a new idea. He thought of all his starving colleagues at the research station. If he could just manage to grab ahold of

---

15. *Ganbare* is Japanese for "Do your best!"

this freshly dead pig and keep it in place till he could get to an area without any water, he could fasten the rope to the pig and get his colleagues to pull the rope back in with the pig attached. It would startle them, sure, but that afternoon, they'd have a large barbecue feast! As he thought of this, his spirits rose and he continued to walk forward, being careful to take notice that the pig hadn't floated off downstream. He took a closer look and realized the pig was a typical farm stock that had been caught in the flood. It looked to be about four or five months old, so the meat would be so fresh and tender. His mouth began to water. He could see himself being tempted by his pangs of hunger, but he wouldn't let himself be distracted for a moment. He had to use the bicycle to block the pig in place on the bicycle frame. The waters had already dropped from his chest to just above his belly button. His footing became slightly easier, but the waters were still running swiftly. The body of the pig seemed to be rolling and sliding. If he wasn't careful, the pig would be carried away by the river flow.

He had only gone five or six more paces when he realized that he could feel the handlebars of the bicycle growing heavier. He looked over at the pig again. Its stomach was bloated like a small cow as it bobbed up and down in the current. Sometimes, it would float towards the back seat of the bicycle from where it might float quickly away. Tsín-suī had to take several steps back so he could pull the pig back towards the center of the bicycle frame. He kept on like this in the rushing water, moving a couple steps forward and then having to waltz a couple back. He'd already done this several times. The pig seemed constantly to have been plotting its escape, but Tsín-suī corralled it back into place every single time without any problem. It was a battle. Tsín-suī used what strength he had in his wrists, his waist, and his willpower to fight with the rolling and bobbing pig. Having to keep his hold on the bicycle, the webbing between his fingers started to tear from overuse. The pain in his back made him feel that he was about to break in half. His entire body was exhausted to the point he just wanted to lie down as soon as he hit dry land. "Little piglet, listen to me. Don't slip away. You ran into trouble, but it was the typhoon that hurt you, not me. Please don't blame me. I want to send you to save my colleagues. I beg you!" Tsín-suī pleaded with the carcass.

Tsín-suī was determined to get the pig up onto dry land. He would take two steps backwards and then forwards five. The dry road was just up ahead, and the waters had receded to below his knees, but a heavy rain suddenly started to fall again. The rainwater was just too much for his hat and began to seep deeply into his hair and then flowed into his mouth.

Why does this rainwater taste salty? He moved his lips around and tasted to see if the briny flavor was from his sweat or his blood. It didn't matter. He had finally made it to shore. It was a rise in the section of the road. He wanted badly to just take off the rope but just then, he felt sapped of all energy. He brought the bicycle up onto land and then tossed it to its side. Fortunately, Tsín-suī had already pulled the pig halfway out of the water. Its lower half was still sitting in the muck. He got up from where he had collapsed and grabbed firmly onto the pig's ears. He heaved it towards him, using every ounce of strength to pull this bloated, huge war prize up onto dry land. Then he took a couple deep breaths himself and was so relieved that he then passed out.

Tsín-suī was awoken from the constant rocking. He realized he was sitting in a military transport truck. His bicycle was propped against one side. In front of him sat two Japanese soldiers.

"Oh, you're awake now. *Aiyee*, Ngôo-san, we're almost at the city center. Can you get up and tell the driver where your house is?"

"What about the pig? Where's the pig?"

"Oh, you mean the dead pig that was lying next to you? Our platoon leader kicked it into the water, and it floated away."

"Nooo! Nooo!" Tsín-suī lightly beat his thighs with his fists. "I worked so hard to get it up on the shore."

"What were you planning on doing with a dead pig?"

"I was going to use the rope to tie it up and send it back to my colleagues at the research station. They're all starving, so I wanted to give them something to stave their hunger."

"Haha, what a pity. Who'd want to eat that dead pig! Who'd be willing to?"

"It had only drowned ten minutes earlier. I saw it die with my own eyes. It was still fresh meat. It was still warm."

"Oh! Is that so? But when we got to where you were, the pig was already bloated, and it had transformed into something...not so good. It looked like nobody could eat it. It's probably already made its way down to the sea where the fishes will make a feast out of it, haha!"

"Did you come to send food supplies?"

"Yes. We're using the rope as a cableway. Two soldiers went over to check on the labs. Your colleagues are all doing fine. Dr. Nakamura asked us to use the military truck to send you back to your home."

***

The wedding was held in the courtyard in front of the central ancestral hall of the Ngôo household. Each one of his colleagues had made it out to the wedding ceremony. The Ngôo patriarch noticed that many of the relatives on the bride's side were from the Phênn-ôo islands by way of Takao. He realized that there was a very strong cohesiveness among these migrants from other Taiwanese prefectures.

Among the Phênn-ôo relatives, Tsín-suí's father was already acquainted with Tông Tsuān-tsong. Tsuān-tsong was introduced to him as "Thong A-Ing's older son." At first, Tông Tsuān-tsong had thought he was a relative of the bride, but as soon as he saw that he was sticking close to his son the whole time and then saw him stand with the groom's entourage going from table to table for toasting, Tsín-suí's father felt as if Tsuān-tsong were a part of his own family.

Ngôo bowed his head and took Tông Tsuān-tsong's name card. The professional title printed on the business card said "Tông Îng Metalworks Foundry/Managing Director. Department Head." "When did your metalworks foundry open?" he asked in a soft voice.

"My father is sending me to Japan to learn some advanced smelting techniques and then to open up the foundry." He then went ahead and explained, "I made the name card in advance. It's to make it easier on myself when I go to some of the foundries in Japan for consultations."

"Oh, I see. Your father's thought this out pretty well."

Uncle A-Huàn and Uncle A-Tsòng were early to the wedding. The two of them made a pact to go check on Tsín-suí's water buffalo before the feasting began. The horizontal wooden slats of the pen were decorated in red ribbons. Uncle A-Huàn lightly tapped on the water buffalo. It opened and closed its mouth, seeming to talk to itself. After A-Huàn had finished his checkup, Uncle A-Tsòng told Uncle A-Huàn under his breath, "When Mari looked at me, she seemed not to have any ill feelings toward me anymore. It looks like she already sees me in a better light."

"Our Taiwanese water buffaloes are always quick to forget a transgression," Uncle A-Huàn replied.

"They won't hold a grudge against you for long. That's the nature of an ox. Their lives are preordained to drive plows for man, to be a beast of burden. They work hard for their masters from the time they're young till the time they go out to pasture."

"Their demeanor's naturally like that, *honnh*, good-natured and easygoing."

"They are temperamental, though! In spite of that, no matter how temperamental they can be, they won't gore their owners."

"You don't know that! If a buffalo does get testy, they can kill their owners."

"So then, the next time when you're whipping them, maybe have some restraint, don't overdo it," Uncle A-Huàn continued.

"OK. I'll change my ways then."

6

The sky was still dark when the newlywed Giok-ìn awoke from her slumber and groped around in the dark. A couple minutes later, the Ngôo kitchen was abuzz with the sound of crackling firewood and kindling. Another few minutes passed, and a wisp of white smoke rose from the vent in the roof and floated off into the ether.

Another person stirred from their sleep. It was Tsín-suí's mother. She called out in a hushed voice to Giok-ìn, "A-Ìn-á, what are you doing up so early making *muê-á* (rice porridge)? Go back to bed!"

"But didn't you say I had to be up early today?"

"Yes, my dear, but it's fine to get some more shut-eye. Go back and rest for a bit longer. I'll take over."

Giok-ìn's porridge was just about done, so she went out to fetch some water. She glanced over at the cow pen and saw that Mari was also awake now. Mari stuck out her tongue, curling it around several mouthfuls of grass, freshly cut the other day, and then chewed nonstop. Several saliva bubbles formed at the corners of her mouth. They were all white. In the early morning that was about to turn bright, Giok-ìn could see the foaming bubbles clearly. She stood there, just staring intently at the water buffalo chewing its cud. Ever since she was a little girl, she'd never seen any draft animal eating as single-mindedly and as calmly. It was a relaxing sight to behold! This was what properly chewing one's food was about!

Entranced, Giok-ìn watched the buffalo as it ate until others started waking up. She was startled to hear the sound of people inside the house squabbling and shuffling around. The whole Ngôo household was awake now. It was just yesterday that Tsín-suí's father declared to the entire party that he had signed a leasing agreement for three *kah* of the reclaimed land over in Lîn-lok. He'd already gotten ahold of a bunch of seedlings, and they were going to start planting them in the fields today.

Right as she was about to step over the threshold and back into the house, she spied a man with a long chin—an oval-faced middle-aged man striding towards her.

"Are you the bride, Ông Giŏk-ìn? You aren't acquainted with me. My name is Soo Tsòng-phik."

"Oh," Giŏk-ìn was startled for a moment, then she continued, "I've heard A-Suī-á talk quite a lot about you. I thought that—"

"Oh, you probably thought I was far older than A-Suī-á, right? To be honest, I'm only older than him by about eleven or twelve years. My name is somewhat old, but I'm still pretty young. People often call me 'Uncle,' so I'm sorry to create any misconceptions, haha!"

Tsín-suī at this point poked his head out of the door and took a couple paces forward, "Who's calling her name? You're probably here just to take advantage of her!"

"Haha! I'm of a noble name, but I'm not very noble," he said, his face full of sarcasm.

"Well, I wouldn't know. My father says A-Tsòng is just some random guy in the Green Fruits Collective."

"Hah!"

That day, Tsín-suī personally drove the oxcart to work. His father, Uncle A-Tsòng, Tsín-suī's brothers Tsín-sing, Tsín-bûn, Tsín-lîng, his older sister, his second youngest sister, and four hired hands were on the oxcart, as well. Before they'd gone to bed the night before, Tsín-suī said that he couldn't take any days off from work at the research station. The heavy responsibility for driving the cart switched back and forth between A-Tsòng and Tsín-suī's second youngest brother, Tsín-sing. The whole purpose of the trip was to get Uncle A-Huàn. He wanted to ask Uncle A-Huàn to teach Mari to be accustomed to different people taking the reins.

When the great load of people had reached the banana tree fields, the sun had already begun to peek out from behind Mount Tāi-bú. Mari was being led by Uncle A-Huàn. A-Tsòng was following behind them. There was a small embankment near the work area. Uncle A-Huàn stopped next to it and began speaking, "Before we drain the field, we should let the buffalo first bathe for a bit. Her *kimochi* (Japanese for 'feelings/disposition') will be a lot better afterwards."

As the buffalo entered the water and submerged her entire body in the mire, for a moment the water level rose. All you could see was her tail swishing two or three times. Then she gulped a big breath of air and exhaled forcefully. The sound of her powerfully expelling air through her nostrils sounded like a tropical whirlwind blowing from a cavern and sent more ripples toward the embankment. It didn't take long for her to finish her mud bath. Uncle A-Huàn led her a little way out into the water. Then he used an index finger and middle finger to lightly tap on the back of her head and lowered his head to say a couple sentences into her ear before passing over her lead.

Uncle A-Tsòng took the lead a little timidly as he whispered, "Uncle A-Huàn, what kind of language are you speaking with this buffalo?"

"What kind of language? Why, I'm speaking Taiwanese, you dolt. From now on, you're to call her Mari. Don't call her 'this buffalo,' do you understand?"

"Yes, clear as crystal," he responded in a loud voice. But under his breath, he muttered, "I don't believe any of these buffalos can understand Taiwanese! I'm no Ngôo Tsín-suī. Uncle A-Huàn's just painting up a great canvas full of nonsense. All he does is just believe, believe, believe."

But strange as it might seem, Mari then very obediently let Uncle A-Tsòng lead her, slowly lumbering towards the banana tree fields.

About an hour later, Tsín-suī stopped his work for the research station for a moment and rode his bicycle over to the field to check up on everyone. He didn't say hello to anyone—he just wanted to see Mari. She was plowing the field with A-Tsòng behind. It looked as if they had made a secret pact. They were tearing up the earth in very neat, orderly rows and lines. They'd already made five or six rows. One line was piled earth, and the other was the freshly made furrow. Hah! Uncle A-Tsòng had finally gotten the hang of it and was plowing furrows as straight as a calligraphy brush. It was a beautiful sight to behold. Banana trees don't need to be planted in straight rows. It just so happened that the topography and soil quality here were quite special, and Tsín-suī's father did well to take his son's advice and take up this line of work. Ever since he found out that Uncle A-Tsòng was a graduate of Heh-Lo̍k and a very knowledgeable member of the Green Fruits Collective, Tsín-suī looked at him as if he were a master of the plowshare, and his respect for him grew by leaps and bounds. Tsín-suī didn't have a lot of time to hang around though, but before he went back to the research station to continue his work, he spotted Uncle A-Huàn and his father off in a patch of shade, sipping tea and having a chat. It was all a very serene scene.

***

Tsín-suĭ was rushing to and fro. Several of his younger brothers spotted him running about. *Nii-san* is always going through all sorts of pains to take care of everything, they thought. But after their older brother had left, another young man that they didn't know came by. He kept walking around the perimeter of the field as if looking through shop windows here and there, wanting to step into the field, but seeming to hesitate for some reason or another. The third eldest Ngôo son, Tsín-bûn, mustered up the energy to go up to him and asked him what he was doing, "Hey, young man, who are you looking for?"

"Oh, nobody, it's not important," the man responded harried.

"It's pretty obviously you're here for someone, speak up. You're being kind of...strange...," Tsín-bûn's face seemed to contort into a grimace.

"*Pháinn-sè*, I came here to find the older daughter of my employer and Ngôo Tsín-suĭ."

"Oh!" Tsín-bûn's scowl quickly changed to a smile, "Come on down, then. What business do you have with them?"

"Oh, it's fine. I won't come down," the stranger responded again.

"Oh, what's the matter? Tsín-suĭ is my older brother. He's over in the research station. Are you wanting to go get ahold of him or not?"

"Oh! Don't let Ngôo-*san* know that I've come. The shopkeeper just told me to come watch for her elder daughter to see whether she's working in the field or not, is all. She ordered me to, saying if I didn't see her older daughter, to come back quickly and not to let the Ngôo family know that I come around. Only somehow I just said, 'Sorry,' then asked you and started talking."

"Oh, is that all there is? I still don't quite understand what you're talking about. You came all this way. Why don't you sit down for a spell and have some tea?"

"Sure, it's much appreciated, but it'd be better to make my way back to the shop now," he said, after which he turned around and quickly left.

After the man had gone, Tsín-bûn went over to his father to tell him what had happened. Old Ngôo began to laugh at his son, "Oh, she must have a soft spot for her daughter and miss her dearly if that's the case. She's worried that since her daughter's married into our family, that we'd work her to death out in the fields, so she sent her little shopkeep over to spy, hah!"

"Oh! So that's all it is."

"Ahahaha," Uncle A-Huàn began cracking up at this.

Today just so happened to be the one day of the year when Ông *thài-thài* would invite her family from the Phênn-ôo Islands over for a family feast. She sent out a pedicab to Thâu-tsîng-khe to fetch her eldest daughter and son-in-law. After the cab had arrived at the Ông household, Tsín-suī delicately took his wife's hand and helped her down out of the pedicab. Everyone in the Ông household had their eyes on him. They not only saw him acting like a proper gentleman, but they also noticed that Giȯk-ìn was already pregnant.

Tsín-suī hadn't even sat down yet and he asked, "Did Tsuān-tsong come out tonight?"

"He barely has any time for anything other than work lately and couldn't make it out, though his younger brother, Tsuān-tik-á, is here. He's off chumming around with the younger Ông son, Hōng-thiam."

"Oh, Tsuān-tik-á came. That's great."

Everyone's conversation naturally turned towards bananas: "Ha! Ngôo-*san*, your family's got a lot of guts investing in that kind of crop! Bananas... More than three *kah*. Well, all you've gotta do is plant them once. You don't know if those *Ji̍t-pún-á* are gonna rip you off. What if they turn around and say they don't want Taiwanese bananas? Aren't you worried that—"

"No, no. They won't. That's not gonna happen. The Japanese have just set up a marketing system for bananas. As soon as I heard about it, I knew that this wouldn't be a flash in the pan. It's gonna be around for a long time."

"What system? Well, let's hear it."

"Well, first off, the Japanese government is encouraging businesses and the green fruits collectives all across the island to form Green Fruits Marketing Cooperatives. The marketing cooperatives are going to separately establish banana research labs. I'm working right now in just one of these labs. In these labs, the *Ji̍t-pún-á* and us islanders work together. We work very hard to improve the crop varieties and carry out disease and pest experiments. It won't take long for our Taiwanese bananas to become a delicious variety in their own right. At the same time, it'll be an industry for making good money."

"But our own bananas are already tasty enough. What else are you changing about them?"

"Well, our bananas originally had a faint astringent taste to them. We've already gotten rid of that taste, and then we added a bit of sweetness. We're able to do this with our techniques and technology...to improve our crops. What's more is that there's still a 'core' in our bananas, despite them being so yellow and ripe. When you chew on one, it feels a bit hard. This is what we're working so hard on improving. Once we're happy with how it's turned out, it ought to be much more tender and sweet."

"Wow, that sounds pretty amazing," one of them said with a little whiff of sarcasm.

"I'm not pulling your leg, it's true."

"So has your family made any money off of it in the last year?"

"With the first crop, our family almost broke even. This next season coming up will be very good, but my father's the one watching the finances."

"We Phênn-ôo'ers have very good seafood. The *Jĭt-pún-á* ought to set up a Seafood Marketing Cooperative. Maybe we could sell some of our catch in Japan."

"You're a dummy! The home islands are all surrounded by water. Their fishing fleets are already far more advanced. They can go out much further to catch fish. They rake in tons and tons of seafood each year. They don't have any real need to come to our waters for fish," said someone else at the table.

"Selling things off to Japan is easier said than done. They're not only working on improving bananas, they're also expanding the research equipment in our labs. They take basket after basket and inspect whether they're good enough to be exported to the home islands. When they're shipped to the port, the officials have to give the crop an inspection. Lately, the Green Fruits Marketing Cooperative is short on hands to get the work done. They're giving farmers the right to do the inspections themselves. If your land for bananas is larger than three *kah*, you can make your own *hojō* (Japanese for 'plantation'). You can choose your own quality levels, make shipping baskets, and stick on your own *phiau-thâu* (trademark stamp) and then ship it to the pier. This is the reason my father first rented out three *kah* of land for planting his bananas."

"Oh, right, that reminds me! It's like with us over in Phênn-ôo. You have to have a stable income. Otherwise, why would you invest so much money into a large fishing boat?"

"Won't banana farmers just put shoddy produce at the bottom of the baskets and then cover up the bad bananas with good ones?"

"The *hojō* already use their own *phiau-thâu*. If they were to do that, the officials would figure it out pretty quickly. As soon as they find out, they'll send the inspectors. Later, that farmer wouldn't want to do any more banana planting. After they implemented this system, the *Jĭt-pún-á* government discovered that the bananas being produced by the *hojō* are a much better quality than those from the research farms."

"How exactly are the Japanese testing these bananas? When they're put into the baskets, they're still all green and unripe. Do they just cut one open and eat it right there on the spot?"

"They're quite fussy about all this. For example, let's say that when the bananas are harvested and shipped, they get damaged. There's a chemical inside the bananas called tannins which will leach out. At first you don't see it, but after a while, it'll oxidize and turn black. They don't want them if they're bruised."

"Ah-ah! I haven't seen you in an entire year and you're now a banana expert. What a feat!"

"Sure! When we first met a year ago, I thought you were just a *ka-kàu sian-sinn* (tutor)."

When Ông *thài-thài* and Giok-ìn arrived back home, they went straight in and started talking about mundane affairs with her family members out back in the kitchen. Her mother was the first to say, "I asked A-Hiông recently to go over to Lîn-lok, to that banana farm of Mr. Ngôo's, to check up on you and see if you were out doing backbreaking work out in the fields."

"*A-Bú*, you don't need to do such a thing..."

"I want to ask... Did Tsín-suí already know about your condition on that day?"

"I didn't say anything to him about it. He probably doesn't know."

Giok-ìn fired back, "*A-Bú*. I'm being serious... Don't do that again. They're not like that. They're not going to treat me like a slave."

"Fine. If you say so, then I'll believe you and set my mind at ease," she scoffed slightly.

"I'm married into their family. I've only been out to the field once since marrying Tsín-suí. How would you know? They have a water buffalo, and it even has a name. It's called Mari."

"Oh, that's an English name, no?" two teenaged boys, Tông Tsuān-tik and Ông Hōng-thiam, yelled out in unison.

"There was one day when the weather was sweltering. The cow pen was filled with mosquitoes buzzing around, and Mari wasn't feeling well at all. Her legs were trembling and her tail was swinging all over her back, her hindquarters, and the outside of her thighs. My husband told me that buffalo and oxen are afraid of mosquitoes. Mari was so distressed because she was trying to get rid of all of them..."

"Buffalo are afraid of mosquitoes? You're joking, no?"

"Yes, it's true!" Giok-ìn continued, "A-Tsín-suí told me, 'Quick, we need to go to the field and dig out some mud to bring back and then plaster it all over Mari. That way, she'll be able to cool off.' When I heard that, I went out to the field barefooted with my head covered. The first time, it was just to get some mud for Mari. When we headed back, we added some water to make a slurry. It was like painting and plastering a wall. I massaged it into her back and kept plastering it over her. When I was finished, I took a look at her from a couple steps back and she looked at me with these beautiful golden eyes. I felt like she was using her eyes to tell me to-siā! (thank you)!"

"*Wah-sai*! Ahahaha, fat chance."

"Heh heh heh! It's true. Amazing!"

Ông *thài-thài* was all smiles. She turned back to the boys, "If your older sister is saying that, then of course it's true. She wouldn't just make it up." She continued, "Come on now. Let's all go out and start dinner. They're all starving. I want to make my rounds with everyone, say hi, ask them how things are going, toast them, and all that. OK?"

"What about Giok-bí? Why haven't I seen her at all since we got here?" Giok-ìn asked puzzled.

"She went to a client's house to pick up a payment. She'll be back after a bit. She seems to be back to normal now. Let's not bring up the matter of what happened."

"Of course."

When the four of them finished their little chitchat and walked out to the kitchen table, Tsín-suī was in the middle of his conversation about bananas and the exchange was getting pretty lively. It was well past nine o'clock when the dinner was over. Tsín-suī and Giok-ìn were walking out to the front gate with Ông *thài-thài*. There weren't any streetlamps. All they had was the lamplight from inside the ceramics shop storefront. The street wasn't that dark out though. Occasionally, a bicycle or a pedicab went whooshing by. They had lights affixed to their fronts, and the circle of light would shoot out intermittently, bobbing up and down, flickering on and off with every bump in the road.

Tsín-suī and his wife were already sitting in a pedicab, but two blinding headlights shone from behind them. It was equipped with a very loud engine and the acrid stench of burning diesel. It was a small shipping truck that had been driven just to the front gate. Tsín-suī turned his head back to look out of curiosity. Giok-ìn, rather indifferently, just said, "Oh, that's a truck that's come to deliver goods for mother. It belongs to the Tsín-Lâm Shipping Company. They're the only people in all of Pîn-tong that have that kind of truck."

The chauffeur began to pedal, but Tsín-suī yelled at him to stop. "What's wrong?" Giók-ìn asked.

"I think I just saw one of my old classmates, A-Tshiu-bók." Tsín-suī looked back with rapt attention into the dark. There were two men there. One was young and seemed to have a familiar face. He was very carefully unloading wares from the back of the truck; the other man was an older fellow. He got out of the truck cab and was holding an account book, walking into the ceramics shop.

Giók-ìn, now annoyed, pressed on, "Go! Go! It's late! Let's go home!"

Tsín-suī wouldn't go, "Is the owner of Tsín-Lâm Shipping surnamed Iàp?"

"I think so, but the owner is very old. How could it possibly be your classmate?"

"I'm going to walk in just to see. I'm pretty sure it's Iàp Tshiu-bók." He hopped down from the pedicab and went back to the store. Just a few seconds later, waves of excited voices flowed out from the open shop door.

Ông *thài-thài* and Giók-ìn followed him into the store and she saw that her husband was firmly grasping the other man's hands. For a long time, the other man put his arm around Tsín-suī's shoulders. The two of them were misty-eyed.

They saw Giók-ìn come into the shop, and Tsín-suī went over and took her hand, introducing her, "This is Iàp Tshiu-bók. He was in the same grade as I was in the common school and my higher subject courses.[16] We were in the same class together. We were thick as thieves back then."

"Should I call her *A-só* (sister-in-law)? My name is Tshiu-bók."

"What do you mean call her *A-só*? You're only a year older than me," Tsín-suī feigned annoyance.

"Oh, you don't know? I was born in Meiji 41 (1908)."

"That's true, and I was born in Meiji 42 (1909)."

"Oh, so you actually are a year younger than me."

"This fine lady here is my wife, Giók-ìn. She's a graduate of Tainan Women's Secondary."

"Oh. I went to Tainan No. 2 Secondary."

The three of them kept babbling on and on like this. When the young man had finished unloading the ceramics from the back of the truck, he called out, "A-Suī-á."

---

16. "Ko-tíng-kho." (高等科) Going by the educational system under the Japanese, it would now be the equivalent of middle school in present-day Taiwan.

Tsín-suī turned, and he realized it was A-Tsòng's son. His name was Tsìng-tik-á. With his friendly, "Hey, hi," he told Iap Tshiu-bok, "this is Tsìng-tik-á. His family's farmland is next to ours. From when I was little, we often did our homework together in the fields and talked and played."

"Is that so! Tsìng-tik-á is one of our laborers."

Ông *thài-thài* had finished settling the bill for the shipment and hadn't said anything yet when Tsín-suī made an introduction. "This is my mother-in-law."

"Oh, so you're the son-in-law."

Ông *thài-thài* then began to speak.

"Since when are you, the young master, now driving the truck?"

"Our manager took the day off, so I came out to help."

"Well, that's a coincidence. You don't often take the truck out, but you just happened to run into your old classmate. Please, sit down! Sit, and chat some more." She continued, "A-Ìn-á, if it's too late, you can stay here for the night. You can go back to Thâu-tsîng-khe tomorrow."

"OK," Giok-ìn responded. She seated herself and listened as Tsín-suī and Tshiu-bok waxed poetic about the good old days.

"I had heard someone say that when you had graduated from Takao Secondary, you were given admission to a university."

"*Aiyee,* that! I'm quite tired of talking about it. My father adamantly refused to let me go, and so I didn't!"

"That's such a shame!"

"So did you go off to Japan to study in a professional field?"

"I went to Chuō University in Japan to study law."

"Oh wow! You could get a position with the Governor General's office."

"My father told me I had to come back to the farm to help work." Iap Tshiu-bok stopped and fidgeted a bit, then brought up another topic. "When we graduated from our higher subjects courses, you got the award. It was an encyclopedia. I was so envious of you for that. Later, when I went and graduated from Tainan No.2, I got my own encyclopedia."

"I've heard they print a new edition every year."

Right then, Tsìng-tik-á walked in. "Master, it's quite late. We ought to be heading back."

"Right, well, let's head home then." Iap Tshiu-bok fished out a small ledger and put it on the table again. He said his goodnight and then said to Tsín-suī, "Now that I know you live out in Thâu-tsîng-khe, I'll be sure to come find you when I have some time and we can chat some more."

Tsìng-tik-á was already out the door and pulled out an N-shaped iron crank from the driver's side of the truck cab. He jammed it into a hole in the front of the truck and then began turning it. Both his hands were gripped tightly around it as he turned the crank a few turns. After about seven or eight rotations, the engine finally roared to life.

Tsín-sūi, his wife, and his mother-in-law all walked out to send Tshiu-bo̍k off, all the while looking at the cloud of heavy, sinking diesel fumes as the truck went on its way.

***

Tsín-sūi worked diligently at the research station for a full four years. In the fifth year, he was transferred to the Pîn-tong Banana research station, where his work hours grew longer than his time spent at home. His wife had more reason to go back to her mother's house more often, and her mother would ask about this arrangement. Gio̍k-ìn would often make excuses for her husband, saying, "That's the meaning of an apprenticeship! Probably, the Green Fruits Marketing Cooperative believed A-Tsín-suī can do an apprenticeship and sent him out to take care of shipment inspections and has directed him to lead the banana farmers in Pîn-tong part time."

"How could he be an inspector and a director? Does that mean he can earn twice the salary?"

"No, not much chance of that! A-Tsín-suī just has a very inquisitive personality. He told me when he's at the inspection office, he can tell right away when someone sends in a sample with blighted bananas, right as soon as he sees it. Sometimes it's because the fertilizer is inadequate, other times it's because of pests. Sometimes it's because they need to improve the harvesting time and method. He's started teaching some of the banana farmers these things. To be honest, he doesn't have to be so concerned about that as an inspector. The job is a matter of passing or not passing inspections and then slapping a stamp on the shipping baskets. But he spends a lot of time teaching others. He's told me he's even gone out to some farmers' fields to help solve issues in person."

"Well no wonder! Whenever I'm doing business with someone and I mention Ngôo Tsín-suī, they all sing his praises. I feel honored to be his mother-in-law."

"Well I don't know if it's good or if it's bad."

"Oh well, his career seems to be growing brighter all the time. That's a good thing for a man—for a family and his wife though, maybe not so much."

One evening, Tsín-suī got home very late and the smell of alcohol lingered on his clothes. He shouted out, "The head of the Taihoku branch of the Nomura Life Insurance Company made a special trip south and came to try to poach me. He said he wanted me to establish a Pîn-tong branch office and be the head manager."

"Nomura's a huge enterprise in Japan. How did they ever find you?"

"How would I know?"

"*A-Pa*, how is it you don't know? *Nii-san* is very famous outside of Thâu-tsîng-khe."

"Famous how? Only people working in the banana industry know his name." He then asked, "Well, are you going to quit your job with the banana inspection office?"

"Yep, I've already responded to the head of the Nomura branch in Tâi-pak."

Several months later, Giok-ìn thought something about her husband had changed. He suddenly went out and bought an *oo-tóo-bái* (motorcycle). The day Tsín-suī brought it home, everyone in the whole village came over to check it out. He had added a gas canister to the bicycle frame and mounted a motor above the pedals and chain ring. It was something a wealthier villager could afford. When she needled him about how he could afford something so expensive, her husband replied, "It's from working for Nomura. All of the area south of Tâi-lâm is my management area. Having a motorcycle is much more convenient."

Not only that, he'd also often come home at midnight. Seven or eight days out of ten, he smelled like he had fallen into a bathtub full of liquor. Sometimes he wouldn't even come home. Ngôo Giok-ìn wasn't very pleased lately with her husband living like this. She went back home to her mother's ceramics shop to beg her to try to persuade Tsín-suī to go back to the banana business, but her husband simply refused every time his mother-in-law pled with him.

One day, Ông *thài-thài* took a pedicab out to the Ngôo household to invite the older Mrs. Ngôo out for a visit to the local Má-tsóo temple. She made a prayer for Tsín-suī since they were already there. After the two matriarchs had obeisantly gone around the temple, bowing with incense and kneeling down in front of various avatars and statues, they then went to do divining with the poa̍h-pue moon blocks and beseech Má-tsóo's guidance. They asked three times about the fate of the banana business the family was embarking on, and all three times, the response was overwhelmingly auspicious. Any other questions asked came back not good or inauspicious or...well...best not to say.

Right then, Tsín-suī's mother decided she should take care of the matter. When she returned home, she tactfully brought up what had happened. Tsín-suī immediately answered that he'd throw his hat back into the banana business, but no matter what she said, he wouldn't give up the Nomura insurance company.

They made a lot of money in those few years with their banana crops. A single yen turned into tens of yen, which in turn became hundreds. A lot of other farmers also started taking to the fields and working with a green thumb at banana planting. The price usually stayed in tandem with the rise and fall of market demand, the severity of typhoons, and the frequency of pests and blights. Tsín-suī was working hard at Nomura on the one hand and planting new trees every now and then on a plot of over four *kah* in Thâu-tsîng-khe when he had the spare time. He'd often go right before dawn or right at dusk to carry out supervision in the plantation. His wife took care of most of the management of the farm while her husband was off in a stuffy office. Mother and mother-in-law both kept Má-tsóo's divine instructions in mind and looked on very optimistically upon the crop Tsín-suī and his wife were harvesting. But Giȯk-ìn divulged a secret— the crops for the last two seasons weren't great by any means, and the price wasn't ideal. Not only did they not break even, but they were already a little bit in the hole. Both matriarchs' hopes were naturally dashed away like breakers rolling over a shipwreck near the shore.

By the end of the year, an old farmer by the name of Lí, over in Bān-tan New Village, said he was no longer going to grow them because of drastic drop in the last two years. He was going to sell off all the unripe bananas[17] on his plantation of over eight *kah*. After word got around, nobody wanted to buy them, nobody dared to, that is, except for one person. Only Tsín-suī seemed to be scattering money this way and that. Both his mother and mother-in-law were starting to get nervous at his supposed recklessness. They pleaded, using Giȯk-ìn as their messenger, "It's just way too risky an endeavor. Whatever you do, stop throwing money into bananas."

"Has he been possessed by a ghost? If he invests big, he's going to fail big. You absolutely HAVE to stop buying that land."

"Well, that's funny. Weren't you all falling over each other to have me throw everything into this business at first? Isn't buying unripe bananas

---

17. 買賣蕉青 "Bé-bē-tsio-tshinn." When a banana tree had already grown and was about to blossom or has already blossomed, but the fruit hadn't ripened, and wasn't ready for harvest, the farmer could sell them to a designated buyer, but the future harvest would belong to the buyer.

the same thing as planting them?" His succinct response seemed to quiet down both matriarchs.

In the end, Tsín-suī bought all the unripe fruit from that massive plantation. That year, the price of bananas rose dramatically. It was a historic high that year. Tsín-suī raked in over twenty thousand yen from the deal. At the time, the salaried pay for the colonial government higher-ups wasn't even a hundred yen.

Tsín-suī was on his way. That motorcycle had already become a part of his identity. Each morning, he put on a nice-looking suit and wheeled out his motorcycle. He straddled the seat and pedaled hard for a meter or two before the engine sprang to life. Each time was like a grand launch ceremony. There was always a group of little kids behind him, giggling and shouting. They ran along and chased after the black exhaust fumes spewed by the motorcycle. They'd chased him until their trousers had nearly fallen down.

Tsín-suī's mother-in-law grew more fervent in her beliefs and began telling everyone, "My son-in-law, ooh... Má-tsóo is more often right than wrong. As long as his business sights are set on bananas, there's nothing but auspiciousness ahead of him."

Japan had already been at war for many years in China and throughout Southeast Asia by that time. The peoples living on Taiwan were only receiving news stories about victories through the newspaper and radio station broadcasts. As such, their lives hadn't been touched by the war yet. Their future was looking up. On the island, the horses kept racing and business kept going on as usual—Tsín-suī's hometown of Thâu-tsîng-khe was next to the settlement of La̍k-tè-tshù, where they had a horse racing track.[18] They'd hold races pretty regularly. Spectators could make bets with *ba-ken* (horse tickets). The winner could exchange them for prizes ten times the price of admission.

Tsín-suī had an uncle on his mother's side who was the director of the Pîn-tong Happy Farmer's Credit Cooperative. One day, that motorbike came puttering up the credit collective. Tsín-suī's uncle had already long before heard the gossip about Tsín-suī's sudden fortune and asked him, "A-Suī-á, are you here to make a deposit?"

---

18. 競馬 (けいば) "*Kei-ba* in Japanese. The Chinese equivalent is *Sài mǎ*, meaning horse racing. During the Japanese era, there were seven horse racing tracks across Taiwan. Taipei, Hsinchu, Taichung, Chiayi, Tainan, Kaohsiung, and Pingtung. The Japanese Governor General of Taiwan made a "Taiwan Horse Racing Decree" to establish the rules and regulations.

"I was thinking about it, Uncle."

"A-Suī, your mother-in-law came in here the other day. You happened to come up in conversation. She thinks you ought to put your money into a house or buy some land. I also think that'd be a sound plan."

"Isn't your credit cooperative a safe investment?"

"That's not what I mean. Our Empire of Japan is off fighting everyone, and they're all slaughtering and butchering each other. It's risky to put all your money into a bank. Oh, that reminds me, how is the Nomura Life Insurance Company coming along? Surely, you've already felt the pinch."

"Yes, of course we have."

"What sort of impact? Well, tell your uncle."

"If I keep it simple, the profit isn't worth the expense. How could you not know that?"

"Oh, don't I know it. Oh and how. The war's going on everywhere. The number of claims and payouts has gone through the roof. It's going to create massive inflation. Ugh... The clients just aren't going to be covered at all, or they'll just cancel their policies."

"I love my job with Nomura, but if this trend keeps happening, I'm afraid I'll have to throw it all away."

"Well then, give it up. That's the only way. Don't gamble away your own future."

A couple days later, Ông *thài-thài* made a special trip out to the Ngôo household. She wanted to take Tsín-suī out to go look at a piece of land. Tsín-suī asked that his wife go look in his stead since he was quite swamped with work these days. When she asked what he was so bogged down by, he just mumbled something and wouldn't say clearly.

He wanted to wait and see first and then negotiate the price. Tsín-suī then meekly mentioned that he was having a little bit of money trouble lately. His wife and mother-in-law seemed to catch the drift of what he was saying. They asked his uncle what had happened. After a long while of trying to twist his arm, it finally came out that Tsín-suī had gone crazy in betting on horse races. He'd already gotten addicted to gambling for the past year or two. Well the mystery to Tsín-suī's hesitation was finally solved. Tsín-suī's father was getting older and didn't have the same spark he had when he was younger. Tsín-suī-á was nearing forty and had already made a name for himself in society. It wasn't likely he could kick his son out of the clan home with a roar again, could he? And what about Tsín-suī's wife? Giok-ìn was a gentle and traditional lady, apart from shedding tears in silence when nobody else was around. What else could she do?

His mother-in-law and Gio̍k-ìn were still trying to figure out a day to invite Tsín-suĭ's father, mother, uncle, and others to come together and convince Tsín-suĭ.

His father was the first to speak. His voice had clearly grown hoarser with age, as if a bit of phlegm was stuck in his throat, "A-Suĭ-á, your old man heard a while back that there's a horse racing track over by La̍k-tè-tshù. I'd never had the chance to see it. Well...have you been there recently to watch the races? Were they worth watching?"

Stern as ever until now, his father was trying to use softer language to assuage his son. It was the first time Tsín-suĭ sensed his father was becoming more and more accommodating and circumspect, if not outright warm and friendly. Is this what aging does to you? Make you senile and soft? Or does it make you naturally bow your head down in wisdom like sheafs of rice bend downwards out in the paddies as they ripen? Tsín-suĭ didn't think about it too much in detail. He was no longer a child now. He didn't have to cower in front of his father. He just had to let himself seem to be a man about society now. After giving some thought to this, he very calmly replied, "I have... I honestly have. *A-pa*, you already know. I've always been alongside cows and water buffalo since I was little. After I grew up, there was nobody in this village who could plow a field better than me. When I had spare time, I could go over to Uncle A-Huàn's and ask him to teach me some new things about veterinary care for buffalo or some such, but lately I've gone with some friends to the horse races. I've gone so many times, but it's become a great irritation for me. Horses and buffalo aren't at all the same. Buffalo can recognize themselves, recognize life, take things in stride. All their movements are slow and deliberate, but they have patience and strength. Horses? Horses are also powerful, and the way they show their power is through their speed. And their legs all move in a certain order when galloping. They're very fast, and their manes seem to fly when they run. This massive difference has hit me deeply—"

His father cut him off and interjected, "Horses aren't animals that we Taiwanese originally had, buffalo are—"

"You two have been talking for so long, but you're not getting anywhere close to the main point at hand," Tsín-suĭ's uncle sharply cut in. "A-Suĭ-á, when you went to see the horse races, did you put any money down?"

"Yes...I did. Recently, I just happened to have a bit of spare change on me."

"You can take it from me and my experience with all that I've seen working in finance, all the stories about getting mixed up in horse racing end the same. Now you listen well to what I have to say: It all starts with a small win, followed by a small loss. You then decide to keep betting, and you win a little more, and then you lose a little more. Then you just lose more and more. Next thing you know, you have nothing left to your name." When his uncle had finished speaking, he was silent for a time. Nobody else uttered a word, either. He continued, "A-Suī-á, I want to ask you, on that path I just told you about, what stage of that do you think you're at now? Can you tell us?"

"I'm going to take my money and put it back. Your story's not going to play out with me."

"Good. That's a good man."

A bit more time had passed. Tsín-suī switched to riding a bicycle again. His wife asked him what had happened to the motorcycle. He said he'd sold it. "I'm glad you were able to sell it. I never liked the damned thing one bit." This is what she said when they were over at her family's, but her mother felt there was something else amiss.

"He's definitely been possessed. The spirit's taken control. Otherwise, how could such an up-and-coming person change into someone like that?"

By this time, Ông *thài-thài* had already switched over the banking accounts for her ceramics business to Tsín-suī's uncle's credit collective. Another stretch of time had passed. Then one day, Tsín-suī's uncle had made a call to Ông *thài-thài*. "A-Tsín-suī came looking for me yesterday. He said he wanted to withdraw five hundred yen from the credit collective."

"So how did you deal with him?"

"I'll put it bluntly. I was not polite about it. I grew very stern with him and rejected him outright."

"Oh, that's good. Do you think he'll snap out of it? If so, maybe the demon spirit in him will finally give up and leave."

When Tsín-suī returned home from his uncle's, he was in a completely sour mood. He talked about it with his wife. He had wanted to take Mari out for a stroll so she could take a mud bath. Giȯk-ìn went with him, following a couple paces behind.

Husband and wife were silent as they walked along the dirt path. When they got to the riverside, the buffalo immersed herself into the waters and abandoned herself to tumbling around and flicking her tail. Giȯk-ìn didn't say anything to reveal her recent dissatisfaction towards her husband. Tsín-suī walked with her, hand tightly grasping hand. He wanted several times to tell her, "I'm sorry for how I've been lately," but these words were stuck in the middle of his throat. He tried several times, but he just couldn't get the words out.

After Mari had had enough of the mud bath, husband and wife led their buffalo home. When they got to the fork in the road, they were about to turn right when Mari forcefully swung her head to the left. Tsín-suī had an odd, unsettling feeling. He decided to follow Mari and look off in the direction she was looking. The road forking to the left was the way to Uncle A-Huàn's. Did she want to go see him?

Not long after following the left path, they reached the old man's home. Tsín-suī deliberately walked Mari straight, not turning into the courtyard house grounds, but Mari pulled on the rope lead, heading towards Uncle A-Huàn's instead. "You're acting so strange! Why are you being so obstinate all of a sudden?" Tsín-suī's curiosity was piqued, and he followed Mari into the farmhouse courtyard, wanting to see the old buffalo-whisperer.

Giȯk-ìn was walking by his side. She couldn't sense at all the pull between her husband and the buffalo. She thought her husband was deliberately going to see Uncle A-Huàn. "It'll be fine to let Tsín-suī chitchat for a bit with this sweet old uncle," she thought.

Tsín-suī called in from the outside. Uncle A-Huàn came tottering out to the door. Tsín-suī felt he'd aged a lot since they last saw each other. As soon as he got out to the door, Uncle A-Huàn asked, "Well, what's wrong with this buffalo?"

"Nothing, nothing's wrong. She just was so intent on seeing you that she dragged us over."

Giȯk-ìn didn't quite understand what her husband was saying, yet she saw Uncle A-Huàn tilt his head to one side and hum a bit through his nose. He looked deep into one of Mari's eyes, lightly pinching and pulling at one of Mari's ears. He used an index finger and middle finger to draw circles on her temple, pressing down a few times. Then he used a knuckle to rap lightly a couple times in the space between her two horns. Mari lowered her head and bellowed out a *uiiii uiiii* twice. Next she puffed out two drafts of air from her nostrils, *hu-honh*. Each time she made a sound, her tail would wave back and forth. The first time, it just swung left and right, but the second time, she whirled it in a circle.

Tsín-suī thought of the first time he'd looked Mari in the face. The old man had said that he himself could talk with buffalo, "But it's just bits and pieces here and there. It's not a full-blown conversation."

Even so, it was amazing enough. Tsín-suī was a man of science. This time, he didn't feel so cold towards the old man's beliefs. No surprise, Mari had some words to share with the old codger, but she knew Uncle A-Huàn was the only human in the world who could talk with her. Was that why she dragged us all the way out here? In the last ten years or so, everything he'd gleaned from Uncle A-Huàn was advice on protecting a bovine's health or medical treatments. "He hasn't taught me the art of conversation yet."

"A-Suī, the reason this buffalo has dragged you here is because she has something to tell you. She just needs me to help relay the message."

"Oh, is that so? What does she want you to convey?"

"I'm still not completely sure I understand. I'll think about it for a bit and keep thinking until I've come up with something. One day soon, I'll have an awakening—a *bāng-kah* vision. Then I'll give you your answer. So you'll have to wait as I let it stew in my noggin."

"Is it like the last time you wanted to tell me something from your dreams?"

"It's a *bāng-kah*, not a dream."

"OK, OK. I promise I'll call it a 'revelation.' How long do you have to wait for it to reveal itself to you?"

"There's no telling. Sometimes it comes on in an instant, and sometimes it takes forever."

Giok-ìn was off to the side listening intently, staring hard at the two of them. By then, she had kind of figured what these two men and a cow were up to. She was flabbergasted and shocked deep down. She couldn't help giving a sideways, condescending glance towards Uncle A-Huàn. His hair was all disheveled and looked as if it were a wild, thousand-year-old thicket of weeds. His face was a field of crevices and trenches—all wrinkles. He had an upturned nose and extremely thick lips. One eye was clear as could be and healthy; the other was a milky gray from blindness and aging. His head was naturally cocked slightly, and his spine, gnarled and humpbacked. The longer her eyes lingered on him, the more she felt he was some kind of ghostly, unsettling phantasm. She unconsciously leaned just a little closer to her husband.

On the way back to the Ngôo household, Mari seemed to be very obedient, not pulling at all. Giok-ìn talked the entire way home. She let loose on how she felt and about Uncle A-Huàn. Tsín-suī replied, "The old man often seems empty-headed. It's only when he's inspecting a water buffalo that he seems to have direct line to the heavens. It's like he's half-god, half-demon or something."

This time, Uncle A-Huàn's *bāng-kah* came to him with unusual speed. On the morning of the following day, Tsín-suī had just woken up when he heard the sound of worn-down oxcart wheels squeaking to a halt by the front gate of the compound courtyard. It was A-Huàn's son who had driven his father over. Tsín-suī quickly said good morning to the both of them and invited them in to sit down. His wife also came out to greet them, but A-Huàn and his son hadn't even bothered to come through the gate before the old man started up. "This time, my *bāng-kah* came to me very quickly. If I hadn't rushed over to tell you as soon as I could, it would've been lost to the depths of my mind for the rest of my days."

"Dreams when you are sleeping are all too easy to forget, but your *bāng-kah* happened when you were already fully awake. You'd be able to remember it, I'm sure."

"I came over as soon as I woke up. You better not call it a dream, or I'm going to go right back home and leave you wondering what I saw, and I won't tell you. It's not a dream, it's a *bāng-kah*—a revelation."

"Yes, yes, yes... Right, right, right. This time you had a *bāng-kah*. Take your time, Uncle."

"It was a tunnel. It was pitch-black all around. There was a crowd of people in this tunnel. Some of them were holding kerosene lamps, looking at a lot of venomous snakes slithering all around. Taiwan habu vipers, all with their triangle-shaped heads. Couldn't miss 'em. There were also hundreds of millipedes and centipedes crawling every which way and over everything. There were boars, too, very fearsome with great big tusks, ready to charge. The people inside, scared to death, called out to be saved as they ran for the mouth of the tunnel, jostling with each other. Because there was sunlight at the entrance it was very bright—" A-Huàn suddenly stopped here. He cocked his head to one side and used his one, crystal-clear eye to avert Tsín-suī's gaze and looked up into the sky. Then he said, "That sun was extremely bright and shone into the tunnel. Under that blazing hot sun, everyone, both inside and outside, was cowering in fear. It was startlingly silent... Too silent," he continued.

Tsín-suī and Giók-ìn felt like they were on a mountain road in the middle of enshrouding mist, seeming to understand the little bits and pieces here but ultimately unable to piece it all together and see the whole picture. They stood there silently and strained to make sense of it. They were both stumped and silent for a while.

"I'm done. That's all I have to say. I'm going back now."

"If you're all done, come in and have breakfast with us," husband and wife said.

"There's already breakfast back at my place."

"Come in! We insist! My old man doesn't have anyone to chat with. Come have some tea at least."

Giòk-ìn lightly tugged at Uncle A-Huàn's wrist, half forcing him into the house.

A couple days later, Tsín-suī accompanied his wife back to her family's house. When they were dining, Giòk-ìn went into great detail with her mother about Uncle A-Huàn's peculiar goings on with the buffalo, and then she began to regale her mother with a description of the old man's *bāng-kah*. Ông *thài-thài* kept interrupting her daughter, inquiring about every little detail, no matter how trivial they seemed to Giòk-ìn. When she had finished asking her questions, she stood up and put her hands together in supplication, facing the direction of Uncle A-Huàn's hamlet. She made a bow and was beginning to recite some prayers. A smile crept up over Tsín-suī's face. He asked her, "*A-Bú*, what do you reckon about all the stuff Uncle A-Huàn had to say in his *bāng-kah*?"

"I can't guess. I don't know what any of it means."

"So, what did you just pray for this morning?"

"I don't know. I just felt that I should pay some respects to that Uncle A-Huàn fellow."

"Hah! Well isn't that something?"

"But...I can guess a little bit. When an arrow misses its mark, it hits the side."

"What do you mean?"

"That *bāng-kah* means that your Tsín-suī is in a bind and in danger but there's definitely a bright path out of it, and a good future is laid out for you." His mother-in-law stopped speaking for a second to think and then started up again, "When I think about it, when you went back to farming bananas, it was like you found that bright, bright exit."

"You're wrong. I can't go back to farming bananas again."

"Why not?"

"Japan's war has spread to the Pacific. They've begun a war with the United States. Japan's military is already taxed as it is. All of the boats used for shipping bananas have been requisitioned by the navy... All exports have stopped. Japan's government is now encouraging banana plantations to let their fields simply go fallow and switch to planting rice and other grains, sugarcane, beans, or other vegetables."

"Oh, a war in the Pacific. I heard someone talking about it already, but I didn't think it would impact banana exports." Tsín-suī's mother-in-law's concerns seemed to be endless. "Well then, what are you going to do with the land you're renting?"

"I've already followed the government's orders. It's all I can do. Part of it will be used to plant beans, and we can begin to harvest them soon; the other part will be used to make organic fertilizer, and I'll be biding my time."

TWO

The War in the Pacific enveloped all of Taiwan. *Tsau-khong-sip* or "fleeing the air raids" became the norm before too long. One afternoon, Tsín-suī took Mari out to the riverbank for her regular mud bath. He left her to her own devices while he took a relaxing walk over to Uncle A-Huàn's house. He intended to get a lesson out of the old man that day. This time, he wanted to learn the basics for talking with buffalo, but they got no further than a few sentences before the air raid sirens began to blare their eerie call. He quickly raised himself up off the courtyard patio and helped shoulder Uncle A-Huàn into the dug-out air-raid shelter built into the hillside. Not long after, the bombers came on like rolling waves of thunder, throwing down their terrible cargo with its ever-lower-pitched whistling as each salvo made its descent, followed by a shattering explosive sound moments later. Tsín-suī listened closely and made a rudimentary judgement that the main target for the bombs must have been near the airfield. He patiently waited until the siren alarms had died down, then invited Uncle A-Huàn to go with him down to the riverside to see whether anything bad had befallen Mari, whether she had been frightened by the sounds of falling ordnance.

The two men hadn't even reached where Mari was when they heard high-pitched mooing, accompanied with the sound of clattering oxhorns striking each other. Taking a few steps closer, they saw the water in the river was being splashed all around. Tsín-suī called back to Uncle A-Huàn, telling him to take his time while he ran over to get a better look. There were three bulls fighting each other, eyes ablaze with rage, their horns interlocking and stabbing. Mari was standing over to the side, silent, her head low, as if she were waiting.

When Uncle A-Huàn strode over, the violently thrashed waters in the river had calmed. The bull that won was a stout one with curved but crude horns, short but curly locks of hair, and he had forced the other two away. His horns were like sharp, majestic, impossibly tall mountain peaks. The beast puffed angry air out of its nostrils, creating waves in the water around it. What was peculiar though, was that even though he had won the three-way fight, he didn't go to claim Mari. He seemed to silently permit one of the other bulls, rotund around the stomach, whose hair was course and sparse, to amble its way over towards Mari. The bull ambling over was already covered in scars, its gait was staggered as it tottered along, but it was still willing to pursue love under the bright sun.

Mari had finished her mud bath by this time and was standing off to the side on the riverbank. Her eyes did not show even the slightest amount of bashfulness. She waited for the more boorish of the bulls to make its way behind her. She bent her hind legs down slightly, allowing the bull to mount her. It was now a grand, wild, theatrical performance, being played out in front of her owner and Uncle A-Huàn.

Tsín-suī didn't want to look over in that direction anymore, and so he lifted his head up towards the sky, began to whistle, and looked off into the distance at two dark clouds up in the sky. It must have been the exhaust trails from the bomber squadron that had just unleashed its terrible wrath. Two clear lines, like a pair of giant scissors slicing its way across the sky. Off to one side, the trails looked very light, to the point they'd already nearly faded away completely. Tsín-suī felt deep down as if he were at once both moved and unmoved—unsettled really—as he watched this overt bovine performance. Meanwhile, Uncle A-Huàn kept his cold, stony face as usual. He began to speak as if they'd already been long in conversation, "The one who's mounting here is a Siān-huà bull. You can tell its breed as soon as you see it. Did you know Siān-huà isn't that far from An-pîng Harbor in Tâi-lâm? That kind comes from abroad. As for the one that won the fight, take a closer look. It has a large head and face. When it's standing up, its legs are just ever so slightly bent. It's got a stature like it's about to get down to work. It's got fearsome horns, short hair, a thick hide. It's a proper Tai-tang buffalo...Why—hey, are you even listening to me at all?"

"Yeah! I'm listening—"

"I'm telling you... Tai-tang buffalo are a lot stronger and hardier than the stock from down in Hîng-tshun, but when you're plowing fields or having them pull a cart, Hîng-tshun stock are better."

"Oh, I know that. So which one of these is Mari, then?"

"Frankly, she's what we'd call a *lak-kue* (six-tortoise) heifer. They're the best kind of buffalo in all of the south. They're headstrong and strong-willed. All four legs are slightly bent, they're resilient, and they're even-tempered. You've seen all of this in her, no?"

"Actually, I have, yeah."

"And also, I honestly forgot to tell you... The bull cavorting with Mari right now, that Siān-huà stock, if you take a better look, there's two tsheng (爭) on his head.[19] There's one on each cheek. This kind of bull, from the outside, looks rather ferocious. When they're angry, they're apt to gore you to death if you get on their bad side."

When the master and student reached this part of the conversation, the owner of two of the bulls came rushing over to the scene. He recognized Uncle A-Huàn and walked up, respectfully bowing to the half-blind senior and greeting him. He then waded into the wet field to take his buffalo home. Once the Siān-huà bull was done with its business, it lay along with Mari in the water. Its tail swished back and forth, and it forced air out of its nostrils into the water, making ripples here and there. There was a bit of exhaustion present in its eyes, some indolence, and yet at the same time, the bull seemed to exhibit some satisfaction.

The two beasts of burden couldn't enjoy their time together for much longer though as the owner of the bull then came along. He didn't bother saying anything to Tsín-suī or Uncle A-Huàn. He simply waded straight into the muck to collect the bull and go back home.

As the bull waded out of the muck, its member was still showing, and as it walked along the road, it urinated everywhere along its path.

Tsín-suī then felt he ought to take Mari home, as well, and just before hitting the dusty trail, he asked Uncle A-Huàn to impart some more wisdom. "If a buffalo 'has a body inside it,' how many months will it take to give birth?"

"For an ox, ten months. For a water buffalo, up to a full year."

"Oh, I see... So I should remember it started since the time we fled from air raids, right?"

Not long after fleeing from air raids, the sky above was quiet for a long stretch, and already Taiwan was changing from a crimson sun to a silver one. The colonized people on the island were about to get a new boss. Tsín-suī knew what was going to happen. After breakfast, he broached the subject with his wife. "Did you hear it, A-Ìn-á? The news today. We're going to be studying *Han-gi* (Chinese) real soon."

"Well, I know a little already. It's not like I'm starting from scratch. They taught it to us at Tainan Girls' Secondary."

---

19. 爭 "Tsenn/tsinn," or "tsing" which literally means "to struggle" or "to fight," in contemporary Taiwanese Hoklo means a whorl in one's hair, or "curls." According to traditional Taiwanese tales, people can also grow "horns" or "swirls," with people sometimes growing one or two.

"I also took it when I was at Takao, but we need to learn how to speak it. We need to learn their *Han-gi*."

"Well, who's going to teach us?"

Giȯk-ìn's sister-in-law poked her head out of the kitchen and said in a high-voice, "The village head has a class. From nine until ten thirty in the mornings."

The next day, Tsín-suī and his wife arrived promptly on time. There were already a dozen people crowded around in the village head's living room. All of them were people they knew. Each of them had brought a stool to sit on. They'd already taken up the best spots. Not long after, their teacher arrived. As soon as Tsín-suī saw him, he rubbed his eyes and looked again. "Oh, dammit," he said deep down inside. He had half wanted to yell it out loud. He lowered his voice and bent over to his wife at his side, whispering into her ear, "We ought to leave. This person has absolutely no business trying to teach us."

"What's the matter?"

"Before we needed to flee the air raids, he was the police officer dispatched to the area. Oftentimes, he'd act as a cudgel for those *Jit-pún-á*, to the point anyone would shiver when they saw him coming their way. He used to swagger and throw his weight around, harassing us villagers...shaking us down..."

"He's a policeman? So why didn't he go back to Japan?"

"No, he's from our island. He lives in the next village over."

"Oh, he's a Taiwanese 'inspector.'"[20]

"This person's very bad news. He goes into other people's homes unwarranted and takes whatever he wants. A-Tsòng's son was minding his own business one day when this very man came over, made up an excuse on the spot, and then arrested him and threw him into the clink over at the dispatch station. He beat A-Tsòng's son till he was all black and blue and had hardly any life left in him." Tsín-suī managed to say this all within one breath. He squeezed his wife's hand, "Let's go. We have to go. Now."

"Don't worry. Let's see what he has to teach us."

That "teacher" was around the same age as Tsín-suī, and his hair was slicked back with fragrant oil. All of it neat and shining. His face was dark,

---

20. During the Japanese colonial period, each police dispatch station employed local Taiwanese. They were tasked with "going out on patrol" and "helping" to keep order. In the end though, these Taiwanese mostly acted inappropriately and evaluated who would then be their victims. They were far crueler than their Japanese colleagues when it came to beatdowns. It was a terrible memory for many Taiwanese who grew up in that era.

but his brilliant eyes were scanning the faces of his gathered students. He used Hoklo to teach the course, and his first words were, "Did everyone review the material I taught in the first lesson yesterday?"

None of the villagers gathered before him responded. He lifted up a tattered, thin book in his right hand and slammed it hard into his left palm, creating a sharp popping sound. In a booming voice that accompanied the pop, he asked, "So. None of you reviewed your lesson?"

Still, nobody in front answered. He lifted up the book again and stretched out his arm, pointing at Tsín-suī. "You. The one in the back who didn't bring a stool with you. Stand at attention!" Tsín-suī obliged and immediately stood up. The policeman ordered him, "I want you to read it once. Read what I taught you yesterday."

"I wasn't here yesterday. Today's my first day."

"Oh, is that so? You're not trying to trick me?" As he expressed his doubt, he stretched out his hand, motioning downwards to indicate, "You can kneel down." And then he hit his palm again with the book. It looked like one of those books mass-printed on steel printing presses. He began the lesson with a roaring voice, "I'm going to read you a sentence today. Everyone follow along and repeat what I say. We're starting now... *'Oh-mun, dough shee chong-go-run.'*"[21]

Everyone repeated after him, including Tsín-suī and Giok-ìn. They all repeated the phrase three times in unison.

"Very good. Now for the second sentence: *'Oh Ai Chong-fa,'* ('I love China')," which everyone promptly repeated three times.

"Just what exactly is the meaning of these two sentences?"

"Oh, this is critical. Everyone had to understand. My *kanbun* teacher once taught us that this means, 'I am a Chinese person, not a Japanese.'"

There was a slight commotion down at the front. Many people were trying to speak in a whisper. The police instructor once more slapped the palm of his hand with the book. The crisp pop resounded through the entire living room. He spoke again, "OK. Come. Let's read the third sentence now. *'Oh-mun de go-jia jiao-tzwo Chung-hwa min-go.'* ('Our country is called the Republic of China')." The villagers tried hard to pay attention to the intonation and pronunciation of his words, repeating in unison for three more times.

Tsín-suī struggled to stay until the break period in class, then he dragged his wife away, very relieved to get out of there. All the while, as they were

---

21. Trans.: The meaning of the sentence is, "We are all Chinese," but the instructor's Mandarin pronunciation is so bad that it is near unintelligible.

walking their way home, he kept nagging, "Why would a *kha-se* (little foot) used by the Japanese police be employed again, now that the government's switched over and they've kept the bastard on all the same! And they have the nerve to call him a *sensei*!"

"Speaking of the police back in those days, they were all rotten. One day, there was a bicycle parked kind of askew in front of our shop. As soon as the police came, they told A-Hiông to come out, and then they beat him in the middle of the street—"

"And those were just the Japanese ones. The Taiwanese deputies were at least ten times worse. I heard they'd often go off on inspection tours using that as their excuse to go into other people's homes and force themselves on the women. Nobody dared to speak out. It was no use reporting their deeds. *Baka yarō* (the f***ing bastards)."

A couple days later, Ông *thài-thài* called to say that there was someone teaching *Han-gi* over at the village Má-tsóo temple but they would only teach if paid tuition. Each person had to pay ten thousand for an hour—but they wouldn't accept Japanese yen. They'd take Taiwan dollars and Taiwan Bank bonds.[22]

***

And so it was that Tsín-suī and Giȯk-ìn switched over to the entrance of the temple to seek learning. This time, they'd brought stools to sit on.

The space at the temple entrance was large, and more than thirty students had come to class. Tsín-suī ran into a familiar face. *"Aiyee*, Tshiu-bȯk-hiann*! How'd you come all the way over to our village for classes?"

"Ah, wah! Tsín-suī-á, I didn't think I'd see you here! I've been around to many different areas, trying to find some place that could teach me proper *Han-gi* (Hoklo for 'Chinese'). I've been trying for four or five months already. I heard from someone else that your village had a *sensei* who could teach, so that's why I made the trip out here to see for myself."

"You're a person of prominence now. Sitting on low stools together with us, it's truly beneath you, no?"

"Oh, what are you talking about! I'm just an ordinary person."

---

22. Around the beginning of the post-war period, from 1945-1949, there was terrible inflation. Commodity prices would change drastically within one day. The "set value notes" issued by the Bank of Taiwan were the equivalent of one Taiwanese dollar on the market. At face value, it started at NT$5000, but by the end, the face value inflated to one bill being the equivalent of 1 million Taiwan dollars. They were called "Tâi-kim-kuàn" or "Taiwanese Dollar Notes."

They couldn't chat any longer because the teacher up at the front announced that he was ready to start the class. The teacher was a middle-aged, well-educated looking man, and he only used *Han-gi* for instruction. After he introduced himself with a name that nobody could understand, he jumped straight into teaching. There was a book lying on the table, but he never picked it up; instead he just talked nonstop off the top of his head. He spoke neither hurriedly nor too slowly, and his voice was a bit monotone, neither rising nor falling. There was no end to his lecture. It was as if he were a prisoner in solitary confinement, sentenced to never ever speak again, who, upon being released, opened his mouth and let the vocal floodgates flow. No doubt, the people up close to him couldn't understand a single thing he was saying. Perhaps he knew but had forgotten that they couldn't understand him, or perhaps he hadn't forgotten but just had no self-control? In the village, there was no shortage of this kind of person who prattled on endlessly. From the time people went down into their fields until the harvest came, neither hand nor foot stopped and neither did their mouths stop rambling on.

Since nobody knew what he was saying, more and more of those sitting down at the front were starting to fall asleep, either lowering their heads, nodding off, or letting their heads fall backwards.

Iap Tshiu-bok already had a good foundation in *Han-gi*, but his brow was permanently creased. He kept whispering into Tsín-suí's ear in Japanese, "This is quite odd... This *sensei* is spraying spit left and right, talking up a storm, so it's no wonder why I can't understand anything."

"Oh, that's no good! I was quite looking forward to you being able to interpret for me."

"I heard that there's many different accents and languages in *Shina* (Japanese for 'China'). There's quite a number of differences. Now I've finally gotten to experience it myself."

Ngôo *thài-thài* put a finger up to her mouth and shushed at them, "Stop chattering you two! Have some patience and just give him a listen. I can already make out bits and pieces."

Several minutes later, Tsín-suí and Tshiu-bok began to whisper again, but even quieter. They were still using Japanese, "I could understand a few of his sentences. He said that we Taiwanese should help the Nationalist army more in exterminating something... That something sounds like it's the Eighth Way or something or other."

"Where did he say there was an eighth road?... Tâi-pak just has small alleys and lanes. They're called *ichijō-tsū* (First Alley), *nijō-tsū* (Second

Alley), and *sanjō-tsū* (Third Alley). There's a bunch of *izakaya* taverns, some of them bawdy houses... He says he wants to wipe them out?"

Gio̍k-ìn once again entered into the conversation, "I heard him say clearly, '*bah-lu-tong*' ('Eighth Road')—not '*bah-jō-tong.*' He's said it over and over again."

The three of them quieted down a bit and strained their ears again to listen. Not too long after, Tshiu-bo̍k started whispering again, "Oh. There's something I understood clearly. He's talking a lot about this Legislator Jiang guy. Turns out he was actually saying '*Kang Kai-chioh*' ('Chiang Kai-shek')."

"*Kang Kai-chioh*? *Shina*'s version of General Nogi Maresuke?"

"No. He's much, much more famous than General Nogi."

"So does that mean he's the emperor of China?"

"Also wrong. He's not high enough in stature to have people falling to their knees and pressing their heads to the ground." He lightly slapped Tsín-suī's thigh and said, "I think I've put it all together. He's not saying '*bah-tiao-tong*' or '*bah-lu-tong.*' He's saying '*Ba-lu-jun*' or the 'Eighth Route Army.'"

"What's the Eighth Route Army?"

"It's China's Red Army. They believe in communism."

Aside from the three of them whispering and discussing what the instructor was teaching them, everyone else in the room was already fast asleep. The "Chinese cram course" became a "sleep cram course." At long last, the instructor realized that something wasn't right and he picked the book up and slammed it down several times rapidly on the table. *Pah-pah-pah*! It sounded like firecrackers going off. He added in some swears and some yelling, but nobody could understand what he was cursing. About half the people who had nodded off were now awake again. Those who hadn't woken up kept on dozing. The instructor saw all these village folk trying hard to listen to him and then he went on "teaching" again, sentence by sentence. His voice was monotone, neither high nor low. No level or oblique tones. It was a performance perfectly well-suited to helping people fall asleep.

In the end, the custodian for the temple came up to the front and reminded everyone of the time, at which point they wrapped up their "class."

On the road back home, Tsín-suī and his wife began reviewing what had happened in class. "That Ia̍p-*san*, Tshiu-bo̍k-*hiann*... He's quite enthusiastic. He's been attending a lot of events in the area. I think I'll recommend him for county representative. I heard some other people saying that most people want him to be the representative."[23]

Giok-ìn sighed, "For an intellectual like him, an important local figure, to come and listen to that *Tiong-kok-á* (Chinese) *sensei*—what a giant waste of time."

"It truly is."

Afterwards, Tsín-suī and his wife never went back to the cram courses at the temple gate. They had lost their zeal for learning *Kango* (Japanese for "Chinese language"). Several months passed and Tshiu-bok came to visit them, but this time in his capacity as a council member. He brought up the topic again, seeming to be beaming in good spirits, "My *Kango* has improved quite a lot, you guys."

"I'll introduce you both to my private cram class, though it's a bit expensive. An hour will cost you twenty thousand yuan," he encouraged them.

The fee was a bit high, but both Tsín-suī and Giok-ìn decided it was worth a shot. They wanted to get the hang of it as soon as possible since studying Chinese had become a necessity. The cram school class was over in downtown Pîn-tong. The three of them met up before the class and headed there together. The room looked like a proper classroom, with its small blackboard nailed to the wall. There were about a dozen students in total, and none of them had idled very long in their seats before the instructor made his entrance. He was a man of about fifty years old, tall and gaunt, with a slightly ruddy complexion. His *Hanyu*, or *Kango*, was at least comprehensible to the young couple. Tshiu-bok whispered into Tsín-suī's ear, "This is what real, standard *Kango* actually sounds like."

Right as the class was to start, the instructor wrote out three characters on the board: "*Gong-sun Li.*" After he finished the last stroke on the character for Li, he had the entire class read it along with him in unison, and then he began to introduce himself by saying that this was his name. He made sure to emphasize that Gong-sun was a special two-syllable surname, and that his surname was not Gong. Gong-sun, according to the instructor, was a complex surname that had existed for millennia from dynasty to dynasty in China. This string of explanations was largely incomprehensible to the young couple and would have been indecipher-

---

23. The committees and committee members from this era were early post-war "Taiwan Provincial Government Officials" who were indirectly elected. It wasn't like the actual, locally elected county committee members who were directly voted in through general elections starting in 1951.

able had it not been for Tshiu-bok acting as an interpreter. That Tsín-suĭ could understand it at all was thanks to him.

Afterwards, Mr. Gong-sun gave every student a piece of cardstock. The top side was filled to the margins with Chinese characters. They were printed with a steel press. There was still a slightly oily ink scent to them. Holding the card in his hand, Tsín-suĭ's fingers started to get stained with the navy-blue ink. Tsín-suĭ was straining his eyes at the content when he heard the instructor speak. "These are our teaching materials, and these are what I am going to teach you with today. Let's recite the whole thing once. Repeat after me. '*Zhe shi jiang-yi.*' ('These are teaching materials'). Once more: '*Zhe shi jiang-yi.*'"

The young couple was excited and happy. They'd finally found a sincere, caring *sensei*. When they were studying in school under the Japanese, *kanbun* was a mandatory class, though it was taught in secondary school using Japanese, and so both husband and wife were able to read Chinese characters, but they were helpless when it came to speaking and listening. Now the two of them began to read the cardstock. It was split into three verses. The topic of the first verse was "*Wei ren xu zhi*" ("What one must know about conducting themselves"):

Line one: "*Ge chu xue-tang, jie gong Kongzi. Wo shang xue-tang, wo bai Kongzi.*" ("Each hall of learning must pay reverence to Confucius. As I enter the hall, I pay my respects to the Master.")

Line two: "*Fu zhi fu yue zu-fu. Fu zhi mu yue zu-mu. Fu zhi xiong yue bo-fu. Fu zhi di yue shu-fu.*" ("My father's father is referred to as my zu-fu. My father's mother is called my zu-mu. My father's older brother is called my bo-fu. And my father's younger brother is called my shu-fu.")

Line three: "*Yi Guo zhi min, ge you zhi-ye; Xu ying zhi-ye, bi-xu du shu; xu wei guo-jia, bi-xu wei bing; ren neng du shu, zhi-ye bi liang, ren neng wei bing, guo-jia bi qiang.*" ("A state's citizens shall all have their lot and professions; if they wish to engage in a profession, they must first study; should they wish to protect the state, they must become soldiers; should the people be capable of learning, and their profession be good, the people can become soldiers, and the state must be strong.")

***

There were many other lines following these. Tsín-suĭ couldn't contain his excitement and he skipped over to the second verse. The topic was the *Selections from Poetry*. There were ten poems stamped on the card in total.

He breezed through them very quickly. Of all the poems on the card, there were only two that he hadn't read when he was at Takao Secondary School. He read the poem in his mind with Japanese: "*Chuang-qian ming yue guang, yi shi di shang shuang, ju tou wang ming yue, di tou si gu-xiang.*" ("The moon shines on my bed brightly, So that I mistake it for frost on the ground. I gaze upwards at the moonlight; Then I look down and my thoughts turn homeward"). After he read it in silence, he tapped his wife on the hand and softly recited another poem in Japanese: "*Ō-tō-sei-nan-koku, shun-rai-hatsu-ketsu-toku, kin-gun-ta-sai-tō, ko-butsu sai-shō-shi.*" ("The red beans grow in the south; and as spring arrives, they begin to sprout; I urge you to pick them more and more; this is what I think of most.") This made his wife smile.

The instructor had very keen hearing and was able to hear Tsín-suī using Japanese to recite the poem, and his face became dour and pink. The true color evinced menace and ire. Then he gave a stern warning. Tsín-suī couldn't understand his warning, but from the expression on the man's reddened face he understood that it was one. Tshiu-bok quickly turned to him in a low voice and interpreted for him. "This *sensei* says that when you are in his *Hanyu* class, you are not allowed to speak Japanese, not even half a sentence."

Having heard Tshiu-bok's explanation, Tsín-suī immediately stood up straight and faced the instructor repeating "yes." It was a Japanese *hai*, (yes) and in Tsín-suī's experience, it was best to say it immediately and in a loud voice. Only then would it express, "Yes, I understand," or "Yes, I will respect your command." However, he didn't anticipate that this *Kango* instructor's reaction would become even more emphatic. The slight red tinge to the man's cheeks had now become a deep crimson, covering his whole face. The man shot out his right hand and shouted several times at Tsín-suī, "Get the hell out of my class! I won't suffer myself to have a lowly Japanese like you in my class! Japanese devils. Get out. GET OUT!"

Tsín-suī could feel the severe tension in the air, but he couldn't understand the man, so he turned to Tshiu-bok sitting next to him to help interpret. This *sensei* was ordering him to leave the school and abandon his lessons. How did this turn out so wrong? Since he was a small child, all the way from the commoner's school to his high-level subjects, to secondary school, Tsín-suī was a stellar student. All sorts of awards adorned the walls of his family home, with nowhere else to place any more of them. All of his former *sensei* had adored and valued him. Why did it have to be this way now, though? How could he possibly make it better? Tsín-suī felt like a small ship being tossed on gigantic ocean waves. The *Kango* instructor once more berated him, "What!? You're still here? Get the hell out!"

The mortification and disappointment that Tsín-suī felt originally now turned into grief and anger. He lifted his chair with a sense of dignity and quickly left the classroom. Giok-ìn followed in hot pursuit.

Husband and wife pushed their bicycles as they walked back home. They didn't feel like riding. They felt drained of energy and that they wouldn't be able to push the pedals. They walked on the dusty path in silence. Occasionally, they would lift their heads. The sky was a bit overcast. There were grayish-purple clouds. It looked as though it would rain later in the day.

The evening of the following day, the Ngôo household was all sitting around outside trying to cool off from the stifling summer heat. A-Tsòng had just sauntered over and was talking about some matter of banana farming with Tsín-suī's father and mother. Tsín-suī and Giok-ìn were off to the side listening to a Chinese-language broadcast on the family radio. The putter of a motorcycle cut in and out from the distance and drew ever nearer. It was Tshiu-bok. His motorcycle was much fancier and newer than the one Tsín-suī had owned.

"I made a special trip out to see you A-Suī-á. I saw how that piggish *sensei* kicked you out pretty quickly. Are you wanting to do anything about it?"

"No, no. I don't want to. I'm feeling a bit down, but it'll all blow over after a while."

"Well, in that case, everything seems fine then." Tshiu-bok sat down. He accepted a freshly poured cup of tea from Giok-ìn with both hands.

"Tshiu-bok-*hiann*, yesterday in class, I was only reciting the poem using Japanese pronunciations for my wife to listen to, that much is true, but I was showing that I accepted that *sensei's* teachings. I wasn't trying to start anything, and he just went off on me like a rabid dog."

"Haha! Oh, that. I was right next to you, and I saw it all play out." Tshiu-bok took a long sip of his tea, then continued, "I think he really lost it after you started saying '*hai*' back to him."

"I think so too," Giok-ìn added.

"Why would a *Tiong-kok-á* teacher not want his students to respond?" Tsín-suī started to be deprecatory. "Early on, when the *Jit-pún-á* teachers were here, no matter what it was for, you had to give them a response. And the only one they would allow was '*hai.*' You had to say this with gusto, with a spiritedness to it. If you did that, the *sensei* wouldn't mind your mistakes. They would like you, trust you even. Wasn't that how it used to be?"

"It was. You're right." Tshiu-bok added, "However, that *Tiong-kok-á sensei* might prefer that we just keep our mouths shut, just nod our head, make a slight bow, and sit down."

"They'd rather that we kneel down, kiss their feet and stay quiet, *baka yarō* (the bastards)." Tsín-suī took his own tea mug and heavily plunked it down on the tea table between them.

Tsín-suī huffed angrily then began ripping the instructor once more. The conversation happening on the other side of Tsín-suī was cut short. A-Tsòng and Tsín-suī's father brought their ratan stools over and faced Tsín-suī, Giok-ìn, and Tshiu-bok.

"Ah!" Tsín-suī's wife began lamenting, "It's such a far cry from what it used to be like."

"It's not such a big change," Tshiu-bok began. "Our council here in Pîn-tong receives all sorts of civil complaint cases every single day. There was one just the other day where, if I describe it, nobody will possibly think it was true. The sugar company has a new manager from China. When he started working there, the workers realized that he couldn't even read any characters. He's an illiterate—"

"He's an illiterate? Then how the hell does he read documents or write correspondence? There are progress reports that need to be written every day. Reports on incoming materials and outgoing goods..."

"His helper can read and write. All he does is put on airs as if he were a manager, walking this way and that around the company, berating people, 'inspecting' every little thing, swaggering around in every direction."

"Is that so?"

"And then there was another case. There was a person who had applied, saying he had seen a job listing in the newspaper for a position at the Hong-suann Horticultural Institute. He had to take a placement test, and he came out on top. In the end, he wasn't selected. When he went in person to inquire why, it was because he hadn't sent them a *red envelope* (monetary gift)."

"So how do you handle these complaints in your position as a council member?"

"Our council leader is—"

"Oh! I had thought you were the council head."

"I'm an islander. How would they ever possibly give the position of council head to a Taiwanese!? The council head is named Chang Ji-fu.

He's a Hakka Taiwanese man who went to the mainland to celebrate the retrocession."

"Ha. It's just the same as it was under the Japanese. Absolutely the same! There's no lead position prospects for people from the island."

"I only got my position because I went early to attend the 'youth group for studying the Three Principles of the People.' And what's more, it means that he was one of the receiving committee members who came to Pîn-tong on behalf of the new government. He only reluctantly gave me the position of deputy head."

"Oh, is that so? Do you have any power as a deputy council head? Did you have any power to help those two complainants?"

'No. I have no power at all. When it comes to those two cases, our council head told us that for the first case, that illiterate manager wasn't the only one of them who couldn't read in a position of importance. As long as he could manage, he would do. 'Well, for a person with a background such as his, I just don't think anyone has a right to blame or castigate him.' That's what the council head said."

"And what about the second case?"

"The council speaker said that he doesn't know whether this event ever truly occurred. The council meeting has no power to carry out an investigation. I reminded him of other similar 'red envelope' problems. It's happening everywhere you go. It's endangering our new government and tarnishing its image. And it's not just small places out of the way. In this case, we have a name and a surname, as well as a job position title. I told him that at the very least he ought to turn these cases over to the city government for review. He said 'fine' but he never did. He took the complaint and threw it into the trash bin."

"What an awful turn of events. What a scoundrel. Just awful."

Up to this point, A-Tsòng was quietly listening. Then he cut in, "All of these issues that you're bringing up... A lot of it is essentially because we don't have the same culture. These cultural differences are going to make themselves known at every level." He paused for a second. Nobody objected or said otherwise, and he continued his point, "There was a time before when I went to the airport. When I was passing by the residences of those Japanese—I saw it with my very own eyes—right before those Japanese were repatriated back to Japan, the entire neighborhood, residences both large and small...all of them got together to sweep up the streets and clean everything. A lot of us locals from Pîn-tong saw this. Aha! Even these losers of the war had enough respect to sweep the streets of their former empire before they said farewell!"

"It truly is such a stark difference. Like night and day," Tsín-suí's father rejoined.

"*Aiyee*. There's shit and rubbish in the streets everywhere now. It's all a mess!"

"It's quite a shock."

After discussing the subject for a while longer, A-Tsòng introduced himself to Ia̍p Tshiu-bo̍k. "My name is Soo Tsòng-phik. My eldest son is Soo Tsìng-tik. He's working for your company, Tsin-lam-sia."

"Oh, Tsìng-tik. He's a good kid. I heard you want him to be promoted to assistant manager."

8

Not long after Tshiu-bok's visit, it was the Lunar New Year, and not much long after that, there was a night where the moon was high and shining brilliantly over the swaying shadows of the trees. Tall shadows cast in the moonlight in front and behind the house. Outside the home, frogs croaked out their songs, and insects buzzed and made their calls. Everything seemed as they always did. Tsín-suí's father, who was a light sleeper, was half-awake. Suddenly, he heard a heavy truck turning into the farm road nearby. He strained his ears to listen, but he felt unsettled. Ever since the Japanese government had left Taiwan, the peace and security of the island had fallen into disarray. There were often thieves who roamed around in the middle of the night to ransack places. He crept off the bed and quietly got to his feet. He first thought he'd take a peek at the doors and windows to make sure they were locked, but he spied a truck off in the distance through one of the windows. It was a military-style truck with a canvas cover over the back part. There were about five or six brutish-looking men right in the middle of digging a big hole.

Apart from the oddity of it all, he felt a pang of fear. He lightly inched his way over to his eldest son's room to wake him up and tell him what was happening. His son was a lot braver, and Tsín-suí picked up a carrying pole and snuck out the front door, barefoot. His father held on to his cane and walked slowly after him. Both father and son lay down in a thicket of grass and shrubs and spied on the men. It was as if they were spying on some momentous secret execution. Their hearts raced, and the hair on their necks stood up in fear.

A single flashlight would occasionally act as a searchlight, shining this way and that. It was through the strange men's sporadic light that father and son could make out what the men were doing. There were six military police and soldiers, all in uniform. Each of them was carrying rounded shovels and pickaxes. They'd already dug a deep hole, and then they offloaded something from the truck. But what was it? Two of the men were standing guard. Unexpectedly, their cargo turned out to be several stocks of rifles and a dozen or so wooden crates.

Tsín-suĭ had received military training when he was at Takao Secondary, including target practice. He expected the crates to be filled with boxes of ammunition. Both father and son were scared out of their wits, so much that they breathed lightly and slowly, having to slow their breathing to the point of passing out. The soldiers made quick work of their digging. Quickly, they put the guns and ammunition into the hole and then covered it back up. They started up their truck and ran back and forth over the hole. When it was sufficiently compacted, they re-covered the area with weeds and dry branches and then left.

The rest of the night went by without any similar incidents. Tsín-suĭ headed back to bed but continued to think of what had happened. This kind of thing wouldn't be possible to report to the authorities. He knew two people in the local government. One is the district head, Lim Kian-bun. The other was Vice Head Councillor Iap Tshiu-bok. Maybe he ought to go tell them and ask what it was all about.

The sun hadn't yet risen, but Tsín-suĭ had made his way to Tshiu-bok's residence. He hadn't even finished describing what he and his father witnessed during the night when he noticed that Tshiu-bok's face evinced deep-seated feelings of heaviness weighing on his heart. He began to speak, "This kind of thing must mean that the authorities don't trust us Pîn-tong'ers—or me, in particular."

"What makes you say that?"

"The chaos in Tâi-pak has swept its way down south. They've started to make barricades and other preparations in Pîn-tong."

"You mean the protests over that poor woman selling cigarettes in Tâi-pak? How did it turn into violence?"

"Oh, it was such a massive thing! All everyone's pent up rage and frustrations from the last year or two finally erupted violently like a volcano. It started up in the north and the central part of the island. People organized one local group after another and plundered guns and ammo from police stations and military police. A lot of the corrupt local governments were overturned, and these civilian groups began managing things. Ka-gī (Chiayi) and Tâi-tiong (Taichung) even made proclamations for the founding of 'militias.'"

"Oh! So it's that serious. I had no idea!" Tsín-suĭ scratched his head, then continued, "I was listening to it on the radio yesterday. I used it as learning and practice listening material for *Han-gi.* That's pretty funny."

"In a moment, I'll have to go to meet with the mayor and the city council and see what new developments there are."

"Oh, that reminds me. My fourth youngest brother, Tsín-bú, is in Tâi-tiong. He's a pretty lively, rambunctious character. If you can, please see if you can find any news about him. I don't know if he's been caught up in things or not."

"Ngôo Tsín-bú. I've heard of him before. I'll definitely be able to ask around for you."

As Tsín-suī was on the way home from Tshiu-bo̍k's home, he stopped at a newspaper stand and bought a couple papers. From the first line on the head page to the last line on the last, the violence Tshiu-bo̍k mentioned had only taken up simple columns buried deep in the papers. There was nothing about Tsín-bú. The older Mr. Ngôo fidgeted and muttered while reading through. "How could those newspapers switch from being bilingual to just Chinese? *Baka yarō!*"

Tsín-suī's brother, Tsín-bûn, came back home and took the radio out into the living room to appease their father. "It's quicker to listen. The radio stations are all still a mix of Chinese and Japanese."

But as the whole family sat around the radio to listen, they slowly switched through the stations—it was all in *Han-gí*. Mr. Ngôo was incensed, "*Baka yarō!* When did they completely stop programming in Japanese? I can't understand a damned thing! The f***ing bastards!"[24]

On the morning of the next day, the sun hadn't yet risen when Tshiu-bo̍k came to the Ngôo household. He was talking in hushed whispers with Tsín-suī at the dining table. The Ngôo patriarch knew that Councillor Ia̍p had come over, but he didn't make his presence known. He sat by the door in the next room over and listened to his son and the friend speak.

"I'll tell it to you straight... The situation is growing much larger, and it's becoming more complicated. You'd mentioned the soldiers from the other morning and how they had buried all those guns and ammo on your property. They've been reported as having been stolen by someone."

---

24. At the beginning, when power was being handed over by the Japanese to the Chinese Nationalist Party in the early post-war period, all official settings, education, media, were originally conducted in both Chinese and Japanese, but on December 31st, 1946, the Chinese Nationalist Party banned the use of Japanese in all public services and only allowed for Chinese to be used. There was a lot of debate afterwards that the policy was implemented far too early. It would be one of the catalysts for the 228 uprisings and subsequent massacres that occurred just two months later in 1947. Officials and civilians often misunderstood each other, and were guessing at each other's moves and intentions, which was one of the factors that led to the uprisings.

"Oh? What kind of person would steal them?"

"It all started yesterday afternoon. There were a lot of us Pîn-tong'ers that came out to answer the call—youths, middle-aged fellows and old geezers—they all came out. They formed a large posse and divided themselves into different units, medium and small. They came in, dug up and ran off with all the weapons and ammunition. I heard that General Peng Meng-chi,[25] sitting over on Siū-*san* in Ko-hiông (Kaohsiung), is so angry at the protesters that he began to *khí-siáu*.[26] He declared an order to seek out whoever leaked the location of the hidden weapons caches to the protestors."

Tsín-sūi lowered his voice, "That evening, aside from my father and I, who else might have seen what those soldiers were doing?"

"If your family is suspected, I'm deathly afraid they'll all be executed."

"I just don't get it. Why are they so hell-bent on burying their weapons caches?"

"You wouldn't know it, but these uprisings are large enough that neither the police nor military garrisons can keep the people from making their way into the stations and garrisons and taking weapons and ammunition. Because of this, the police chief in the south, Peng Ming-chi, has ordered our mayor, Gong Lyu-duan, to take the weapons and bury them in advance so civilians can't get their hands on them."

"Are we civilians truly that terrifying to them? Can the military and police really not win?"

"That's right. The *Tiong-kok-á* government armies have most of their forces amassed over on the continent, and they're duking it out with the *a-kong-á* (Communists) in a civil war. Their military power here is limited. It's not so easy to defeat us."

"Oh, I wouldn't have guessed."

"I made a special trip out here to tell you all though, and I'll tell you again. If anyone comes here to ask questions about the weapons, asking if you know anything about the weapons buried, you must unequivocally deny it. You can never speak of it or admit to it for the rest of your life. Do you understand what I'm telling you?"

"Of course, of course. I won't admit to it."

Right then, Tsín-suī's father walked out from the next room over. After everyone had wished each other a good morning, he asked, "Iap-san,

---

25. Peng Ming-chi is also known as the "Butcher of Kaohsiung" for his role in the Chinese Nationalist Army's indiscriminate slaughter in Kaohsiung during the March Massacres that followed the 228 uprising.

26. *Khí-siáu*." Taiwanese Hoklo. To become crazed or demented with rage.

which day did the uprising in Tâi-pak happen? Was it on February 28th or was it on March 1st?"

"February 28th. *Bin-kok 36* (36th year since the founding of the Republic of China)."

"Oh, you mean *Showa 22* (the 22nd year of the Japanese Showa Emperor's reign)."

"*O-tsi-sang*, we can't use the era name 'Showa' anymore. We have to use '*Min-kuo*' now."

"Oh, it's just a force of habit. I don't think I'll ever adapt to the new way." The elder Ngôo-*san* lowered his voice, "Maybe, just maybe...after the movement is over, those greedy pigs will flee back. Just maybe."

"I'm extremely pressed for time. Those mainlanders, such as our mayor, police chief, organization heads, all *soo-khai'ed*.[27] Even our own Hakka council chief has headed for the hills. It looks like control of all of Pîn-tong is going to turn over to us. There's a whole lot of things that have to be taken care of. I need to take my leave now. I'll see you later."

Tshiu-bók was already walking over the threshold to the main door when Tsín-suí's father came running up to him and speaking in a low voice, dejectedly and panicked, said, "A-Suí-á asked you if you could find out anything about our A-Tsín-bú. Did you manage to at all?"

"No, unfortunately. Nobody had a clue about his whereabouts at all."

"*Aiyee*. I'm wracking my brains over this. I can't eat or sleep not knowing what's become of him."

The following day, Tsín-suí went down to the family fields as usual. He hadn't yet started working when he heard A-Tsòng calling out, "A-Suí-á, your friend A-Tshiu-bók said there was going to be a citizen's rally today. Aren't you going out to attend it?"

"Oh? But he never told me or invited me to go."

"There's no need to invite anyone. People are going just as soon as they catch wind of it."

"Where's it at?"

"I heard it's in the council hall."

"Well, do you want to go?"

"I'm going with your father elsewhere."

Tsín-suí suddenly didn't have it in him to continue working. He rinsed the mud off his hands and feet, went home and changed his clothes, then

---

27. A Taiwanese Hoklo pronunciation of a Japanese loan word meaning "to flee" or "vamoose." After the Japanese colonial period ended, Taiwanese continued to use this word often.

raced off towards the meeting hall. As he got there, he saw all the seats were already full. There were lots of students in attendance. He saw Tshiu-bok sitting up in the highest position where the council head would normally sit. Tsín-suī noticed it didn't seem to be just council members. There were also several locals up at the committee table. He asked someone next to him, "Is Iap-*san* already the council head now?"

"No, he's just the vice head councillor. The head councillor, Chang Ji-fu, said he was feeling ill, so he took leave and didn't come. Everyone knows he's just faking it though."

"Ugh, some head councillor he is. Running off to attend that Taiwanese Retrocession Group. He went right over to the mainland to fondle their family jewels for them and then came right back with their approval. He's a clever one. It's just not right, putting all that responsibility on Iap Tshiu-bok."

"Right. They're not being clear at all. Today's event isn't a councillor's meeting. It's a Provisional Governance Meeting of Pîn-tong being convened by city residents."

"Oh, so that's what it is."

Tsín-suī stood silently, listening to the agenda items. It turned out that the residents of Pîn-tong did actually want to rise up. Everyone was congregating and forming units out in the city park, distributing guns and ammunition and swearing oaths. Of those on the provisional committee, the majority of them were advising the use of restraint, and those who were encouraging people to wage war were few. Tshiu-bok decreed in imperfect Chinese that "we're formally preparing a resolution that should any citizen wish to express their opinions, they must do so peacefully and must refrain from military force or violent means. Does anyone object?"

Nobody objected. Then Tshiu-bok, as vice head councillor, switched to Hoklo. "We will need to send someone as a representative to go to the park and convince them to not use military force or to shoot anyone. Does anyone want to volunteer?"

"Vice Head Councillor, you're the chairman of the provisional committee. You would be the best for this task, right?"

"I have to stay here and occupy this place for the security section. All of Pîn-tong's security is our responsibility. The mayor and the head councillor have all *soo-khai'ed* (fled for their lives). The security section for the city can't just give up the city or let things run rampant." He used the word 'soo-khai' but then immediately corrected himself, using Chinese. "What I meant to say is that the council head and the mayor are 'not here'—not the Japanese word *shōkai*. The pronunciation is similar. Please, nobody misunderstand me!"

Several of the attendees had slight grins on their faces, and then they all quieted down. They stayed silent for quite some time, then someone began calling names off a roster. Several of the more well-known councillors, such as Li Ming-chia and Lin Mian-shun, were called, but they all shook their heads and hands to say no. They were adamant in not wanting to be one to go out and face the crowds. The head of the fire department, Kang Kim-tiunn, was also called, but he, too, refused. Ia̍p Tshiu-bo̍k, sitting in his high place of power, was at a loss for what to do. Tsín-suī stood up from off to the side and called out, "Fire Chief Kang Kim-tiunn would be the best because he already has a team he can call on. Don't refuse. Come on. Go!"

Several people in the hall turned to get a look at who had called out the fire chief for his cowardice. Nobody knew who Tsín-suī was. Tshiu-bo̍k made an introduction, "This man's name is Ngôo Tsín-suī. He's a classmate of mine from the time we were in the common school and special subjects classes. He's a graduate of Takao Secondary, worked as a technician at a banana research station, and was the head of the Pîn-tong branch of the Nomura Insurance Company."

"Ngôo Tsín-suī would also be perfectly suited to act as a representative. It looks like you've got a lot of talent, can speak well, and have accomplished a lot of types of work," Fire Chief Kang cleverly took the opportunity to say.

"I don't have any experience as an official. How could I possibly be a representative for the council?"

"It doesn't matter if you're a public worker, don't worry. The important thing is that you pass yourself off as an important person. And what's more, you're one of Tshiu-bo̍k's classmates—his good friend! Go! You're the best person for the job," Fire Chief Kang urged him once more.

Tsín-suī was filled with deep rage. All of these public figures were downright fearful of sticking their necks out! All the people gathering in the park had guns and bullets. If they started shooting, how would that be any good? How many people would die? If they didn't take care of the problem quickly, it would be much harder to take care of things after dark. As he thought of this, he finally burst out, "Fine. My answer is 'yes,' but Fire Chief Kang has to go, as well. I will need your help."

He was surprised when Kang answered, "OK. My answer is 'yes.' My fire brigade will be a wall behind you. We'll collect information and try to communicate with all sides. We'll be your shield. If we're done speaking, then it's settled."

"A-Suī-á, try your best, OK!" Tshiu-bok suddenly added.

Tsín-suī's busybody personality was on full display, and he tacitly accepted this plan. He had to represent the peace advocates to go and negotiate with the war makers, but he was just a defenseless farmer with no name or position.

More than a thousand people were gathered in the city park, and there was a giant pile of weapons and boxes upon boxes of ammunition stacked on the running track. Several people were crouched over, wiping the dirt off the guns. Tsín-suī knew that they had been dug out of the makeshift hiding spots all around the area.

As soon as his tall, gaunt figure appeared, about seven or eight youths came up. He began to address them, "My name is Ngôo Tsín-suī. I was ordered to come here on behalf of Pîn-tong's provisional committee."

Many eyes darted to him like arrows, sizing him up and down. Someone picked up a rifle. Tsín-suī quickly made a self-introduction, "I'm from Thâu-tsîng-khe. I'm a banana farmer, and I used to be the head of the Nomura Insurance Company's Pîn-tong branch."

"Oh, I know you." He looked like he was the leader. "How is it that they ended up choosing for you to come out here?"

"I went over to the council meeting to hear them speak, and I heard them trying to call on people to come out, but none of them had the balls to do so. I thought it was pretty pitiful, so I foolishly tried to make a suggestion. It just so happens that the person convening the council is an old friend of mine, Iap Tshiu-bok." Tsín-suī smartly decided to be a little cruder in his speech to try to ease the tension with these regular joes. He could sense the intense gaze of the gun-toting civilians soften a bit.

"Ahahaha, so they sent someone with some actual balls to come out here!" someone in the militia crowd blurted out half-jokingly. "That damned committee. They're not worth even a wad of spit."

"Well, it's not the same as it was. It used to be headed by the mayor and the council head, the chief of police, the garrison police, and the gendarmerie, but now it's only the provincial assembly that are our own countrymen." Tsín-suī's tone of voice and attitude gained from being the oldest child and elder brother in his family flowed naturally, "Right now, with the committee as the basis, we've formed a Pîn-tong provisional representative committee. Everyone pushed for Iap Tshiu-bok to be the chairman. At the same time, they've set up a security team. They want to manage all of Pîn-tong's defense."

"So, what is the provisional committee doing now?"

"They're acting as our shield. With them acting as our shield, we can win."

"So you're saying none of those committee members have any balls and aren't willing to show their faces here?"

"At least Ia̍p Tshiu-bo̍k is concerned with the broader picture, and he's pretty adamant."

"OK. Speak your peace. What instructions does Ia̍p Tshiu-bo̍k have?"

"First of all, the provisional committee's resolution to 'use peaceful means to express ideas. You can't use violence.' So everyone please respect this order. You may make your move as soon as the resolution is handled."

"We can't do that. We can't accept that. What do you mean we 'can't use violence'?! Our two militias have just beaten the police, and they've got more weapons and ammunition. Right now, the police are on the run. Each dispatch center, as well as government bodies, all want the city emptied out. Each of our units should immediately go and occupy those abandoned posts and stations."

Tsín-suī was silent for a moment. He was desperately casting about for a way to calm down the conflict. "Hmmm... OK. I suggest each unit occupy a station or post, but they need to carry a Security Keeping Force flag. They can't use guns or knives or other weapons. Collect the guns and ammo. Don't even shoot a gun for practice. That's the only way we'll be able to occupy these spaces."

Now it was the militia commander's time to go silent. Tsín-suī quickly tacked on another condition. "Should the time come, if we need to *tshia-piànn* (fight to the death), I swear I won't run away."

The most senior ranking of the militia members was called the commander. He gave an initial agreement to Tsín-suī's suggestion. He and the others talked it over for a bit. The main group would prepare these security force flags, and then the entire militia would leave the park in an orderly manner, just like those Japanese soldiers who were expatriated. The militia walked from the park towards the first ring neighborhood of the governmental center.[28] It was just a short road of about forty meters. Tsín-suī walked next to the militia. He noticed many of the locals cheering them on. Some of the people's hands were placed on their hearts as if to say, "Thank goodness. They're not about to start shooting up the place." Still, others just wanted to come out to see all the commotion. They thought it was some sort of official parade.

They were just about at the intersection. Tsín-suī suddenly looked off and saw his father and A-Tsòng standing in the crowd. His father's lips

---

28. The area around present-day Zhongzheng Road and Gongyuan Road in Pingtung City.

were pressed tightly. They were curved up slightly in a faint smile. He couldn't guess what his father was thinking. He thought then of just going up to his old man and calling out a hello, but when he looked up again after collecting his thoughts, he couldn't find his father in the throng anymore... He couldn't find him at all.

Because the commander was leading a bunch of men into the police station, Tsín-suī decided to follow them too. It was convenient for him to be close by to help negotiate and calm things down. He asked the commander for his name.

"It's Tsng Ing-bin."

Apart from the notice on the outside door to the station, there was a red piece of paper tacked on with writing in large characters: "Police Team Headquarters." The characters were written using sternly written, blocky characters that gave off a sense of authority.

After entering the building, they found no traces of anyone in the hallways. He poked around in all the empty offices, but a vague fear began to rise in his heart. Just then, he thought of the old performer who did opera performances in front of his village's temple. He sometimes sang about the story of Zhu Ge-Liang entering an empty city and his plot to scare off the enemy army of Wei. These were the performer's words: "Grabbing hold the military's flags, the great gates of the city are cast wide open. The soldiers disguise themselves as ordinary folk. They only need to concern themselves with sweeping through the streets. Should the armies of Wei arrive, there is no need to fret and fear. I have my own wits and guile. Hahahaha." After just a few verses, the song concluded with the *dong* *dong* *dong* crashing of cymbals and the chirp and twang of a shamisen.

Tsín-suī sang a bit of the rest of the song in a low voice, but then he couldn't continue on with it. The fear kept rising within him. He was surrounded by a strong, foreboding sense of emptiness and loneliness. So just where were Fire Chief Kang and his men? Not a single one of them was to be found! And what of those committee members all dressed up in their Western suits? Not a single one of them was here either! He thought about how he had stuck his stupid neck out for this and wasn't able to succeed in getting the committee's demands accomplished at all. Not only were the men not dispersing, but they were also now forcing their way into the police station. He was on a razor-thin edge between both the war supporters and the peace supporters. If he wasn't careful, he'd surely end up hurt somehow.

He felt fortunate that he had managed by some stroke of luck, good or bad, to have earned the trust of the men in the war-supporter camp, but now he was being dragged away by the situation. How could a lone, little songbird be able to lead everyone else? The next moment, the situation became like the recent outbreaks of dysentery and cholera. One after another, villages succumbed to the spread.

A group of militia men had only occupied the district's police dispatch station for a few moments before they went off to attack the soldiers. Shots were fired. The soldiers were routed entirely. Tsín-suī rushed over immediately. Assuming the guise of the commander, he managed to convince the group to stop their advance.

A fried bread and dough stick shop run by a Chinese mainlander was attacked. The chairs and tables in the store were thrown out into the street and set on fire. Calls to "*Phah à-soann-á*!" ("Beat the mainlanders!") rose and fell, one after another. Tsín-suī and the commander hadn't even arrived at the scene yet, and a blaze was already roaring with sparks and smoke flying up into the air. The flames reflected back on the faces of the citizenry surrounding the bonfire. Some faces were filled with excitement, others looked reluctant.

A group of Indigenous Taiwanese came by, shouting that they were Paiwan warriors and were here to join the war supporters. A few more mainlanders were dragged out and beaten. The entire scene was chaotic and filled with screams. Tsín-suī's youngest brother, Tsín-lîng, was riding around the city on a bicycle and saw that there was chaos everywhere about. He kept asking strangers, "I need to find my oldest brother, Ngôo Tsín-suī. Do you know where he is?... Sorry, but have you seen my brother, Ngôo Tsín-suī?"

After a long time searching, he finally managed to find Tsín-suī at the police station. "*Nii-san*, our Mari is about to give birth. It looks like it's not going to be an easy one either. She's in a lot of pain. She keeps crying out. A-só is scared to death. She's asking that you come back home immediately," he panted.

"Oh yes... It's already been a year, hasn't it?"

"*Nii-san*, it's heartbreaking to watch. Mari can't stand up on her forelegs. She keeps shaking and trembling. And then she looks like a house that's ready to collapse. That face of hers looks like she's enduring unbearable pain."

"Did you already go over to ask Uncle A-Huàn?"

"*A-só* already asked *jī-hiann* (second-oldest brother) to go over to Uncle A-Huàn's to bring him over to the house. At the same time, she ordered me to come out here and tell you to come back home."

"*Ai-yee*, you tell your sister-in-law that I'm extremely sorry. I honestly can't leave the area. *Ai-yee*! Why did this have to happen to Mari on this of all days?"

"*Nii-san*, Mari's in a lot of pain. *A-só* is next to the cow pen. She's crying and bellowing all the time. *A-só* said that this stuff happening here in town has nothing to do with you, that you should come home now! Your home and family are more important than anything else."

"OK, OK, as soon as I've settled the problem here, I'll go back immediately. You go back first."

"Don't make your wife even more upset, *Nii-san*!"

Tsín-suī had decided he was going to go home and had packed up some of the sundry items he had brought with him. Just as he was about to leave, a group of people, obviously locals from Pîn-tong, brought a dozen mainlanders into the station. Among them, six or seven of them were clearly injured. What exactly was this? One look and he realized what was going on, but Commander Tsng then shouted, "What do you want coming here?"

Tsín-suī quickly took a couple steps forward. He recognized two of the local men. One was a well-known doctor by the name of Kueh It-tshing. The other was an employee at the Huanan Bank, a young man surnamed Lîm. He didn't recognize any of the others. Dr. Kueh ignored the commander and went directly up to Tsín-suī and said, "You here, find a room. We need to put these mainlanders in one, and quickly."

Dr. Kueh was at least a decade older than Tsín-suī, and he was a man of great reputation about the town, so Tsín-suī responded to him immediately with a Japanese-style "*Hai*!"

"Oh, that's excellent. You're still doing well." Dr. Kueh had praised him, then he eyed the commander, who was sitting in the on-duty officer's chair. He asked Tsín-suī, "What's the matter? *Daijōbu ka*? (Japanese for 'Is everything OK?')"

"Wait a moment." Tsín-suī moved towards the commander to bargain. "Well? We should prepare a room to house them in, OK?" The commander was silent. Tsín-suī waited at his side for a second, not moving an eyebrow or strand of hair. Then, collecting his wits, he changed tack. "These mainlanders... We need to lock them up in the cell. We should lock them up. What do you think?"

Of course, as soon as the commander heard it, he shot back a quick, "Yes. Lock them up."

After the mainlanders were led to the jail cell, Dr. Kueh began administering some light treatment to the victims. He expressed a quick thanks to Tsín-suī, "Locking them up might actually be the best thing that could happen to these folks in these times." He continued, "Are you Ngôo-*san* Tsín-suī? I've heard Tshiu-bok-á mention your name before."

"Oh! You know Tshiu-bok?"

"He's my son-in-law."

"Oh! I had no idea!"

After Tsín-suī and Dr. Kueh busied themselves attending to the patient-prisoners for a bit, they stepped outside, then realized that the commander and his men were nowhere to be found. There wasn't a trace of anyone else around besides the two of them. Tsín-suī thought it was quite puzzling. A young doctor on a motorcycle accompanying Dr. Kueh came riding up to the station doors and told everyone, "Iap Tshiu-bok has gathered all the men and they're heading to the airport to fight to the death!"

Tsín-suī was absolutely stunned. "You're lying! Tshiu-bok was the one advocating a peaceful resolution. How is it that he'd lead everyone to attack on the airport? What would they achieve by attacking it?"

"Well, it happened like this Ngôo-*san*: All of the troops and police from in and around Pîn-tong fled to the airport. Since Iap Tshiu-bok was made the interim mayor by the committee, he's using his position as mayor to demand all of the soldiers and police hand over their weapons. Iap-*san* was concerned they wouldn't heed his order, so he gathered everyone up and went off together. It looked quite imposing."

"Oh, so they're going to fight to the death?"

"If they don't go out to fight to the death, and it doesn't look imposing, will anyone obey them and hand over their weapons?"

The younger doctor then started speaking again, "I rode over on my motorcycle to see, and sure enough, a large mass of people went with Iap Tshiu-bok as his 'soldiers.' I heard Tshiu-bok proclaiming that 'the people here must also give up their weapons. Neither side is allowed to have rifles. That's the only way to preserve the peace.'"

"Ah, so what's the situation now?"

"Both sides are still sticking to their guns."

When he heard this, Tsín-suī started walking as he spoke, "Well if that's the case, I ought to be going now. I have to go support Tshiu-bok."

But then Dr. Kueh called out to him to stop, "Ngôo-*san*, I think it'd be best if you didn't go. There's already plenty of people there to give their support to Tshiu-bok. They won't miss you not being there. Quite frankly, we need your help here to patch people up."

"I must go. But I need to go home first, and then I'll go to the airport." As he finished speaking, he hopped on his bicycle to go.

He was tall and thin, so when he leaned forward and peddled hard, he kicked up clouds of dust.

After he had ridden a distance along the road, a motorcycle caught up to him. It was the young bank teller from Huanan Bank surnamed Lîm. He kept the engine running and shouted out to Tsín-suī, "Ngôo-*san*. Dr. Kueh told me to catch up with you and have you come back to the police station."

Tsín-suī was still straddling the bicycle saddle, one foot on the ground. "What's the matter now?"

"A truck is parked outside the Pîn-tong train station. There's a machine gun at the front of the truck and about twenty or thirty people riding in it. They're all regular folks from the island, and some people from elsewhere too. The station master said that they've come from the Pîn-tong airport, and they want to help with the self-defense. Dr. Kueh is urging them to go back, but they won't listen. Dr. Kueh says that you've got a knack for speaking and calming things down, so he wants you to go over to the station quickly."

"I thought you said there wasn't anything happening at the airport?"

"They're saying it's already better."

"But I have to go back home. My family's buffalo is right in the middle of giving birth. I heard it's a difficult delivery."

"Do you know how to deliver a calf? Just go ask Uncle A-Huàn to help. Have you asked him already?"

"Yes. Uncle A-Huàn is friends with my family."

"Well then, there's no problem. I'll drive you back to the police station. Dr. Kueh is waiting for you."

"But I don't have anywhere to put my bicycle."

"Just leave it on the side of the road."

"No, I can't. It's lawless out there. It'll be stolen quickly if I leave it here."

"They're all gone. Those who haven't fled for the hills are already locked up in the jail. Don't you remember?"

"OK. Fine. Let's go." Tsín-suī straddled the back of the motorcycle seat, adjusting his balance, and then said, "I used to have a motorcycle a while ago. This one looks like it cost an arm and a leg."

"This is Dr. Kueh's. I'm not rich enough to afford one."

The motorcycle kicked up a lot of dust as it sped on through the wind, so the two of them had to squint, their hair fluttering behind them as they rode. They reached the train station in no time. The Japanese name *eki* (train station) had been replaced by the Chinese *chezhan* on the sign. The truck was still waiting in the plaza in front of the station. It in fact did have a machine gun mounted on the front. Dr. Kueh was talking with the leader right at that moment, demure and soft-spoken. Over a hundred people were at the scene, looking on from all around, and more people continued to draw in off the street. As soon as Tsín-suī saw the scene, the first thing he did was decide on a strategy. He went up to the men in the truck and interjected strongly, "Why do you think we need your help with self-defense here in Pîn-tong? We have plenty of men as it is. The *Tua-liok-á* (mainlander) leaders have all fled away. The ones who haven't are already locked up in the jail cell. If you don't believe me, I can take you to see them right now—"

"We believe you, but we need to stop them from sending troops down from Ko-hiông. We need to work together to stop them."

"The issue at the airport is already taken care of. We're going to start collecting rifles and guns. All of the people here for the past two or three days are heading back to their homes," Dr. Kueh responded.

Someone in the crowd surrounding them responded in a booming voice, "There's no proof they're going to stop. We're going to stay where we are. We'll move out and attack at any hint of trouble."

Tsín-suī had to shout loudly and keep his tone the same, "This man who was just speaking now is none other than Dr. Kueh It-tshing. He's Iap Tshiu-bok's father-in-law. We've already gotten word back from the airport from Tshiu-bok-*hiann* that the police and soldiers, as well as our own, are going to agree to a cease-fire and give up their weapons. They're not allowing anyone to take weapons. This is Iap Tshiu-bok's order."

"OK." The other man stepped up onto the truck and warned them, "You Pîn-tong'ers are saying you don't need our help then. We'll be going now, but I'm warning you that you're truly going to regret it. The mainlanders aren't going to just simply stop like you mistakenly think they will. Don't say we didn't warn you."

After the truck drove off, more and more people came up to help Dr. Kueh and Tsín-suī. The peacemakers had convinced each squad to give up their weapons and urged them to go on home. However, Tsín-suī himself never had the chance to go home because the peacemaker party gave him the responsibility of keeping watch over the police station and guarding the stored armaments.

He kept watch until very late at night when a military truck parked outside the doors to the police headquarters. Several troops with rifles and bullets jumped down from the truck and rushed the police station. The lead officer shouted out, "Where are they?"

Tsín-suī was startled. He responded half in Taiwanese, half in Chinese, "Who is the commander referring to?"

"To the people you've locked up."

"They're not locked up. They're being given refuge. They're in the jail cell."

The officer quickly dispatched some of his men into the station to free the mainlanders and then pointed at Tsín-suī, "Seize this bastard."

Two soldiers came forward and manhandled Tsín-suī, grabbing him roughly by the arms. Tsín-suī was frightened and enraged. After trying to struggle, he wanted to speak, but all he could manage was to shout out a furious, "You!" before his tongue froze. He wasn't sure if trying to talk his way out gently would be better, or if he should angrily curse them.

Right then, a group of mainlanders walked out. They saw the situation unfolding and spoke a couple words to the officer in Mandarin that Tsín-suī couldn't comprehend. "OK. Let him go." The officer remained quite brusque with Tsín-suī, "Get yourself home quickly and don't come back. You have nothing to do here."

"*Baka yarō*! F***!" Tsín-suī cursed the soldiers deep down in his heart as he walked. He was also cursing himself. He ought to have gone home long ago. Why should he have remained standing guard over this place alone? "*Baka ne*!" He berated himself and left quickly.

He heard someone calling from behind him. It seemed like they were calling to him, "Hey, mister." He didn't turn his head. Then they said, "You, Mister! Thank you. Thank you for your help."

It was still a bit cold at the beginning of March. The coolness issued from his heart and over his skin. He walked quickly along, thinking about the words of the guy on the truck. "You Pîn-tong'ers are saying you don't need our help then. We'll be going now, but I'm warning you now that you're truly going to regret it. The mainlanders aren't going to just simply stop like you mistakenly think they will." He turned into a small lane to take a shortcut. It wasn't long before he had found his own bicycle. Luckily, it hadn't been stolen.

As soon as he reached the house, he went first to see Mari. She was lying down on her side, resting. Her horns were inclined against the wall. "Are you still in pain, Mari? You're probably exhausted, aren't you?" he thought deep down. He spotted a small calf, half-laying and half-leaning. It still hadn't grown any horns yet. In the dark of night, he couldn't make out its face and nostrils clearly. Its outline was faint and gave off an air of youth and tenderness. Such extreme good fortune! Both mother and child were safe and sound.

After a quick brush of his hair and rinsing off some of the grime, he went to bed, but he had woken up his wife. Tsín-suī just managed to say a faint, "I'm sorry," and then he slipped beneath the covers. He lightly clasped his wife's hand and quickly fell asleep. The next day, when he woke up, all had seemed like it was normal. Giok-ìn wasn't very angry with her husband. He'd come home safe, which was all that really mattered. He'd just stay in the house for the morning. It wasn't long after he'd finished eating breakfast that he began to feel very uneasy, vexed. His eyelids wouldn't stop twitching. He then hopped onto his bicycle and rode towards the town. He hadn't said a single word to his family.

He went racing off all over the place, intentionally going back to the police station, which he rode a circle around. Everything was quiet. Eerily quiet. It was like the calm before the storm when all the soldiers and police from a couple days before had fled out of the city. Most of the doors to the shops and homes along the street were open as usual. He looked around. Just as he thought about riding over to his mother-in-law's for a respite, he suddenly saw a group of soldiers slowly advancing from another part of the street. The military was coming out in force now. It was a bit strange. Especially those up at the front of their file. One of them had a long trumpet and was blasting away some military tune. Whatever the song was, Tsín-suī had never heard it before. It almost seemed like a marching song, and also like a funerary send-off.

He leaned his bicycle against a wall and quickly took a few steps forward. He was dumbstruck. In the middle of the troupe, he saw an uncovered military truck. There was a person on the back of it, tied up and bound. There was a wooden two-by-four tied to his back, and on it were written some grass-script characters that read *"bao-dong shou-kui"* (Leader of the Riot) in gigantic red characters. Those were Chinese-styled characters, not the ones used in Japanese. While it was true that there were violent outbursts in the previous few days, who exactly was this "leader"? Was it that "commander" he had run around with? He shifted forward just a few steps more and saw that the man's face was unrecognizable because of all the blood. His two ears were cut off and they were still bleeding, all the way down his shoulders. Blood had seeped into his shirt and shirt collar and was spreading everywhere. His nose was also cut clean off. Oh my God! He's still alive! His whole body was shaking. Was he shaking from the pain, or was he shaking from the cold? Tsín-suī began to tremble uncontrollably. He tried looking more closely. It didn't look like it was the militia commander. It was then that he snapped out of his stupor and shock and realized it was Iap Tshiu-bok. His ensanguined face, covered in thick, congealing blood looked all too familiar now.

Tsín-suí felt a massive surge of terror. Was it really Tshiu-bok-*hiann*??? It couldn't be! It couldn't be him. It just couldn't.

The parade of soldiers moved at a snail's pace. They were deliberately slow because they wanted to ensure that everyone in town could see Tshiu-bok paraded through the streets as an example. Several minutes later, there came a shrill cry from behind the last of the soldiers at the end of the procession. The sharp voice kept calling out, shouting until the voice became hoarse. He focused on the voice again. Oh! It was calling out, "Tshiu-bok-ia! A-Bok-á! A-Bok-á!"

Tsín-suí got the sudden urge to move towards the back of the procession. It was Tshiu-bok's wife. Of course she'd be there for him! Just as Tsín-suí was about to make his way, he heard the continuous wails of small children. *Wah-sai*! It was his two children! They had already made their way up to the soldiers. They kept crying out "*Tō-san!*" (Japanese for "father") and "*Ka-san!*" (Japanese for "mother"). Tsín-suí quickly stepped forward. He saw three or four women trying to drag them away from the soldiers and the truck. He caught one last glimpse of Tshiu-bok's wife's face. It was a face lost to an unbelievable stupor. There was no spirit in those eyes, and they were not weeping any longer. Her mouth was wide open and her neck was stretched, but she couldn't call out anymore. All Tsín-suí could hear was a hissing sound.

About an hour had passed and Tsín-suí had grown despondent. He was being pushed forward along with the crowd. The faces of the people in the crowd were filled with terror, but nobody cried out, they didn't even dare to sigh, they just kept pushing forward to observe this horrifying spectacle. People exchanged glances and silently mouthed words to convey their alarm and the abject terror in their hearts, and quickly established a consensus—a consensus that enveloped the whole street—utter silence. Nobody at the scene made a sound. All they heard were the trumpet blasts from the head of the column of soldiers. That screeching, piercing sound of the trumpet. As Tsín-suí walked and walked, he felt a vague pain in his stomach. That pain gradually spread throughout his body until it reached to his heart and then spread all up and down his spine.

The soldiers had reached the triangle park in front of the Taiwan Bank, and then they stopped. Tsín-suí was tall, so he lifted his head above the other people gathered and watched as several soldiers crudely shoved Tshiu-bok off the back of the truck and forced him to kneel. People emerged from all around to watch. Tsín-suī pushed forward to the front. From the gaps in the crowd of people, he could see Tshiu-bo̍k-*hiann* had lowered his head. It was being pressed down by the heavy two-by-four tied to his back, so he wasn't able to lift his head up. Tsín-suī tried hard to make eye contact, but he couldn't see clearly. All he could see was that Tshiu-bo̍k's lips were pressed tightly. He was closing them with all his might making an upward crescent shape.

The soldiers raised their rifles and marched towards the crowd surrounding the park to try to disperse the gathered throng. Several minutes later, a line of soldiers appeared from behind the soldiers, trying to block the bystanders. An officer shouted out, "Raise your rifles! Aim at his heart! Fire!"

The awful burst of gunshots echoed painfully in everyone's ears. In a flash, the word *soo-khai* (to flee) floated to the top of Tsín-suī's mind. He decided then and there that he had to flee. Ia̍p Tshiu-bo̍k was the main leader of the committee. He was the one who had made a resolution for a peaceful solution. If someone like him could be so brutally dispatched and dragged out to be publicly executed as he was, then what about Tsín-suī, himself? "I was the one who tried to carry out the resolution. Won't I be in serious peril?" he worried. He made a flash decision. He ran to the nearby Hong Tsuân-tông bakery where he spent every last bit of money he had on him and bought four large loaves of bread. He rushed home, and after making a simple relay of the morning's events to his wife, he sought out a mosquito net and a cotton quilt and raced towards a dense forest by the river, about three *li* away from his home. As he was racing down the road, he felt pangs of pain. Wave after wave of vague pain ripped through him, from his stomach into his back.

This was a densely forested area that nobody from the outside looking in could easily see, but Tsín-suī could easily peer outside. A creek gurgled its way through the thickets and groves of this forest. He was hunched over on his hands and feet, trying to flatten a bit of the ground. Sitting down, his heart was racing, *ka-thunk* *ka-thunk* *ka-thunk.* The pain moving from his abdomen into his back again assaulted him. This time, even his head and throat were feeling it. He wrapped his arms around his head in a panicked daze and bent over. Everything around him was serene. Occasionally, a frog jumped here or there along the creek, but he rarely heard the chirping of birds. This only added to the placid effect. This kind of tranquility was just enough to make the hairs on one's neck stand up. Right then, the pain grew even more intense. It had spread throughout his whole body. There wasn't any part of him that didn't feel pained. The dull pain had morphed into stabbing pain. It was like his skin was being pierced by searing hot acupuncture needles. *Okashii ne?* It was strange, no?

Was he seriously ill? Would he die in the wilds on the outskirts of home? He opened his eyes wide and looked off in every direction. There was no sign of anyone else. He began to shout out and cry. Angrily, he cried and wailed. He cried for a long time and was suddenly alarmed that the leaves in the trees all around him had begun to rustle. He stopped wailing, then felt that the pain in his body had begun to leave him. He stretched out one arm to try to feel the breeze. There was no wind though. Why were the trees and leaves moving?

Was it monkeys, squirrels, or birds up in the boughs and limbs just then? He wiped the tears from his face and looked around. No. There was nothing. Nothing at all. Was it just a fluke? A small earthquake? It couldn't have been. He remained sitting on the ground. His butt would have felt the earth's tremors if there had actually been a quake. Could it have been a phantom in the forest?

"I was the best student in my science classes. How could I possibly believe in such a thing as ghosts and spirits? Maybe it's just the sound reverberating from all my cries and wails that shook them," he mused.

He was still sitting there, dumbstruck, when he thought of the role he had played in the previous day's chaos. His mind was haunted by the mask of misery worn by Tshiu-bȯk-*hiann*'s wife, and the two Iȧp family children running after and calling out, "*Tō-san!*" "*Ka-san!*" His mind had switched over to thinking about how Tshiu-bȯk's wife was Dr. Kueh's younger sister. He fixated on how Dr. Kueh was such a well-respected, publicly minded person. He had thought and thought till all the pain in his body had built itself back up again. His bowels felt like they were tied all up in knots. He was experiencing constant spasms. The pain in his back felt like the kind of pain you feel when your fingers are clamped in a pair of steel pliers. He felt as if the pain was radiating from the top of his head all the way down to his rectum, shooting out left and right. The longer he thought about it all, the more pain he felt. He felt so awful he began shedding tears and wailing all over again. He cried out loudly because there was nobody around to hear him anyway. He wailed and wailed for a long time, then he was startled to notice that the tree leaves all around him had begun shaking and rustling again. At the same time, he once more felt like the pain was lessening.

"It's strange, isn't it? Crying out all my sorrows can heal my pain!" He didn't understand why this was.

He went on like this forever and ever, tormented, and the sky had begun to darken. Tsín-suī then felt a strong urge to go home. It hadn't even been a day and he had felt homesick. He stood up with determination, embraced the still-rolled-up cotton quilt and mosquito netting, and started to walk out of the forest. Ah! It was still quite bright outside the edge of the forest! He wondered, "Would they really come after me next? Wasn't I running every which way in order to stop the chaos? He tried taking two steps forward, looking left and right several times." He took three more steps, then looked again. Then he retreated back to where he had originally been and sat back down. He sat, looking at nothing in particular, striving as hard as he could not to think of the horrors he had witnessed that day in town. The pains didn't come back.

"No. It's not right. I can't spend the night out here!" He gritted his teeth, drummed up his courage, and walked out again. This time, he walked a full thirty meters down the road. When he got to the intersection where he should turn, he thought better of it and turned back again into the forest to where he had been sitting.

The forest had already darkened to a pitch-black. The gurgling sounds of the creek had gone silent. The frogs had stopped their calls. The buzz of insects was only faintly discernable. It was deathly quiet. He felt extremely afraid. Even though he'd grown up in a country village, having to spend the night alone in the wild made him more fearful with every passing minute. All around him, ethereal shadows seemed to float on by, sometimes to the left, and sometimes to the right, until his whole body was covered in goose bumps and the top of his head felt numb. Eventually, he discovered it was the leaves—moving despite the lack of wind—that were casting their shadows. It was just too quiet. He was hoping that something would screech out from the nothingness, but suddenly a small tree branch fell into the creek, with the faintest *plop* sound, startling him and making his heart pound. He started to wonder if Giók-ìn-á could feel her husband's loneliness and terror at this moment. Would she try to sneak out and comfort him? What a dream that would be!

He looked far off into the distance from the edge of the forest once more. Giók-ìn-á wouldn't come. It was better if she stayed back at the house, anyway. Right here by the creek edge in the wilds, he didn't know if a rat or a snake might come up beside him in the middle of the night. That would without a doubt scare her witless. She was a city girl, through and through. What would possibly make her want to endure such hardship as being on the run out in the wilds? In any case, she hadn't done anything wrong! "I'm the one who had gone out and done something, even though I thought it was the right thing to do."

Thinking of rats and snakes, Tsín-suī decided to enlarge this area where he'd be sleeping. He used some tree trunks to hang up the mosquito netting. He busied himself for quite some time, and as soon as he'd gotten under the netting, he felt a slight sense of security. The netting, made of gauze, would give him some small semblance of peace for just a night, at least until the warm rays of morning sunlight filtered in. He tried to lie down under the netting. Looking through the gauze, he could see a natural curtain up at the canvas of sky woven by the leaves and branches of the trees. Through the gaps in that tattered curtain, he could see bits and pieces of the sky. The moon hadn't yet risen. The stars hadn't come out yet either. He was hoping that bright moonlight would shine in. Just at that moment, he thought of how he should have been sitting around the dinner table with his family. He felt around his pack for the bread he'd bought that morning. He held one bun in his hand and eyed it, but he had no appetite whatsoever.

He curled himself up, half-reposed, half-sitting under the mosquito netting. He didn't want to eat, and he couldn't fall asleep. His mind was full of thoughts, but he stopped himself from thinking about how his whole body had been inflamed with pain. At some point, frogs started their croaking. Much later, a nighthawk began to cry out repeatedly. Their calls would sometimes stop completely, almost as if they had some secret pact with each other. It was already a terrifying hour of the night. Tsín-suī's hearing became especially acute. He carefully looked to find the sources of noises, almost as if he were searching for some comfort for his life. Ants were crawling around on dried leaves that had fallen to the forest floor. Tsín-suī was so tuned into the noises around him that he could hear their extremely light shuffling. These frightful moments of quiet came only once in a long while, and he couldn't remember after how many times it had been that he started to feel famished, so he ate two of the buns. After filling his stomach, he began to feel sleepy and very quickly fell into a slumber.

He wasn't sure just how long he had been asleep, but he was awoken by a succession of *pah, pah, pah* sounds. It was dark as could be all around him. The moon and the stars were shining, and they brought with their light the flickering dance of ghostly shadows. Sometimes the sounds came in quick succession; at others, they were spaced apart. Tsín-suī pricked up his ears and concentrated on what he heard. There was also a *nuuuu* sound that penetrated through the empty forest space. The *nuuuu* was relatively weaker than the *pah*. The *nuuuu* came on first and then the *pah*. Tsín-suī was a believer in hard science. He tried his best to think of what exact kind of bird species or frog was making this call, but he could make neither head nor tail of it. "Ah forget it! I should go back to sleep!" He had just closed his eyes when he was awoken again, *nuuuu-pah, nuuuu-pah*. It started off weak then ended strongly. It seemed to be trying to warn him. Or maybe whatever it was was trying to summon something. This time, he didn't open his eyes. He just focused on trying to get back to sleep. In his half-lucid state, he thought that he could hear the advancing steps of soldiers. He thought of when he was at Takao Secondary doing target practice as part of his military preparedness training. As the bullet left the chamber, there was an explosion next to his ear which then brought with it the smell of burning gunpowder. The sound of a row of soldiers executing Tshiu-bo̍k abruptly forced its way into his mind.

Nuuuu-pah, nuuuu-pah. Weak, then strong again. The calls were incessant. Tsín-suī felt as if his blood were running cold. His entire body was covered in goose bumps! Another sound resounded around him this time. It was a long, drawn-out *jiiiiiiii* chirping noise. Every three to five seconds, whatever was making the sound seemed to be darting in and out and making this sharp whistling chirp when he wasn't prepared for it. By now, he had been awake more than he was asleep. He recognized the sound as the call of a nighthawk. He didn't open his eyes. He didn't dare to. The bullets had shot out of their gun barrels, and they had penetrated right through Tshiu-bo̍k's chest and out his back. The spray of blood had painted the air. In a movie, they wouldn't have used *jiiii* but rather a *shiewww* sound. "I'm not afraid. I must not be afraid. It'll be light out soon. All those sounds—the frogs, the birds, ghostly wails, and celestial shouts—will stop as soon as the sun's rays come out."

The unfortunate thing was that at this critical time when he should have been asleep, his whole body started to be racked with pain again. It started along his spine and then radiated out to his waist, then rose up to his upper back, shoulders, head. The pain was so great that he thought he ought to bash his head on a tree trunk to end the pain, but the *nuuuu-pah* sound continued to resound not too far away from him. It scared him. It was vexing and infuriating. "*Ah-hai*! If I'm going to be in this much pain, I ought to just be dead." He turned himself over and laid flat on his stomach, wincing in pain, with tears streaming down his face. He wailed out in terror. He didn't know how long he cried.

When he woke up, his wife was by his side. The sun's rays were out in full force. There was a kettle of tea, some rice balls, and a fishing pole outside the mosquito net. Tsín-suī's first words to his wife were, "I was here alone last night. It was extremely frightening!"

"I couldn't fall asleep last night either."

"I wanted to come back around midnight to at least wash myself."

"*A-Pa* says that they're out trying to catch people. They're doing it in the middle of the night. You need to be more careful."

"What's the purpose of that?"

"Never mind. It's not important for you to bathe."

"Giok-ìn, when you came here, were you followed?"

"No. I had both the buffalo with me. I was pretending to take them out to the creek for a mud bath."

"Mari and her calf—are they both OK?"

"The calf is growing very quickly. Uncle A-Huàn was saying when he went out to the field to do plowing after she gave birth, Mari had aged a lot. She didn't have any more strength left in her."

"Considering her age, Mari is already very old. Giving birth at such an old age, it's no surprise that it caused her so much pain."

Tsín-suī took his wife's hands in his and held them tightly. Giok-ìn squeezed his hands in return. Both husband and wife were silent for some time. Tsín-suī then asked her, "When we both went to study *kanbun*, do you remember that character for 'fear'? Was it pronounced *pah*?"

"Yes, that's right. It was stressed as *pah*." Giok-ìn used one hand to draw the character in the dirt. "It's this character. An 'upright heart' over on the left side, and the character for 'pale' on the other. A pale heart (怕)."

"This character, *pah*, is something I had learned a long time ago," Tsín-suī was muttering to himself. "When your heart stands up, your face grows sallow and pale, like lead. This is called *pah*."

"Why are you suddenly asking such a question?"

Tsín-suī lost some of the color in his face as he responded, "Last night, there was something out there in the woods calling out. It kept crying out *nuuuuu-pah, nuuuuu-pah*. It just wouldn't stop calling out. It was terrifying. It kept crying out so much that I had the worst luck trying to fall asleep."

"It's definitely a bird. You slept badly last night, but you should be able to sleep pretty well tonight," Giok-ìn said.

After his wife had left and headed back home, he was utterly alone once more. He began to start digging for earthworms and night crawlers to go fishing. There were a lot of fish and freshwater shrimp in this creek. He didn't have to wait long after placing the line in the water before making his first catch. He didn't have any matches on him, but if he roasted any of his catch, he'd inevitably be creating firelight and smoke. He thought for a bit. He couldn't risk it. He took the fish on the line, unhooked it, and returned it to the water. He kept hooking fish left and right, and he kept setting them free. This is how his weeks went. He felt that his days were getting better. He was especially thankful for his wife having brought him a fishing rod to pass the time.

He couldn't even bathe! He began to feel that this forest was a prison, and he was in solitary confinement. He didn't know how long he was going to be hemmed in by these branches and leaves. He stood up and searched for a sharp stone. He carved a horizontal line into the trunk, and then under that line he carved another one. He was talking to himself as he made each cut into the bark, "Today is the second day." This was his habit of counting ever since he was a little boy. He didn't know where the practice had originated. He didn't know whether it was done originally with Japanese renditions of Chinese characters or the Chinese characters used by the Qing. Nobody had ever told him. All in all, he carved out a *tshiann* character (正) to represent five days. Two *tshiann* became ten days. Ten *tshiann* became fifty. He had hoped he wouldn't have to stay that long and that things would have died down enough for him to leave this place peacefully. He hoped.

On the second night, he had slept for a while but then that *nuuuu-pah*, *nuuuuu-pah* sound woke him up again. With the previous night's experience fresh in his mind, he tried to ignore it. He tried and tried for a long while. The ghostly voices and sounds of the previous day were still clawing at his mind. The more he tried to ignore it, it more able it seemed to penetrate into his ears and nose and into his brain. Tsín-suī decided he had to try to fight it. "*Kann!* (F***)! *Nu-pah, nu-pah* must mean, 'You're scared,' huh? Yeah. I am afraid. I'm afraid. Well! What are you waiting for?"

He sat up. Each time the *nuuuu-pah* resounded, he used Mandarin to respond, "*Oh-pa-le*. (I'm afraid)."[29]

"*Nu-pa*."

"Yeah, *oh-pa-le*."

---

29. In that era, before the widespread usage of the Bopomofo system for writing Mandarin Chinese, Taiwanese people who spoke Hoklo as their mother tongue all tended to pronounce the Mandarin Chinese "wo," meaning "I" or "me," like the word "oh."

"*Nu-pa.*"

"Yeah, *oh-pa-le*," Tsín-suī kept replying.

He started to compete with whatever was making the sound, getting into a shouting match with it. Several times, the scene had calmed down, but he just couldn't get to sleep. He started thinking up random, crazed thoughts.

What he feared most was thinking about the melancholy, distraught scene that must have been Tshiu-bok's family. He was afraid that his own body would start aching again, so he had to continue to fight the fear. His resistance turned out to be useful. Lessening his fears started to work, and he shouted back at whatever was making the noise. Half-awake, he kept on responding to the calls.

Tsín-suī went fast asleep as soon as the sun had risen, and it was light all around. When his wife had reached his spot in the forest, she saw her husband was still fast asleep, so she didn't try to wake him up. She just sat alone next to the mosquito netting and recited a Buddhist sutra in silence. A long time after, her husband woke up. His eyes were bloodshot, and his voice was hoarse. She made him drink some boiled water she had brought from the house. After his mind was fully awake, she told him, "There was a man, someone by the name of Kang Kim-tiunn. He said he was the fire chief. He went over to my mother's shop. He said they told him to go specifically and send you a message. You absolutely had to flee. You have to flee to someplace nobody could find you."

On the third day, as soon as she got to the secret grove, she warned her husband, "A policeman came to the house searching for you."

"What! They did?"

"They visited twice. The first time was yesterday afternoon. It was just the policeman. The second time, they came in the middle of the night, but that time there were soldiers with them. They accused you of fomenting 'blind hatred and violence,' and they wanted you to go to the police bureau for questioning."

"To hell with those bastards! When the hell did I ever blindly engage in any violence?!" Tsín-suī was shaking violently from the shock of it all. He grabbed at some mud and flung it hard towards the creek.

"They asked me, but I told them that you had left the village, that you had gone to another city in another county to get a payment for my mother's shop."

"*Aiyee*! Ah! So it was for the best that I fled all the way here then."

Giok-ìn moved close to her husband and spoke softly to try to calm him down. "You don't have to curse and get all worked up. We need to turn things around. Since you've fled all the way here, we have a lot of time to be alone together, no?"

Tsín-suī then embraced his wife, pulling her close and dropped back onto the ground and said, "Of all the things of the world, there's fortune in misery and misery in fortune." Nobody else was around to see or hear them. They had time to spend, but his wife wouldn't be able to stay there forever. The sound of a truck off in the distance was growing closer. Tsín-suī heard it first. He got up hastily, like a frightened dog that had been lying down on a hot road. Gio̍k-ìn sat up. They kept trying to listen to the noise and got up to walk towards the forest edge to take a look. It turned out to just be an ordinary delivery truck. It wasn't a military truck. Both husband and wife breathed long, heavy sighs of relief.

Since he couldn't get to sleep very easily, many times, Tsín-suī would lie down with his head in his wife's lap, using her thigh as a pillow to try to help him get some shut-eye. He would sleep until Gio̍k-ìn's legs had started to hurt from the pins and needles of falling asleep.

After his wife had gone back home, Tsín-suī took his fishing pole and began to have a conversation with himself. "*Aiyee*, I've got all this time on my hands to go fishing since I've 'fled!'"

He went down to a bend in the creek every day. The water flowed by peacefully and he placed his rod firmly. He would sit there for several hours at a time. For the most part, he used earthworms and night crawlers as bait, and the little minnows kept rising to the hook. He always went to the trouble of unhooking and setting them free each time he caught one.

One day, he decided to use a chunk of sweet potato his wife had brought him as bait. It was so fragrant and sweet smelling. It wasn't on the fishhook for too long before the bobber was violently dragged down into the murky water. He pulled lightly on the fishing pole. It felt like he had snagged a piece of wood. He pulled again. No. It wasn't a piece of driftwood. Something was struggling on the hook, pulling and dragging. He gripped the pole tightly with both hands and stood up. This was the moment the fish would be most energized. The slender, tapered end of the rod had already been pulled down into the water. The rod momentarily thrashed about violently. It must be massive!

"Just how big are you? Are you trying to get rid of the hook? Are you trying to swim away? Now I want to pull you in to get a better look."

The next moment, the surface of the water was placid and peaceful. He felt as if the air around him was muggy and stifling, just like the days right before a typhoon makes landfall. The hook seemed to have loosened.

"So did you make your escape? Or are you just taking a breather before continuing your fight? Or maybe you're just testing my patience, playing dead, seeing if I'll let go of my grip, huh?"

The tenseness between man and fish eased up for a long time. He looked everywhere at the shadows in the forest for movement. He'd reckoned that at least an hour had passed. Gradually, the fish's movements had obviously slowed, but Tsín-suī couldn't get careless. If he pulled too hard on the rod, the fish might use Tsín-suī's tug to pull the hook straight, in spite of the pain, then make its escape. It could have also been that this fish was very heavy, and he needed to use the buoyancy of the water to keep the line from breaking. After running all sorts of factors through his mind, he decided to pick up the fight! He'd see who had the most strength and endurance. After another long moment passed, the shadows of the trees shifted slightly. Tsín-suī decided he had to move. First, he gripped the rod and shoved it firmly into the ground. He took off some of the bamboo leaves and bark from his conical *leh-á* hat and made a small net with what remained of the frame. Then he slowly waded into the water. The water in early March in this forest creek was icy cold. The water in the middle of the creek went up to his chest. He stood by, waiting. He was waiting for the fish to tire out and finally rise to the surface in surrender. It was only a few minutes before the lower half of his body began to ache from the chilly waters. His quarry finally floated up. He scooped it up with his *leh-á* "sieve net." He used all his strength to heave the fish up onto the creek bank. It probably weighed at least two or three kilos.

The fish flopped every which way in the mud. Tsín-suī had already decided to let his wife take it back home to cook it with some vegetables, and so he ignored it. He moved a few feet towards the sunlight to warm himself up, then pulled his pants off to dry them in the warm light. Then he'd put them back on and walked back into the middle of the forest. As he recalled his battle with the fish, he couldn't figure out how he had won. He felt extremely pleased with himself. He thought of everything that had happened, and especially the crucial point at which he had resolutely sacrificed that *leh-á* hat to ensure his success. At this, he couldn't stop himself from laughing aloud.

Right then, he thought of commemorating the feelings that he had experienced. He found a sharp stone and began to carve characters into the tree's smooth trunk. He spent a lot of effort to carve out in Japanese, "If you want to succeed: bait, skill, patience, sacrifice." A slight smile spread across his face as he was carving the words. As he dug into the bark with each cut, he forgot about the sticky sweat that was drenching his body.

He remained in his forest prison for days on end. His wife brought news to him every day. It was obviously still not OK for him to show his face in town. On the afternoon on the twenty-first day, he was again shocked when his father arrived with Giok-ìn, supported by his younger brother Tsin-liong. His father was also carrying a cotton blanket and his own mosquito netting, along with his walking cane.

It had turned out that the weapons the military police had buried were immediately dug up the next day. The cops were going door to door to figure out who had done it, but the entire village was suspected. If anyone who was taken "out for tea" didn't give quite the right response, they'd be tortured. Tsín-suī's father was quite up there in age. He thought he wouldn't be able to stand harsh treatment, so it was much easier for him to hide out and keep company with his son.

Tsín-suī helped his father to clear a patch for him to lie down on, and his father said, "I've taken care of Mari since you weren't at home. She was quite old."

"What! What do you mean you 'took care of her'?"

"I know you were close with Mari, so I couldn't just deal with her carelessly."

"What exactly did you do?"

"I didn't quite know what to do either. I just told Uncle A-Huàn to take her and deal with her."

"Oh." Once Tsín-suī knew that Uncle A-Huàn had come to take her, his anger subsided a bit.

"Don't worry. That calf of yours is growing stronger day by day."

"Before I fled and hid myself away, I only got to see it once at night. I didn't know whether it was a bull or a cow."

"Your guess is as good as mine."

"It's actually kind of simple. If the horns are large, then it's a bull. If they're small, then it's a cow."

"Oh, is that so? Then it's probably a bull."

Tsín-suī's father was much more suited for surviving in the wild than he was. The first night, he had slept soundly.

On the morning of the second day, both father and son began chatting. Tsín-suī's father asked, "While you were asleep last night, you kept crying out, '*Oh-pa-le, oh-pa-le.*' Were you having a nightmare?"

Tsín-suī replied dispiritedly, "I wasn't dreaming. I was half-awake."

"*A-Pa*, did you happen to hear a weird *nuuuu-pah, nuuuu-pah* call last night?"

"I did. It was very noisy. Late at night in a place like these, you hear all sorts of strange sounds." Tsín-suí's father was focused intently on his son. "I think that deep down you have had a tremendous shock, and that is why you've been crying out in your sleep."

The topic of the conversation took a slight turn. "This bit of chaos is now being called the '228 Incident' in the newspapers and on the radio. We Pîn-tong-ers are calling it the 'March 4th Incident,'" his father said.

"Oh, right. Do you know what these two characters '*shi-bian*' (Chinese for 'incident') mean?" Tsín-suí opened up and went into great detail with his father about all the things that had happened those few days, what had sparked it all, and what had transpired in the end. Then he finally reached the part of his recollections where he talked about seeing with his own eyes what had happened to Iap Tshiu-bok-*hiann* and the man's utterly distraught wife and children. Waves of pain began to wash over Tsín-suí's entire body again. The more he talked, the sharper the pain grew. Tsín-suí's father listened intently to his son's story. He saw the color leave his son's face and a look of terror take over. Now his son was shaking, and his teeth were chattering as he spoke. His son lost his voice and began to sob.

Tsín-suí's father knew that his son and Iap Tshiu-bok were like two peas in a pod since the time they were both very little. He just let his son continue to cry until he couldn't anymore. He didn't say a word or make any movements to try to console him. He just patiently waited for Tsín-suí to settle down, and then he decided to tell his son something important. "A-Suí-á, you might not have known it, but Iap Tshiu-bok started off supporting a peaceful resolution to the chaos, but in the end he had to harden himself. Especially after he had been made the chairman of Pîn-tong's provisional committee. He led that group of people to the airport to wage a battle. He was brilliant."

The Ngôo patriarch mused, then he added a touch of fatherly love, "I'll ask you, when you think of that 'incident' from over twenty days ago, have you ever thought of which side—the war supporters or the peace supporters—were right?"

His father's question dragged him out of his pain and sorrow, but this question was something he kept turning over and over in his mind. He started to reply to his father, "If we look at it from what the result was, then it seems like the war supporters weren't right; but from what I feel myself, those men in the war faction had real grievances and real anger and frustrations. They should have been able to vent it all out. When the Chinese came, they just made it worse for us islanders. We're completely without hope. To be honest, deep down, I can sympathize with the war faction's proposals and actions."

"It's a shame you didn't support them!"

"When I think of the peace faction, their thoughts and actions are also something I sympathize with. I looked out at the chaos in the streets with wide, startled eyes. They were burning everything in the street. I saw how the mobs were. My heart couldn't take it. I rushed out to help people and tried to convince people not to fight. I think this came from my love for our hometown and everything we know. I was at the scene and could sense that people on both sides were fully committed to what they thought was best. Neither seemed to be overly ambitious."

"You made two big mistakes in that process."

"What mistakes?"

"The first one was when that truck carrying the machine gun came into town. They said that they wanted to help us Pîn-tongers to defend ourselves. You never should have told them to leave. They should have stayed till the end. The second was that you shouldn't have told them to give up their weapons. If you had organized all the forces and drawn a consensus, what's to say this wouldn't have changed the outcome."

Tsín-suī felt a great disconnect with the image of his father he held in his heart. "*A-Pa*, I didn't know you were so much in support of the war faction."

"When the *Tiong-kok*-á first arrived, I was filled with a lot of hope. What else could I say? They are Han peoples too. The *Jit-pún-á* are foreigners, but after two or three years, I've completely lost all of that hope. I want them all to leave. I wouldn't want the *Jit-pún-á* to come back... Maybe switching to the Americans would have been fine. It would be even better if we had none of them and if we just stood up on our own."

Tsín-suī didn't know what to say and stayed silent for a long time. His father started up again, "It's too bad, all of you who had received military training under the Japanese—"

"Even with military training, if a civil war took place, it wouldn't necessarily help. In any case, most people would probably close themselves off to it and watch from the sidelines, only wanting to protect themselves."

"The important point is the leadership's will. If they had the will, then they could change the entire situation."

Tsín-suī shot back, "Iap Tshiu-bok had heart! Initiative too. He had a strong will. But then this all happened."

"The kind of 'will' I'm talking about is the kind of thorough, resolute will and determination to get rid of the *A-suann-á* . Iap Tshiu-bok didn't have that kind of will or drive. His thoughts stopped at keeping the violence away and protecting the villages. That's just not enough. Not at all."

"Frankly, *A-Pa*, that kind of drive and determination is something we islanders somewhat lack. We don't have the training. We don't have that kind of ability."

"*Aiyee*! Since we're on it…I just want to bawl." Tsín-suī's father looked as if he was about to cry, but he kept quiet for a few seconds before continuing. "For the most part, we Taiwanese are used to being conquered. Whenever we run into horrible rulers, we all turn into scaredy-cats. Everyone's just out to save themselves… *Aiyee*… Our last Japanese governor, Gotō Shinpei, said it best, 'Taiwanese only care about money and face, but they're afraid of dying.'"

Tsín-suī didn't want to talk any more about this topic, so he switched tack again. "*A-Pa*. Since you mentioned Japanese military drills in school, have you heard anything from Tsín-bú?[30] How is he faring?"

"Last week, there was a phone call for us. He said he hoped your mother and I were safe. I asked him how he was recently. He said he was doing excellently and that he asked me not to worry. Then I told him I wanted to go to Tâi-tiong to pay him a visit. He then responded that he was going to go to the Chinese mainland any day now. He was about to depart Tâi-tiong. I then asked him what he was going to do there? He wasn't very clear about what he was going to do, but he told me not to worry. He said he'd write us as soon as he got there." When his father finished relaying

---

30 Ngôo Tsín-bú (吳振武) was Ngôo Tsín-suī's fourth youngest brother. During the Japanese colonial era, he became a naval officer in the Imperial Japanese Navy and made it to the rank of lieutenant. He was the highest-ranking Taiwanese ever in the Imperial Japanese forces. After the end of the War in the Pacific, he returned to Taiwan from Hainan Island in southern China. At the breakout of the 228 uprisings, he was nominated by a war-seeking faction in Taichung to be the leader of the "27th Brigade." He initially said he would, but then before he even left the city he was shot in the thigh and sent to a hospital. It's still a mystery to this day whether somebody else shot him or if he shot himself. After he was discharged from the hospital, he headed to Shanghai to join the Republic of China Navy where he became a teacher at the Naval College. He was a lead captain on an underwater demolition brigade. Later, due to his role in 228 being found out, his military career didn't go so smoothly. After he retired from military service, he became a physical education teacher. His own life story is no less elaborate than his older brother, Tsín-suī.

the story, he raised his head and looked towards the canopy above them and just began talking to himself. "He was a proper Japanese military officer. I don't know if he ever could sense my real feelings about all this."

"Don't give him a reason to worry, *lah*. He was always going to go abroad and—" Tsín-suī stopped mid-sentence. He picked up on the sound of feet shuffling through the forest floor. "Someone's coming, *A-Pa*." He stood up quietly, straining his ears again, listening. "Damnit. There is a person coming." As he said the words, he grabbed his father's arm and was about to run off somewhere, but a single person came climbing up from the riverbank. Father and son were startled at first, but they quickly felt some relief. It was just A-Tsòng, and he was covered completely in fetid mud, all the way up to his neck.

"I'm sorry, did I frighten you?" he said, panting, trying to regain his breath from the climb up the embankment.

"How did you find us?"

"I got it out of your youngest son, Tsin-ling."

"Aren't you afraid you were being followed?"

"Just by water ghosts! I got all the way here by wading up the river, not by land."

"Oh well, do you have any news?"

"No. There's no damned news! Uncle A-Huàn is just worried about you both. He wanted me to see with my own two eyes that you both were OK. After he hears you're fine, he'll start to eat and sleep again, so I absolutely had to come."

"*Aiyee*! This is too...," Tsín-suī's father sighed.

"Have you had anything to eat, being all the way out here?"

"Yes. Giòk-ìn-á has made sure I've had lots to eat."

"That's good then. I'm relieved for you."

"Come. Have a seat and rest a bit. When you're ready to leave, be careful."

"Yes. I'm aware." A-Tsòng sat down cross-legged and, after settling down for a couple minutes, he began, "A-Suī-á, the Iáp family business is completely dead. That Tsin-lam Shipping company was forcibly liquidated and all their assets stolen. F***! My son, Tsìng-tik, has to find a new job all over again."

"*Baka yarō*! F***! They're terrible!" Tsín-suī gritted and gnashed his teeth.

"I'd like to ask a favor of you... Can you recommend my Tsìng-tik-á to Tông Tsuān-tsong?"

"Sure, no problem." Tsín-suī thought for a moment then added, "I'm going to go home first and tell Giòk-ìn to use my name to write a letter of introduction and then run quickly to find Tông Tsuān-tsong. I think you should be able to get in touch with him. I have to stay hidden still for some time. After I've left the forest, I'll immediately give Tsuān-tsong-*hiann* a telephone call."

"Oh, thank you very much in advance, Tsín-suĭ. *To-siā, lóo-laṫ.*"

"You're welcome, no need to feel indebted. It's my pleasure."

At this, A-Tsòng quickly said, "I'd better head back now," and then he slowly waded back into the water and swam. He didn't make any large waves, and there was almost no trace on the water's surface.

With his father at his side to keep him company in his forest prison, Tsín-suĭ's days passed by a bit more quickly. After a few days, they probably wouldn't be able to hide out here anymore since the weather was becoming hotter and more unbearable. The snakes that were hibernating for winter had begun to wake from their slumber. A light early summer rain fell, so father and son decided to go back home. As they were about to go, Tsín-suĭ made a quick note of all the "diary entries" he had carved into the tree trunk. He had eight five-stroked *Tsiann* characters. He'd been out in the wilds for exactly forty days.

When they returned to civilization, they found that the situation wasn't as tense as it was a month earlier. Tsín-suĭ had to vigorously scrub himself to become clean. When he came out of the wash house, he told his wife, "I wasn't able to bathe for forty days, and my whole body was coated with a thick layer of dirt. It was like a protective film, and now it's been washed away, I feel kind of naked, like I'm not used to being clean anymore."

Giȯk-ìn laughed at him, "You're being silly!"

The both of them went to the cow pen. It was empty, because it was bereft of Mari. Tsín-suĭ stepped into the pen with a great stride. A small buffalo calf huddled in the corner timidly raised its head. He moved towards the calf and crouched down about halfway to stare it in the face. Ah! The calf has got its mother's great, big expressive eyes. It was like a mix of fear and grace. Tsín-suĭ couldn't help but think of Mari. He stretched an arm out and lightly patted the calf on its cheek. He followed the soft calf's hairs up towards the top of its head and patting it on the head around where its horns would grow out. He lightly tapped on each spot three times and then with both hands together, smoothened out the calf's fur, beginning to speak with it. "We sent your mom away too quickly. I'm so sorry for you, little one. We've hurt you by making you lonely. I'm so sorry. You're safe here. You can grow up nice and strong at your own pace. My wife and I will take great care of you." He tapped at the calf's tailbone three times, as if finishing some sort of ritual. He took his hands back and clapped them three times. It was a bit strange to Tsín-suī. The calf suddenly tried leaning towards him and then began head-butting and nuzzling Tsín-suī along his thigh. Its little tail swayed left and right and then made a circle as if painting with a calligraphy brush.

Giŏk-ìn had a moment of mother's intuition and understood this calf's love deep down in her heart. That was the secret to Uncle A-Huàn's teachings on the art of training cattle. Truly, he must have been half-god, half-demon. The next day, Tsín-suī went back home with his wife. His mother-in-law had cooked up a delicious meal of roasted pork knuckles and thin noodles. But they hadn't even finished dinner when they heard something ominous: there was trouble at the Tông Îng Steel Mill.

"I don't know who reported him. They said that after the Japanese navy left, they had sold the Tông Îng Steel Mill over in Tsó-iânn (Tsuo-ying). I don't know how he was suddenly seen as a collaborator against the Chinese. The president of the company, Tông-A-Tsuān-tsong, was arrested. Such a massive factory like that was just confiscated in plain sight."

Tsín-suī simply stopped chewing and couldn't eat anymore. His face turned from red to purple, and he began to yell, *"Baka yarō*! This *A-Suann-á* (derogatory name for Chinese) government is absolutely rotten to the core!" Then he lowered his voice a bit. "Tsuān-tsong-*hiann* doesn't know what to do now. I'll have to visit him in the stockade and try to console him."

"You still have a case against you, and it hasn't been settled. If you go, they'll just throw you in a cage at the earliest opportunity."

"*Baka*!" Tsín-suī's anger was almost uncontrollable. "The entire factory was confiscated??? So how does that help any of the employees in the company? There are several thousands of them! All these people's hard work, their property… Just like that… It's just taken away, just like that??? Where the hell is the reasoning behind any of this madness? *Baka ne*!"

"The big boss, Tông A-Îng, and many of his friends were hit hard by the confiscation and nearly swept away. They were hoping to be able to salvage the insurance first."

Suddenly, Tsín-suī dropped his head and pressed his hands deep into his scalp. He then began holding his chest, then he pressed down on his right shoulder. Giŏk-ìn looked at the beads of sweat growing on his forehead and how his face looked twisted and contorted. "*Aiyee*! What's wrong!?" Tsín-suī couldn't speak. His wife asked him again, "It's that pain you were talking about. It's back now, right?"

Tsín-suī just nodded in response. She heard her mother calling for the pedicab chauffeur. Giok-ìn stopped her while helping her husband towards a guest room. Not long after, his despondent wails issued through the door.

Ông *thài-thài* and everyone else in the Ông household gathered at the bedroom door to try to listen. They made out that it was Tsín-suī's wails and not Giok-ìn's. Pained grimaces of curiosity and doubt filled everyone's faces as the sound of wailing quickly affected all of them. Ông *thài-thài* and Giok-ìn's brother's wife began to shed tears when they heard his pained sobs.

Several minutes later, Giok-ìn went into the room alone. "Should we send him to see the doctor?" her mother asked, right before her daughter went in.

"No. We don't need to." Giok-ìn lightly patted her chest and then said, "It's the first time I've seen him cry out like this. Hah. It's quite a shock to see his hurt and pain morph into this." She took a deep breath then began speaking again, "He said when he fled into the forest, he thought about the tragedy that had befallen Iap Tshiu-bok. He said it had happened three times. Each time he would wail, and that same pain would well up in him again."

"It looks to me like he needs to go see a doctor to see what kind of illness it is."

"I told him he needs to go see a doctor. He keeps saying he doesn't need to." Giok-ìn continued, "It's not just that. Ever since he came back from the forest, whenever he's sleeping at night, I can hear him talking in his sleep. I keep trying to listen carefully to what he's saying. He keeps calling out, '*Oh-pa-le*,' in his dreams. 'I'm afraid.'"

"*Aiyee!*" Ông *thài-thài* sighed.

Giok-ìn's sister-in-law pointed out, "There's no sound coming from the bedroom."

"Right. He's quiet now. Let him rest. Let's go over there," Giok-ìn said.

Tsín-suī hadn't even been back for more than two days before the district chief, Lîm Kiàn-bûn, came over looking for him. The two men had been longtime acquaintances. The district chief just came out with the topic point blank, "Where did you go to *soo-khai*? Everyone's been searching for you for a long time. You have a legal case against you. You need to try to resolve it as soon as possible."

"That's strange! What case do I have against me? Well, tell me! What is it I have to settle?"

"You know very well what you did. If you don't, then why did you go on the run for so long? I came here to give you some good advice and help you resolve your case."

"Then how should I resolve it?"

"You need to write a 'Letter of self-reform' is all."

"And how do you write one of those?"

"You don't need to write anything. I've already prepared one for you." The district chief pulled out a stamped letter from his briefcase and handed it over to Tsín-suī. "Sign your name and put your name seal on it, and then you're done."

Tsín-suī looked down to give the letter a closer look. When he saw the words "Blindly involved in violent acts," in large font, he flushed up in anger. "*Baka yarō*! I was one of the people trying to STOP the violence. How could I possibly be charged with being 'being blindly involved in violent acts?'"

"That's just what those at the top have specified."

"I was never 'blindly involved in violent acts.' Why should I sign?"

"This is just a formality. If you sign it, then the case is finished."

"I won't sign. Even if you dragged me out to execute me with a gun, I wouldn't sign it."

"If that's the case, I'll take you to the party headquarters tomorrow to meet with a councillor. His surname is Chen. You can directly consult him on the matter." The district chief took his leave after he relayed this to Tsín-suī, and then, after he'd already stepped over the threshold to the main entrance of the Ngôo household, he turned back and said in half-Taiwanese, half-Chinese, "A-Suī-á, I'm warning you in good faith—I'm begging you, actually. You need to stop using that phrasing from now on. You need to stop saying '*Baka yarō*,' especially when you're speaking with Chinese officials."

Tsín-suī practiced using Chinese to respond to the district chief. "Su... su de. (Yes...yes.) Thank you for your concern," he said as he led the other man to his car. Right as they reached the passenger door, he asked him, "If I can't say '*baka yarō*' to yell at people, then what's the Chinese phrase I should use?"

"They've switched to saying '*ma-la-ge-bi*.'"

"*Ma-la-ge-bi. Ma-la-ge-bi.* Seems like a good phrase."

On the second day, Tsín-suī arrived on schedule at the party headquarters. He sat meekly in the guest room and waited for a very long time, but he was fidgeting, unable to stand waiting for this Chen councillor fellow to ever appear. He wondered if there was some sort of trap. He was just thinking that maybe it'd be smarter to flee, when he saw District Chief Lîm Kiàn-bûn accompanying a middle-aged mainlander out of the office. The district chief was at their side, bowing to the man with clasped hands and with a fake smile on his face. Tsín-suī stood up from his chair and walked towards him, "Pardon me, are you the councillor? My name is Ngôo Tsín-suī."

The councillor's face was like a coffin. He said, "Mr. Ngôo, your case has been made clear, but we still need to settle the matter of your father's case."

"My father?"

"Don't ask me. Your father's case is being handled personally by the mayor, Hong Lyu-duan. He's over in the next room right now. He wants to set up a time to meet with you."

He was taken aback when this Mayor Hong, whom he'd never met before, called out his name as soon as he saw his face. "Mr. Wu Chen-jui, your case is pretty simple to clear up...but your father's..."

Tsín-suī very nervously searched for words, and in broken Chinese, he said, "My father? He's such an old man who's not all quite there. What could he have possibly done?"

Mayor Hong's expression was deeply serious and grave, and his response was as sharp as a sword, "The police bureau buried several weapons and ammunition caches in your village. Your father and his friends had the nerve to dare to give those weapons and ammo to the rioters."

Tsín-suī shot back as if his fingers had been burned, touching a hot clothes iron. "That couldn't be. It's absolutely impossible! He's already got one foot in the grave, he's deaf, can't walk properly, and can't see clearly. Our village head over in the local temple even refers to him as 'old saint.'" He thought of what Iap Tshiu-bok had told him before, that this was a maelstrom that would swallow up and destroy entire families. Tsín-suī felt he had no choice but to flat out deny everything.

"We heard about it through the confession of a rioter. There's no mistake."

"Who was it that told you that? I want you to tell them to come out and look me in the eye when they say that."

"That hooligan was already executed. Damn it! The bastard died way too fast! However, we'll have to verify it through other means. We'll wait three days and if nobody goes to your house to arrest him, then the whole ordeal is over."

And just like that, Tsín-suī went once more with his father to hide in that stretch of forest. The entire family was petrified for three days and nights, but the military police never came. In the end, they went back home, greeted by happy people who were grateful to heaven for this stroke of luck. Even the calf was brought out to celebrate.

On the way home, Tsín-suī caught wind of a new bit of information. The Tông Îng Steel Mill case judgment was overturned and settled. The mill was returned to the Tôngs, and Tsuān-tsong was set free. Tsín-suī reminded his wife, "We should arrange a time for my mother and several of the migrants from Phênn-ôo to take a car over and pay them a visit. We should go see Tsuān-tsong-*hiann*, console him, and give him our support."

"OK. I'll arrange it with my mother, then."

9

All in all, there were about a dozen or so of the Phênn-ôo family members and kin who had been led into Director Tông Tsuān-tsong's office. His father, Tông Ĩng, had a great big smile on his face as he greeted everyone. Tsuān-tsong just stood at the door shaking hands and exchanging a word or two with everyone as they came into the room. Each of them was greeted very swiftly and not with much warmth to give.

The warm and inviting sounds of the Phênn-ôo accent floated around in the spacious but plain office.

"Hah! A-Tsuān-tsong, you haven't changed a bit since you were a kid. You look great. You're still just as gracious and grounded as ever, the spitting image of a great industrialist!" they poked fun at him.

Two men came forward. One man grabbed Tsuān-tsong's hand up and said, "Aiyah! A-Tsuān-tsong! We thought you were a goner for sure. We kept hearing others saying that 'traitors' would be executed. This government loves nothing more than to shoot people. I'm extremely grateful that you're alive."

"They're still killing people in Pîn-tong!"

A burst of loud crashing noises suddenly erupted from outside the office. Tông Ĩng shouted excitedly, "*A-Ha*! We've started up the furnaces again today!"

Tsuān-tsong shifted his feet as someone else moved forward and tightly gripped his hand, "There's been enough trouble already! You're a sincere and loyal businessman. This government's got shit for eyes!"

"It wasn't anything too bad! They only locked me up for a week or two. Fortunately, they let me go rather quickly."

Tsín-suī stood at the back of the group of the Phênn-ôo friends and relatives. He noticed that Tsuān-tsong-*hiann* was wearing a Western suit and necktie. His hair was slicked back with pomade, but these things couldn't conceal the sense of the painful ordeal that he had just endured still lingering on his face.

Tsín-suī took both Tsuān-tsong's hands in his and was silent for a while. Finally, he spoke, "Ha! You almost never wore a *se-pit-lô*[31] before. You're looking very dashing today!"

"I wear it for work. I look more fit when I wear it."

Tông Îng called out in a loud voice, "Yes! You have to look like you're in good spirits. Everything has to be started all over."

Two workers came in carrying trays of tea and light snacks. Tông Îng gathered everyone around, "Come! Sit! Sit! Let's sit. Our A-Tsuān-tsong has always managed to pick himself up and dust himself off when he's fallen down. Everyone, rest assured."

A relative who had just plopped himself down in a chair spoke, "But... This *Tiong-kok-á* government is truly monstrous—"

Tông Îng stopped the relative from continuing in his deduction. "We were incorrect in our own behavior. It's because we were too greedy and wanted to acquire the place for cheap, having gone to the Japanese before things were settled. The Japanese were our enemy. Their property was meant to be for the public. How could our rightful government just let anyone help themselves to what the Japanese had left behind?"

Everybody just sat in silence and stared at Tông Îng. He continued, but this time with more force in his voice, "Our government was right. Our company was in the wrong. That we should be punished was the upright thing to do. We deserved it. We have no right to complain."

Tsuān-tsong, seemingly unsettled by his father's continued praise of their new government, decided to switch the topic. "Everyone, keep drinking your tea and keep the conversation light. A-Tsín-suī and Giȯk-ìn would like to take a tour of the mill. I'll take them and show them around."

The three of them bantered a bit as they walked along, visiting every nook and cranny of the mill. When they got close to the great gate to the factory, Tsuān-tsong was in high spirits. He opened up a bit in relief, having gotten away from the oppressive presence of his father. "Over here... Let me show you... Right where we're standing now, they've just changed the name of this main street here. It's now called San-duo Road. All the way to our right, there's another big road which has just changed names. It's called Chung-shan Road. Far to our left, can you see it? That over there is Cheng-kung Road. Right... And over behind, to the south, is Hsin-Kuang Road."

---

31. *Se-pit-lô*; originally the Japanese word, "sebiro," or business suit thought to have derived from tailor shops in Seville Row in London."

"Hah! This road's bigger than half our village in Pîn-tong! How did you all manage to buy such a massive factory and the land?" Tsín-suī followed up and asked.

"Because this is the closest place to Lêng-ngá-liâu. It's farmland all around, but it's not as fertile as the fields in Pîn-tong. You can hardly grow anything out here, so the land value was extremely cheap. I had suggested it to my father. If we were going to set up a factory, we had to prepare to buy up a big chunk of land."

"You were importing pig iron. Are you able to smelt steel yet?"

"No, unfortunately. Right now, we're just making steel parts. Later, we're planning on designing our own machines and making steel parts for building cars and locomotives."[32]

"During the time that the Chinese government confiscated the factory, was there any damage done to it?"

"Of course, we took a hit. Our losses were massive. I started to think we wouldn't be able to open up, and I didn't know what to do. Who could I possibly have gone to in this rotten government about the troubles we were facing? When they brand you with some frightful name and confiscate your factory, and then they have the gall to remove your property. Hunh! We were staring death in the face." All of the good spirits had left Tsuān-tsong by then. If he were a sunny day, there were now storm clouds all around. "Afterwards, my father convinced me that I absolutely had to open the factory. He said, 'They're over on the mainland fighting a civil war with the Communists. They need a lot of war supplies on the front. Give them what they want! We'll have to spend a lot of money trying to have better relations with them!'"

Tsín-suī stayed silent in response. Tsuān-tsong repeated, "Man! Once is enough. It was enough to scare you out of your wits."

"Is it because of that mainlander secretary over in the office next door that your father took it upon himself to confess?" Tsín-suī asked.

"It wasn't necessarily because of that. I believe that it's his business philosophy. He's often told me that no matter who's in charge of the government, there will always be lions and tigers waiting for a slipup. We businessmen have to contend with them."

"You're a parent yourself now, but you've only said a few words. Can you truly just accept that and put it behind you?"

---

32. At the time, Taiwan didn't have any industrialized areas. China Steel Corporation hadn't yet been established. There were only two companies at the time engaged in the business. People called them "Bei-Tatung" (the predecessor to Tatung) and "Nan Tang-Ying" (Tông Îng here in this novel). They were the trailblazers to Taiwan's industrialization.

"My father's tried convincing me nonstop to just forget it, that I should just completely push it out of my mind. After today, I will need to keep trying to placate them. I'll have to work extremely hard to kiss up to them, until everything's smoothed over. We have work to do under their heel. We must kiss up to them. We have no choice."

Hearing Tsuān-tsong talk about things in this way, Tsín-suī and his wife had lost all enthusiasm to continue on their tour. They went silent. The three of them walked along without seeming to look at anything in particular. Without knowing it, they'd walked all the way to the back side of the steel mill. The back of the mill was next to Hsin-kuang Road. There was a farming village right nearby. There were row upon row of fields spread out before them. Just as they were thinking of going back to the chairman's office, they suddenly heard the plaintive cries of an ox. It was the call of an ox crying out in excruciating pain. Tsín-suī felt most sensitive to it, and his eyes scanned every which way to seek out where the cries were coming from. He realized the calls were coming from beneath a cluster of banyan trees next to a farmer's hut and shed. Frantically, he said, "Tsuān-tsong-*hiann*, I'm going to go take a look. You should take Giok-ìn-á back first."

As he spoke, he had already begun running along the embankments between the paddies, slipping this way and that. His shoes and the bottoms of his pants were now completely caked in mud. He hadn't even reached the banyans when he spotted a farmer holding a long needle meant for sewing up heavy grain sacks. There was a brazier with coals burning hotly. The needle point was already glowing red-hot. He was right in the middle of trying to pierce the ox's nostrils for placing a leading ring. The farmer obviously hadn't succeeded the first time and he was just now gearing up to try piercing the bull's nose again. Tsín-suī was paying so much attention to the scene that he fell right into a paddy. It took a lot of effort to get back up on top of the embankment, and then he noticed that coarse ropes were tied to both of the ox's horns, which were then tied up tightly to a tree trunk. The ox was extremely vexed and was trying desperately to escape. It kept shaking its head to the left and right. Tsín-suī was nearly out of breath from rushing over, but he began to curse the farmer, "F***. You absolute fool. F*** you for being so stupid."

It still took him a while to finally reach the trees. "Stop! Stop, stop!" Tsín-suī was waving his hands in the air. He forgot he was just some stranger from the street, shouting out like a crazy person. "*Wei*! You can't treat your ox that way! What you're doing to it is absolute torture! You shouldn't do that!"

The farmer then put down his work. A group of villagers had come out to see what all the fuss was about. The farmer kept thinking, "Who the hell is this person?" None of the crowd wanted to make eye contact. Tsín-suī took great strides towards the buffalo, knelt down, and after inspecting its face, saw that its nose had very obviously been stabbed and seared into an ugly, painful pulp of red and black, bleeding quite profusely. Its nostrils, which were originally a chocolatey mousse color, had been dyed a very fresh crimson. He didn't know where exactly the rage had come from, but as soon as it surfaced, it burst forth like a volcano. "*Baka yarō*! What the f*** did this buffalo ever do to you?! Why did you have to torture it!? *Honnh*! You have no idea how to pierce an ox's nose. You can't just stab it any which place. You don't know what the f*** you're doing, do you?!" As he was berating the farmer, he wanted to reach out and grab the rope and free the bull from its torture session.

Having just been strongly berated by some stranger from nowhere, the farmer erupted in anger too. He took a giant step in front of the buffalo, gestured at Tsín-suī to get away, but he didn't have the strength to do anything. Instead, the man shot back at Tsín-suī, "And who the hell are you? This is MY business. You can f*** off! *Honnh*!"

The farmer was growing more irritated by the second. Tsín-suī followed up by taking two steps back, then softened his tone. "I'm trying to teach you. You have to first feel an ox's nose with your fingertips. You'll feel there's two bits of soft cartilage. There's a soft spot between that cartilage. That's where you can pierce its nose and run a rope through. You have to pierce it with effort and strength, and you have to be able to pierce it within one or two seconds. You absolutely cannot use an awl or needle that's been fired up red-hot, like you did just now. It's just like randomly stabbing it. Your ox is in a lot of pain. It's too much for it to handle. It's absolutely barbaric... You're a monster."

The ox could sense that a savior had made its way over to relieve its suffering, and it bellowed out in a pleading cry. It kept trying to sway its head and horns. It wanted to break free from the ropes tethering its horns to the tree branch. Just then, Tsín-suī calmly said, "The buffalo's in too much pain. It's in too much pain." He took another glimpse at the buffalo as it was crying out and struggling, and unconsciously, his anger burst forth from deep down in his belly again and he began to berate the farmer. "You're so cruel to that buffalo. *Ma-la-ge-bi*! You truly are a *ma-la-ge-bi*!" He then regained control of himself after he cursed him twice, then switched back to imploring, "Please. I'm begging you to quickly cut your buffalo free, OK? I'm begging you."

"You can go f*** right off! Who the hell are you? *Honnh*? This buffalo has nothing to do with you. You're f***ing demented!" The farmer's voice cracked as he screamed back at Tsín-suī, flying into a fit of shamed rage. It didn't look like he was going to let up on the rope tied to the buffalo's horns.

Tsín-suī tried once more to reason with the farmer and convince him. He said in a soft-spoken pleading tone, "*Nii-san*, hey. I'm just seeing that your buffalo is in great pain. It's unhappy. Its voice is agitated. It's asking you not to be cruel towards it. Who am I? I'm the pupil of a *gû-sian-á* (ox whisperer) named Uncle A-Huàn, who lives over on the opposite side of the Lower Tăm-tsuí River. He's taught me much about buffalo—"

Someone off in the crowd of farm villagers cried out, "Oh, A-Huàn-tsik-á. I've heard of him."

Tsín-suī looked at the man's body language as he was speaking and felt that he could finally do something, so he slowly stretched out a hand to untether the buffalo from the rope. The farmer gave up his protest. The villager in the crowd that had spoken up came forward to give Tsín-suī a hand. Both Tsín-suī's hands were preoccupied, but he continued speaking and switched to yet another tone. And in his own brotherly way of speaking, he told the villager, "Please bring me a bowl of clean water. We need to wash the buffalo's wound first. After two or three days, the wound should have scarred over. Trying to pierce its nose again will be much more difficult, so I might need to get my teacher to come out himself to do it. Two weeks from now, I'll give Uncle A-Huàn a ride out here on my motorcycle. He's got a special pair of piercing needles. Once it's done, he won't charge you anything. Until that time, please don't try to pierce the buffalo's nose anymore, OK?"

As he relaxed the lead rope, he turned his gaze and saw out of the corner of his eye that his wife and Tsuān-tsong were standing in the middle of the crowd of people. His wife seemed to have a slight look of embarrassment on her face, but Tsuān-tsong-*hiann*, on the other hand, was beaming with a smile. He then saw the farmer taking the brazier back into the house. As everything wrapped up, he told everyone gathered around, "I'm sorry. I've bothered you enough already. I'm leaving now," in a loud voice. He made a ninety-degree Japanese-style bow at the waist and, with Giòk-ìn and Tsuān-tsong at his side, headed back towards the steel mill.

When they were up on the road, Tsuān-tsong began speaking, "The two of us should take a different, easier road back. I wanted to tell them I was the president of the Tông Îng Steel Mill up ahead. I thought they'd be a lot more polite. A lot of them work in our mill."

"Well, if you had said something earlier, it would've saved me a whole lot of trouble."

"Next time, I think you won't try to barge in like you did. Your temper's gonna get you into trouble. Once you lost your reasoning, you had to try hard to get everything back under control. I thought you did a pretty good job though. I've got to admire your skill."

Tsín-suī didn't respond. Tsuān-tsong kept talking, "I can't figure out though what it means... What did you mean when you kept shouting 'ma-la-ge-bi' those two times?"

"Oh, that. Our district chief, Lîm Kiàn-bûn, told me that we can't use Japanese insults like '*baka yarō*' anymore. He said the *Tiong-kok-á* are used to '*ma-la-ge-bi*.' The two words are supposed to mean the same thing."

"These two words aren't exactly the same, Tsín-suī. What's important is that when that '*ma-la-ge-bi*' comes out of your mouth, it just sounds off! It's like an ox trying to speak as if it were a horse. I think you ought to not use that anymore when chewing someone out."

"Oh! Well, OK then!"

***

Two weeks later, Tsín-suī went to see Dr. Kueh It-tsing. As soon as he saw him, he felt a huge difference in the doctor's disposition. Where was the Dr. Kueh who was helping people out in the street during the March Massacres? He hadn't seen the good doctor in just a handful of months, and yet he looked like he had aged twenty years! His cheeks were no longer filled with a warm, pink of life. His eyes had become sunken and sullen. The corners of his mouth were wrinkled and sagged down deeply. His lower jaw and his neck seemed to have shrunk slightly. Tsín-suī felt stiff as a corpse in his presence. He couldn't bring himself to speak. He wanted desperately to ask the doctor about his younger sister. He wanted to know how she—Iap Tshiu-bok's surviving wife—was holding on. But he just couldn't get the words to come out. Dr. Kueh very quickly took Tsín-suī by the arm and pulled him into the clinic. He very warmly asked Tsín-suī, "Did you come to me because you are ill?"

"No. I wanted to ask you if I could borrow your motorcycle. I would just need it for a day."

"Where are you going to ride it off to?"

"I'd like to take Uncle A-Huàn over to another village to help someone put a nose ring on their water buffalo."

"Sure. Go ahead and take it. It's out back." Dr. Kueh fetched a key from out of a drawer, and then said to Tsín-suī as he handed him the key, "Put in a good word for me wherever you go."

"I owe you a lot for this, Dr. Kueh." Tsín-suī was already standing up, but then he sat back down. "I have a strange illness... I wanted to see you about it, but I didn't feel I could come to you earlier."

"Oh, what's the matter?"

"The day the thing happened to Tshiu-bok-*hiann*, I fled off someplace and hid away for over a month. I only just recently had the case against me closed."

"What case against you?"

"They said that I had 'blindly committed violence.'"

"*Baka yarō*, those *Tshing-kok-lau*" (Chinese)."

"When I was hiding out, each time I thought of Tshiu-bok-*hiann*, his wife, and their two kids, my entire body would be washed over in pain. It was an excruciating pain."

"Does it cover your entire stomach and head in pain?"

"Not just that. It's my entire body. It's like being pierced with needles. It's worse than being burned."

"And how about now? Are you still feeling this pain?"

"It hurts so much sometimes that I cry out, and after I've shed my tears, the pain begins to lessen."

"Oh, that... I've experienced it. It's just about the same as what I've been feeling."

"You're also feeling the same?"

"I've had serious stomach cramping, constant diarrhea. I had diarrhea practically for a month. My head... Oh... It was like being split open with an axe."

"So how did you get better?"

"This is a matter of the heart, I'm afraid. There's no medicine that'll cure it. The only thing that can mend this kind of pain is time. However, there's no hope for my younger sister. It's just too much for her. She's completely beside herself and has lost her mind. It's too painful to even think about..." Dr. Kueh didn't want to keep speaking. He couldn't. He just kept choking on his words.

Tsín-suī stood up once more. He knew if he kept on talking about Tshiu-bok, the pain was going to come back as swift as a specter to haunt him and tie up his mind like some demon. But he couldn't help but pry for just a little bit more information, "Ah, so what about the two children then? What's become of them?"

"They're living with me. I'm trying my best to watch over them and to console them, but their wounds and terror will haunt them for the rest of their lives. That I'm sure of."

"*Aiyee*! Well, I just needed to come for the motorcycle, Dr. Kueh. We'll have to find another day to sit down together again and catch up."

"I'll take you around back to fetch it." Dr. Kueh obviously wanted to keep talking, so they talked as they headed out back. "A-Suī-á, there's something I regret very greatly."

"What's that?"

"That day when we were in front of the Pîn-tong train station and a large truck came by with a bunch of armed men. They had mounted a machine gun up at the front. I think you probably remember it. It was just the two of us telling them to leave. That was a massive mistake."

"How strange! That's exactly what my father thought."

"What did your father have to say on the matter?"

"He said that we should have kept the men and the weapons and reorganized our troops and not only protected our own homes here in Pîn-tong but drive the *Tshing-kok-lau* out. He kept saying that over those several days—if there had been real, strong leadership, then we would have had a chance to change the entire game."

"Ah! They were right when they told us we'd regret it. If we could relive this event, I'd definitely have picked up a rifle and joined them in the fight."

"Dr. Kueh, I have another pain that I haven't told you about. Since what happened to Tshiu-bo̍k-*hiann*, after I returned from my hide-out, I keep talking in my sleep, screaming. I keep calling out, '*o-phah-le, o-phah-le.*' I'm in quite a bind. My wife is starting to sleep more and more in her own room, away from me."

"Is your talking in your sleep beginning to lessen at all?"

"Sometimes I feel like it's getting better, and sometimes I feel like it's getting worse."

"Come back when you have more time. I'll take you to see a specialist."

***

It was the first time Uncle A-Huàn had ridden a motorcycle in his nearly seventy years on this earth. The wind whipped at his face, scaring him and making his heart thud almost audibly. He also seemed to be farting along with the rhythm of the motorcycle engine out of fear. Or maybe that was his age catching up with him. After they had crossed the bridge over the

Lower Tamsui River, the old man glanced down at the vast riverbed expanse spread out under the bridge. He held on to Tsín-suī's waist very tightly, nearly clawing into him. He had to strain to speak, "A-Suī, next time we come to Kaohsiung, we ought to take a cart and hitch it up to a buffalo."

They had reached the village located behind the Tông-Îng foundry, and the news had spread that the motorcycle had arrived. Nearly half the village crowded around Uncle A-Huàn. They were all shoulder to shoulder just to catch a glimpse of this famed "ox-whisperer." The people at the front of the crowd relayed his features, one by one, passing along descriptions of him to people further back who couldn't catch a glimpse of the man. They all said, "He looks hideous. He's so old. One of his eyes is completely glazed over white, blinded." Since the paddock was very small, only Uncle A-Huàn, Tsín-suī, and the buffalo's owner could go in. The villagers were clamoring over each other to try to see what was happening.

Uncle A-Huàn pieced the buffalo's nose cartilage even quicker than it took to ride the motorcycle out there—even before the owner's wife brewed tea for their guests from Pîn-tong. She had caught a chicken to kill. Then everyone heard a vigorous shout, "OK, OK! A-Suī-á, let's head back now."

The rumors among the villagers immediately began flying left and right. "Ah! So it is the '*gû-sian-á*' ('buffalo saint'). He did it in just two or three swift moves! What a master! I heard someone say he's so skilled that only a single, tiny drop of blood fell, and the buffalo didn't even make so much as a grunt!" The villagers' sighs rose and fell.

The buffalo's owner tried everything to get them to stay. But when Uncle A-Huàn heard him, he didn't respond to these tales of his skills. He just cocked his head slightly to the side and began to critique them. "Your buffalo here is already eight months old. It's a bull. Usually, a bull will have its nose ring put in while it's still four to six months old. This bull will be very powerful and strong when it's older. You need to treat it very well. When it's older, it can bring you back a lot of wealth. You should take it often for mud baths and make sure to feed it lots of grass until it's completely full." As he finished speaking, he pointed over to Tsín-suī and said, "A-Suī-á told me that you were torturing this poor bull. You absolutely cannot do that! Don't you hurt it again! This buffalo came into this world to bring you wealth, so you have to treat it well. Do you understand me?"

"I understand. We understand. We'll definitely treat it well. We most certainly will."

The bull owner's family didn't have any money to pay him, so they grabbed two chickens. They used strings made from grass fiber to tie up their wings and feet, then stuffed them into a large sack. They hung it from the back of the motorcycle. One bird on each side. Uncle A-Huàn didn't protest their gift.

The motorcycle started up again, and the engine's roaring to life startled the chickens so much they kept squawking and squawking, livening up the little farm village. Several of the smaller children followed behind the motorcycle as it leisurely slipped away. They ran after it jumping and touching it as a kind of sending off.

Uncle A-Huàn was still clinging tightly to Tsín-suī's waist. The first thing he said was, "Both those chickens are so heavy. They keep moving around too. Are you sure this motorcycle can get us all back to Pîn-tong in one piece?"

"Sure it can. Don't worry, Uncle."

"And what about your own calf? Have you figured out how old it is? How many moons have passed?"

"More than five months. We're coming up on half a year old, soon."

"You can get a nose ring put in too. Do you want to do it yourself, or do you want me to help you do it?"

"I can do it myself. It's no trouble." Tsín-suī brought the motorcycle to a full stop for a moment. "That calf... I've given a lot of thought to what I want to name it. I'm going to call it Masa. It's a Japanese name. It means something like 'enduring bravery and righteousness.'"

"You truly are a strange man, do you know that? I'll never understand why you want to give a buffalo a name."

They had arrived at Uncle A-Huàn's in one piece, just as Tsín-suī had said, and he drove them up to the gate of Uncle A-Huàn's house. Tsín-suī carefully and slowly helped his old neighbor off of the motorcycle. He asked him for some advice, "Once I've pierced his nose and given him a rope ring, how soon do you think I can start putting him in the field to work?"

"Don't do it so soon. Before a buffalo is a full year old, its spine and hind legs still aren't strong enough. They're too supple and tender. Wait for its horns to come up, and then it should be OK. At first, you need to have it pull an oxcart. Later, you can train it to plow your fields and paddies."

"Sure. I see now."

Three days after they had made their day trek out to Ko-hiông, ill-received news had arrived at Tsín-suī's doorstep—Uncle A-Huàn had passed away and gone off to the Western Paradise. He wasn't sick, nor was he in any pain. He just naturally slipped away in his sleep and dreams. He had lived a full life, having reached the ripe old age of seventy-one.

Tsín-suī was completely beside himself. Although there was a great gulf between them in terms of age, they had been good friends for decades. He was Uncle A-Huàn's unacknowledged disciple for the past few years. He decided he would read a eulogy in front of the memorial altar with Uncle A-Huàn's spirit plaque and other funerary effects on the day of the funeral to send him off on his journey. Tsín-suī sat, neck craned over pieces of paper in front of his desk, mired in thought. How should he write the eulogy? Should he write it in *Han-bun* (Chinese)? He could write out all the characters he'd need, but he couldn't pronounce them correctly. Uncle A-Huàn wouldn't have understood it anyway. Japanese then? Uncle A-Huàn didn't really know that either. So should he write it out in Hoklo? This all-too-difficult decision was racking Tsín-suī's brain.

Tsín-suī strained to write one character, then one sentence and pull them together. He worked on it into the early hours of the morning before he finally finished.

The day of the funeral, the mourning hall was set up in an open lot next to the family home. It was essentially a tent made of canvas. There seemed to be an endless stream of mourners who came out to send off Uncle A-Huàn. They'd all received his help back in the past. They were those who had heard of his fame. They all crowded the street. When Tsín-suī's family finally made their way up to the spirit altar under the tent, they offered flowers and burned incense for Uncle A-Huàn. Tsín-suī began reading his eulogy, calling out loudly into the ether, wanting Uncle A-Huàn to hear him. None of the other villagers and friends and guests had heard a eulogy read as loudly, and everyone stopped to listen curiously as Tsín-suī read.

> Uncle A-Huàn, you're an 'ox-whisperer' of the first rate. Your A-Suī-á is here. He wants to tell you *sayōnara* (farewell). Please go easily on your road home.
>
> You've helped so many people to treat their sick oxen and buffalo. You helped them all, those with money, and those without. Whenever you heard that there was an ox somewhere in a great deal of pain, you always went out of your way, whether you had a cart to carry you or not. Oftentimes, you just went right on foot, going as far as it took, sometimes crossing over bridges, fording streams. All of this was to care for precious animals. Oxen are us farmers' best helpers. They're strong and resilient and patient, and they are forever being ill-treated

by their owners. In all my life, I have only ever seen you learn about, love, and care for buffalo and oxen with the spirit of a whole generation. You were their best friend. You were their best veterinarian. You were their greatest defender. When you defended them, it was out of a farmer's spirit and mindset. Us villagers can't go on without you. And there will never be anyone else like you ever again.

Uncle A-Huàn, great changes might be happening all around us, but you always lived in your own world, living in a world for buffalo and oxen. When the Qing dynasty was trying to lord over you, you didn't bother studying Manchurian. When the Japanese were here for half a century, you didn't bother learning their speech either. Even in these most recent years, the Republic of China has come to rule over you, but you also didn't bother to learn their national language. You've used the language of your parents for your whole life, and now you can rest easy and bask in relaxation for once. When you were with us, you were running off every which way. You wore the simplest of clothes and ate the plainest of food. Not once did you ever know that you were such an important person to all of us.

Uncle A-Huàn, today, I'm here. I want to solemnly tell you to-siā, *lóo-làt* (thank you). You've labored hard. As a member of a later generation, I come here to offer you incense, pay my respects, and offer you some of the most delicious bananas that we've planted with our own hands. Alas! all is lost for us with your presence missing. I wholeheartedly hope that you are able to enjoy what we offer to you.

Tsín-suī did his best to finish his elegy. He sat kneeling on the soft cushion in front of the altar, with his head bowed and his shoulders shaking. Two others slowly and lightly walked forward. Giòk-ìn came up to his right and A-Tsòng to his left. They both took him by the hands and helped him up and walked him back to their seats. The entire funerary tent was solemn and silent. It was as if the entire venue was steeped in the emotions of his elegy.

"A-Tsín-suī, you forgot to mention something. Uncle A-Huàn could speak with buffalo and oxen. And beyond that, he spoke to them in Hoklo," A-Tsòng said in a voice that was neither too loud nor a whisper.

Many of the other mourners heard A-Tsòng speaking, and their faces warmed.

The funerary procession meandered along the country roads towards the burial site. Tsín-suī and Giòk-ìn walked shoulder to shoulder. A few moments later, A-Tsòng walked up beside them. He asked something completely unrelated to the funeral, "A-Tsín-suī, have you ever been involved in the Ko-hiông Green Fruits Collective?"

"Yes! What about it?"

"I'd like you to run as our representative. As long as you put your hat in the race, the employees are bound to pick you."

"So, what would I be doing as a representative?"

"At the moment, the Kaohsiung Green Fruits Collective is split between the Khe-tong (east river) and Khe-sai (west river) factions. Khe-tong represents Pîn-tong, and Khe-sai is Kî-san. We need someone of our own to represent Pîn-tongers in the organization."

"Oh, that would be good."

Tsín-suī thought of what his father had told him years ago. "This A-Tsòng was a heavyweight in the organization back when Taiwan was a Japanese colony."

10

It was now already autumn. Today was the first day that Masa would be pulling an oxcart. The sun was shining ever brilliantly with a blue sky overhead. Tsín-suī very cautiously walked Masa out of the paddock. He patted Masa on the neck and top of his head. His horns were already grown out about three inches now. They resembled fresh bamboo shoots rising straight out of the soil. Tsín-suī used some spit to massage Masa's neck where the yoke and harness would be placed. Giók-ìn had just come out from the house, where she had fetched a heavy hemp bag. She struggled to drag the massive bag along, especially as she crossed over the three-inch-tall door threshold. She was gritting her teeth, and the veins in her right temple were starting to pop out from the strain.

Tsín-suī had just finished hitching Masa to the cart, and he ran back over to help his wife. The two of them dragged the massive bag up to the cart and, using Japanese to count, they shouted out, "*Ichi! Ni! San,*" in unison, then lifted it into the cart.

Masa began walking and picked up the pace. He moved along so gracefully. As Tsín-suī drove the cart, he mumbled under his breath, "Frankly, maybe we should switch to speaking in *Han-gi*. So I think we ought to be saying, '*Yi, Uh, Shan.*'" He tried reciting the numbers about two or three times.

Giók-ìn sat next to him, ignoring his comment about the numbers in Mandarin Chinese. She brought them back to the real issue, "We have two million, three hundred seven thousand. And then we'll go take my mother's thirteen million. Do you think it'll be too heavy for Masa to pull?"

"I think he can do it. It shouldn't be a problem," Tsín-suī responded, without giving it any real thought. As the cart rolled down the country road, he remembered when he was kicked out of the Ngôo household all those years ago in his younger days and he had pulled an oxcart all on his own down this very road. There was only a pile of high-school textbooks that he had used for his job tutoring. "If I could pull this cart on my own, it should be very easy for Masa. He's probably not even breaking a sweat." He reminisced again. It was just him back then on this same road. Now he had a wife at his side. It was already dark out the day he was kicked out. Right now, it was a bright and sunny early morning. He lifted his head to take in the scenery. Mount Tāi-bú was sitting silently over to the east. The sun was blazing away from the peak as usual, spreading its rays across the earth. He looked off in another direction. The sky far above was an expanse of deep azure with a few puffs of calm, lazily floating white clouds. These days, everyone all across the island was unsettled and didn't feel any sense of security! Everything was in flux, and it was rapidly changing by the day. It was all too painful. Nobody dared to complain now. And there wasn't any way to redress their issues now anyway.

The oxcart was slow and jolted up and down from time to time. They hadn't even arrived at the Ông household when Giȯk-ìn spotted her mother and older brother waiting anxiously outside the main entrance. They had four bulky hemp bags clumsily piled on the ground next to them, all of them bulging at the seams.

Putting all four bags onto the cart was a whole family affair. "Do you want to come with us?" Tsín-suī asked.

"I'll go. *A-Bú* can stay at home and mind the shop," Tsín-suī's brother-in-law replied. Tsín-suī watched from a distance as his mother-in-law made her way back to the shop. "I think *A-Bú* has aged a lot recently!" he said in a low voice to Giȯk-ìn. All Giȯk-ìn could do was sigh.

Tsín-suī and his wife were worried that Masa couldn't pull the load. Fortunately, there was only about two hundred meters or so to go. The Taiwan Bank wasn't too far from the shop.

The three-corner park was in front of the Taiwan Bank branch. The sound of voices rose until it was more boisterous than a marketplace. Tsín-suī quickly scanned the area. There were several families who had brought their burdens on carrying poles. The ends of the poles drooped down under their loads, and the poles were clearly cutting into these people's shoulders. They looked like farmers who had just harvested several bushels of rice and were about to toss them into a granary for storage. There were those who had wobbled along on bicycles heaped up with bags. There were also those who had hired pedicabs and had stacked up their own bags and sacks in the back seats. Then there were two other families who were using oxcarts like Tsín-suī's. They had just arrived when they heard the sounds of cursing shouts directed at the bank employees.

"Those with millions or more, keep to the back. All we have are a couple hundred thousand at most. Let us trade in ours first, *honnh*?"

"Hey! You can't do that! If you're going to have them count out all of your money, they won't get to us until long after the sun's already set!"

A bank manager came out from behind the teller's wicket and shouted, "Everyone! Please bind all of your money into stacks of forty thousand! If you do that, it'll be easier for us to help you."

One of the tellers immediately questioned it, "But vice manager, if you let them count and bind their own money and they miscount it and lower the amount by two or three bills, then won't that cause problems?"

"These old Taiwanese dollars are worthless! Four hundred thousand dollars can only get you a scoop of rice. You can't buy a bowl of noodles for less than one hundred thousand dollars. It doesn't matter if you give or take by a bill or two. There's no difference. Efficiency is extremely important now."

"There's crowds and crowds of people in front of us, though. If we don't do it that way, even if we count for three days and three nights straight, we'd never be able to finish converting their money."

The teller faced one of the soldiers at the entrance to the bank who was gripping a rifle. He shot him a look pleading for help from the soldier. The soldier in turn, dressed in a green uniform and helmet and wearing grass-woven shoes, took his rifle down, seeming to recognize the order. He whistled with great force. The entire crowd in front of the bank hushed up very quickly. The soldier began to bark out, "The government policy is to allow for bills to be changed before the year's end. You do not have to change your bills today."

Some people understood the Chinese the soldier was speaking. Others just stared at him in complete silence, not having understood him at all. People interpreted for others, going in waves from those up closest to the soldier all the way out to those standing out at the back, near the park. As soon as others heard what the soldier said, a common complaint was, "They're as worthless as cut grass, but they're as heavy as iron ingots. It was such a hassle to get these bills out here in the first place. Why should we have to wait for another day just to have to come back and face the same situation?"

In the end, the bank's deputy manager's suggestion gained traction. A wave of activity swept through the crowd as people counted and tied up their banknotes until their fingers went numb. Occasionally, some of them would stop and wave their hands like a fan. They didn't have enough string to tie up their bank notes. Some people began fighting each other and, amid the squabbling, the sound of the soldier's whistle was occasionally heard. Tsín-suī was struck dumb and thought, "Even the sparrows in the trees in the park are annoyed with all of you noisy, bothersome people!" He thought, "These people are pretty impressive. Even amid all this extreme disturbance they can still count and tie up their bills. They have to be quick and accurate, as well."

An elderly man shouted out and brought Tsín-suī back to the present moment, "Pardon, Mr. Deputy Manager. If our family has already counted out and wrapped up our money into units of forty thousand, then can we go ahead and be served first?"

"Sure, if you've already bound them up, then you can come up first."

Five or six families then raced each other to the bank teller windows, struggling to get to the front of the line. Tsín-suī was forcefully shoved by another person, and anger quickly flared up in him. With one hand on his hip and a finger raised in the air, he faced everyone and started berating them, "We islanders shouldn't be like this. Don't let those Chinese have a reason to ridicule and abuse us. Don't give them a reason to belittle us! In the Japanese era, we used to line up respectfully and considerately, right? We are Taiwanese, some of Asia's most civilized and advanced people. We shouldn't be acting like this!"

When his words—like those of a *sensei* or a brotherly *Nii-san*—rose from the midst of the crowd, people unconsciously organized themselves politely into a queue and began to treat each other respectfully. Giŏk-ìn gave her husband a glance and then subtly nodded.

They were rather quick to be seen and exchanged their bills and left. First, they returned to his mother-in-law's home. Ông *thài-thài* grabbed her daughter's arm and pulled her into the storage area of the shop. Giŏk-ìn called out in shock, "*A-Bú*! I'm shocked. You've stocked up on so many things!"

"Haven't you and your husband stocked up at all?"

"Yes, but not as much as you, *A-Bú*. You bought a ton of stuff! Aren't you worried it'll all rot and spoil?"

"It won't, no. Who knows how long the chaos will continue on for."

When Tsín-suī got back to the house and was just about to take Masa down to the river for a mud bath and to eat some grass, the postman arrived with a registered letter. Tsín-suī told Giŏk-ìn, "A-Ìn, you take care of it. I'm going to take Masa out for a walk." With these instructions, he set off.

He hadn't walked more than a couple of feet before his wife came racing after him. Her tone of voice was very stern. She began to interrogate him, "A-Suī, you built up your business so large. How could you not have told me anything about how the business was going?"

"What do you mean, 'large'? Before 228, I was only able to buy a little sugar! You know it, too, as does your mother! A couple days ago, I let it go. It'll probably fetch a profit of a few dozen percent. Why? What's happened?"

"Well apart from this, you never told me about the other business you were working on."

"Just spit it out! What's this large business I was running? What about it? What's written there in that letter?"

His wife passed him the letter, "Take a look for yourself. It's massive! Your account has one point fifty-four *billion* dollars in it!!!" She especially emphasized the "*billion*."

"Hah! There's no way! There's no way there's that much! Maybe it's just a promissory note from Huanan Bank!" Tsín-suī shouted as he led Masa back in his pen. "This has to be some big mistake on the part of the bank. Come on, let's go over to the bank and ask them."

The couple cycled alongside each other and rode for about half a mile before they noticed that there was a pedicab approaching them. It wasn't just one either. Then Tsín-suī and Giȯk-ìn quickly went to the side of the road to make way, riding along the shoulder. Just as they were about to be overtaken, they heard a familiar voice calling out to them. Ah! It was Tsín-suī's mother-in-law and a young man sitting up in front. The second pedicab's passenger seating was empty.

Ông *thài-thài* and the young man quickly stepped out of the pedicab. She then gave an introduction for the man, "This young fellow here is an employee of Huanan Bank. He's the employee who manages all our accounts there."

"Oh, ha! Huanan Bank! We just got—"

The bank employee gave a quick bow and cut in, "Yes. I've come all the way out here especially for your particular case. The bank has sent a car expressly to find you so we can manage the matter."

"Sure. Fine. Let's go." Tsín-suī and his wife rode back to the house, and after storing their bicycles away, they calmly got into the bank's pedicab and rode into Pîn-tong.

Once they reached the bank, they were quickly ushered into the manager's office. The men at the table were right in the middle of a tense discussion, harried and flustered almost. As soon as the guests entered, a gentleman wearing a Western suit and leather shoes rose from his seat and, smiling, stuck his hand out to shake Tsín-suī's hand. "And you must be Mr. Ngôo Tsín-suī, I presume? I'm happy to make your acquaintance. I'm the bank's manager, Chiou Ch'ing-hwa. These two are my deputy manager and assistant manager." He spoke very stilted Mandarin. Tsín-suī could pick up that he was a man of Hakka stock by his accent.

"Hello Mr. Chiou. I heard that I have a massive sum of money in savings here?" Tsín-suī responded in Mandarin, mixing in a couple words of Hoklo.

"Well, this is the situation, Mr. Ngôo. Our central bank office has received a telephone call saying that the Taipei branch had bought a one point fifty-four million Taiwan dollar promissory note; however, there was a clerical error, and they had accidentally written it in as one point fifty-four billion dollars. The Taipei branch hadn't inspected it, and it wasn't until we had discovered it that we went to try to fix the error, but the central branch had already disbursed the money. They sent it by express mail to your residence."

"I've already received it," Tsín-suī responded.

A man burst into the room without knocking. Manager Chiou stopped speaking with Tsín-suī. This person seemed to be someone Mr. Chiou knew well. He spoke with the manager for a bit, all in Hakka. He then faced Tsín-suī and extended his hand to shake it. The man's face was all smiles. He shook Tsín-suī's hand and introduced himself. He spoke in heavily Hakka-accented Hoklo, "Mr. Ngôo. My name is Hiu Kin-ded. I'm from the village next to yours, Hué-Sio-Tsng. I currently run a small business here in Pîn-tong City. It just so happened that I was off of work today. Mr. Chiou doesn't know how to speak Hoklo, so he sent for me to help him interpret. We're cousins."

"Oh, Mr. Hiu, nice to meet you. That's probably for the best then. Mr. Chiou speaks Chinese quite slowly. I can understand about half of what he says."

Ông *thài-thài* butted in, "Why don't we use Japanese to speak instead?"

Mr. Hiu and Mr. Chiou looked at each other and then peeked outside the room, saying, "*Pháinn-sè*, the manager is worried that someone might be listening in on us. If the security personnel hear us, I'm afraid it might impact our future prospects. Please forgive us this inconvenience." After he explained this, he spoke to his manager-cousin, "A-Hua, just speak slowly. Mr. Ngôo said he can understand more than half of what you're saying. If he doesn't understand you, then I can explain it for you."

Manager Chiou then continued, "Mr. Ngôo, if you look at the amount written on the bill, you've probably been shocked. There's been a massive mistake..."

Tsín-suī butted in, "You only want to give us one point fifty-four million dollars not one billion, five hundred and forty million. I'm pretty clear on that."

"Mr. Ngôo, you're well ahead in understanding our predicament. I have great admiration for you! Our bank though...," the manager hesitated.

Manager Chiou was speaking too slowly in Chinese, and it was tempting for others to interject. This time, the one who butted in was Ông *thài-thài*, "However, this is a promissory note issued by the bank." She only stopped for a second and then strengthened her intonation. "This promissory note is as good as gold. It's cash, right in hand, is it not?" The whole room went quiet. Nobody spoke for a while. Ông *thài-thài* spelled it all out for everyone, "I'm Ngôo Tsín-suí's mother-in-law. I'm a businesswoman, and I've been doing business with this bank for a very long time."

Manager Chiou was stunned for a few seconds. He then immediately switched to speaking in fluent Japanese with Ông *thài-thài*, though he spoke almost in hushed tones, as if he was a school pupil afraid to be caught by his teacher talking with another classmate. "Ō(Ông)-*san*, please give me a few minutes to explain. I'll contact the head office in Taihoku."

The vice manager helped him to place a call through. Mr. Chiou spoke in stiff Chinese to relay Ông *thài-thài*'s intention and then stayed on the phone just listening. Mr. Chiou did nothing after that point except repeatedly agree, "Yes... Un-huh... Yes, I see... Understood, yes."

After he hung up the phone, Mr. Chiou continued speaking with her in Japanese, and in a soft voice still, "Ō-san, I'll give it to you straight. Our central bank is willing to give thirty million in return for the promissory note."

"Just thirty million?" Ông *thài-thài* reached over across the table at the pocket abacus over on the general manager's desk. As she made her nimble-fingered calculations, she kept talking to herself, "I'll count it out myself. How much do you have after you exchange forty thousand old Taiwanese dollars for one New Taiwan dollar?"

As soon as he saw her calculating, Mr. Chiou quickly said to Ông *thài-thài*, "Ō-san, it's only as much as what the central bank branch has told me. I can increase it by another ten million."

"Just forty million?" Ông *thài-thài* shook the abacus in her hand, resetting all the beads. It made the same subtle, gentle clicking sound that pearls made when lifted up. "I'm going to recount it." She began flicking the abacus beads with furious speed. Obviously, she could have divided forty million by forty thousand. She shook up the abacus once more...and then was about to start her counting again.

The general manager's room became abnormally quiet. The hand Ông *thài-thài* was using to flick beads on the abacus froze in mid-air. It seemed that she was pondering some difficult mathematical problem. Not long after, Mr. Chiou let out a deep breath and broke the silence, "Ō-san. Our general branch gave me the highest rate at fifty million. If you don't accept, then I will have to go back up to Taipei to deal with it myself."

"Fine. I'll confer with my son-in-law for a moment."

Tsín-suī was off to his mother-in-law's side, just sitting in silence. And then his expression changed. "*A-Bú*. I'm very appreciative that you're trying so hard to fight for me. I've given this issue a lot of thought, and I think that I just want to take my one point fifty-four million and call it a day."

"Huh!?" Several of the people called out in exasperation. There was a strange calm immediately after.

"A-Suī-á, in the business realm, this is something you often have to face and contend with. There's no need to feel awkward or sorry."

"I know. But if you do things in a bad way, you'll have to pay the price at some point. And in any case A-Bú, deep down, I don't think this money belongs to me. It would be better not to take all of it."

"Oh, this simple-minded child! This stupid, lovable fool!" Ông *thài-thài*'s eyes, full of years of wisdom, opened wide in surprise. She stared at Tsín-suī. "How could such a smart and driven person decide to do such a stupid thing?" she kept thinking to herself. And what about her own daughter? At this moment, her daughter was sitting right next to her husband. She was leaning in close to her husband. Ông *thài-thài* couldn't tell what kind of thoughts her daughter had cooped up in her own mind.

THREE

UNDER THE HEEL OF THE
CHINESE NATIONALIST PARTY

11

That day, an afternoon thunderstorm rolled in and when the sun finally came out, the great earth was as if washed anew. Everything was bright under the sunlight, and even the air was especially clean and fresh smelling. There was a horse cart on the old dirt road heading towards Thâu-tsîng-khe, and it seemed to rival the speed of a motorcycle. A great cloud of dust was kicked up as it sped on by.

Giȯk-ìn looked off into the distance. She wanted to see who had come by, and she didn't expect them to actually stop at their front gate. A middle-aged man hopped down from the cart. To Giȯk-ìn's surprise, it was the Hakka man whom they had met two days prior at the Huanan Bank branch in town. He had said he was the bank manager's cousin or some kin, surnamed Hiu. His first name escaped her memory for a moment. He kindly walked forward and called out a greeting to her. "Pardon me, but is this Ngôo Tsín-suí's residence? Oh, wait. Never mind. I've seen you before. You must be his wife. My name is Hiu Kin-ded. We met over at the bank a few days ago," he spoke in fluent Japanese.

"Oh, so you're Mr. Hiu. Right, that day at the bank…"

"Sorry to bother you all unannounced, but is your husband home?"

"He went out with the laborers to the banana fields. You just missed him. Come, please come in and sit down for a bit. I'll call for my son to drive your cart out to the side."

"Oh, there's no need. You see, I came out here today to speak with Mr. Ngôo about some matter. The bank manager is aware of it, and he asked me to send you a small gift. He'll come himself on another day to express his thanks for your help." Hiu Kin-ded finished speaking and then turned back to the horse cart and lifted items down from it. They were boxes and boxes full of fruit and dried goods. Giȯk-ìn was dumbfounded, "Oh, you shouldn't be so kind. That's unnecessary. That's too much."

"Oh, it's no problem at all!" Apart from noticing that two of the baskets were filled to the brim with apples, the other baskets and boxes were filled with all sorts of gifts that Giok-ìn couldn't clearly make out. Giok-ìn just stood there not knowing what to do. She wasn't exactly sure of how to treat this situation. Fortunately, Mr. Hiu was a very jovial man. He helped her to bring the boxes and baskets into the house and then got straight to the point. "Ngôo *thài-thài*, I had told you a little while ago that I have a matter to discuss with your husband, Tsín-suī. If you could call your son to hop up onto my cart and show me the way, then I think I should like to go find your husband myself. As I'm already here, I'd also like to take a look at your family's banana farm, if that's alright by you."

"My son doesn't know the roads around here. If you'd like to go, then I'll have to show you the way myself." Giok-ìn went back into the house and explained what she was doing, then gladly got up onto the cart. She often saw this horse cart at her mother's store, mainly because they were using it to deliver goods. It stood higher off the ground than an oxcart, and the wheels had tires made of rubber instead of iron worked around wood. All the same, it was still the first time she had ever ridden on one, and it was much faster than their household's oxcart, and it turned on a dime. When they had quickly made their way to the fields, the road narrowed. Right at about the point the road narrowed, she saw Mr. Hiu make a U-turn without any trouble. She called out in amazement without realizing, "Oh wow! Your cart[33] can back up!"

Hiu Kin-ded said back with pride, "*A li-ah-kha* can reverse because it's got two wheels. Backing out with a four-wheeled oxcart would be difficult."

As soon as he saw him, Tsín-suī knew that it was Mr. Hiu. The two men went into the field to chat and take a stroll. Mr. Hiu was also a banana farmer, so the two of them talked and talked from the start of the field to its end and then all the way back again. All they had talked about the entire time was bananas. When they got back to where the horse cart was parked, Hiu Kin-ded asked Tsín-suī, "What kind of acreage are you working with here?"

"This field is about one and a half *kah*. I also have another field that's close to two *kah*."

---

33. 'Li-ah-kha' is an extremely common expression in Taiwan's rural villages. The original meaning is 'horse cart,' but later, any cart, whether pulled by a human, a bicycle, or a motorcycle, could be called a 'Li-ah-kha'.

"Ah, OK, so it's more than three *kah*, right?"

"Of course it is."

"OK. Let's sit down for a bit and talk some more."

Along with Giŏk-ìn, the three of them sat by the embankment and talked about business, while the sun continued to shine splendidly.

"*Ngai kin-fun-lit loi...*," Hiu Kin-ded then seemed to realize he was speaking in Hakka and switched over to speaking Hoklo. "I came today because I wanted to give you a proposition... I'd like to invite you to take over as the inspector for the Kaohsiung Green Fruits Export Association."

"Oh, why's that?"

"I'm the current inspector. I've been wanting to resign from the position for a long time, but I could never find someone who was suitable to replace me."

"Why do you want to resign?"

"It's just too much work."

"What career are you trying to move into afterwards?"

"I make shipments by *li-a-kha*. And I also hue-long. Aside from that, I'm also working a three- or four-*kah* banana farm." He paused for a second, then continued. "I'm sorry... to be honest, my Hoklo isn't up to snuff... I meant to say '*bí-kă*' (rice milling) when I said '*hue-long*.'"

"Oh, I see." Tsín-suī then asked him, "But, are you saying I could start right away if I want it?"

"I can arrange that for you. The chairman of the board is one of my own men. You've got the qualifications, at least you can manage a farm over three *kah* in size."

"There's plenty of banana farmers though. Why me in particular?"

"When you were managing the incident over at the Huanan Bank, your honesty and sincerity deeply moved me."

Tsín-suī didn't say anything in response, so Kin-ded continued, "The inspector needs to be a man of just such integrity. You absolutely have to come out and take the job, *honnh*!"

It was like an angel had been sent from heaven. It was incredibly smooth sailing for Tsín-suī, the moment he entered the association. It was a large building next to the wharfs of Ko-hiông. As soon as he stepped inside, he went straight up to the boardroom up on the top floor. There was a very old chairman standing at the door to welcome him on board. Who else would it be but A-Tsòng? He was dressed in a white dress shirt and black dress slacks. His skin was still as sunburnt and darkened as ever. His beard and mustache were unruly and unclean. He had a musty odor to him that belonged more on someone working out in the middle of a field.

Taking his place at the inspector's table. Tsín-suī noticed that A-Tsòng took the seat diagonally across from him. The desk plaque in front of him said "Chairman Su Chuang-bo" (Mandarin pronunciation of Soo Tsòng-phik). He kept staring at A-Tsòng. He then smiled a little and gave A-Tsòng a nod. In an instant, Tsín-suī finally had a feeling of security, that he was safe here. This man—a neighbor companion who went together with Tsín-suī into the fields, one of his father's longest-standing friends, would somehow end up being at the same table in this conference room, discussing important matters.

He couldn't help but have mixed feelings. He was formerly a member of the Green Fruits Association when it was under the Japanese. Tsín-suī himself was once nothing more than a low-level technician at a banana farm research station. He was only twenty at the time, but now he was already forty-two. That year so long ago when he had first set foot into this field, there was another Hakka man by the name of Chin Fo-sen who led the way for him, and then there was his brotherly friend, Tsuān-tsong, whose words of encouragement had never faded from deep in Tsín-suī's mind: "I think this is a good thing. Lîn-lok is just to the east of Pîn-tong, so you'll be heading east. You'll be heading in the direction the sun rises from. Maybe you'll be walking right into sunlight if you keep going."

When he was just starting out in farming, Tsín-suī worked hard to learn the ropes. He studied techniques for planting bananas. Now his humility and diligent attitude of that time crept up in him again. There was no lack of discussion of items to go through at the supervisor's meeting. They were right in the middle of talking about how to break past multiple gigantic monopolies in the Japanese market for bananas. The next item was a discussion on a letter from the Executive Yuan's foreign trade committee. These were all fresh subjects for Tsín-suī.

After the first meeting when he had returned home, he reeked of booze from head to toe. Giok-ìn immediately wanted to know her husband's impressions on being a "new official." What she didn't expect to hear was, "Being a supervisor is boring work. No wonder that Hiu Kin-ded wanted to ditch the job so fast and was clamoring to give it to me."

"What's so boring about it? Well? Speak up."

"Inspectors are responsible for looking into incidents. Everyone talked about duties during the meeting, mainly duties related to the chairmen."

"Inspectors aren't allowed to express their own opinion?"

"I'm still not quite sure. It was my first time in one of these meetings. I did my best to listen to it all." He then continued, "I figured out today that A-Tsòng is truly a very knowledgeable chairman."

"He's just like a bottle made of black glass filled with soy sauce... You'd never expect him to be such a knowledgeable, useful person by appearance alone."

"So I'll just get to the point... Why is it that you left the meeting and then had to go out drinking so much?" Giok-ìn asked more pointedly.

"This is just part of the company culture. There's nothing else to it. How else would you be able to get your foot in the door and make acquaintances?"

"I don't believe you. I absolutely don't believe you."

After several of these drinking parties, he finally made inroads. He also went everywhere to inspect the conditions at different farm sites. Once when they were holding a meeting with very few topics to discuss, Tsín-suī raised his hand to speak.

"Back in the Japanese era, farmers who had plots of land larger than three *kha* were considered *hōjō* (plantations) and they could do their own export inspections. The farmers grew the bananas themselves. They selected them, packed them, and used their own trademarks. All of the costs were borne by the farmers themselves. Back then, the Green Fruits Collective didn't need to go out to do inspections in person. They just had to send someone to the wharfs in the harbor to make the inspections.

"Well, now we have a new government. They want to send officials out to inspect even the smallest patches of scrub land. All in all, we have more than two hundred and eighty farms. Each one of them has to get their product out the next day. Because of this demand, they have to employ more than a hundred and forty inspectors. Ordinarily, each farm's output is about a hundred baskets or so. That's not so much of a problem, truth be told. If there's a big bumper crop, each farm might produce four or five hundred baskets' worth—maybe even a thousand at some. During such times, the inspectors won't be able to keep up with the demand. And they're not allowed to receive any help from our organization. I found out that the bananas they're taking from the farms for inspection sites are being checked too early, compared to when they were shipped directly from the plantations when we were under the Japanese. It's such a massive difference in quality!"

Chang Ming-suh, who was executive chairman of the meeting, spoke up, "Supervisor Ngôo, when you're speaking, just make your point. You don't have to compare our current government to the Japanese."

When the chairman finished speaking, he lifted a tea cup and made a gesture to one of the workers. The worker went up to him carrying a kettle and filled his cup, then took the opportunity to fill the cups of each of the supervisors and inspectors. When he got to Tsín-suī, he secretly passed him a note. On it was written, "Please do not mention the government ever again. Someone will report it to the Party."

Tsín-suī was very agitated now. He decided he'd ignore the note. He continued speaking just as he had been, "Fine. I won't mention the Japanese era, but I'd like to discuss something, and that something is how are we having officials going to every single farm now? Isn't the quality declining? This is because first, many farmers are paying off these officials so the standards are slackened and there is no realistic assessment; second, when their bananas are selling in great numbers, there's not enough hands around to carry out the inspections. Even our colleagues are going out to help do the counting and quality checks. They don't even know if the bananas are round or flat."

"OK. Speak your mind. What do you propose we do to make things better?" the chairman responded.

"We first have to treat the root issues. We'll have to notify all the members of the banana association that they shouldn't use *oo-se* (bribe) or *pho-lan-pha* (literally: hold their family jewels for them, give them special treatment). If we're selling shoddy, substandard products abroad, doubtless that's going to come back and bite us in the butt if the Japanese companies think that we're not being honest or trustworthy. It's the farmers in the end who are going to bear the brunt of that kind of behavior. Secondly, the way to treat the disease itself is to work hard to give suggestions to the government. We need to revive the old system where farmers carry out the inspections themselves. Make a system where the farmers are fully responsible for their own produce—"

"So are there any among us who are opposed?"

"It's very easy to convince them. Since the income for banana farms is calculated as a combination of both domestic and foreign prices, once they're responsible for their own produce, if they bring their bananas to the port for export and we find that they're not the quality we want, then we'll just sell them in the domestic market. Our association will still keep spending money as it normally would, and the farmers' income won't decrease. Sometimes the internal marketing price is better than the foreign one, no?"

Tsín-suī made a polite bow, sat back down into his seat, then scanned the meeting table. The executive chairman silently regarded him with a fixed gaze, but the directors and supervisors looked at him with different expressions in their eyes. The whole room was waiting for the chairman's proverbial gavel to come swinging down in judgment. Just then, a certain director with extensive experience, one A-Tsòng, spoke directly without raising his hand. "I feel a lot of resonance with what our new inspector Ngôo A-Tsín-suī has said. I'd like to add a comment. The governmental policy at this time has gradually taken away the ability for banana farmers—I'd even venture to say everyone on the island—to monitor our own quality. We've lost the ability to govern ourselves and at the same time, there's more and more opportunities for government officials to commit acts of graft—"

As soon as the words left his lips, the chairman cut short A-Tsòng's rousing speech. "Inspector Ngôo has made a very convincing argument. I'll look further into his suggestion. Let's adjourn our meeting here, gentlemen, shall we?"

The meeting room relaxed instantly. A-Tsòng walked over to Tsín-suī and whispered into his ear, "Did you see the attending cadres over next to the chairman? There's a lackey with suntanned skin. The one with the unruly mop of hair. The *khah-se* (running dog). He had his head buried in his notebook, scribbling away. He's our association's security commissioner. His family surname is Ouyang. He was sent here by the Party. I noticed that when you were speaking, he was giving you dagger eyes. He just kept looking at you and jotting everything down that came out of your mouth."

"Oh. The chairman passed me a note to remind me that if I brought up anything related to the government, there would be someone who would make a report to the Party. So, he's the one, then?"

"Exactly. So long as you are aware."

After the meeting wrapped up, they filed out to go for a meal. Tsín-suī's ideas continued to ferment in his mind. How would he be able to convince the authorities to change their inspection system?

Like a divine oracle, A-Tsòng told him with complete confidence, looking as if he was a fortune teller revealing a gigantic secret. He went right out and said it to Tsín-suī, "This system that the *Tiong-kok-á* have come up with... I'd wager everything on it with any of you... They won't budge."

"Why?"

"If it's changed, there's gonna be a lot of people who don't get to *kua-loo-a* (getting their cut of the profit), so they're not gonna lift a finger to change it." He looked around and saw nobody was arguing against him, then kept going on with his grand hypothesis. "This is what their culture is all about. It's buried deep down within every one of them."

"Haha, ah... You're so astute, A-Tsòng."

One day, Tsín-suī and A-Tsòng took a pedicab home together. A-Tsòng suddenly posed a question to Tsín-suī, "A person such as yourself would be good at being a director. Are you interested in taking over the helm?"

Tsín-suī didn't immediately answer him, trying to conceal his excitement. He just grinned and nodded slightly.

"I'll just come out and tell you then. We Pîn-tonger's are headed by a director named Lim Mian-shun. He doesn't want to run for a second time after his term is up. You can start preparing your campaign."

A couple months later, Tsín-suī made his move and took over Lim's directorship, winning it handily.

After biding his time on the board of directors for a term of three years, then being reelected for a second term, he'd gained enough knowledge to be elected as member of the bargaining committee. The first time Tsín-suī had attended it, it was being held in Taipei. It was led by head of the directors, Chang Ming-suh. Before the meeting was held, Giok-ìn made a special point of going out to buy a tie for her husband. It was a blue tie with green fringe. The two of them stood in their bedroom for a long time, trying to figure out how to tie it. A long time after, Giok-ìn learned how to do it. She first fastened a good knot, then pulled it directly down over her husband's head to his collar, gave it two light, affectionate tugs and made a little adjustment, then happily announced, "There now. All done. You look so handsome!"

A look of happiness spread across Tsín-suī's face, though he slightly muttered to himself, "Our association was set up for banana farmers. I'm also a representative for banana farmers. Why can't I just go around barefoot wearing a sedge hat?"

Before they left, he went in his Western suit and tie to the cow pen to see Masa. He realized there was deep fear in the water buffalo's eyes. They were wide open, and he had also tilted his head slightly to the side.

Because it was the first time Tsín-suī was attending one of these meetings, as they sat on the train heading north, the chairman of the board, Chang Ming-suh gave him a bit of guidance. "The objective for the trip is to convince the exporters. They're called the Green Fruits Association. There are two top leaders in the organization. The higher-ranking of the two is a lady. She's the organization's director. She's not at all someone who can easily be won over. Her name is Tân Hīng-tshun—"[34]

"Oh, I've definitely heard others mention her before. They call her the 'Banana Queen.'"

"Right. She's the very one. The second person's name is Tân Tsa-bóo.[35] But despite the name, they're not a woman. They're a man."

"He's one of those exporters. They've been siphoning off the blood of us farmers for a long time."

"They're all impressive rich people. With you being a poor country boy, when you're negotiating with them, you might want to—"

"Hah, don't worry Mr. Chairman. I'm not so weak-kneed."

"They've long had relationships with the party government. Lately, they've spent a gigantic amount of money in buying up land around Tsó-iânn over in Ko-hiông. They were ordered to donate it to Chiang Kai-shek's wife, Sung Mei-ling. They're building a gigantic housing complex to house the soldiers and officers who came over from China. They've already given the compound a name. They're calling it the Fruits Trade New Village."

"No wonder, eh! These people are such brownnosers, that's how they can lord it over the profits from banana exports. The f***ing nerve!" Tsín-suī thought for a bit, then asked, "Why did they donate and dedicate it to Sung Mei-ling?"

"Because Sung Mei-ling is currently heading the foreign trade office. There's a general beneath her by the name of Hsu Po-yuen. He's helped her control the foreign exchange trade review committee under the Executive Yuan branch of the government."

Tsín-suī made a soft "oh" in response, then kept quiet. Chang Ming-suh tacked on some more, "Truth be told, the largest building in that Fruits Trade New Village over in Tsuo-ing (Tsó-iânn) has a marker over the entrance written by the madame. It's done very nicely; however, very few people know that it was donated by the Green Fruits Association."

The talks on prices were being held in a large conference room in the Jiang-shan building.

---

34. Tân Hīng-tshun (Chen Hsing-tsun) was from Taipei. She was married to a Tainanese doctor, Hsieh Ta-lin, but her husband died very young and she had raised her children alone. She had one granddaughter named Lien-fang who is now a member of the Japanese Diet and once was director of the Japanese People's Progressive Party. According to a report by a well-known Japanese reporter, there was always a picture of her grandmother, Chen Hsing-tsun hanging in her office at the Diet.

35. Trans.: In Hoklo, 'tsa-boo' means 'woman.'

The members from Ko-hiông arrived first. They sat all in a row. The director chairman, Chang Ming-suh, was sitting smack dab in the middle of the file. He had made sure that Tsín-suī was sitting to his left. Not a few moments later, two strangers entered the room. They had just finished introducing themselves when Tân Tsa-bóo arrived and then everything went silent.

Tân Hīng-tshun arrived last. All of the exporters stood up, and the cooperative association members immediately followed suit, as if they were greeting some vaunted dignitary. Tsín-suī felt a deep sense of enmity against this fresh face. Inexplicably, though, the first time he laid eyes on her, he felt a sense of closeness and kindness that countered his enmity.

She began shaking hands and exchanging pleasantries with all those across from her. Tsín-suī kept gazing at her from across the table. He thought deep down that kind of easygoing feeling was something he'd felt before. It was like the first time he had set his eyes on Giok-ìn. The first time he had looked at Mari from across the fields. The first time he had seen Uncle A-Huàn. The first time he had met Tông Tsuān-tsong. The first time he had seen Iap Tshiu-bok after all those long years. All of it was as clear and lucid as a bright, cloudless day. He felt a strong sense of wanting to get closer to them, care for them, and help them. And in all cases, the first time he met these people, he easily fell into conversation with them. He remembered the first time he had met both Tshiu-bok and Tsuān-tsong, they just kept conversing deep into the night, forgetting sleep until the sun had already risen.

Hīng-tshun was tall and slim and was wearing a well-tailored, blue, Western-style suit with an expensive-looking leather belt. This lady spoke elegantly and looked just as much the part as her words expressed. You could say she was beautiful. She had a slightly elongated face and a prominent nose. Her ear lobes were long and rounded, and her lips were full and supple. Her eyes were the most peculiar part about her visage. They were wide and bright, and the outline of her eye sockets only added to the allure her face exuded. Her eyes were elegant—classic almond-shaped "phoenix eyes."

When she got to him, they shook hands but for some reason didn't let go for a full minute or two. The pleasantries they exchanged were also different than those exchanged between the others.

"Mr. Ngôo, this is the first time you've attended. Welcome. We'll have to make more of an acquaintance and gain your insights later."

"Director Chen, hello. There's no need to ask me for my advice on anything. I'm happy to meet you."

"So are you a banana planter or a banana seller?"

"Both. I both plant and sell. I even sell and trade them when they're still green and unripe."

"Oh, so you're an actual expert, then."

"When I was twenty, I worked for many years in a research lab under the wing of a Japanese supervisor."

"You look like you're about the same age as me."

"I was born in Meiji 42."

"Oh, I'm younger than you by a year, then. I was born in Meiji 43."

All those around them had begun talking among themselves in hushed, joking tones. "Oh, how can you do that? The first time you meet a man you tell them your age?"

"She's fallen for him. She's fallen for him. She's fallen for this *Ian-tau-a-san* (young, handsome) Ngôo fellow here!"

"Our Director Tân has gone through so much tribulation to get here. People call her a 'hero among women.' Let's not dwell on the details too much."

Hīng-tshun clearly realized people were talking about her so she quickly finished her handshaking around the table and returned to her seat, then immediately began, "Come. Let's start the talks. What should we speak about first?"

Chang Ming-suh: "Let's talk first about the prices in Kaohsiung. It's a topic that must be settled."

Tsa-bóo: "Chairman Chang is concerned about the seven *jiao* (seventy cents). When we came back from Kaohsiung, we carefully recalculated, and that seven *jiao* is needed to cover the rise in shipping costs—"

Ngôo Tsín-suī: "Have the shipping costs gone up? How much have they gone up? Do you need seventy cents per basket of bananas to cover it? Let's recalculate it. To be frank, we've already run the numbers."

Tsa-bóo: "Mr. Ngôo, how are you coming up with that number?"

Tsín-suī: "The shipping fees should be absorbed by your industry, right? The way I figure it is: one basket weighs forty-eight kilos. If it's just seventy cents short, that's one and a half cents per kilo. This is such a paltry amount for your shipping companies. It's not even worth fussing over. It should be given to the banana farmers."

Tsa-bóo: "Please, Mr. Ngôo, do not bean count for others. I'm going to stick to seventy cents."

Hīng-tshun: "Mr. Ngôo, if the vice-director wants to insist..."

Tsín-suī cocked his head to the side as he looked across the table at the leader of the other delegation. "Mr. Chairman, you must state your position. If you want to persist, you cannot concede even a bit."

Chang Ming-suh remained quiet, indicating he wasn't going to insist. Tân Hīng-tshun then seized the opportunity to declare, "Come. Let's talk about the second agenda item then."

The second item on the agenda happened to be about the number and price for the boats to be used in the next shipping period. The teams negotiated fiercely for a long while. In the end, it was the fruits association that prevailed. The third and fourth agenda items were quite simple by comparison. The fruits association easily won its hoped-for goal. After the meeting was ended, everyone went back to their lodgings.

Tsín-suī had a few words to say regarding the results, "We shouldn't concede to them on the seventy-cent price difference. One basket is seventy cents. A hundred baskets would be seventy dollars. That's not a small amount of money at all for a banana farmer."

"Oh, you wouldn't have known, but I don't support this proposal because it's the only way we can get the prices we want on a few other cases."

"I need to go find that Tân Hīng-tshun to see if I can get that price of seventy cents reversed."

"Well, go then. You're the best one for the job. Everyone will be grateful to you."

"So...this woman... How do I find her?"

"I'll try to contact her for you."

Tân Hīng-tshun was only too happy in her response to hold another talk with Tsín-suī about the price difference. She made arrangements for them to come to her office at her own trading firm. Chang Ming-suh called for a pedicab to take Tsín-suī over.

Hīng-tshun first gave her guests a tour of the company. When they returned to her office, Tsín-suī was the first to speak. "I also have a trade company over in Ko-hiông, over by the Iam-ting district. We import and export leather goods. It's called San-Yi Hang. I run the business together with two friends. It's being managed by them."

"At present, I am only dealing in bananas."

"Forgive me for being a bit blunt and direct with you, but you all have made too much money off of banana farmers."

Hīng-tshun stared at him with eyes like a hawk. Her answer was unexpected, "Well, you're not wrong about that. Our Green Fruits Association has indeed made quite a killing."

"Well, if you've already come to this realization, then why are you all still so adamant about those seventy cents?"

"Sometimes it's not easy to settle things in a formal meeting. Yesterday, I went to seek out Tân Tsa-bóo in person. He was so adamant. As the committee chair, I have no choice but to consider his opinion on the matter."

"Oh, I see... Well, is there still room to talk about that seventy-cent difference?"

"I know you want to go ahead and get down to the nitty-gritty details with Tân Tsa-bóo all in one go, but the reality is that one basket of bananas would be fully covered with just an increase of thirty cents. So I'd like to go ahead and offer you a price raise of forty cents."

"Won't Tân Tsa-bóo be angry about that?"

"No. He won't be," Hīng-tshun continued. "I've already given him enough face during the meeting. In private talks behind closed doors, everyone can be a bit more at ease and speak their mind."

"OK. Wonderful. Well then, I'll be making my way back now. I have something to tell my chairman now."

Suddenly, Hīng-tshun switched to speaking in Chinese. Tsín-suī could tell that she was speaking it fluently and with the standard accent and everything. "You once said you had worked in a banana research station. What exactly was it that you were doing?"

"I was a full-time researcher and farming technician," Tsín-suī tried to speak in Chinese, but he switched back to Taiwanese after two attempts. He began speaking about his past, starting from when he was a student at Takao Secondary.

As soon as she heard him talking about his alma mater, Hīng-tshun stopped him mid-speech. "I graduated from the Taipei Girls Professional School in the Japanese era."

"Oh! There was one evening one year where I once stood outside the gates of your alma mater. I kept thinking, 'Just what kind of thing does this school train women from our island to do?'"

"When I was there, I was studying Western clothing design and manufacturing." She pulled out a heavy folio from a desk drawer, then called Tsín-suī to take a look. It was a listing of important Taiwanese gentry families and notables. It was a sort of white pages of important peoples and who's who published during the Japanese era. She first searched for the pages corresponding to the surname Chin (Tân). Next, she flipped through, paging nimbly until she reached a page exclusively devoted to introducing her. Tsín-suī read her title and saw she was listed as a "Western clothing store owner; fashion designer." There was a footnote underneath that read "Graduated from the Western Clothing Designer's School in the Ginza District, Tokyo."

"Whoa! That's astounding! You were already famous at twenty years old and were included in this 'Taiwanese People's Guide'! What a feat! This is absolutely amazing," Tsín-suī called out, astonished.

"It's just a small introduction only. You're heaping too much praise on me. Please don't put too much stock in it." She then continued, "I'm intentionally speaking Chinese with you because I would like to have you quickly grasp it. We're now run by a Chinese government. It won't be easy. You were wanting to talk about your past just now, but I rudely interrupted you. Please. Continue speaking."

Tsín-suī began to speak. He knew this lady was more of an "uptown girl" than Giȯk-ìn was. As he deliberately described several farming villages and life out working in the fields, he added in a couple tidbits about water buffalo. Hīng-tshun was soaking it all in like a sponge, not shifting her gaze from him as she listened. Then she expressed with some emotion, "My mother-in-law is from Tainan. I lived in the south for a long time, though I never went out to any farm fields."

"Have you ever seen a banana farm in person?"

"Well, from the roadside, but I've never gone down into a field."

"The grass in banana fields is incredibly dense—"

"Ngôo-*san*, you should start trying to practice your *Hua-gi*. Speak it slowly. I'd like to listen to you tell me all about bananas."

"The grass grows very quickly in the banana fields. If you don't cut it for two weeks, when you go down into the fields, you'll find it's overrun with plenty of rats and all kinds of snakes. You have to cut grass with a *tik-thâu* (hoe). I'm not sure how you say '*tik-thâu*' in Chinese. Anyway, oh, thanks, 'a farm hoe.' You have to do the weeding one swing of the hoe after another. You'll be out there the entire day, sweating until your entire body is soaked through and your palms start to blister. Then you'll have to go back through the entire field again two or three more times. The sky will have darkened then, and you hit the dusty trail back home. If you stay at home for two days and come back out, you'll see that the grass has started to grow back again."

"Oh, that I'm well aware of. The entire south is so humid and warm. Keep speaking. Use Chinese, OK?"

"After the bananas are harvested, you often have to spread fertilizer. The best kind is actually all the night soil from people's homes. Then you can add whatever the pigs, chickens, and ducks create to the mix. After that's composted and fermented, it'll be extremely pungent and full of bacteria and life. Farming families, both large and small, all have to help out whenever they can and spread the fertilizer around. They have to drag it from the house courtyards all the way out to the fields. Some families have to take it several kilometers away. Once they've made it out to their plantation fields, then they have to spread it, scoop by scoop, sprinkling it around the stumps of the banana trees. If you spend a day spreading manure, the stench clings to your whole body and doesn't go away, even after a week of bathing."

Hīng-tshun fanned her hand in front of her face in disgust, "Ugh. Don't speak any more about that Mr. Ngôo. Let's talk about something else."

"Hmmm... Do you know how bananas are cut? I'll tell you if you'd like. You use an extremely sharp machete. You start from about midway on the tree stalk, that is to say, its waist. You take aim and cut with a single blow. Then, in the one or two seconds while it is falling, you have to be quick and grab onto the bunch with one hand and heave it onto one of your shoulders. With the other hand, you cut through the top of the bunch. Untrained farmers can't cut through the bunch stalk. The secret is to use the force of the tree falling and cut using its momentum. The bunches are heavy, about ten or twenty kilos. If the bones in your arms aren't strong enough, the weight of the bananas can snap them easily if it hits you in the wrong place."

Tsín-suī was struggling more and more to use his Chinese fluently, but he didn't give up. He worked up a mental sweat trying to practice again. "It's not enough then to just call it a day. You still have to hoist that single bushel out of the field, place it on a cotton blanket, and split it up. You say 'fen-kai' to mean 'divide it up,' right? Oh, wait. I know. You could also say 'zhi-jie' ('cut it along the splitting branches'), and then you have to put one section of the bunch at a time up onto a cart. Then you send it off to the inspectors. All that for one bunch."

"I never would've guessed. I trade and export fruits all the time, but I never knew any of this."

"Oh, wait Ms. Tân, I'm not done yet... There's still a little bit more. So these banana farmers work so hard to grow and sell their crops, but sometimes they can't even break even. Sometimes they don't make a cent for all that effort. Do you know why that might be?"

"You sound like you're asking a three-year old. It's the typhoons. As soon as they hit the island, everything gets destroyed. All that blood, sweat, and tears just goes for nothing."

"Right. There's always going to be a typhoon each year. For all of the loss of produce, exporters and people up in Taipei never put a single thought or consideration into helping us when it comes to that."

"When we first started having this conversation, I told you that our Green Fruits Export Association made piles of money. That's all from those banana farmers' hard work."

Tsín-suī, startled, immediately stood up from the sofa. He made a ninety-degree, Japanese-style bow and spoke, "Committee Leader Tân, hearing you speak so forthrightly, I'm extremely grateful. Thank you. Coming on this trip to Taipei and meeting you has been extremely valuable and productive. I'm absolutely thrilled."

Hīng-tshun didn't bother responding to Tsín-suī. She simply pressed down on a recorder button from a device on the table. She made a command, "I have a guest here. When you send him his meal, give him an extra helping!"

"I didn't ask what you'd prefer to have. We're having Japanese-style grilled Umeko eel for lunch. Is that OK?"

"That sounds great. Excellent... Your Chinese is so articulate. How did you come about studying it?" Tsín-suī then asked.

"Oh, I lived in Shanghai for a very long time."

"Shanghai? When we were still under Japanese rule?"

"Yes, that's correct. I had a benefactor, actually. After the Republic of China was established over on the mainland, they sent ambassadors every which way around the world. Taiwan was a part of Japan at the time, and so the Republic set up its main embassy in Tokyo and set up a general consulate in Tâi-pak. I helped the consul general's wife to design clothing and became good friends with them. The consul general invited me to do business in Shanghai."

She seemed to be enraptured in memory, growing animated as she spoke, and then pulled open another drawer. She flipped through the contents, searching until she had found an old, yellowed photograph. Tsín-suī moved closer to take a look. It was two Japanese military planes. In the photograph, Hīng-tshun was pointing at the words "*Kō-son-maru*" ("*The Hīng-tshun*") on the side of one of the planes. "This was an airplane my company in Shanghai had contributed and bought for the Japanese military. The company decided to use my name for the contribution, and so the military then anointed it with my name."

Tsín-suī took the photo in both hands and carefully examined it. He couldn't believe the woman in front of him was as astoundingly capable as she was. Hīng-tshun flipped through, searching for another aged photograph. Once again, it was those military planes, but this one had her standing next to one of the machines with her shadow cast over the fuselage. She was a lot younger then. She had both her hands resting on her waist in a power pose. She had a regal look of pride on her face as her hair was carried off, floating in the breeze.

"Didn't the Japanese start waging their war in the Pacific at that time?"

"It had just begun. They wanted all the citizens to contribute." She paused for a moment and then began speaking again, "At the time, it was the right time to donate, and it was also the best time to invest."

Just then, one of the servers came in with their food. She said something in a foreign tongue to the man that Tsín-suī couldn't understand at all. Hīng-tshun then sat down with Tsín-suī and explained to him as they began to eat, "I was speaking in Shanghainese, in *Wu*, with him. He's an old soldier from Shanghai who came over with the KMT. When my company donated the aircraft to the military, we received a lot of benefits from the Japanese, but it did turn me into something of a collaborator after the war. My crime was 'helping the Japanese and selling out the country.' Back then in Shanghai, it was seen in the same light as selling out your own family. There were several Taiwanese who were considered as such. Fortunately, the KMT's military tribunals deemed us as not being complicit and they let us go free."

"Well then, that's very fortunate, *honnh*!"

"Back in those years, a couple Taiwanese had come over and they helped us to negotiate and represented us as our lawyers. The reason we were judged not guilty was that we were in fact citizens of the Empire of Japan. Citizens help their own country. How could we be called collaborators?!"

Tsín-suī grew deeply silent, buried his head, and ate his meal quietly. He thought about his own times growing up as a Japanese citizen. He thought about that frequently ordered slogan they were made to recite when they were at Takao Secondary, doing their military training drills: "May the Soldiers of the Great Japanese Empire continue in their fight forever. Banzai! Ban-banzai!"

Hīng-tshun suddenly replied back in Taiwanese, "Oh, hah! If we talk about my past, we could be speaking for three full days and nights and we'd still not be finished."

After their meal, the servant came back with a silver tray with freshly brewed coffee. Tsín-suī had only ever had this drink once or twice in Kaohsiung. Even so, it was still a rarity in Taipei and wasn't so easily bought, let alone found. "Way back in the day, I was one of the first people to import coffee into Taiwan from Brazil," Hīng-tshun told him.

It was already dusk when Tsín-suī made his way back from Hīng-tshun's company to the meeting room with his colleagues from the Kaohsiung Green Fruit Association. Tsín-suī broke the news to all his colleagues there. Even though it was just a modest forty cents, to those banana farmers among their delegation, it was no small victory. Tsín-suī added, "When the Banana Queen told me that 'our Green Fruits Export Association made piles of money these past few years. That's all from those banana farmers' toiling,' I felt extremely moved. Based on my social experience, I looked her in the eyes when she told me this. I couldn't suss out if there was some sort of haggling exchange in her expression or that it was just talk. It seemed like she was being completely sincere."

"You brought back a lot of earnings from Tâi-pak! You've earned something for us all here at the association. And... you also earned something for yourself too."

"And what did I earn myself?"

"You won yourself a girlfriend."

"Oh, you're being ridiculous. She's just a good friend. There's no way in hell it's anything more than that."

12

It was five days before Tsín-suī returned from his business trip to Taipei. He was still wearing the tie Giok-ìn had looped around his neck. This time though, his wife didn't ask him how his trip went. Instead, she was anxious to tell him some news. "The Tông Îng Steel Mill said that they've just built a new part of the factory. They just built an…oh, what was it called now…a 'furnace,' I think? And so they're having an opening party for it. He invited the vice president, Chen Cheng, to attend and preside over the ribbon-cutting ceremony. All of us Phênn-ôo'ers and family and relatives have been invited to attend," she said in earnest.

"I'd like to go too. We'll certainly have to show up."

Giok-ìn went out shopping again to pick up a big red tie for her husband. She wanted to add to the festive atmosphere of the following day's ceremony.

It was a gigantic space Tsín-suī hadn't seen before. A long, red carpet was rolled out from the great gate of the foundry entrance all the way up to the makeshift stage. The Phênn-ôo relatives and workers were all lined up over towards the back on the right side. They could all still see Tsuān-tsong's father standing under the brutal sunlight over by the main gate. There was a bit of a hunchbacked look to him, but he seemed to be in great spirits. Tsuān-tsong was standing to the right of his father, barrel-chested and standing up as straight as could be. There was a row of stern-looking teams of men arranged in lines to each side of the red carpeting. Both rows were just about as long as the carpet. They were all wearing dashing uniforms with the company's logo embroidered into them, all completely the same.

About seven or eight minutes later, firecrackers were set off in a loud cacophony and celebratory music began to play. Five black sedans slowly drew up along San-duo Road from far off in the distance. Since the road had already been cleared of all traffic and untouchable types, apart from the traffic cop with his whistle blowing, there weren't any people loitering about. There wasn't even any dust roiling up.

"They're here, they're here!" Tông Îng slowly walked along the red carpet with Vice President Chen Cheng, who had just stepped out of one of the sedans. "Oh! That's Chen Cheng! The vice president!" He wasn't a very tall man, but the guy wasn't pudgy either for lack of height. Chen Cheng was still a bit skinnier than Tông Îng. Tsín-suī couldn't tell, but it looked like they were chatting about something. All Tông Îng did was give a humble smile without response. There seemed to be some middle-aged mainlander man following closely behind them. The man would occasionally nod his head a couple times at Chen Cheng's side. Looking over at them up on the stage, his pace seemed very relaxed. He seemed to have a look of pride beaming from his face. This must have been something he was preparing for a long time ago. Tsuān-tsong, who was walking behind them all, didn't have any smile to his face whatsoever. He looked quite nervous, as if his nerves were drawn taut.

The guests all stepped forward to the red silken cloth for the ribbon cutting. They stood all in a row. Red flower corsages were bursting out from everyone's coat pockets. The scissors were all placed along the ribbon. The crowd looked on with eagerness and anticipation, not wanting to shift their gaze and miss the moment. Tsín-suī kept focusing on two cameras. One was to the left and one to the right, filming the entire cutting ceremony. He kept thinking of the team he was on over at the research farm station over in Lîn-lŏk, headed by Dr. Nakamura. These two cameras were much smaller than the one used on that torrential night all those years ago. The one off to the left was still using a black curtain to shield the cameraman's face. The one to the right didn't have any cloth whatsoever. The cameraman on the right just kept his head lowered and was gazing through a small box that made him look as if he were a child carrying a silkworm carton out to play.

A man came up to Tsín-suī's side just then, startling him for a second. "A-Tsòng, how'd you get there?"

"They invited all of us parents of employees to come out to watch the ceremony. Tsìng-tik-á has already been promoted to vice-manager."

"Ah, then a big congratulations to you and yours! Tsìng-tik-á's come a long way. You must be so proud."

"Did you see those young men over there? They're busy, madly writing everything down. Their heads are buried in their notepads. They just don't stop writing... They're—"

"They're probably journalists, no?"

"A-Suī-á, did you hear their performance? Don't you know the melody they're playing?"

"No, I'm not familiar with it. Over here, if it were still the Japanese era, it would probably be their navy's anthem, right?"

The two of them kept speaking in low voices and they watched as the ribbon was finally cut. Tsuān-tsong gave a short introduction to the vice president. The first words out of his mouth, "Reporting to the vice president!" came out with gusto. The next few sentences that he uttered were heavily tinged with a Hoklo accent. He would speak a few words here and there and then wait. Just then, one of the two young men who looked like they were mainlanders began to interpret into fluent Mandarin Chinese. After the boys finished, Tsuān-tsong would continue speaking. The guests all looked on, oblivious to the Chinese, collectively scratching their heads. Only Tsín-suī could understand a bit of the speech. He gathered up bits and pieces here and there. "This new electric furnace used to require workers to control the electrodes, and its monthly output was only a mere thousand tons of steel... After installing the dynamic electrode automatic control system, our monthly output has now reached fifteen hundred tons... This control system can be used for producing steel and can shorten the smelting time by more than half an hour..."

All the Phênn-ôo relatives began to speak in hushed tones, "I heard that they have two thousand workers."

"Not just that. I heard it's more than three thousand, and they're about to need four."

"These past couple of years, this foundry's made just about everything. Train locomotives, railroad tracks. I heard they're getting ready to build steel automobiles."

"The Tôngs are supposedly the leading business family in all of Ko-hiông."

"No, they're the leading steel manufacturer in all of Ko-hiông."

A-Tsòng and Tsín-suī were exchanging words, though of a far different nature from everyone else around them.

"A-Suī-á, do you think Tsuān-tsong's going to get a passing grade for the amount of ball-fondling he's doing?"

"You're saying he looks nervous today? Would you say he's acting unnaturally?"

"He doesn't want to be like his father. A-Îng is already an immortal. He has the footwork of an immortal, carefully stepping around on eggshells to cozy on up to these officials, tigers, and demigods."

"I don't quite follow what you're saying."

"Tông Îng is expressing his heart's deepest desire. He absolutely worships Chen Cheng like some idol, right down to the very earth he walks upon. Deep down, he sees him as some 'grandiose, magnanimous leader, a guiding lodestar for the people.' He just wishes he could hold Chen Cheng's family jewels for him. It would come so naturally to him. No clouds of doubt hanging around in the air at all. He'd do it completely willingly. That's what it means to become an immortal."

"Hah! '*Hóo-lān*'... You speak so poetically about sucking up to people, you get to the heart of it. It's like you've heard it straight from the horse's mouth."

"I'm just calling how I see this entire scene, this...arrangement. Just looking at father and son and how they've been acting and standing and walking, I can paint a story for you right away if you'd like, haha."

"Though, when you 'paint up this story,' I might only give you a five out of ten for your final grade."

"It's worth more than a five. It's more like an eight or a nine."

"I need to study your mastery of this scene here. Maybe my company can use it later on."

"Right, right, learning the art of holding others' family jewels requires exhaustive study."

13

After one stint as a director, Tsín-suī ran for another term. One evening, Chang Ming-suh came over to the Ngôo household to pay him a visit. The purpose of his visit? He strode over with a spring in his step and with a lot of pep in his voice. He beamed as he told Tsín-suī that he thought his younger colleague ought to run for the chairmanship itself.

"Uh... So what about you? Where are you planning to run off to after your tenure's over?"

"I want to go and stand for chairman of the national United Daily News Association executive."

"Huh, you're telling me if I run for the chairmanship of the Ko-hiông Association, you think I'd be able to win it?"

"Our outfit in Ko-hiông has an unspoken rule that the chairman must come from Pîn-tong. I'm just here to tell you that at the present moment, there's three from Pîn-tong City and two from Kî-*san* who are more knowledgeable than you, and among those from Pîn-tong, Uncle A-Tsòng has already told me that he would throw his weight behind your campaign. The only other person from Pîn-tong who would be running against you is Hong Hsi. Well, what do you think? Will you throw your hat into the race?"

Tsín-suī just sat in silence for a moment, then replied, "OK. I'm in. Let's see how I do."

As Chang Ming-suh was leaving, he added hesitantly, "The only concern I have is that relationship you have with Tân Hīng-tshun, the Banana Queen. Someone might try to pick that up and make a story out of it."

"There's nothing untoward between me and her. Absolutely nothing. We're just very close friends is all."

"Each time you go off to Japan on a business trip, she also just happens to be going there too. Don't you think that's a bit too much of a coincidence?"

"All we do when we go to Japan is call on lots of people and meet lots of business leaders. It's a great help for me and for the future of our Taiwanese banana crops." Tsín-suī paused a moment before continuing, "Brother Ming-suh, think about it for a second. My friendship with Tân Hīng-tshun is openly known to everyone in my family. When my son, Tîng-kong, and my daughters Bí-siù and Bí-ài go to Tâi-pak, they all stay at Tân Hīng-tshun's house. They call her 'Auntie Hīng-tshun.' If there were anything suspicious between us, it would have to be a very well-kept secret. It wouldn't be possible to have that kind of open relationship between our families, would it?"

"Well, of course I know that. When the time comes and someone raises suspicions, just explain it to them like that."

Not long after, at the beginning of 1960, Chang Ming-suh did, in fact, join the United Daily Newspaper in Taipei where he was elected the chairman of the board. Thereupon, he came back down south to Ko-hiông and convened a board meeting to announce his resignation and declared the election of a successor chairman. In the contest between Tsín-suī and Hong Hsi, Tsín-suī won out with eleven votes to Hong's seven. On the day that he assumed his position as chairman of the board, there was a celebratory meeting and Tsín-suī, of course, had to go up and make a speech. He had been preparing for this speech for an entire day and night, hashing out a draft in a mix of Japanese and Chinese. Once he had finished writing the draft, he tried to read it aloud in Chinese, which took a huge effort, and it didn't make any sense. He switched over to Hoklo, and it was a bit smoother, so in the end, he decided to go with a mix of Taiwanese Hoklo and Chinese.

The meeting was being held in the Great Hall of the Cooperative Association. After the opening formalities concluded and the government representatives had made their remarks, it was finally time for Ngôo Tsín-suī to begin his speech.

> Gentlemen, officials, distinguished guests, inspectors, as well as our managers and vice-managers, welcome! I've received many congratulations and encouragement from Hong hsi-*hiann* and others over these past two days. My heart is full of gratitude and overcome with emotion.
>
> I, A-Tsín-suī, began my work in this field as a mere research technician when I was only twenty years old. Today, at over fifty years old, I've had much time to prepare. But what have I been preparing for? I have been

preparing to take over the helm of the Ko-hiông Green Fruits Shipping and Marketing Cooperative as its new chairman.

In these last several years, I've run all over the place inspecting banana plantations and have often gone to the collection and inspection sites. I've gone to meet and discuss matters with bamboo basket manufacturers. I've also gone off to Japan to meet with all of the big companies, to understand their markets and to feel out how the leaders of the world of Japanese trade think, deep down. During these times, I've often had a *bāng-kah* appear to me. Such *bāng-kah*—such visions—were among the things that my ox-appraising master neighbor, Uncle A-Huàn, used to talk about all the time. He used to say that the *bāng-kah* that used to appear in his mind were a way of seeing images of the future and describing ages past. However, my understanding is different. The *bāng-kah* that have appeared to me in the last few years are my ideals— they are a blueprint for what I am now preparing to bring to fruition.

The most senior of all the directors in attendance, Uncle A-Tsòng, was the first to start clapping, leading everyone else in the hall in a wave of applause. Tsín-suī was forced to pause until the applause died down, so he took a sip of tea and then picked up where he had left off:

My first *bāng-kah* is that there be one truck after another filled to overflowing with bananas, entering the port at Ko-hiông, and one basket after another being unloaded, checked, and loaded onto waiting ships from piers as crowded as the morning vegetable markets. People are shouting back and forth, and everything is noisy and bustling as can be. My friends, this isn't some mere fantasy dream. I want to raise the number of yearly banana exports from Taiwan to eight million baskets, even up to ten million!

At this last part, prolonged *oohs* and *ahs* of astonishment rose from the audience. Current exports were only around four hundred eighty thousand baskets. In the best of seasons, they could barely make five hundred thousand.

So how will we reach this amount? I'll tell you how! All around Kî-san, including the floodplains of the Lower Tamsui River between Kî-*san* and Li-kang, and the broad agricultural lands north of Hong-liau in Pîn-tong are all extremely suitable areas for growing bananas. We can greatly increase the area cultivated for bananas! So... How do we encourage our farmers to increase their yield? The only incentive is price. When there is money to earn, especially when there is big money to earn, everyone will want to grow bananas.

But if everyone wants to grow bananas and the size of banana plantations increases greatly, then the price will drop like a rock, right? Well, not necessarily. The Japanese market still has massive potential for expansion. Right now, trade in bananas between Taiwan and Japan is a seller's market. They'll take whatever amount we have! Several of their big companies want our product, and so...

My second *bāng-kah* is to make sure that at all the food markets everywhere in Japan, as Japanese consumers peel our bright yellow bananas and start to eat them with big bites, chewing then swallowing, their faces will shine with satisfaction.

Friends, do you want to know how Japanese eat bananas? After they peel them, they don't dare eat them straight away. They use a knife to cut them into thin slices, and then they use a fork to eat one slice at a time, as if they're eating Korean ginseng. I'm not pulling your leg...

The whole hall roared with laughter. Someone down in the audience called out, "Sounds like when we Taiwanese eat Fuji apples. They're so precious, nobody dares to just scarf them down."

Tsín-suí continued his speech, slightly raising his voice.

Friends, after I've started my tenure, I want to set up an office in Japan to help spread the word about our produce. I want to change the Japanese mindset that bananas are a 'delicacy' and bring down the price. I want to get Japanese used to happily munching our bananas every day and that way expand Japan's banana market. We'll make our Taiwanese bananas dominate the market and stop them thinking about imports from South America. After we've brought down the price in Japan, I'd first like to increase our exports to eight million baskets a year, and even up to ten million might be possible. I know, some of you may be asking, 'On the one hand, you want us to raise the price of bananas in the domestic market to encourage production, but then on the other hand, lower the price of our bananas in Japan. Isn't that a contradiction?' Well, here's what I have to say to the naysayers: The secret is in the word 'volume.' In addition to increasing the volume of consumption in Japan, we have something important to do on our own island of Taiwan, and it's quite a difficult matter... And that brings me to...

My third *bāng-kah*. In this vision, I have three sets of numbers in mind. They are 'anything more than zero,' 'seventy-five-to-twenty-five,' and 'fifty-fifty.' Faced with these numbers together, some banana farmers might cry out as they wipe the tears from their eyes. So, what does this *bāng-kah* mean? Well, everyone here knows. Taiwanese banana exports were worth six million New Taiwan dollars last year. It accounted for one third of the country's total exports. But it's the exporters who monopolize everything, and we farmers are squeezed and exploited and left with nothing. So that's where 'anything more than zero' comes in. In 1956, we asked the central government to coordinate with us to change the export quota so that for every three baskets sold by exporters, we farmers could sell one. So that's where seventy-five versus twenty-five percent comes in.

Everyone in the audience knew that Tsín-suī had arrived at his main point and they were so quiet, you could hear a pin drop.

Friends, I vow to you here and now, I will do everything in my power to change this senseless ratio. I've set two goals for myself. First, within two or three years, I guarantee to change that 'seventy-five-to-twenty-five' quota to 'fifty-fifty.' I'm asking you to work together with me on this.

The sound of applause rose from the crowd and went on for a full two minutes.

Everyone, hold your applause, please. My second step is that I want to start up a 'unified production and sales movement.' So, what is that, you might ask? Well, it's about abolishing the export quota so that banana producers can export all the bananas that we grow.

Some in the audience began to clap and shout for joy, but Tsín-suī raised his hand and continued.

None of these goals will be easy. We need to strive towards them from three angles. One is that we need to organize our producers and go everywhere and explain our situation—to city halls, to the provincial government. Taipei will be even more important, especially the Foreign Currency and Trade Deliberation committee of the Executive Yuan. We need to petition the governmental departments in charge of these matters to explain these goals very clearly.

The second aspect is that we already know that the Japanese government is preparing to promote trade liberalization and they will choose several items to start with. I'd like to go to Japan to speak with them and suggest that our bananas be one of the first products to be liberalized. That's the only way that we'll be completely free of the export quota system.

The third point is that I hope we can completely break free of the exporters so that they have no control, not even over one basket—

"Isn't the director of the foreign exporters Tân Hīng-tshun? Will you be able to push her aside?" Someone in the audience shouted.

She will support our ideas. In order to help us to realize our goals, she will deal with the exporters as necessary, regardless of who they are, and if it requires overturning some tables, so be it! What is there to be afraid of?!

"Oh, heh-heh, he's very ambitious. There's a lot in what Chairman Ngôo says."
"Haha, he's got balls, that's for sure!"
Tsín-suī wasn't even able to finish his remarks before the entire hall started enthusiastically responding to his ideas, and the din just grew louder and louder. Uncle A-Tsòng, down in the front row, was just sitting silently. After a long, long time he finally he blurted out, "Our Banana King has come! Oh! He is the new Banana King! Oh, Ngôo Tsín-suī from our village will become the new Banana King!"
Two young men briskly walked up from the last row and handed their calling cards to Tsín-suī. One was a reporter for the *Central Daily News*. As soon as he spoke, you could tell the guy was a *waishengren* (mainlander). The other was an especially dispatched reporter with the *Taiwan New Life Gazette* who spoke Mandarin with a Hoklo accent. He didn't know what the difference between the special dispatch reporter and journalist was, so

Tsín-suī just thought of them as both news reporters. Tsín-suī first politely asked the *waishengren* journalist, "My speech didn't quite sound like the Mandarin Chinese, were you able to understand me?"

"I could catch bits and pieces. The parts I didn't understand, I'll just ask him." He motioned with his thumb toward the special dispatch reporter from the Taiwan New Life Gazette beside him.

"Chairman, you said you want to raise Taiwan's yearly banana exports to eight million or even ten million baskets. What's the current number?"

"It's currently about five hundred thousand."

"Incredible! You're aiming for fifteen or sixteen times the current number. Are you sure you can do it? How long will it take to get to your goal?"

"This is my long-term goal—my dream, my long view. We will need to work hard both in Taiwan and in the Japanese market, but when both the objective and subjective conditions have come to fruition, it will definitely be achievable."

"So, Mr. Chairman, can we use what you just said as a headline? Can we call it 'Ngôo Tsín-suī's Banana Dream?'"

"Sure. Just write 'dream.' If you write '*bāng-kah*,' most people won't understand." Tsín-suī felt that these two journalists didn't want to leave just yet, and so he continued to talk with them for a bit. "Truth be told, I have a fourth *bāng-kah* in mind, but I forgot to mention it just now."

"What is it?"

"There are all sorts of bamboo forests all over Taiwan. Since people's lifestyles have been changing rapidly over the last few years, the husks of spiny bamboo and Makino bamboo are no longer being harvested as much as they used to be. There's plenty of wild rattan growing in the mountainous areas too. Then there's also an abundance of straw rope made from rice stalks. Think about it. After banana exports have been considerably increased, it will give rise to a range of thriving peripheral industries—harvesting rattan and making rattan goods, gathering bamboo husks, making rope, and weaving bamboo baskets. If we include the land and sea transportation industry, I estimate that tens of thousands of families will benefit."

"Can we put this *bāng-kah* in 'Ngôo Tsín-suī's Banana Dream'?"

"Of course, by all means. Thank you."

14

Things were especially frenzied in the conference room of the Executive Yuan's Foreign Trade Deliberation Committee. Inside, representatives of the Green Fruit Cooperative and the Green Fruit Guild had been arguing endlessly, and the sound of their voices spilled out into the halls of the bureau.

"What are you basing that off of?! *Honnh*?! We gave you an extra twenty-five percent, then not long afterwards you come back wanting more. We give you an inch, and you want a mile. You're never satisfied!"

"Now we raise it from twenty-five percent, and you're still not satisfied? Before, when your quota wasn't even one basket, weren't your banana farmers still happily growing their bananas and living comfortably?"

"Growing bananas with tears in your eyes is not happiness. You know the damned difference!"

"What kind of bullshit is that? *Honnh*? You're taking advantage of everyone. You've grown used to squeezing and abusing us banana farmers. You're used to drinking our blood! You've been drinking it so long you think it's just that way things are."

"Do you know what fairness looks like? Do you think you're better than banana farmers? All you ever do is just sit in your lavish offices here in Tâi-pak. You never go out and sweat under the burning sun. You sit in your offices all day with the fans blowing. How does that make you better than anyone?"

The foreign trade official was getting fed up. "Both sides need to lower their voices! None of you can speak Mandarin yet, and you're speaking so loudly in that local dialect. Do you have no shame? Hmm?" The meeting room quieted down very quickly, and the official warned them again, "If Chairman Hsu comes and hears you hooting and hollering in that uncouth dialect, he'll be angry and order you all to be kicked out."

The official's rebuke was exactly like that of a teacher who slams his fist on his desk to make the class quiet down.

The representative for the exporters, Tân Hīng-tshun, who hadn't been speaking much at the meeting took the opportunity to make a recommendation. Using Shanghai-accented Mandarin, she said, "Everyone, calm down please. Let's all try to give a little more: sixty percent to forty percent. Six—four—. Let's not fight anymore!"

Tsín-suī extended his hand to the official with his five fingers raised. He turned his hand back to front twice without saying a word.

The official asked, "Are you trying to say five to five?"

Tsín-suī nodded several times.

The meeting quieted down again. After a period of silence, Tân Tshâ-bóo also extended his hand and raised a couple fingers. First, he made a "six," quickly followed by a "five." He stopped for a second and then made a "three," followed by a "five," also without speaking. The official impatiently piped up, "What's going on? What are you up to! Have you both suddenly become mutes? Why are you using sign language?" He turned to Hīng-tshun, "Director Chen, what does your vice-director mean by those signs?"

"It means sixty-five percent to thirty-five percent," Hīng-tshun answered.

As soon as Hīng-tshun suggested the sixty-five to thirty-five ratio, Tsín-suī forcefully extended five fingers. He then flipped his hand over and back twice. After this sign, he spoke in a mix of Mandarin and Hoklo, saying, "Fifty-fifty. If you don't agree, then we'll all regret it later."

The official stared over at Hīng-tshun. "Director Chen,—"

Before the official even finished speaking, Hīng-tshun ungrudgingly replied, "OK, you've got a deal."

Tân Tshâ-bóo, sitting next to her, shouted out, "I oppose it. Director, we can't do that!"

Hīng-tshun said, "Enough. Enough. Don't be stubborn!"

Tshâ-bóo stood up and announced, "I'm sorry, I'm going to take my leave now." Then he strode off. Of the five trade representatives, two followed him out the door.

Hīng-tshun wasn't moved at all by this, and she said, "Would the trade association please make a formal note in the committee record that a consensus has been reached for fifty percent to fifty percent."

The official added, "OK. Our committee will draft a formula so that we can announce implementation as soon as it has been submitted for approval."

After the meeting had broken up, both sides asked the official to make an appointment to see Chairman Hsu Po-yuen. His secretary said, "The chairman is currently in a meeting and is unable to receive guests."

Hīng-tshun had earlier reserved a side room at a Japanese restaurant for dinner. She said that she was bringing an extremely important Japanese guest with her. Who could it be? She wouldn't tell Tsín-suī just yet.

Tsín-suī brought along his general affairs secretary, Tsai Kun-shan. When he pulled back the *shōji* sliding door, the guest was already inside. Tsín-suī was momentarily taken aback, then blurted out in surprise, "*Wah*! Satō-*san*! It's you! Satō Kishin! Haha, it's you!" The two of them shook hands and looked at each other for a moment, sizing each other up. They were both a little excited.

"It's been far too long. How long as it been?" Satō Kishin began.

Tsín-suī pondered it for a moment, "Thirty years. It's been thirty years since we first met. I went to your home in Taipei and slept in your antique-enclosed redwood bed ahaha!"

"How is your mother-in-law doing? Is Ông-*san* still faring well?"

"She's already crossed over to the Western Paradise, I'm afraid. The shop's affairs are being taken care of by my brother-in-law now."

Hīng-tshun told the two men to sit down and began to order, but the flow of the conversation never faltered.

"Satō-*san* has already told me that story from thirty years ago at least a dozen times. It's quite the tale!" Hīng-tshun began her introduction, "However, Satō Kishin-*san* is no longer that small businessman of all those years ago in Taipei. He's now the head honcho of the Tokyo Satō Commercial Company. He's the head of the Japanese trade committee and has had a lot of business dealings with my company branch in Tokyo."

Tsín-suī butted in, "How did you find me?"

"Hah! I've been in Taipei these last two days, and I saw in the newspaper that you were now a big shot yourself. I called up Ms. Tân Hīng-tshun here and learned that you had been good friends for a long time."

"Do you still have your home here in Taipei?"

"I do, but I spend most of my time in Tokyo."

The four of them chatted as they ate, and the atmosphere was extremely jovial. Just as dinner was ending, Vice-chairman Tsai left to go settle the bill. When he returned, he was holding newspapers. One was the Truth News,[36] and the other was the United Daily News. He handed both of them to Tsín-suī and pointed to the headlines. "Mr. Chairman... Look. Take a look here."

---

36. *Truth (Cheng-hsin) News* was the predecessor of the *China Times*.

Tsín-suī and Hīng-tshun took a newspaper each and began reading. A couple minutes later, Tsín-suī's whole body started to tremble. He leaned his head back against the wooden dividing wall behind him. His face first turned reddish black, then pallid green. His forehead was all furrowed and his mouth drawn taut, as if he was enduring acute pain.

"What's going on? What's going on? What's this all about?" Everyone shouted in shock.

Hīng-tshun told Assistant Manager Tsai, "It might be food poisoning, it's quite serious. Go call for an ambulance."

At this point, Tsín-suī grabbed hold of his assistant manager and yelled at him, "No! Don't call one. There's no need!"

A couple of the restaurant staff out in the corridor heard the commotion and entered. Hīng-tshun immediately confronted them, "There's a problem with your food. It might be food poisoning."

But with a trembling voice Tsín-suī said, "No. It's not that. Just slide the door closed. I'm fine." He climbed onto the low table and his whole body began to convulse. Wow! He was crying! He let out sorrowful wails that shook his whole body.

Hīng-tshun drew herself closer to him, lightly patting and stroking his back. Satō Kishin looked startled and at a loss. The longer Tsín-suī wept, the louder he got, drawing lots of stares from those outside the room. Assistant Manager Tsai opened the door a crack and explained to people outside, "He's drunk. Our guest is bawling because he has had too much to drink. It's nothing, OK!" Then he slid the door tightly.

"Perhaps it's because your chairman read that headline regarding the Tông Îng Steel foundry? Would that be too farfetched?"

"The chairman of Tông Îng Steel, Tông Tsuān-tsong, is one of our chairman's good friends."

Hīng-tshun returned to her place and carefully read the headlines and subheadings. "Tang Eng Steel Foundry is being returned to the State / According to Nation Mobilization Laws its loans are being frozen; Tang and his sons were extravagant / Last year they had a banquet with two hundred tables for their son's engagement / Bank of Taiwan issues news statement revealing Tang Eng Steel's debt figures."

Before she finished reading, Hīng-tshun felt Tsín-suī had stopped crying. She looked up and saw that he was wiping his eyes. "A-Suī-á, you scared me for a second, scared me nearly to death. What was that all about?"

"Don't worry yourself. The doctor told me that this is a kind of nervous condition. When it happens, I feel extreme pain throughout my whole body and it makes me weep inconsolably for a time, but after I weep, I get better. The last time I had this happen was twenty years ago. It happens after some major event occurs."

"A major event? Do you mean the thing with the Tông Îng Steel Foundry?"

"It's absolutely terrible. This absolutely has to be a setup, a big setup. They're being persecuted... *Baka yarō!*"

"Do you have some understanding of the situation?"

"I think I know it best. I often work with their general manager, Tông Tsuān-tsong, exchanging business ideas. The steel industry was originally an industry where you had to sink a lot of investments and then got very slow returns. It couldn't be done without bank loans, especially low-in-terest loans from the government." As he spoke, Tsín-suī's voice still had that nasal ring of someone who has been crying. "That Bank of Taiwan is an all-out rotten cabal. How could they publicize Tông Îng's debt figures? The debtholders will all want their money back as soon as they see the numbers. It's not a question of if the company will go under, but when. *Baka yarō!* This is completely deliberate!"

Hīng-tshun just listened in silence. Tsín-suī started to curse again, "F*** them! This newspaper writes about how the Tông family are extravagant, which is just pure libel. Father and son are extremely frugal. To say that they had over two hundred tables for their son's engagement...*Baka!* There are all those different managers within the foundry and all sorts of clients in the supply chain. Then there's that broad network of social contacts... Of course, they'd need two hundred tables."

Tsín-suī remembered that Satō Kishin was in the room and gave him a demure look. "Satō-*san*... I'm extremely sorry for my outburst. I have let you see my nervous condition act up. I feel ridiculous and so ashamed."

"You don't need to feel ashamed. I've seen clearly just what kind of person you are," Satō-*san* said in Taiwanese. He stopped for a moment and then switched over to Japanese. "Thirty years ago, it was your character that I was particularly impressed by. That's why I came to you."

Hīng-tshun chimed in, asking, "The Tôngs...what higher-ups were they engaged with?"

"They were originally on good private terms with Chen Cheng."

"Oh, I see now." Hīng-tshun stopped for a few moments, and then switched to Mandarin. "One definitely has to tread the Chiang path if they want to succeed. The emperor is someone we will never have an audience with, but the empress or the prince—those are some options for you, but you have to be very careful about this in future."

"I heard someone say that the foreign trade committee is headed by Hsu Po-yuen and that he's one of Madame Chiang's generals?"

"That's correct. I'm pretty well-connected with him. When the right time comes, I'll pull a few strings for you."

"Hīng-tshun, Satō-*san*, I think I need to go back to Ko-hiông immediately to help console my friend, Tsuān-tsong, and see how I can help make things better. Let's call it a day and find another day to have a good chat, OK?"

"Sure. Don't feel too hurt by it all. Take care of yourself, ah!"

Mr. Satō stood up to say goodbye. "Whenever you're in Japan trying to sell bananas, if you ever need any of help, please reach out to me."

"Yes. I'll definitely seek you out. I truly need your help at the moment."

After they split up, Tsín-suī told Assistant Manager Tsai, "Let's go. Let's take the night train back to Ko-hiông."

"Mr. Chairman, you can't go back to Ko-hiông. Tomorrow, you have to be on time to meet with the Provincial Council. We made arrangements for a group of banana farmers to send a petition in person. As their leader, how could you forget that?"

"Oh. Yes, I guess I did. Why didn't you mention it to me before?"

"We want to petition for 'unified production and sales.' I wanted to hold off on telling you because I thought it best if Ms. Tan didn't know about it."

"She would have found out about it sooner or later. She usually supports my plans."

"I had figured. She's got a good heart. Sooner or later, she's going to butt heads with Tân Tshâ-bóo."

"That's true. Sooner or later."

The Taiwan Provincial Council had already relocated from Taipei down to Chung-hsing New Village in Nantou County. There was a decent-sized plaza in front of the newly constructed building. Groups of petitioners who had arrived were separated and handled by different representatives accordingly. Just as Tsín-suī's team of petitioners had finished submitting their petition and were about to head back to Tainan, Tsuān-tsong suddenly walked out from a representative's room accompanied by a secretary. Tsuān-tsong saw his friend first. "Hey. A-Suī-á."

Tsín-suī practically ran over to him. They grasped each other with both hands, fixing their eyes on the other. Ah! Tsuān-tsong had suddenly grown much older. He had a patch of white hair and deeply etched crow's-feet at the corners of his eyes and mouth. Tsín-suī could only call out, "Tsuān-tsong-*hiann*," but he was at a loss for what to say next.

Tsuān-tsong lightly patted Tsín-suí's shoulder and said, "Let's go. Let's find a place to sit, and I'll tell you all about it."

The two of them left the council building and happened to see a place over to their left with a small pond and a wooden bench next to it. It was made so people could sit and watch the goldfish in the pond. All around the pond, flowers and trees grew luxuriantly and little birds called from the branches. It was a bit noisy, but that didn't impede their conversation.

"When I went to visit you two months ago, you never told me you might be in danger."

"What danger? Everything's been taken care of. Who doesn't have loans to take care of in the steel industry?" Tsuān-tsong's voice was a little hoarse. "However, Chen Cheng sent someone to tell my father a bunch of strange things. They were very vague and it wasn't clear what they were saying, but it seemed they were implying that the vice president didn't have any time to speak with anyone these days, that we couldn't go to him to report anything. We also weren't allowed to request that he do anything."

"Is that so? Could it be that... Would it be fair to say that...it was a warning?"

"After Chen Cheng's men came, I thought it was a warning to us, but lately we hadn't gone to him to ask him to do anything."

"So how does your father feel about the whole thing?"

"He's absolutely devastated. He wasn't in great health to begin with, and now he's just lying in his bed, refusing to speak with anyone..." Tsín-suí immediately felt a twinge of sadness and he was afraid his own condition would start acting up. He looked up in search of the sparrows in the trees and tried hard to think of other things. He thought of Giȯk-ín at home and whether everything was OK with her. He thought of his buffalo, Masa. The last time he had gone home, Masa had already grown to be quite large and strong. His younger brother excitedly told him that Masa was even easier to drive than his mother, Mari. Tsín-suí immersed himself in his thoughts, but when he heard the sound of Tsuān-tsong weeping, then blowing his nose, he pulled himself back. For a time, he didn't know how best to console Tsuān-tsong. He unconsciously blurted out, "F***, just like that they absconded with a huge steel factory in broad daylight! It's despicable! *Baka yarō*!"

"A-Tsín-suí, to be honest, I'm also quite devastated, but there are still many, many managers and partners that must rely on me. As I sit at my father's bedside, he looks deep into the depths of my soul and has such strong resolve. He wants me to rebound from this, to pull myself back up. A-Suí-á, you know that since I was young, I have been in business with my dad. His way of handling relationships with the government has made a deep impression on me. So... F***! F*** them! I'll just have to grin and bear it for now!"

Tsín-suī slapped his thigh hard, then blurted out, "Yes, we've got to put up with it. We've got to just endure it!"

"A-Tsín-suī, there's nothing for it but to keep persevering, and as long as I can laugh at it, I know I can make a comeback."

"When the war ended and they were being repatriated, my Japanese manager, Mr. Yamamoto, the director over at the Pingtung Banana Research Lab, invited me to his home for a meal. He was a very astute and learned man. He told me, 'You'll go on to do a great many things for your people, but you must always be careful. If you read the history of the Chinese, you'll know that their governments are extremely treacherous.'"

Tsuān-tsong kept listening to Tsín-suī in silence.

Tsín-suī continued, "Yesterday, Tân Hīng-tshun asked me to remind you that when you need to make connections or you need to curry favor, you have to tread the line of the Chiang family, whether it's the empress or the prince, it doesn't matter. As long as it's the Chiangs, it should be fine."

"I recently made this realization myself. It was a deeply painful realization."

"There's more... The newspapers in the last couple of days...you shouldn't read any of them. They're nothing but a pack of lies, just malicious distortions. It's not just twisting the truth. Their newspapers are trying to assassinate your family and its character with words."

"The bastards! F*** them!"

Just as Tsín-suī and Tsuān-tsong reached this part of the conversation, a man walked towards the pond. He threw a couple pieces of bread into the water and watched as the fish fought for the scraps. They were like a pack of hungry wolves devouring a little white rabbit. The two of them hushed up and watched in silence at the commotion being made by the fish. They kept sitting for a while longer. They then got up together without prompt and walked shoulder to shoulder towards the parking lot. The two men's small entourage of officials were in tow. Tsín-suī continued speaking hurriedly, "Tsuān-tsong, when you say, 'keep on enduring and reverse what's happened and be able to smile at it,' it's not at all a simple task."[37]

---

37. In this highly authoritarian period of Taiwan's history, good friends would often privately express their feelings about the government. Historian Hsu Hsueh-yi once recorded an oral history with Tông Tsuān-tsong, which is part of the work "消失的台灣鋼鐵大王" (Taiwan's Disappeared King of Steel), where he was said "to have had great animosity towards the government. He used a lot of expletives at almost every opportunity."

"From the time I was young and went everywhere with my father for business, it gave me a chance to experience the business world a bit earlier than you. There's a secret to it. When you see an adversary that 'wants to kill you' as a good person, as someone worthy of respect, when you spend your own energy in treating this person with amity and respect, you have to 'provide incense and kneel and grovel at his feet.' When you do this, he shouldn't want to hurt you again, should he? They might even provide you with work to do."

"*Aiyee*! That's just downright degrading!"

"It's just what I'm thinking deep down. Even if I want to do it, it doesn't mean it'll succeed."

15

After leaving Chung-hsing New Village, Tsín-suī felt like going back to Pîn-tong for a visit but another task was still awaiting him. The managers had helped him to prepare his documents for leaving the country, as well as a giant ream of materials. His company car stopped outside the office door. He stepped into the car, and the chauffeur sped along towards the airport. Once inside the car, he opened up his briefcase and paged through all his papers.

The materials were briefs and company background information on his Japanese counterparts for the negotiations between Japan and Taiwan on banana sales. As the chairman of the Kaohsiung firm and the United firm's general manager, he was the main representative for the Taiwanese side. Tsín-suī flipped through several pages of these documents and then put them back in his briefcase. He then closed his eyes to rest. He silently thought about all the etiquette, rules of engagement, and manners of interacting with his Japanese counterparts which had been drilled into him throughout his youth—all of his experiences in the past—which strategies worked and which ones didn't.

Tokyo wasn't far and his plane soon touched down. After he and his colleagues had settled into their *ryokan* inn, the head of the Japanese side, Director Shibata, made an appointment to meet Tsín-suī privately. They had a reservation at the Fujimura Restaurant. It was the kind of an establishment where a man could order some liquor and light snacks and be in the company of beautiful women. In spite of that, Director Shibata only ordered up some fruit and green tea, insisting that tonight was strictly for talking about business, not for pleasure.

Two blankets were laid inside the room. Shibata knelt down on one of them. Tsín-suī followed his example. They had just drunk the first cup of tea when Shibata got down to the point. "About how many baskets of bananas do you estimate you can ship us this year?"

"From Kaohsiung, we're estimating an export of about three million baskets. From Taichung, about one million."

Shibata asked, "Does this include the amount from the exporter, Tân Hīng-tshun?"

"That's correct." Tsín-suī felt a pang of anxiety after responding, and asked Shibata back, "Just what exactly is the highest amount that can be marketed in Japan?"

"Eight million."

"So, from a business calculation, how many baskets would bring your companies the greatest profit?"

Shibata muttered to himself for a moment and then said, "Six million."

In his mind, Tsín-suī shouted out, "That's too risky!" But he remained silent. Shibata shifted back to lean on the wood paneled wall and stretched his feet out beneath the blanket. He did not say anything, and his eyes were slightly closed. It was as if he was resting, but he had a thoughtful expression on his face, as if he was pondering deeply. Tsín-suī shifted his position from kneeling to a half-sitting, half-reclined position. He was thinking, "We've got such a huge gap in what our farmers can produce and the amount the Japanese want! If I'm not careful in fulfilling their demands, the Japanese will almost certainly be looking towards a third country to import from." As he was thinking this, he looked up at Shibata. Just at that moment, Shibata also opened his eyes and their eyes met. It was like electric wires with positive and negative charges suddenly connected with an explosion of sparks.

Shibata spoke first, seeming aware of Tsín-suī's inner thoughts. "If you can't yet produce two million baskets, I'm afraid that our Japanese merchants will go to another country looking a solution."

Tsín-suī responded in such a low voice, it was almost as if he were talking to himself. "What other countries can supply that amount?"

"The Philippines, Indonesia, Vietnam, Malaysia, Thailand, China—"

"Those places may have cultivated bananas, but they don't have bananas that suit Japanese palates. If you go off to those countries to buy up their produce, I'm afraid it won't sell here at all."

"Have you done a market survey in Japan?"

"No, but I'm sure of it." Tsín-suī sat up straight, raising his voice, "Taiwanese bananas are hybrids produced by Japanese agricultural technicians. They improved the variety and taste. I myself began in a Japanese research facility. My *enshi* (dear former teacher) is none other than Nakamura Jiro of Kyushu University."

Shibata didn't say anything and Tsín-suī kept adding details. "In all of Asia, Japanese only have fondness for bananas grown in Taiwan. They're the shortest distance to ship by boat and so the shipping fees are also quite low."

"Well, tell me then, how do you expect to make up for the lack in quantity?"

Tsín-suī got up to his feet and said, "Director Shibata, I have a solution that offers the best of both worlds."

"Well, go on. I'm listening."

"With your agreement, I'd like to raise the price of Kaohsiung bananas from seven American dollars a basket to eight dollars. If I go back to Kaohsiung and immediately inform them, it will be a great encouragement for the farmers. They'll increase production many times over, and quickly meet the demand for the Japanese market."

Shibata also stood up and asked, "What about Taichung? Would they also need to increase the price?"

"No. Taichung's bananas are already eight dollars a basket."

"Using a price increase to encourage production isn't a long-term solution. Other companies will object to it."

"One year," Tsín-suī extended one finger. "I just need one year to do it."

"This I can agree to," Shibata replied firmly. He sat down again, kneeling once again, and continued speaking, "But I need to get all of the companies in my organization on board for it to be cleared." Tsín-suī followed suit and knelt down opposite Shibata. Each of them took a sip of tea. The two of them sat in silence for a while. Shibata then started, "In tomorrow's formal meeting, the Fujiwara company will raise some questions about what we've just discussed."

"Tomorrow, neither Mr. Director nor I should say anything at the start. I'll have director Cheng Hsi-chüan give the response for my side."

"When we get to the point in discussion about imports from Southeast Asian countries, you should speak up yourself. What you just told me about the improvement of varieties and flavors will have some power in convincing Japanese. I'm also concerned that my colleagues will blindly begin imports and ultimately be unable to sell the Southeast Asian varieties."

"Understood." Tsín-suī bowed, then said, "Thank you very much for your decision, Mr. Director."

"I heard that the Satō Kishin of Satō-Shōji is an old friend of yours?"

"Yes, that's right. Why did you wish to mention him, Mr. Director?"

"Our company only caught word of it yesterday," Shibata said. "Mr. Ishikawa from the Yamazaki Corporation will also be in attendance tomorrow. He's very well connected to Mr. Satō Kishin. They both hold a lot of shares in each other's companies."

"Yes, thank you for the reminder," Tsín-suī continued. "Tomorrow, when we finally get to a resolution, I hope that you, Mr. Director, will come out in strong support of it."

The day after he returned from Japan, Tsín-suī had held a routine supervisory meeting. After the meeting, he prepared to head back to Pingtung to gather all the members of the producer families together and demand that they find as much land as they could. It didn't matter if they rented it or bought it or leased it, so long as they used the land to grow bananas—the more the better. He cut down on the amount of his official travel over the next two days and stayed at home as much as he could, trying to make related arrangements in person.

When he got back to his office in Kaohsiung, there was a large pile of reports sitting on his bureau awaiting him. Right up at the top of it was the minutes of the board of directors meeting from just a few days before, to be kept on file after he had read through them. This was the simplest matter, and there couldn't be any mistake with it. All he had to do was read them and then add his signature.

Case One: Chinese Nationalist Party, Tokyo Branch, is requesting that our association pledge donations to fight the Communist bandits. The Japanese companies in question are willing to pledge money on our behalf. Please agree to the item.

Chairman's explanation: After this company has obtained its export quota, it provided the Japanese banana importers with a listed price, in accordance with our government's stipulated price of seven American dollars per basket of produce. The Green Fruits Export Association's listed price is listed at one and a half to two dollars more. Therefore, each Japanese company has expressed friendship that goes beyond that of what they would hold for an ordinary company. In addition, the Japanese market for bananas is a seller's market. The Japanese side, in recent days, under the leadership of Mr. Shibata, has proactively proposed that they would cover the increase in the fees to "fight the Communist bandits" without any additional conditions. The pledged donations are in the amount of twenty-five million Japanese yen. The way in which these Japanese companies are offering to pledge this amount is by making a small deduction of thirty Japanese yen from each basket of bananas, thus creating an amicable, friendly business relationship with this company.

Resolution: Agreed.

As he read to this point, he began to smile slightly as an expression of pride appeared on his face, but his eyes didn't stop as he read on.

Case Two: How to manage the results of the Sixth ROC-Japanese Banana Trade Negotiations.

Chairman's explanation: After these negotiations with our Japanese counterparts, we obtained their agreement. Starting next month, the Kaohsiung company's sales of bananas will be adjusted from seven American dollars to eight dollars for each basket sold. (Chairman Wu and Executive Cheng hsi-chüan and others have elaborated in detail on the meeting and thus we omit it here.)

Resolutions:
1. The management department will discuss the results of this case and promptly notify the local companies and agencies of these changes, as well as notify all members of the organization.
2. All supervisors of the organization, including Manager Lee and his subordinate departments, shall go to all of the counties and townships to publicize it for implementation.

Tsín-suī lifted his gaze towards the ceiling and watched the hanging fan slowly whirling around, lost in thought. Then he fished out a small notebook from his suit coat pocket and made a couple of rough notes in Japanese, returned the pen to his pocket, and continued reading Case Three.

Case Three: Adjustments to worker pay.

Explanation: Due to the thriving exports of Taiwanese bananas to the Japanese market in recent years and area of banana plantations and number of banana cultivators has expanded greatly, this company's workers have increased from ten thousand workers to more than sixty thousand. This is due to the leadership of the chairman of our board of directors as well as the supervisors and the fruits of their labor. Presently, the company's internal financials are in good standing, and to reward all the departments and workers for their hard work in the company, we propose to give salary raises to all employees, to be effective with first payment to be made on the fifteenth of each month.

Resolution: Agreed.

As he was reading this case, he opened a drawer in his bureau and took out a pocket abacus. He flicked the beads, calculating, and calculating some more. As the corners of his lips curled into a smile, he quickly put the abacus back and continued reading.

Case Four: How to break the bottleneck in the association's "unified production and sales" movement regarding banana exports.

Explanation: This movement is an important phase for our company, and the petitioning activities for the various committees and local governments have already been concluded. Although the action-related units agreed to put the proposals on their agendas, the proposals have been met with much opposition and it is urgent to find a way to make an amicable breakthrough.

Resolution: Despite lively discussion, a concrete case has yet to be arrived at. We will discuss this at the next meeting.

As he arrived at this section, his expression changed. He grew serious, put his pen down, and leaned against the back of his rattan chair. He took several deep breaths, then lowered his gaze and sank deep into thought. He remained that way for a long time, and it looked from his posture as if he had fallen asleep.

The phone rang, and Tsín-suï picked up the receiver after one ring. It was Hīng-tshun on the other end. After a few quick exchanges, Tsín-suï looked excited. He called over Manager Lee T'u-chen and Vice-manager Tsai Kun-shan and told them, "Go out and prepare a car, quick. We're going to take a trip to Tsou-ying. We need to head out as soon as possible."

"What's the occasion?"

"I'll tell you the details when we're in the car."

16

It was a sweltering end to May. Even the night air across the southern part of the island was unbearably hot. Tsín-suī awoke with a start. He lightly rapped on his daughter's bedroom door. Bí-ài was already a second-year student in middle school by this time. She was a heavy sleeper and after her father shook her, she opened her eyes just slightly, then turned over and went straight back to sleep.

Tsín-suī didn't want to keep bothering her, so he stepped out and stood by the living room window and looked through the hazy moonlight at Masa asleep in the cow pen behind the house. Masa was now a juvenile bull with a gigantic appetite, constantly needing to chew on lots of cud. Right now, he was as still as a boulder and must have been in a deep sleep. "There's so much labor that needs doing during the day, you have a good sleep," Tsín-suī thought to himself. As Tsín-suī stared at the beast, he noticed some strands of white foamy bubbles around its mouth.

Whenever Masa slept, he would always lie down on his side with his front legs tucked inward. The clock on the wall chimed twice to signal the hour. It sounded especially clear in the late-night calm. He was just considering going back to bed, when he saw his daughter Bí-ài trudge out of her bedroom.

"*A-Pa*, why haven't you gone to sleep? Were you trying to wake me up just now?"

"Mmmhh. Your *A-Pa* just can't go to sleep. He has something on his mind."

"What's the matter?"

"Are any of your classes at school tomorrow important?"

"English and mathematics... Of course they're important. Why?"

"Well, don't worry about it. It's nothing."

Bí-ài lightly stamped one foot on the floor. "*A-Pa*, what do you need me to do? Tell me!"

"Oh, it's nothing. You just go to school in the morning like normal."

"*A-Pa*, tell me!" Bí-ài stamped her foot lightly again.

"Your *A-Pa* is going to be receiving an extremely important guest tomorrow at the Cooperative Association. I wrote a welcome speech, and I'd like to recite it to him in person. The key point I want to explain to him is included in the welcome address. I thought that it might be clearer that way... But your *A-Pa*'s Mandarin is not very good. No matter how hard I study, I can never get my speech to sound right. It's bothering me so much that I can't go to sleep."

"Who's so important?"

"His name is Hsu Pai-yuen. He's the official in charge of managing all banana exports. You'll understand when you see him tomorrow."

"*A-Pa*, so you mean that you want me to skip school tomorrow, right?"

"Would that be OK?"

"Ok, fine then. It's no big deal."

"OK, that settles it. You'll come with me to the Cooperative Association tomorrow and when Hsu Pai-yuen arrives, you'll just stand beside me and read out the speech loudly in standard Mandarin."

"Sure. I can manage that, no problem. So can I see that draft you wrote of your welcome speech?"

Tsín-suī crept quietly back to his room. When he came back out, he had two sheets of yellowed paper with ten lines of characters running down each page. Bí-ài turned on a lamp and softly read them through, then looked up and said, "*A-Pa*, this is too strange. You can't read off the Mandarin, but you can write it very well. This is like the classical Chinese in our Chinese textbook."

"When your *A-Pa* was studying at Takao Secondary, we had a required course called Chinese Letters. Our teacher from Japan used Japanese to pronounce the words and then used Japanese translations to explain the meaning to us. So, for your *A-Pa*, I have a grounding in Chinese, but I can't pronounce the characters correctly. A few years ago, I went to one of those remedial Mandarin courses taught by the Nationalist government, but it didn't help me much. The pronunciation is just so hard!" Tsín-suī paused for a bit before continuing, "Well, do you think you can read it for me?"

"Of course, I can." Bí-ài continued reading, this time in a slightly louder voice, "Chairman Hsu, whom I have long heard of, is a diligent administrator who loves the people and cares for their plight. He constantly keeps in mind the livelihood of banana farmers and the development of international trade. All of our banana farmers are grateful for your benevolent governance. I, Ngôo Tsín-suī, kneel before you, and beseech thee... " Bí-ài read down to the end of this line and stopped to ask her father, "*A-Pa*, are you really going to kneel down in front of this guy?"

"That's right. When you get to this part, I want you to stop reading off the page for about half a minute. Let your *A-Pa* kneel down and once I'm down on my knees, start up with the reading again."

"*A-Pa*...," Bí-ài softly called to her dad with a tinge of sorrow to her voice. She stared her father deep in the eyes and continued reading the speech, "I beseech thee to support our association in unifying the production and marketing... *A-Pa*, what is 'unifying the production and marketing?'"

"This is such an important thing. I'll give you a more complete explanation some other time. If there are no problems with the speech, then you should head back to bed. We both need to have clear minds for tomorrow."

"OK. *A-Pa*, you need to go back to bed soon too. You absolutely need to get some rest."

At this point in their late-night rendezvous, the sound of their voices was too loud and woke up Giȯk-ìn. A hoarse voice called out from the pitch dark in a bedroom down the hallway, "A-Suī-á, who are you talking to?" Tsín-suī walked slowly back to his bedroom without saying anything in response.

Before walking back through the doorway though, he took one more peek at Masa, who was still sleeping in the same position with his front legs bent inwards, but he had turned over. Just a few moments ago when Tsín-suī had passed by, Masa had been facing inwards, but now he was facing towards the outside.

The next day, the Kaohsiung Green Fruits Export Cooperative Association was bustling with all the supervisors, the managers from each department, and their workers, even the dock workers from the No. 31 wharf. All of them were crowded outside. There were two files of men outside the three-story office building on Kaohsiung's Hai-bian Road. Tsín-suī and his two well-versed directors were standing bolt upright in front of the two files, in their Western suits.

The sun was high over the city, and everyone was sweating heavily. Even the wind that occasionally blew from the south was hot and was no real relief. The throng of people began chatting amongst themselves as they waited for the special guests to arrive.

"I heard he was still at the Tsuo-ying Naval Base playing golf!"

"That was yesterday. Today he's coming directly from the reception hall at the Naval Command Center."

"Just who's so powerful that we hear about them coming to Ko-hiông?"

"Well it's his lady friend who directs the office up in Tâi-pak, Tân Hīng-tshun. She came down the other day to relay a message. Our chairman went to the golf course by Tsuo-ying yesterday to meet her. He went out of his way to invite her to guide him on some matter—"

"Oh, so that's what it is... No wonder! But... I've gotta say, you need to be careful what you say. Tân Hīng-tshun is our chairman's friend. She isn't his lady friend."

"They're here! They're here! I think I just saw the chairman on the move up ahead."

The two human columns looked off to the right in unison. It looked a bit like a row of puppets moving like a row of dominoes.

"No way, you're talking nonsense. There's no sign of them at all."

"I saw the chairman's daughter arrive this morning. Do you know what she's doing here?"

"Couldn't tell ya."

"The daughter quite resembles her old man. She's super tall. She'll grow up to be a great beauty someday, I'll bet."

"They're here! They're here! This time it's for real!"

"I dunno if it's true or not—"

"Hey, you need to start clapping! Everyone clap! Clap, clap, clap!"

"We have to shout, 'Greetings, Chairman.' Everyone shout, 'Greetings, Chairman,' together now!"

It was true—Tsín-suī had arrived accompanying someone respectfully. Applause resounded like bursts of firecrackers. A round of "Welcome Mr. Chairman" in a Taiwanese Hoklo accent also rose from the welcoming crowd. Ah, and what a powerful-looking official he was! He was a bit shorter than our chairman, wearing a pair of glasses with thick black rims. His face was a bit wide and looked prosperous and refined—he managed to look the part of a great official. The man was smiling the entire time, occasionally waving to the welcoming crowd on either side, returning their greetings and showing his appreciation. His expression seemed to indicate he was very satisfied with his reception.

After they entered the building, a female worker gave the distinguished guests and the Chairmen hand towels to wipe away their sweat. Chairman Ngôo began to give an introduction as he wiped his face. "This is our manager, Lee T'u-chen. He is the association's chief executive officer." It was obvious the guest was used to being a senior-level official. With a practiced smile, he stepped forward and shook hands as he asked a question that was a bit specialized but also a bit general. His body language suggested that he was listening carefully to the answers given to him. Tsín-suī, standing next to him, felt quite impressed. He thought back to the time before he was thirty-five to times when he was questioned by a Japanese official or a teacher. There was a difference between the Chinese and the Japanese, almost down to their very nature, and now he was feeling tense and uneasy. For a while, he couldn't place why his experiences with Japanese officials and this man, Hsu, were different, but they certainly weren't the same! He figured it out just then. The difference was a matter of being stern or being amicable. It was a degree of sincerity in a person's eyes.

As he faced the Cooperative Association's officers and the great crowd of banana producers, Tsín-suī was now thinking how he wanted to learn this Chairman Hsu Pai-yuen's ways of responding to others. "I can try to mimic this Chinese official's manner of speaking and attitude, but my questions will be more specialized than his, like Japanese officials who research matters so carefully." He continued to observe and ponder.

The guest reception room was on the second floor of the association's headquarters. Tea and fresh fruit had already been set out for the occasion. The suspended ceiling fan and an oscillating Tatung Electric fan hummed loudly as they blew blasts of hot air over everyone, up and down, left and right.

After the guests had been seated, Tsín-suī started to speak in stiff Mandarin, "I have prepared a welcome speech, Chairman Hsu, but I'm afraid you might not be able to understand my Taiwanese Mandarin, so I've especially invited my daughter to assist me. I hope the Chairman doesn't object to this?"

"Haha! Fine. Fine. There's no need to be so polite!"

Bí-ài stepped forward and stood at her father's side. Timidly, she glanced over at Hsu Pai-Yuen and then, as if suddenly remembering something, she quickly lowered her head and made a perfunctory bow, at the same time raising her girlishly natural, tender voice, "Greetings, Chairman. As a humble representative of all the inspectors and office workers of the Kaohsiung Green Fruits Export and Marketing Cooperative Association, and all the banana producers, I warmly welcome your visit." Just as Bí-ài reached this point in the speech, Tsín-suī stood up and made a bow; the directors sitting on both sides of Tsín-suī followed suit. They bowed deeply from the waist in the manner of those who had received a Japanese education.

Hsu had an intuition. The way that the girl gave a bow just now is how it is taught in schools since the Republic of China's takeover of Taiwan, but it seemed as though those directors in front of him still couldn't get out of the habit of bowing like Japanese!

Bí-ài's narration continued, "I have long heard of your diligent governance and love of the people and your care for our plight, always keeping the livelihood of our banana producers and the development of the nation's foreign trade in mind. Today bananas are listed as free trade items in Japan. It's a pity that our domestic organizations have not yet changed to meet this challenge. Banana exports are still controlled by the shipping industry. To advance our nation's goals of unifying production and marketing, I, Ngôo Tsín-suī, kneel before you, and beseech thee..."

Just as Bí-ài said the words "kneel before you," she stopped reading. Without the least hesitation, Tsín-suī stood up and then got down on his knees. Hsu, astonished by the sight, immediately stood up, walked over, and then tried to lift Tsín-suī up with both arms, saying, "No. This isn't right. There's no need. There's no need for you to be so polite! It's just too much. I will support you in the unification of production and marketing. I'll support you. I will."

Tsín-suī was a towering giant of a man, and when he knelt down on his knees, he was still about as tall as his daughter was as she stood. He looked as if he was going to bow down again, but he was quickly lifted up to his feet by Hsu. Tsín-suī was fifty-two years old at the time. Even though he had been a farmer since he was small, his knee joints still seemed strong and he was able to kneel down with ease, but when standing back up, it looked as if it took great effort. He first tried to stand with his right leg half bent, but his body clearly listed to the left. The association's directors off to his side hurried to help Hsu to bring Tsín-suī to his feet. Beside him, Bí-ài just looked at the scene, not knowing whether to feel moved or hurt. Tears welled up in her eyes as she tried to finish reading the last two lines of the speech as clearly as possible before she retreated to the back.

Then Hsu Pai-yuen asked Tsín-suī about the Japanese market situation, as well as local banana production issues. Tsín-suī and his advisors and directors gave thorough explanations, and the discussions were animated. There was even the occasional sound of laugher. Nobody noticed Bí-ài sitting in a rattan chair off in the corner, quietly wiping away her tears, still trying to regain her composure.

An older man who looked a bit rustic moved a chair over next to Bí-ài's side. "Aiyah, Ah... A-Tsòng, you came today!"

"Uncle saw you trying to wipe the tears from your eyes. What's wrong? What are you upset about? Your father's done a fantastic job here. The *Tiong-kok-á* officials are all just eating it up."

Bí-ài gave the older man a stunned look. She wasn't sure how to respond. A-Tsòng continued where he left off, "We in Taiwan... This is a time where everyone's clamoring to kiss up to each other."

Bí-ài still wasn't sure how she should respond. A-Tsòng brought up what seemed at first like a nonsensical question. "Over the last few years, I've been hearing this phrase, 'all stand up respectfully,' being bandied about. What the heck does that mean?"

"It means that everyone stands up, and they stand up straight."

"Ah, so does 'all stand up respectfully' mean the same as 'all stand in silence'?"

"No, they're not the same by any stretch. 'All stand in silence' means that everyone is quiet and nobody utters a word."

"Oh, so that's what it means. It was the same under the Japanese."

***

A few months later, the leader of a theater troupe in Kî-*san* named Kua Tsìn-hu traveled all the way out to Pîn-tong with an assistant. He searched far and wide until he found A-Tsòng. He then explained his reason for coming.

"More and more of us in Kî-*san* are growing bananas. In the last few years, everyone's been lifted up. Everyone from the top down in the village is praising Ngôo Tsín-suī. They see him as a god. Our theater troupe wants to make a performance about him, and we heard that you know the most about him of anyone around these parts, so we came to pick your brain."

"It'd just be better if you go and find Ngôo Tsín-suī yourself. What's the use in seeking me out?"

"I went looking for him. Twice already. He went off to Japan, and I don't know when he'll be back."

"Fine. Well, how can I help you?"

"We want to write a script, but when we got to Ngôo Tsín-suī's part, we only wrote two or three lines before we got stuck. We were hoping to ask you about some of his latest exploits—"

"Let me take a look at the parts you've already written."

The troupe leader, Koa, handed the script over. A-Tsòng looked it over, muttering to himself, "It's a good thing I can read Chinese characters."

[Ngôo A-Tsín-suī (short cymbal crash), a native son of Pîn-tong, (short cymbal crash), has the gift of knowing heaven's will (*suona* and cymbals). One day, a vaunted official made a visit, and Tsín-suī startled the heavens by kneeling down (*suona* and cymbals). The heavenly court above shook (a short burst of the cymbal), and from that time, the banana farmers who prayed for a wind were granted wind. If they desired rains, they got rain (southern-style suona tune playing). The bananas grew bountifully, especially fragrant, and delicious beyond compare (instrument ensemble).]

This Ngôo Tsín-suī brought money to our world (a short cymbal crash). As soon as he knelt down, heaven and earth shook (*suona* with clappers and gong). This allowed everyone to make money, and all the villages began to be much better off for it (instrument ensemble).

Farmers in Kî-*san* and Pîn-tong all grew rich (an erhu accompanies the cymbals), taverns and theatres abound in all directions. The fields and hamlets are thriving, and the people are in high spirits (southern *suona* accompanying quick hand-drumming). One *kah* of banana trees can earn a salary of two hundred thousand, and the civil servants only earn five hundred a month (one short cymbal crash). In the morning, they cut their harvest; by early afternoon, it's shipped off to market. They hope that by nightfall they'll be bearing bags of rice and pockets full of silver aplenty back to their homes. Hah hah hah hah (instrument ensemble).

There is one such Lôo Á-Tîng of Kî-*san* (a short burst of cymbals), they call him Banana-Tîng (a short burst of cymbals). He wears his banana fiber shirt, with drips of banana juice from collar to hem (a strummed shamisen accompanies a small drum). Oh! He earns half of what the whole farmers' association makes. If he withdraws his money, the farmers' association will surely go half-bankrupt (instrument ensemble).

When he got to that point there was no more. A-Tsòng slowly looked up and gave his appraisal, "The third and fourth lines are written very well, but the first two parts about Ngôo Tsín-suī are too fanciful. You might want to cut back a bit, I'm afraid."

"Yes. It's a bit fanciful, no doubt about it. I'm thinking though, an operatic performance needs to be a bit flowery and exaggerated, no? I want the audience to be interested in him."

"Well, that makes sense. I'll give you some real-life examples if you'd like. First, you only need to mention him kneeling once. If you must sing it twice, you need to say that after Chairman Ngôo arises, the number of exports jumps to 1.07 million baskets; after he kneels, the banana farmers are filled with gratitude, and their banana production jumps. In the second year, the number suddenly jumps to 3.04 million baskets, three times the original crop."

"Sure. This is the reason why we traveled so far to seek you out. Please keep going on. Please instruct us."

"Second, early on, the banana farmers were selling their bananas and only earning fifty-five New Taiwan dollars per basket, but the price was later raised to one hundred and four. Now they're earning one hundred and sixty-three. They're earning a lot more money now. These two points are mainly concerned with numbers. If you add it in, won't it detract from the interest of the play?"

"It should be OK to throw a few numbers in. We can always look it over again and revise it if it doesn't flow well or fit. Thank you, thank you, A-Tsòng."

"Oh, and one more thing. I just thought about it. There's also the bamboo basketmaking industry. They've been doing pretty amazingly these last few years too—"

"Sure, just a second. Let me write it down."

"I'd like to turn the tables on you for one second and ask you a question. That last part in your script, when you mentioned that Lôo Á-Tîng fellow or whoever, who is he?"

"Oh, you guys over here in Pîn-tong don't know much about him. He's a verrrrry famous person from Bí-lông Village over by Kî-san—"

Just as Kua Tsìn-hu reached this point in the conversation, a huge, brand-new motorcycle came roaring up and cut him off. It was Tsai Kun-shan, with Commissioner Ouyang riding pillion behind him. Tsai Kun-shan shouted out as he stepped down from the big bike, "Director A-Tsòng, they're having a big *tsiò* ritual[38] over in the next village, Lak-tè-tshù. A couple people invited me out as a guest. Commissioner Ouyang here went out with me to pay a visit to that farmer, A-tsong-tsú. After we ate, we decided to turn down your road and call on you too."

---

38. A *tsiò* (Mandarin *jiao*) is a major ceremony in folk religion in Taiwan that often last several days. *Tsiò* are intended to propitiate the local and heavenly divinities and involve ritual sacrifice and the formal rites performed by Taoist priests.

"Come, come sit. Have some tea," said A-Tsòng. "I know him. Was it a lavish feast?"

"Hah. Very much so! It was a big outdoor banquet, and he invited a huge crowd."

"He's gotten a lot richer now. He can afford to invite lots of people, or at least he ought to."

Commissioner Ouyang walked up, exchanged pleasantries, and then in half-Mandarin, half-Taiwanese Hoklo, asked A-Tsòng, "Director A-Tsòng, we took the liberty of visiting you since we were all the way out here. I hope we're not imposing on you right now."

"Not at all, not at all. Please, feel welcome to the utmost," A-Tsòng responded in Mandarin.

His two guests laughed. "Nobody says 'Welcome to the utmost,' *lah*."

"Oh! Then what should I say instead?"

"You should say, 'You're extremely welcome.'"

"Haha! That's a big difference, huh?" A-Tsòng continued, "I heard the government sloganeering, saying, 'Oppose the Communists to the utmost, saving the country is the top priority,' and I thought I'd try to copy the grammar of it."

Everyone laughed except for Commissioner Ouyang, whose lips didn't move.

Once his new guests had made themselves comfortable, tea was brought out and everyone introduced themselves. A-Tsòng turned his head towards the opera troupe leader, Kua Tsìn-hu. "Let's pick up where we left off. How did that Lôo Á-Tîng fellow make a name for himself?"

"Oh, him... People call him 'Banana Tîng.' The reason for that is that he's a very plain but ardent worker over in Kî-san. When he heard from the Green Fruits Export Cooperative Association that farmers were madly buying up farmland to grow bananas, he also invested big. My playscript has that line about people going to sell their bananas and 'coming back carrying shoulder poles loaded with bags of rice on one end and piles of money on the other.' Well, Lôo Á-Tîng himself came back with piles of money on both ends, and he went directly to the farmers' credit association to deposit it. One day, his wife went into the credit association dressed in her usual working clothes and asked to withdraw some money, but the credit association teller thought that she didn't have the means do so, and he treated her horribly. Well, Lôo Á-Tîng heard all about it and was ready to blow up at them and withdraw all his savings. After the credit association had calculated all his money, oh my God, it turned out over half the money deposited in the credit association's coffers was his! If he took it all out, the association would go bankrupt!"

"Oh, I've heard that tale about Lôo Á-Tîng," Tsai Kun-shan chimed in.

The troupe leader stopped talking, stood up, and cleared his throat, then out of nowhere, very excitedly started belting out an opera song for everyone.

> Cutting bananas, shipping bananas, making big bucks, making money so we can eat our fill, eat our fill;
>
> Cutting bananas, shipping bananas, counting out the numbers, counting out the money, 'til our fingers are sore, oh so sore;
>
> Cutting bananas, shipping bananas, bank and credit union, both vie to treat us well, everyone's feeling so fine, oh so fine.

He sang these three lines and everyone around was delighted. Commissioner Ouyang asked him, "Director Ko, you said something about a playscript. May I borrow it from you for a bit?"

"Sure," Director Kua very cheerily handed his playscript over.

Ouyang took it and looked it over once, then asked, "May I make a copy to take with me?"

"It shouldn't be a problem, but the script isn't finished yet. I came out here to find A-Tsòng to research some material to finish it," Kua finished explaining. Then he asked, "What do you want to copy it for?"

"I'm going to write a report for my superiors."

"Oh... Your superiors?" Kua thought for a moment, then said, "That script of mine is too simple, and a bit superficial, and the most important parts haven't even been written yet."

"For example?"

"Well, the bamboo baskets and packing makers are constantly working day and night to keep up. They're also doing very well."

"Oh, I know, I've gone to interview them and observe them."

"There's one more thing. Most people won't notice it though."

Something wasn't sitting right with A-Tsòng. He seemed somewhat unconvinced. "What's that?" he asked.

The troupe leader cleared his throat, then said, "These past few years there's still one other group of people who are working day and night—those are the carpenters helping to put up people's houses. Some call them brickmasons, I think. Just take my own village in Chi-shan, for example. Every household wants their old earthen homes to be upgraded to brick-and-tile homes. It's because the farmer families all now have the ability to do so. Those brickmasons are constantly being sought out. They've got their work cut out for them for weeks and months already, all the way through till the end of next year. They'll never be finished."

Everyone's eyes lit up. A-Tsòng sighed in admiration, "Hah! Director Kua, Pîn-tong's undergoing the same changes you're talking about, only I didn't think of it momentarily." Then, sounding a bit boastful he said, "Oh, Commissioner Ouyang, there's one more thing. You can write it down too. Before, the dropout rate for students in primary schools and middle schools used to be astoundingly high. Why was that? Well, it was because these families couldn't afford the tuition to give their children an education, or they didn't have enough hands to help around the farm, or they needed another person to go out and help earn money. Often they'd force their kids, especially the oldest sons and daughters, to discontinue their studies. But nowadays, to my knowledge, families everywhere are encouraging all their kids to study. They think the higher the educational achievement, the better, and so when the bananas are doing well, it brings the dropout rate down a lot."

"*Wah*, A-Tsòng, when I was a kid, I never got to finish school. When I hear you speaking about these kinds of changes, I feel quite touched. It just makes me want to sing another song."

"Please! Don't stop! Please keep singing."

Director Kua stood up again. He swept his right hand through the air, lightly raised his foot, then began to sing.

> Cutting the rice stalks all day long, *dong dong cha*! Going out before first light, dong dong cha! Watching people go to school, eyes full of tears, these eyes are full of tears, *tshe cha tshe cha*!

Then he held his hands up to his mouth and pretended to play the pipes of the hsiao. He took a big step and began singing again.

> *Hoo—ooo, oooo*, oh Mom and Dad... Let me go to study, let me go to school, OK? OK? *Ooo- oooo—hoh*.

He only sang these two lines and then stopped and said with a bit of embarrassment, "I'm sorry, I have to keep working on this draft section. I need to write the stage play before I can continue trying to sing this section."

Commissioner Ouyang stood up, took out a notepad, and moved over to a stone table not far away. He put his head down and started writing quickly, like a good student diligently doing their homework.

Director Kua lowered his voice and asked, "This Commissioner Ouyang fellow said he needed to write a report for his superiors. Who are those superiors? Does he mean someone at the Co-op Association?"

"No. He has another higher-up—the Party," A-Tsòng responded.

"No. His real higher-up is actually the Bureau of Investigation," Tsai replied.

"Oh! Oh!" terror tinged his response.

"Oh! I didn't realize!"

17

A-Tsòng took a fall at the office one day. His right wrist was lightly fractured and, worrying that he also had a concussion, Tsín-suī took him in a car to the hospital.

Traffic was backed up at the roundabout at the intersection of Kaohsiung's San-duo Road and Chung-shan Road. The reason was that there was construction going on in the roundabout. The scaffolding was built up tall and wide. Tsín-suī couldn't see what it was in the middle the structure, just that it was something towering.

"Hey, A-Tsòng-á, up ahead at the San-duo roundabout, they're putting up an equestrian statue of President Chiang. It looks so massive and impressive."

"I know."

"But the builder is Tông Tsuān-tsong. Did you know that? He had to spend four or five million dollars on it."

"Oh?! Is Tsuān-tsong trying to climb his way back up?"

"After the government liquidated their company, Tông Îng, and cleared away all of the assets and debt, they gave Tông over seven million dollars. Later, Tsuān-tsong sent out petitions every which way and was able to scrounge up forty million dollars, so he's still got plenty of money. The money for this copper statue was given as compensation by the Kaohsiung city government in lieu of payment for the land expropriated from Tông Îng."

"Oh, so that's how it ended!"

"The Tông family have been punished and abused over and over by the Chiangs. Why are they wasting their time with building a statue of Chiang?" A-Tsòng continued in a low voice.

"Tsuān-tsong isn't sure. It isn't them that the Chiangs are concerned about; they're hoping to undermine Chen Cheng's base in the civil economy. So, as soon as Tsuān-tsong found out, he was frightened and began to walk the Chiang path."

"Amazing! They're going straight for the emperor. Tông Tsuān-tsong's giving you a run for your money."

"What's he competing with me for?"

"For who can do the most ass-kissing."

"Haha!" Tsín-suī felt a little awkward as he laughed. "When my old man was still around, he once told me, 'That A-Tsòng, he's got a mind sharper than a sickle.' I guess he wasn't wrong!"

"Hah! Well, are we at the hospital yet?"

When A-Tsòng was discharged from the hospital, Tsín-suī went himself to pick him up. The two of them took the long road home. He wanted to see Tsuān-tsong. Just as they arrived, he looked over and saw that Tsuān-tsong was sending off three official-looking men. He walked them right up to the side of a fancy black sedan, bowing and waving his hand until the sedan slid of sight. Tsín-suī's eyes were very keen, and he could pick out that one of the three men was the Kaohsiung city mayor, Iûnn Kim-hu. He knew instantly what was going on.

Tsuān-tsong's face had already regained its former robust color, "Yes, that was Mayor Iûnn. He brought the heads of the labor and the finance bureaus out to do an inspection and to coordinate the equestrian statue's construction."

"We saw that statue when we drove by. It looks like it should be complete in about a month or two."

"Once it's been raised, there will still be lots of work, sculpting and *shiage*.[39] It won't be done in less than half a year."

"This here is Soo Tsòng-phik. He's from my village. He's a director of the Green Fruits Export Cooperative Association, although he's not serving at the moment."[40]

"My oldest son, Soo Tsìng-tik, works at your company as a manager."

"Oh, that's right! What a surprise to meet you, a pleasant surprise! A-Tsìng-tik is an outstanding talent. He's always helping me with something."

"Thank you for your kindness."

"It's true."

The workers were coming in just then, and there was tea and snacks.

---

39. *Shiage*—Japanese for "the finishing touches."

40. There was an equestrian statue of Chiang Kai-Shek at the roundabout intersection of San-duo and Chung-shan Roads in Kaohsiung. Including the base of the statue, it was three stories high. It was completed in 1971, and then demolished in 1994. It was an important landmark in Kaohsiung at the time.

"So, tell me, are you stopping the military veterans from coming into your organization?"

"Yes. It's best not to talk about it. It's a pain. My inner working circle of workers are all our local men." The three of them talked on for a bit longer.

Tsuān-tsong opened a desk drawer and pulled out a sheet of paper. He handed it to Tsín-suī, saying, "A-Suī-á, I have a favor to ask. Someone at the top is putting together a Mr. Chen Cheng Scholarship Foundation Collection Committee. I'm duty-bound not to refuse. I was wondering if you would be able to help out an old friend and join the committee?"

"Your wish is my command. I'll definitely join."

"All of the people fundraising for the committee are big shots. The main organizing committee chair is Huang Chao-ch'in. There're also two vice-chairmen—Li Kuo-ting and Wu San-lien."

"After I join, about how much money should I give?"

"It's more than just the money. You'll be responsible for fundraising for the whole green fruit industry. If you agree, they'll send you a letter of invitation to be the head of the Green Fruits Cooperative Association's fundraising team."

"Don't worry. Well, does that mean you're already the fundraising head of the steel industry?"

"That's right."

The two of them chatted for a little longer and then parted ways. On the road back home, A-Tsòng's narrative began again, "This is such a wonderful era."

"What do you mean?"

"There's just so many people out there who are willing to donate, happily donate. Those receiving the donations are even more filled with joy. They're so happy to receive money, and that's what makes others happy."

"Hah! A-Tsòng, that sickle mind of yours is just as razor-sharp and cutting as ever!"

18

It was a scorching Sunday in August. Hīng-tshun replied to say she was coming to Ko-hiông to take part in some military dependents' village event. Tsín-suī changed his plans to accompany her. She was a representative for the donations collected for the high-rise apartments. She was bedecked in a deep navy-blue suit, but the purse that she carried and her shoes were both a deep forest green. Tsín-suī's suit was also paired nicely with a tie, and he had a light bit of pomade rubbed into his hair. He stood by her side the whole time, not trying to avoid being seen with her. They looked as if they were a proper couple. He was only introduced as the chairman of the Kaohsiung Green Fruits Export Cooperative Association. There was no mention of him being Hīng-tshun's husband.

After the event had wrapped up, Tsín-suī pressed the question, "It's finally over. Where do you want to go now?"

"Let's go pay a visit to your wife, can we?"

"Sure, let's."

The car turned south, and before long they could see the massive Mount Tāi-bú towering over everything around. "It's a lot different from that mountain of yours up in Tâi-pak."

"How are they different?"

"Your mountain here is high and massive, strong and powerful, and also clear to see. Tâi-pak's is dainty and delicate and also has some beautiful feminine mystique."

"The face of Mount Tāi-bú changes anytime. Whether the weather is good or bad, scorching or frigid, before the rain or after. It never looks the same."

"You just stare off at that mountain after you've eaten your fill and feel bored, huh?" she gently teased him.

"Well, I've lived here since my childhood, and when I was older and went to work in the fields, whenever I'd look up, Mount Tāi-bú was there."

As the car headed south, they crossed over the bridge connecting Kaohsiung and Pingtung counties and arrived at Thâu-tsîng-khe.

Mrs. Ngôo Gio̍k-ìn definitely wasn't expecting her husband would be bringing some fashionable beauty back home with him, and she was alarmed at first. Fortunately, Tsín-suī-á made a proper introduction. So this is Tân Hīng-tshun, the "Auntie Hīng-tshun" the children so often spoke of. Moreover, with her feminine intuition, Gio̍k-ìn started to feel at ease about her after exchanging just a few pleasantries.

Several neighbors came over and hung around by the courtyard, peering through the door and windows. That's just how life in the countryside is. The way Hīng-tshun was all dressed up and everything she did immediately became the topic of gossip.

"Those Tâi-pak'ers all have such white skin. Our A-Ìn-á just can't compare!"

"Just one look and you can tell that woman from Tâi-pak is something special. But by comparison, our A-Ìn-á is plain and old-fashioned—a good wife and mother."

"If you were A-Tsín-suī, which of those two women would you choose?"

"What the heck are you talking about, huh? She's a business associate of A-Tsín-suī's. He's not brought another bride home. Don't talk nonsense!"

"How so? How do you know?"

Inside the house, Hīng-tshun and Gio̍k-ìn were having an animated conversation, when Tsín-suī suddenly got up and looked out the window. There was a guy out there who looked a bit rugged, like a field hand, leading a buffalo back towards the house. "Huh?" Tsín-suī asked. "Why does Masa look so dispirited?"

Gio̍k-ìn answered him, "It started yesterday. He won't eat. He just doesn't have any appetite."

Tsín-suī quickly threw off his Western suit and switched into some everyday farmers' clothes, pushed the door open, and went outside. Hīng-tshun was curious and followed him with her eyes. She saw him kneel down and use his fingers to open up the buffalo's eye to examine it carefully, then look at the other eye. Then he felt Masa's belly, then worked gradually back until he got to the animal's hind quarters and lifted up its tail. He felt around its anus and then lifted his hand to his nose to smell for anything that seemed off.

Hīng-tshun turned her head back, looking at Gio̍k-ìn. "Auntie, what exactly is it A-Tsín-suī is doing?"

"This buffalo is sick. A-Suī-á is examining it."

"He knows how to doctor a buffalo?"

"He does!"

"Wow, he's truly amazing!"

When Tsín-suī came to a diagnosis for Masa, he called out in a loud voice, "Masa has heat stroke. He's overheating. A-liang, come here for a sec. I need you to do something for me." The field hand walked quickly over, and Tsín-suī told him what he wanted. "I need you to go over to the graveyard and pick up some *na-tāu* (pandanus) leaves and bring them back. What I need is the leaf hearts. You'll need to use some gloves because they've got sticky nettles. Ah! Go quick!"

After he gave the order, he reached out and rubbed his buffalo along the back. Masa could hardly stand. His knees buckled and he slumped to the ground, but he kept nudging Tsín-suī with his head cocked, as if nuzzling a loved one. Tsín-suī let Masa nuzzle him for a while, then he went back to the guest room to drink some tea and chat.

Hīng-tshun had all sorts of questions for him, "You gave your buffalo a name? You call it Masa?"

"Yes, that's right."

"You said the animal was 'expiring from heat'—that's 'heat stroke' in Mandarin, right? Buffalo can get heat strokes too?"

"Yes, they certainly can. Buffalo can get heat strokes—and colds too."

"Where did you learn how to doctor a buffalo?"

"Well, it's a long story. I had a neighbor when I was younger. His name was Uncle A-Huàn—"

At that point, his field hand A-liang came back. Tsín-suī stared at the plant in the man's hand carefully to determine that it was definitely *na-tāu*. Then he gave another order, "Take the leaves, and carefully roll them into a paste. When you've macerated them well, place them in half a bowl of water and then add some rice wine to it. Once you're done, hand me the bowl."

After a while, Masa's medicine was ready. Tsín-suī had already gone to the cow pen to wait. Hīng-tshun and Giok-ìn also walked over and watched how Tsín-suī administered the medicine, as if they were watching a play.

Giok-ìn first stepped into the storage shed and pulled out a carved, flat, tongue-shaped bamboo cylinder and handed it to her husband. Tsín-suī then lightly pulled upwards on Masa's lead rope to get him to face upwards. His beast raised its head to look up at him. Oh! He was talking to his buffalo. It wasn't clear what exactly he was saying, but he touched the buffalo on its neck lightly with his left hand. Masa became very obedient. He opened his mouth wide and when Tsín-suī calmly poured in the watery mixture, Masa swallowed it. Though it didn't take any more than about two minutes, Hīng-tshun was moved by what she saw. With her woman's instinct, she could sense that Ngôo Tsín-suï had a rare gentleness to both his speech and actions. Was he just as soft and gentle towards his wife? What a touching sight!

After the issue with Masa had been dealt with, Hīng-tshun began a round of questions, "Should we go out and see the banana farmers harvesting their crop?"

"Are any of our fields ready to be harvested?" Tsín-suï asked his wife.

"The cutters always go out first thing in the morning. It's almost high noon and it's stiflingly hot," Giok-ìn replied.

Tsín-suï thought for a moment, then continued, "Oh! Well then... Fine. Let's go! I'll take you to Siâ-phī near Wan-Tan. We can pay a visit to one of the local farmers, A-Thiam-hok. He's one of the bigger producers out this way."

"It's almost eleven in the morning now... It's a bit...late," Giok-ìn hesitated.

"No worries. Let's go out anyway. They will have gone to deliver their bananas and they might be coming back just now."

"Mrs. Ngôo, let's go together, shall we?"

"Sure. Let's go," Giok-ìn gave a slight smile as she replied.

Once they were on the road, Hīng-tshun tried to encourage Giok-ìn. "You're doing better these days, but your house looks kind of simple on the inside. Maybe you should think about moving to Ko-hiông or coming up north to Tâi-pak. A-Tsín-suï might not be so harried having to run every which way."

"Hah. I'm a bit set in my ways living out in the wilds here. My parents live in Pîn-tong. It's a bit easier to take care of them from here."

Tsín-suï's car was a large, American-made sedan, which brought all the villagers out, along with clouds of dust. A-Thiam-hok lived in a large, courtyard-style house with a broad threshing ground in front of it. Two metal carts were parked off to the left side of the threshing ground, and on top and beside them were piles and piles of soiled, padded-cotton quilts. There must have been ten or more of them. Tsín-suï had just gotten out of the car when a middle-aged man charged out of the house barefoot, wearing shorts and calling out as he headed towards them.

"Oh, it's the Chairman Ngôo! Ah! Ngôo Tsín-suï's come to my house, hah! Why didn't you tell me earlier you'd be coming!" As soon as he came up to Tsín-suï, Thiam-hok gave a ninety-degree Japanese bow and Tsín-suï responded in kind.

"Representative Tiunn, A-Thiam-hok, we were on a little tour, and I wanted to show my friend from the capital around."

A-Thiam-hok turned back and shouted an order towards the house in a booming voice, "Go slaughter two chickens, OK!" He turned back towards the group and let Tsín-suī introduce Hīng-tshun. When he heard she was the director general of the Taipei Green Fruits Exporting Company, Thiam-hok could only stare with wide eyes and greet her, giving her a ninety-degree Japanese bow and calling her "Madame Chairman."

Hīng-tshun didn't mind this clearly hot-and-cold attitude. In fact, A-Thiam-hok's singlet and shorts piqued her interest, just as the cotton quilts by the threshing ground had, completely covered with banana sap stains as they were. There were dark spots and light spots, but all of them were brown. She strained to think, was what they called 'banana milk' really a viscous, sticky kind of sap? What could these farmers possibly use to wash it out of their clothes?

More and more farmers gathered around. Tsín-suī turned to his wife, "Go into their house, and tell Ms. Tiunn not to kill the chickens. We're just going to take a walk around and then go."

Someone in the crowd called out to try and persuade them to say, "You have to kill the chickens. Chairman Ngôo, you don't come out this way often. Stay and have some food!"

"Thank you, thank you, but we're going to look around and then be on our way." Tsín-suī nodded towards the gathered the villagers, smiling in appreciation of their welcome and respect.

Hīng-tshun's gaze shifted towards the threshing ground. She saw two girls who looked like they were students busying themselves with those dirtied cotton quilts, working to flip them over. She walked forward but didn't ask any questions.

Giȯk-ìn walked out of the house with Ms. Tiunn, who was explaining, "These cotton quilts are for cushioning the bananas. We're sunning them to make them a bit softer."

"Oh, I thought so. Mr. Ngôo has told me about this, but this is the first time I've seen it in person." Hīng-tshun crouched down to touch one of the quilts laying on the ground. It was pure cotton.

"It's for cushioning the bananas so their peels won't get bruised. If they're unbruised, they won't be sold on the domestic market and can earn a higher price abroad," Ms. Tiunn added.

"That's right. For foreign exports, they want pristine, undamaged fruit," Hīng-tshun said with great seriousness. Then, in order to sound a bit more informal, she added, half joking, "Even though the weather is so scorching, the bananas still need to be covered with heavy cotton quilts."

"I've heard there's refrigerated cargo ships nowadays. Bananas get pampered more than people do. They get air conditioning all the way till they reach Japan," Ms. Tiunn also half-jokingly replied.

"Haha, it's true."

Noon came by, and they stuck around for lunch after all. It opened Hīng-tshun's eyes. Several neighbor women came over to help with the cooking, and the kitchen buzzed with activity. The chickens were dispatched with early on, and now the women were cutting up the meat, chopping up sausage, frying up some eggs. It didn't look like anyone in the team of women was acting as head chef, but there was no disorder to the kitchen work, either. One of the older women in the group called out, "OK, this eggplant's pretty much all tender now and ready to go out to the table." Immediately, someone passed it down a line and freshly sliced shallots, chives, and soy sauce were added. How was it that they were all so well coordinated? Heh heh! There was a little girl helping to peel garlic cloves. She stealthily plopped an unboiled fish ball into her mouth and chewed slowly and lightly, her cheeks bulging. She swallowed the morsel and, when nobody was watching, stole a thin slice of cooked sausage and popped it into her mouth. Wasn't she afraid of burning herself? As Hīng-tshun watched, it made her smile inwardly and it wasn't long before the smile rose to her face.

Not long after, dish after scrumptious dish was sent out to the table with startling efficiency. Hīng-tshun looked on with deep satisfaction. All of this farmer's fare was something that people living in Taipei rarely had the luxury of eating.

They had only eaten two of the dishes, when two of the neighbor representatives heard the news of Tsín-suí's visit and came to join them. Soon enough, the topic of conversation was all "banana talk." Hīng-tshun was a veteran when it came to the banana trade, but even so, hearing these villagers talk shop was something of a novelty to her.

While the adults around them were busy talking, that little girl who had been outside turning over the banana quilts stole off to the edge of the table and began playing a radio. It was turned to the channel for information from the banana depot, and then she tuned it to a channel that was playing some tunes in Mandarin. It only took two minutes for Thiam-hok to realize it wasn't his regular station and he yelled out, "*Wei, wei*! Don't touch the radio! Turn it back!"

The channel was quickly changed back, but it was hard to tell what kind of station it was. It mostly broadcast Taiwanese opera, Taiwanese songs, and Japanese *enka* ballads. About every ten minutes, there came a bit of information about the time of operations for the Ma-lu-bing, Malu-Tan, Malu-ji, which were some of the neighboring shipping trucks. Hīng-tshun smiled to herself again. This radio station was very clever! These time advertisements were placed here and there, so you wouldn't change the station. They may have been making a little bit of advertising money that way![41]

After they had left Tiunn Thiam-hok's house, Hīng-tshun said several times, "It's been so interesting this time coming south and seeing all these banana farmers!"

"If you think that's interesting, let me take you again to see where they make the packaging and baskets," Tsín-suī replied.

"Excellent. Just excellent," Hīng-tshun said.

"The packaging industry can be split into four groupings: grass rope-spinning, Makino bamboo cutting, hemp rope spinning, and bamboo basket weaving. The most interesting of the four is the bamboo basket weaving workshop."

"There's one of those workshops right by the public park near our home, isn't there?" Giȯk-ìn reminded her husband.

"Sure, let's go!"

The workshop factory was housed in a large shop with a sprawling floorspace. There were several steel carts parked by the doorway. Workers were going every which way, trying to do their tasks. Moving closer to them, the heavy pungent stench of sweat and body odor exuded from the skin of each one of the workers. There were several workers sitting on low, round stools, looking downwards, busily working at their tasks. Hīng-tshun happened to hear the soft wails of an infant. Her eyes followed to where the sound was coming from, and she saw a little infant being rocked in a corner. Next to it was a young female worker, busy with the work at hand. She would occasionally stop, put down the bamboo strips,

---

41. *Malu* comes from the Japanese word *maru* meaning "circle." In all the goods collection depots in rural locales across Taiwan, they used to use the surname of the location owner as the depot name. At the entrance to the venues, and on the crates and baskets, they used circles to stamp the name of the venue inside the circle. It was a trademark, which is how the "-maru" call-sign came to be. This originated in the Japanese colonial era, and you could hear Taiwanese farmers calling out "-malu" all the time. Such practices gradually disappeared in the 1970s.

and rock and hum a little lullaby to her baby, and the child seemed to drift off to sleep again.

The factory-owner's wife was the first to discover the Ngôos had come to pay a visit and called over to them, "*Aiyoh*, it's Chairman Ngôo. Chairman Ngôo is here!"

The owner, sitting behind a simple business bureau, was startled. He sprang up to his feet and took giant strides over giant bundles of Makino bamboo like a monkey. He made a bow and shook hands with the visitors, then turned around and shouted, "Everyone, stand up! Stand up! Show our Chairman Ngôo some respect!"

"There's no need, there's no need! Everyone, just keep on with your work. I'm just here to bring a friend to take a look around. It's no big deal."

"This here is my friend from up north in Tâi-pak, the Director of the Green Fruits Association, Tân Hīng-tshun," he added solemnly.

Hīng-tshun politely extended a hand and lightly shook the factory owner's hand. Although her facial expression hadn't changed, the people around her could sense there was some change in her. She was shaking a hand that was as rough, course, and calloused as crocodile skin, and it gave her a start.

Giok-ìn went with Hīng-tshun, to look all around the factory. When they had reached one of the women workers, Hīng-tshun very curiously crouched down. Ah! The worker was handling the bamboo strips with her bare hands! She was snapping the bamboo with twists to the left and right. The raw edges of the bamboo strips were as sharp as knives! Why aren't they wearing any gloves to protect themselves? It's as if they have to make a living with their skin and flesh!

Hīng-tshun just couldn't bear to look and stood up. She saw that Tsín-suī was with the boss over at the main doorway, in the middle of a conversation with the driver of a metal delivery cart. The doorway was like a vegetable market, with carts coming and going. The small carts delivered hemp rope, while bundles of long bamboo strips were being unloaded from the large ones. There were even larger shipping trucks parked outside, and finished bamboo baskets were being loaded onto them. It was a bustling scene that was a joy to behold, alive with the vivid rhythm of life!

Through the din, the infant's wails from earlier started up again, but this time, its cries wouldn't cease. Hīng-tshun's innate love for children spurred her to wind her way around all the moving workers and piles of bamboo until she came upon that little babe now in its mother's arms.

The young mother had turned towards the wall and unbuttoned part of her dress and pulled out one of snow white her breasts filled with milk. Seeing that its mother had pulled out her breast, the infant skillfully latched on with its tiny lips. It seemed as if Hīng-tshun could hear the gentle sound of the child vigorously sucking and swallowing. It was a beautiful picture of a country woman nursing her child. The young mother calmly looked up and gave an open smile to Hīng-tshun, who was standing right next to her. It was a pure smile, like flowers blossoming in a meadow. Hīng-tshun was intoxicated by the woman in front of her and watched as she reached out to caress the infant's head, stroking the babe's head over and over. The infant then unlatched from its mother and began to wail again. The woman began rocking her upper body ever so slightly, "*Sit-lé, sit-lé*, sorry, little one. Momma forgot her hands are so course and they've stabbed you. Don't cry sweetheart. Eat. Eat," the woman said as she pushed her breast back into her babe's mouth.

This scene was heartbreaking to Hīng-tshun. She returned to Giŏk-ìn's side and asked in a whisper, "I want to go buy some gloves for these workers. Do you think that would be a good idea?"

"I don't think they'll accept them. I once asked about it a long time ago. They told me that wearing gloves would make their hands clumsy and unwieldy and slow down their work."

"Oh, I see... I think it's a bit too much to bear!"

"They all have rough and hardened skin now. They're not afraid of being sliced by bamboo slivers."

"What is their income like?"

"They're doing exceptionally well. Much more than in the early days, so they have nothing but thanks and praise to give to A-Suī-á. They see him as a god."

Just as Giŏk-ìn had said this, Hīng-tshun suddenly heard the owner shouting and berating someone. "F***! The distributor said he would take five *kak* off each basket!"

"I have to lower it temporarily by five *kak* silver. I'm trying to unify all the prices." After this, Tsín-suī lowered his voice a bit and explained, "The problem is, the son of a former national minister wants to get a foot in the door of our industry, and he's going through certain related agencies to demand a transfer fee—"

Hīng-tshun and Giŏk-ìn made a quick beeline over to Tsín-suī and heard the factory owner say in a low growl, "That little bastard the chairman is talking about, I know just who he is. F*** him!"

Giok-ìn gave her husband a light kick. "Come on. Let's go. We still need visit another place."

After they left the bamboo basket shop, the three of them had walked a short distance when they saw a group of men at the foot of a tree, crowded around looking at something. As they drew closer, Tsín-suī told Hīng-tshun, "It's called 'slicing sugarcane.' It's a kind of game and a form of buying and selling."

Two young men were in the middle of the people circled around them. One of them was holding a sharp blade. There were several dozen dark, unpeeled sugarcane stalks leaning against the trunk of the large banyan tree. "I don't understand the point of it," Hīng-tshun said.

So Tsín-suī explained, "The guest pays in five silver coins and gets a chance to slice a sugarcane stalk. See the person with the knife? He's about to start. First he takes the stalk and stands it upright. Ah! Look! He's using the back of the blade to press down on the tip of the stalk. He's not allowed to let it fall. And then, hah! He flips the knife blade around and slices down as quickly as he can and, before the stalk falls, he has to use all his strength to cut through to the lowest part of the stalk he can. Oh! Ah! His knife sliced off to one side! He only got through one and a half sections! So he only gets one and a half sections."

The onlookers around them burst into an uproar of applause and shouts. The man with the knife fished a copper coin from out of a pocket and declared that he wanted to try at it once more. But a lot of people urged, "Enough. Let's give someone else a try! Give someone else a turn!"

There were a lot of people around, gnawing on pieces of sugarcane. They bared their teeth as they tore away the sugarcane bark before biting into the flesh. Hīng-tshun was deeply impressed, "What strong teeth they must have!"

The sound of crunching and chomping on sugarcane rose and fell. As they chewed away, they spat out the chunks of chewed sugarcane wherever they pleased, so the ground was covered with piles of sugarcane fibers and sugarcane bark.

"He still might not be quick of hand enough to do it. That's why he let the stalk fall without cutting it all the way through to the bottom," Tsín-suī added.

"If someone's skilled enough and they can cut down—down the entire stalk—that would be the same thing as buying a whole sugarcane stalk for five *kak*," Hīng-tshun argued.

"I've seen the best of them. They could only ever cut down halfway and then the stalk fell over," Giok-ìn joined in.

A large group of flies was dispersed everywhere, dancing and buzzing about the sugarcane stalks and the spat-out little mounds of bark and juicy fibers scattered across the ground. They were an especially large variety. Their crystalline heads with their giant, beady eyes bobbed up and down, left and right. Their wings were also amazingly agile. They were drawn in by the sweet aroma and taste of the sugarcane juice. It was a delicious manna from heaven, they probably thought (if flies thought), and so they flitted every which way they could, trying to suck up all the leftover juice. When someone shuffled a foot or a sugarcane stalk fell, the flies would immediately take notice and buzz away, flying into the crowd of human onlookers. They parked themselves on the heads, necks, shoulders, and clothes of all those standing around. They were waiting for the chance to take their fill of fresh sugarcane.

A swarm of them were buzzing all around Hīng-tshun's head now, and she felt flustered and suggested that they leave.

The trio had decided to walk back to the Ngôo household, giving Hīng-tshun a chance to better appreciate this small, agrarian township tucked away in the southern countryside. They talked as they walked along. For someone living up in the capital, Pîn-tong city had hardly any busy roads, and once you got to the Thâu-tsîng-khe-á district, it was no more than a placid little farming community.

"A-Suī-á, when you were in the bamboo factory, you had mentioned something about having to take five *kak* off every basket. I'm worried someone might have overheard you, and they'll report you." The road they were on was empty, and Giok-ìn was the one who brought this up.

"It won't happen. Don't you worry."

"The transfer fee of five *kak* is probably known to everyone by now, so I've heard, but," Hīng-tshun asked, "is the guy behind it actually the one you're talking about?"

"Yes. He is. He exists."

"The sugarcane juice at your cooperative is so sweet, it brings all the flies out."

"That's exactly right. And that's not all. I'll tell you what's what. The KMT Central Party has a Sino-Japanese Anti-communist Alliance Committee. They formally sent a request for our organization to freely contribute a hundred thousand American dollars each year. They must have thought that we were so filled with joy to fork over that amount of money that two years after they first asked, they then asked for three hundred thousand dollars. *Baka yarō*!"

"Ha! I've not heard someone swear in Japanese for such a long time!" Hīng-tshun responded. "Our Green Fruit Association also has to give out a donation each year of about a hundred thousand dollars American, but they've never given us a shakedown for three hundred grand. I remember the names on the letter were for a Ma Shu-li and Chang Yen-yuen. Does that ring a bell?"

"Yep, that's right. And what's more," Tsín-suĭ continued, "the National Women's League also sent us a letter asking us for one dollar American per basket of bananas sold. That's three million dollars a year right there. So who do you think the National Women's League is a front for? How could we not know? If there were people in society who were worth a million, they'd call them 'millionaires,' but this bunch siphon away three million a year. F***!"

"They're not letting off our Green Fruits Association. We also have to donate a dollar per basket."

Giŏk-ìn chimed in to make him stop, "A-Suĭ-á! Don't use such vulgar words! You're a person with position and status now."

"Fine, fine. I'll be more careful about what I say. Don't worry." Tsín-suĭ stopped for a moment but couldn't keep himself from continuing, "The truly detestable thing is that when our workers in Japan get their paychecks, they're all forced to donate a hundred thousand yen, every month! They're targeting our employees!"

"That's far too much! What cause are they using?" Giŏk-ìn asked.

"It's all the same. They're calling them campaigns to 'Fight the Communists.'"

"Lately, our company received a letter from the Father of the Nation [Sun Yat-sen] Birthday Memorial Preparation Committee, asking us to donate ten million dollars to build some Sun Yat-sen Memorial Hall," Hīng-tshun added.

"That ten million dollars... We got their letter, too, but I was relatively happy to make that donation."

"Why?"

"Because the donation letter came from Wang Yun-wu and Hsu Pai-yuen. Hsu Pai-yuen is helping our organization a lot. As long as it comes from him, I immediately respond. For example, there's Tamkang Humanities and Science Institute. They want to build some chemistry building. We donated a million dollars to them too."

The three of them kept conversing as they strolled through town. Before they knew it, they had reached the Ngôo home. Tsín-suĭ invited

Hīng-tshun to take one more look at the banana fields, but she said she couldn't. "I'm sorry, I had better start my way back now. First, I'll need to take a car to the airport in Hsiao-kang and then catch a flight up to the capital on a China Airlines flight."

19

The next day was a Monday, and Tsín-suī had just woken up when he had to field a telephone call from Li Kuo-ting, the head of the Ministry of Economic Affairs, asking him to go to the Rural Revitalization Committee to meet face to face with a representative of the American Lawton Company. They arranged a time over the phone.

He arrived earlier than planned. The Agricultural Revitalization Bureau official pulled Tsín-suī into a lavish but small meeting room. A tall, gaunt foreigner was waiting for him, standing alone in the middle of the room. He watched as Tsín-suī entered the room and walked forward to shake hands with him. Tsín-suī could only speak a few words of greeting in English. The Agricultural Revitalization official did simultaneous interpreting for the two.

"This man here is Mr.— from the Lawton Company. He's an American, and he's specifically sent to us here in China. He wants to help us to consolidate the business of banana harvesting."

The official said the American's name, but it was a name unfamiliar to Tsín-suī. He'd never heard of it before in any textbook. Tsín-suī couldn't remember it to save his life. He had a strange feeling about the man. "Why hasn't this guy given me his business card yet? Don't these *a-tok-á a* (foreigners) ever exchange business cards?"

That foreigner then directly and familiarly used his hand to motion at Tsín-suī to look at the paper box sitting atop the table. Oh! This was something the guy must have brought. He wanted to market a paper box for banana packaging. Tsín-suī lowered his head and looked for a while at the box, realizing it was too thin and the center of the box was divided in two by a piece of cardboard. It looked like it wasn't very suited to packaging bananas at all. "Foreign guy, have you ever tried packaging bananas before?" Tsín-suī thought to himself.

Tsín-suī hadn't said anything. The American still had a cordial attitude as he motioned to Tsín-suī, "Have a seat, please." Tsín-suī could understand this sentence at least, and so he sat down as invited. Shortly after that, the meeting room dimmed and a film began playing.

It was a black-and-white film clip. He immediately could tell that it was showing harvesting operations on a large banana plantation in South America. The bananas were being cut down by farmworkers and then strung along a motorized cableway next to them. The bananas traveled along the cableway, sliding towards a packaging plant. Workers took the fruit off the line, cut them into smaller bundles, washed them, and then packed them into this kind of paper box, then put the boxes onto a shipping truck.

Tsín-suī pondered as he watched this documentary, "It's ideal to use a mechanical cableway to transport bananas. It can keep them from getting damaged while they're moving along. This kind of system isn't a problem for a massive plantation like in this video. We Taiwanese, though, we don't have fields the size of the one in the video. One *kah* or eight *hun* of land is large enough for us. How could you possibly call on any Taiwanese farmer to sink a bunch of money into a cableway?!"

As he sat there lost in thought, the lights were illuminated again in the meeting room. The American didn't come back over to Tsín-suī's side again for further discussion. It was as if he believed his mission was complete, and so he began packing up his briefcase and prepared to leave. "So just who was it that was trying to push this system onto Taiwanese farmers, if it wasn't the Lawton Company? Was it our own officials?"

A man came over to Tsín-suī and handed over his business card. He was the secretary for the Economic Cooperation and Development Council. His surname was Liu, and his manner of speaking wasn't like a salesman. He had the mannerisms of a government official. "Chairman Wu (Ngôo), you can work well with the Lawton Company, but you will need to sign a contract first."

"Are they selling the paper boxes?"

"No. They're a company that specializes in selling ideas. His idea gets a commission after it's been agreed to."

"So, what does he want to sign? What does he want us to agree to?"

"You can't go wrong if you agree to work with them. The terms of the contract will be written clearly in the agreement."

Tsín-suī tried hard to maintain the smile on his face, but he didn't say anything in response.

Perhaps it was because Tsín-suī hadn't been the least bit enthusiastic about agreeing, but he got a visit several days later, again, from the Lawton

Company representative. Tsín-suī was then serving as the chairman and director of the Kaohsiung Green Fruits Export Cooperative Association, as well as the nationwide United Fruits Exports Company general director. The United company office was up in Taipei, and his office was both spacious and newly built. When he received his American visitor, the person in the firm who could speak English the most fluently was the enterprise planning department vice manager, Wu Chih-tsung. He was introduced to Tsín-suī by Chiang Yen-shih. Chih-tsung could work as Tsín-suī's interpreter for this meeting. This time, the Lawton representative tried his best to make a brief presentation, showing the film for the other company administrators. Tsín-suī still wouldn't give him an enthusiastic response.

A long time passed by after this second meeting with the American. Then a phone call came in from Li Kuo-ting's office. This time, they had arranged for Tsín-suī to come over to the Ministry of Economic Affairs for an in-person chat. The first time Tsín-suī had seen an official of this stature and power, he felt a deep sense of respect and admiration for him, but his heart was also filled with trepidation. The main government organ responsible for banana marketing was the foreign trade inspection committee of the Executive Yuan, and it was headed by Hsu Pai-yuen. The banana subcommittee was convened by Chiang Yen-shih. Why would he be getting two phone calls from the Ministry of Economic Affairs? And this time, being summoned to come alone, in person?

All it took was a couple of brief greetings for Li Ting-kuo to know that Tsín-suī's Chinese left a lot to be desired. He called in an assistant who could speak Taiwanese Hoklo and kept his sentences brief, speaking one sentence then waiting for translation. "Your Green Fruits Association absolutely must accept the offer from Lawton."

"This is quite a serious matter. It's got a lot of complexity to it. I need to think it over and look into the details more before I can decide on it," Tsín-suī summoned his courage and replied boldly.

"Fine. You go back and think about it for a bit. But be quick about a decision," the assistant interpreted the terse response and shuffled Tsín-suī out the door.

On the way back, they hit a gigantic traffic jam. The car would jerk forward then stop. It went on like this for a while. Tsín-suī's mind seemed to be keeping pace with the jolt and stops of the car as it crawled along. Up and down. Up and down. "A person like Li Kuo-ting," he thought, "most people would flatter the man just out of fear of falling out of his good graces. How the hell did I find the courage to face him down and refuse the request? What's wrong with me? Is it because I have to care for my industry and all the people I work with and not upset the banana cart that I refused his demand to change the status quo? Is it because I don't want to see those poor bamboo basket makers lose their livelihoods to paper boxes?" Outside his car window, a large bus was lumbering by, swaying a bit from side to side. Right at that moment, his head cleared. He thought to himself, "I honestly can't accept that proposal from Lawton. The cartons could be redesigned, but that kind of industrialization is so unsuitable for Taiwan's fragmented, scattered banana plantations. But I need to think about it some more. What will the consequences be if I offend Li again? Will he start spreading lies and rumors about me to Hsu Pai-yuen? Will he try to get Hsu to stop supporting me?"

The car came to a halt at the association offices. He stepped out of the car and felt his head spinning. Was he carsick? He had never been carsick before!

Tsín-suī brought Lawton's proposal to the board of directors for discussion. No matter whether it was the Kaohsiung or the National Fruits Export Association, his colleagues on the board of executives all supported his thinking. They all decided to ignore Lawton for the moment, but the national branch supervisors had decided on a side resolution to send Tsín-suī off to South America to do his own field inspection. They made an itinerary for him and selected a week for him to fly off. He would be going off to Ecuador.

First on the agenda was for Tsín-suī to stop off in Tokyo and attend a regular meeting with Japanese businesses before flying again towards the other side of the world. On this trip, Tsín-suī was accompanied by the chairman of the board for the national-level export association, Chou Fang-Chi; the contact point for the Taipei Green Fruits and Green Fruits Cooperative, Lu Kuo-Hua; the manager of the Kaohsiung Green Fruits Association sent to Japan, Hsu Te-lang; and others. Lu Kuo-Hua was recommended by Hīng-tshun. "Mr. Lu is from the mainland. If you and the chairman use Japanese to communicate, you'll have to interpret for him!" Hīng-tshun pled with Hsu Te-lang.

The meeting in Japan was only halfway through when a phone call came in from Taipei. The person on the other end asked Chou Fang-chi to take the call. Tsín-suī's heart skipped a beat. Was Lawton trying to change its tactics by going through Chou? The meeting carried on. Chou only returned after the meeting had wrapped up. He was holding a piece of luggage in one hand. He had apparently checked out of their hotel. "What's the matter?" Tsín-suī asked, flustered.

"Chiang Yen-shih told me to go back to Taiwan immediately. He said I needed to have a talk with the man from Lawton."

"And you were just going to up and leave without telling me first?"

An expression of pained awkwardness was scrawled on Chou's face, as his eyes looked downcast at the floor, and he nodded slightly. "Mr. Chairman, *pháinn-sè*." Chou Fang-chi was Tsín-suī's longtime subordinate from the Kaohsiung association. Tsín-suī did not want to be the chairman of the board of directors for the United Association, so he made a point of arranging for Chou to take the position, but Chou still called Tsín-suī "Chairman" in private.

"Fine. Since you have no choice but to go, then go. I'm afraid I'll have to ask you to politely decline Chiang Yen-shih's request though." Even though Tsín-suī was speaking to someone who was technically his superior, his voice carried a sense of authority. "But be extremely careful. If you absolutely have to sign anything, do not do so without careful deliberation. Do not treat it in some light fashion, am I clear?"

"Yes. Crystal. You can rest assured, Mr. Chairman."

As Tsín-suī gave Chou Fang-chi these instructions, Lu Kuo-Hua and Hsu Te-lang were standing off to the side. Tsín-suī didn't see any sign of dissatisfaction from either of the two. Tsín-suī had nothing but prestige behind him in this industry, and Chou ought to be reverent and respectful.

Although Ecuador is on the equator and should be a tropical country, because of its high topography and the cold winds coming up from Antarctica, its weather all year is warm with a bit of coolness. People were wearing long-sleeve shirts in the middle of June. As soon as Tsín-suī got off the plane, he asked what the weather was supposed to be like for the next day and then called out to his entourage, "This is one of the most suitable lands for growing bananas I've ever seen!"

After they'd made it to the hotel and rested up for a while, their host chauffeured them to an Ecuadorian banana plantation. The man on the entourage tasked with interpreting was a local who could speak Japanese. Soon after, the car had reached a high point in the road with a clearing and everyone was amazed by the wide vista. *Wah-sai*! It wasn't simply some plantation—it was an entire ocean! A veritable sea of green banana leaves, the huge, fan-like leaves fluttered gently in the breeze. Looking far off into the distance, they looked like waves, churning and rolling on the ocean.

They stepped out of the car and asked just how large the field was. "It's about three thousand hectares," the farm owner replied.

Tsín-suī and Te-lang gave each other a look. Hsu spoke in Japanese first, "Our *kah* are just a little bit smaller than a hectare. One hectare is about 1.03 *kah*, so this means that you have more than three thousand *kah* of land for this plantation." Lu Kuo-hua stood at the side and gave Te-lang a swift, light jab with the tip of his foot. Te-lang switched over to Chinese, awkwardly tinged with a Hakka accent and repeated the information.

"The interpreter is saying that this plantation isn't even the largest of them." Tsín-suī said this to Te-Lang in a low voice, using Japanese. Lu Kuo-hua once more kicked at Te-lang's leg. Hsu once more interpreted into Hakka-accented Chinese.

Tsín-suī strode towards the plantation. He randomly picked up a few clumps of dirt. He was startled. It was all black humus. He asked to borrow a shovel to dig deeper, to about two meters. It was all still the same soft black earth. "You don't need any fertilizer to plant bananas in this soil at all."

"It doesn't need to be weeded either because there are no weeds competing with the banana trees for nutrients," the interpreter responded.

"There aren't any typhoons here are there?" Te-lang asked.

The response was, "None."

"With plantations of this size, where are you shipping your harvest to?" Tsín-suī enquired.

"America, Canada, and Europe," was the response he got.

After he got his answer, Tsín-suī's mind was hooked by another issue. After he had visited several more similar banana plantations, his focus turned to the Ecuadorians' business model. Electric cable ropeways being used to harvest the bananas and paper carton boxes for packaging were no longer the main point for him. Tsín-suī asked to change their itinerary. He wanted to inspect their shipping methods, what kinds of harbors they were using, their cargo ships for transport, etc. After he had seen it all and put all the puzzle pieces together in his mind, Tsín-suī and Te-lang carefully made tabulations, calculating the Ecuadorians' overhead costs for production and the shipping fees. They kept running the numbers and finally stopped. "We need to thank our lucky stars that the Pacific is as vast as it is. It's the only thing saving Taiwanese bananas," Tsín-suī said to Hsu with some lamentation.

Lu Kuo-hua didn't understand this sentence in Japanese. "What's that? What are you saying Mr. Chairman?" he followed up.

Tsín-suī responded half in Taiwanese, half in Chinese, "South American banana farmers have such a low overhead. Fortunately for us, the Pacific is extremely vast. They don't have any way of shipping their fruits to Japan."

"If there's faster cargo ships or refrigerated ships in the future, then they'll become a direct competitor for us."

"So we need to keep thinking of better strategies to keep our hold on the Japanese market. We can't let them enter the market."

Tsín-suī pursed his lips then spoke, "This is something I want to figure out on this trip. It's my biggest learning experience."

Lu Kuo-hua took the opportunity to teach Tsín-suī a phrase in Chinese. "You could say it's your greatest 'warning.'" He even wrote out for him in Chinese characters.

"Oh, I learned this word 'warning' already. Ha! that's for sure."

After Tsín-suī and his entourage had made their way back to Taiwan, the first place he stopped off at was the United Green Fruits Export Association in Taipei. The deputy manager of the planning department, Wu Chih-tsung, came into Tsín-suī's office to report to him after he found out his boss was back. "Mr. Chairman, there's something I think you ought to know. Chou Fang-chi suddenly had a stroke not long after he had returned to Taiwan to speak with the representative from Lawton. His condition is quite serious. He's been in the hospital paralyzed ever since. He can't continue his duties."

"He's always been in good health! How could such a strong person suddenly have a stroke?!"

"Maybe the pressure was just too great for him. Perhaps he just couldn't take the stress from above and he was worried you would be angry."

Tsín-suī sharply sat up, and practically yelled, "What happened with our company while I was away? Speak! Now!"

Chih-tsung slowly presented a dossier. Tsín-suī opened it up. He was absolutely flummoxed. Chou Fang-chi had used his position as the chairman of the United Association to sign a memorandum of understanding with Lawton. He scanned the document in a hurry, slamming the document hard onto the table. He stood up and flung his chair away, glaring at Chih-tsung. He didn't know who to take his anger out on first. Next he paced the room back and forth frantically about ten times. Chih-tsung was off to the side, completely stupefied by fear. This was the first time he'd ever seen a public figure such as Ngôo Tsín-suī angry. They never threw things. They didn't use violence and didn't swear or go blue in the face with veins bulging from rage like this. Chih-tsung thought playfully that his boss reminded him of a bull, like in the Brother Buffalo comic that children often read, whose main character was an angry Taiwanese water buffalo. The comic character's nostrils were drawn very large, and steam shot angrily from them. But in the comic, *Brother Buffalo* didn't make any sounds, unlike General Manager Ngôo, who was huffing angrily, "*Honnh—honnh—honnh!*"

Finally, Tsín-suī seemed to have tired from pacing the room and went back to his bureau to read back through the memorandum dossier. He patiently read it, line by line:

I.   Lawton Company will assist in the systematization of Taiwanese banana farming.

II.   All associated fees shall be paid by the Taiwanese signatory.

III. The fees for all of Lawton's dispatched technicians are to be paid by the Taiwanese signatory.

IV.   The Taiwanese side shall construct a paper products plant.

V.   The paper-producing factory must be unconditionally provided for the use of Lawton Company for twenty years.

VI.   All needed paper boxes will be purchased from the Lawton Company.

VII. Should the amount of paper boxes not reach the equivalent of six million bamboo baskets within one year, the Taiwanese party shall pay to the Lawton Co. 1 percent of the export fees for each basket in the amount of one (1) American dollar per basket as an additional export fee.

Tsín-suī read each term over and over again, mulling it over in his mind. He leaned back in his chair and closed his eyes for a long time. Then he opened his eyes again and made notes in the margins next to each item. Chih-tsung took a couple steps forward, lowered his head, and discovered that General Manager Ngôo was annotating in Japanese. He was wondering just who in the managing department could possibly read Japanese when he was suddenly brought back to reality on hearing Tsín-suī give him an order. "Director Wu, I'd like you to pay Chiang Yen-shih a visit. I want you to arrange the visit for me. It's important!"

Chiang Yen-shih quickly saw him. Now Tsín-suī had realized everything. Chiang and Li Kuo-ting were ganging up on him. But Chiang had given a lot of help to the associations in the past. Now he was in a higher position and was still trying to maintain his grip on the convenor of the banana subcommittees; he couldn't lose his composure in front of him. As soon as Tsín-suī walked through Chiang's office doors, Tsín-suī greeted him in standard Chinese, "Congratulations Mr. Chiang on taking up your post as secretary of the Executive Yuan." His phrasing was something Chih-tsung had taught him before he had left.

"You're here so soon after coming back. Is there anything I can do for you?"

"I've come to ask for your advice on something, Mr. Secretary. I've looked over this memorandum of understanding several times, but I have the feeling that it's some kind of unequal treaty."

Chiang Yen-shih kept on staring at Tsín-suī but didn't respond. Tsín-suī continued, "Our Chairman Chou had talks with the Lawton Company. Were you not in his presence when he signed the memorandum?"

"I was. I was there. But I said nothing from the time I arrived till the time that I left. It was your Chairman Chou who did all the talking with the Lawton Company."

"You're the convenor of the banana subcommittee, no? You have the responsibility of executive supervision! Yet, surprisingly, when there were discussions between a foreign company and a group from our country, you didn't have any opinion on the matter! What kind of managerial oversight is this? Did you forget your position, or did you force Chou's hand without saying anything? *Honnh*!" Tsín-suī's cursed Chiang in his mind, but he didn't dare speak the words out loud. Instead, he led with this, "I'd like to ask the Secretary to invite Lawton back in for another round of talks. I'm not sure if—"

"I'm afraid they can't do that. The previous talks were carried out by people holding power of attorney."

Tsín-suī very quickly took his leave, striving very hard not to blow up in Chiang's face—and to keep his calm.

After he'd returned to his office at the association, he was livid. He thought about the system in place. Hsu Pai-yuen was supposed to be the highest-ranking authority for the banana exporting industry, no? He immediately went to seek an audience with Hsu and was very quickly received.

Tsín-suī very politely presented the memorandum of understanding. Hsu Pai-yuen just gave it a quick glance and immediately pulled out a dossier from a stack of folders. "This deal with Lawton... I still hadn't made any annotations when they were signing. I wanted to ask your opinion on the matter."

"Mr. Chairman, both sides had their discussions and signed the document while I was out of the country. Upon further inspection, all I see is an unequal treaty."

"What is unequal about it?"

Tsín-suī felt it wasn't impossible to change Hsu's mind, but he had to use all his mental energy to express himself clearly, and he needed to do all of this as much as he could in Mandarin alone. "I'd like to report to the chairman that the critical issue in the matter is the unification of banana harvesting proposed by Lawton. That would only be appropriate for the huge South American plantations. Mr. Chairman, you understand clearly that our Taiwanese banana farms are far smaller—perhaps five or ten fen of land apiece—and they are scattered all over the place. In order to implement Lawton's methods, you will end up spending far more money than you anticipate, perhaps several tens of millions of dollars. This would be a burden to the farmers and laborers, and you will end up enraging the public, Mr. Chairman."

"You can speak slower if you'd wish. I can understand you. Your skills in the national language have improved quite a lot."

"If this plan is approved, the second article suggests that we pay for everything. That is something we could bear, but with Article Three, it includes all of the expenses for their technicians, including their salaries, room and board, and so on. All of that would have to be paid for by us. This is utterly unfair. Article Four: we are responsible for establishing a paper carton factory. This would be feasible if not for Articles Six and Seven. Mr. Chairman, could you please take a closer inspection? Lawton's greed is plain for all to see. I hope that..."

"Well?"

"I've already performed the calculations. They want us to build a factory that can produce six million cartons, the fees of which can be no less than one hundred million dollars. After the deal is signed and they receive the money, they demand that we unconditionally provide the factory for their use for twenty years. This would force our banana farmers to buy their paper cartons. This makes almost no sense, Mr. Chairman!"

"And Article Seven?"

"Article Seven states that should the amount of paper cartons be less than the amount of six million cartons, that we will need to pay damages to Lawton. I don't understand what kind of pressure our chairman of the board, Chou Fang-chi, was under that he would sign such a thing. This article isn't just an unequal treaty, it's a hegemonic pact. Mr. Chairman, please reconsider it. If our use of their cartons doesn't reach six million units within any year, it would be due to factors beyond our control. For example, if there are big problems with the buyer or if we're hit by some big typhoon, not only would we suffer damage and loss, but we would also have to pay an indemnity to Lawton. This would be the absolute death of us!"

After hearing Tsín-suī's description, Hsu Pai-yuen once more pulled out the dossier and began to write some notes. Tsín-suī stood off to the side, upright and silent, head lowered and heart thumping away erratically. He saw Hsu's notes added to the very top of the signatures.

I. If you must use the paper boxes, then there must be a public tender for purchase.
II. There are also domestic technicians that can be hired.

Oh! He did it! The table had been turned! Hsu Pai-yuen truly was on the side of good. He could be counted on for some justice. He's standing with us banana farmers. I thought he would have caved, but he hasn't!

This time, Tsín-suī didn't kneel before Hsu but made a bow and said words of thanks.

Tsín-suī felt as if he had just scored a victory. It felt as if this was a battle, with him slashing and hacking randomly with a scythe in a dense fog. He was elated with the kind of elation where your heart is both free of worry and racing. That evening, he made arrangements to have dinner with Hīng-tshun. The two of them ran back through the entire timeline of events with a fine-tooth comb. Hīng-tshun drank several glasses of Japanese sake, but she was still quite lucid and sober. A lifetime of experiences and bitter hardship came and went before her eyes. When they talked about the future, she just had one critical question to ask, "So...that paper carton factory of yours... Is it up and running yet?"

"We touched upon it, but the Japanese side still hasn't officially requested that we change to paper cartons. We're continuing to ship our bananas using bamboo baskets."

"Who did you turn to for it?"

"I went into a Japanese-Taiwanese co-funded International Farmer Workers Company. I want a fifty-one percent stake in the Taiwanese side."

"So, if the talks come to anything, it'll shift to your association and your Japanese counterpart having to build a paper carton factory."

"That's correct."

"So the Lawton Company is going to refuse to trade with your cooperative association?"

"Right."

"If that's so, starting today, you need to be careful how Li Kuo-ting might try to seek his revenge."

Tsín-suī looked pained and he took a big swig of *sake*.

"I can ask on your behalf, if you'd like. You can ask me anytime."

Just as they were about to part ways, he asked, "If I can still subscribe to that International Farmer Workers Fund, let me know."

"Sure. Next time we meet, I'll help you to sign up."

***

The following day, Tsín-suī returned to Ko-hiông, convened a meeting with all the officers, and took care of a few things. After that, he headed over to Tsuān-tsong's company. He wanted to get Tsuān-tsong's opinion. After Tsín-suī had told his friend all of what transpired, the first words out of Tsuān-tsong's mouth were, "I think if you're only relying on Hsu Pai-yuen, he's too weak."

"There's nothing else I can do. Hsu Pai-yuen is one of the good guys. He's been a good friend to us banana farmers."

"Did you ever think that when you work together with two companies, one of them is the International Farmer Workers Company and the other is this Lawton Company? You're standing with one foot planted in one boat each, and they're drifting apart. The devil wants to make a deal with him."

"Lawton doesn't make any paper cartons at all. They're a new kind of American company, specializing in ideas. They tried to siphon off big bucks from us. Any time I think about this memorandum, it puts such a big fire in me that I'd like to go off on someone."

"Although it sounds like Chiang Yen-shih and Li Kuo-ting are on the same ticket, you've already pissed off Li Kuo-ting. You're going to have to do a lot to try to repair the relationship with Chiang Yen-shih."

"I've thought about that too. Chiang had already introduced a Mr. Chou to me, who would be in charge of the planning department. Recently, I had the misfortune of promoting him to manager."

"Was it worth it at all? What I mean is, how is it to be kissing their asses?"

"I wouldn't know. He's treading along the U.S. AID path. When we're in meetings, the representative has long been one of Chiang's men."

"One of us Taiwanese or from the mainland?"

"He's Taiwanese, born and raised in Tâi-pak."

"A-Suī-á, I have to tell you something," Tsuān-tsong's face grew very serious all of a sudden. "If you're going to kiss ass, you should at least pick the right person. I went a bit too early in deciding to kiss up to Chen Cheng! Each time I pass by the intersection of San-duo Road and Chung-shan Road, I see that massive f***ing equestrian statue of President Chiang Kai-shek that I spent four or five million dollars on. F*** it all! I look at it and I ask myself, 'Am I finished kissing the Chiang family's asses yet?' They can all get f***ed!"

"Hey, hey now, no need to be that way. Giok-ìn-á reminds me all the time, we're people of high status now."

"Holding others' family jewels for them is for the purpose of making sure everything's safe. I'm cursing to set my heart at ease."

"My son has been going to Chinese school. One day, he told me a story. It was a book called *Chronicles of the Eastern Zhou Kingdoms*."

"What's the story about?"

"Well, in the story, there was a king named Fu-chai, King of Wu. After he had lost a battle, he called together his officials and ministers. Each day in the morning, he had them remind him in a loud voice, 'Your Majesty! Did you forget who defeated you? Did you forget who beheaded your father?'"

"So why are you trying to tell me this story? My father would have killed them."

"I was just thinking that you and Fu-chai are running along a similar path. Each day you go by that huge copper statue, it's like a reminder, 'President Chiang Kai-shek! Have you forgotten how long I've held your family's jewels for you?'"

"Hahaha, well, f*** his mother!"

"Tsuān-tsong-*hiann*, your words will come back to you. Sung Mei-ling, Hsu Pai-yuen—these people are all part of the Chiang family, no?"

"Of course they are. But...I don't know! I can't quite say for sure!"

After the two had said goodbye and Tsuān-tsong headed home, Tsín-suī went back to Pîn-tong. That evening, he slept like a rock. In the morning over breakfast, Uncle A-Tsòng's son, Soo Tsìng-tik, came rushing in, searching for Tsín-suī.

"My father says he absolutely needs to see you, but he can't get out of bed."

"What? What's happened to your father? is he sick?"

"His entire back and buttocks are covered in abscesses, and he's been running a high fever for the past three or four days now."

They each got on a bicycle and rode quickly together along the country road. On one side of the road was a rice paddy. The other side was a banana farm. Updrafts of the cool morning air rose to their faces. Ah! The smell of the countryside. The light scent of mud and earth, the slight aroma of chicken shit and pig feces, all mixed up together with the fresh dawn air. Tsín-suī inhaled deeply and thought to himself, for the past ten years or so he had been racing around Ko-hiông, Tâi-pak, Japan, riding in cars, traveling overseas on jet planes. But he felt most at home just riding a bicycle around his hometown.

Soo Tsìng-tik spoke, derailing Tsín-suī's train of thought, "Our chairman of the board said it's been a long time since you went to meet with him."

"But I went to see him yesterday."

"He praises you a lot. He said you're so effective in the green fruits world that if you shouted out, water would freeze at your command."

"That's just what it looks like from the outside." Tsín-suī quickly changed the topic, "And what about you? How are you doing with your director?"

"Quite well. He's recently sent me off to help organize a new company."

"Oh, that's quite good. He's keeping you busy then."

They talked and talked, and finally reached the Soo household. When they reached his bed, they saw A-Tsòng lying flat on his stomach. There was a thin banket lightly covering his back. The entire room reeked of a medicinal odor. He saw that Tsín-suī had come and shifted his body to his side. It looked like his whole body was writhing from pain as he turned. His mouth was slanted and wincing, and his eyebrows were wrinkled up in pain. Tsín-suī hadn't seen A-Tsòng in months. It was clear to see that the older man had lost much weight, but there was still a sharpness to his eyes, as ever. Seeing his body pained, the sight of him whipping Mari arose to Tsín-suī's mind. Tsín-suī quickly swept that thought from his mind and said, "A-Tsòng, you should really go to the hospital in your current condition."

"I just came back from the hospital." He slightly raised his head. He stared at Tsín-suī for a moment, "How are you doing recently? Is everything going smoothly with the association?"

"Quite well. Everything's going smoothly."

A weak smile came to A-Tsòng's face. "Well, that's good. You're the chairman now. No annoyances blocking your way."

"Well I wouldn't say that. There are people are coming out of the woodwork from everywhere to ask us to donate. They're asking for huge sums of 'happy donations.'"

"I gather it has to do with the 'fight the Communists' money, no? We were dealing with that a long time ago too."

"Well, now there's even more of them who've started calling on us."

"People say that there's thousand-kilo pigs but no thousand-kilo bulls. It turns out they're right."

What do you mean by "there's thousand-kilo pigs but no thousand-kilo bulls?" Tsín-suī asked.

"Oh, nothing... I'm just thinking of an ancient proverb. I'm just thinking out loud again."

"Anything else on your mind?" A-Tsòng continued.

Tsín-suī sat at the edge of the bed and told A-Tsòng about how he had gone to South America to inspect banana plantations there. The more A-Tsòng listened, the more excited he became, and he wanted to sit up, but as soon as he moved, he winced and wailed in pain. Tsín-suī supported his shoulder, pleading with A-Tsòng not to move. All the while, he told A-Tsòng about the whole affair with Li Kuo-ting and the Lawton Company. A-Tsòng's excitement suddenly drained from his now-white face. Tsín-suī had never seen his expression hardened like this before. A-Tsòng's eyes just stared back, wide as ever, as he listened to Tsín-suī. Tsín-suī had already finished retelling the tale, but A-Tsòng just stared, wide-eyed at him, giving no reply. There was a depressive pall about the room now. Tsín-suī picked up on the dispirited look in A-Tsòng's gaze. His eyes resembled nearly spent cinders in a fireplace, almost about to burn out. A-Tsòng laid there in silence for a long time before he suddenly stretched an arm out, gripping Tsín-suī by the shoulder, and encouraged him, "A-Suī-á, don't fret. As long as you do the right thing and keep plowing along on your course, then that's fine. Just keep moving forward like an ox, tilling your own furrow."

20

In 1964, Taiwanese banana shipments increased to 3.14 million baskets of bananas. In 1965, the number exploded to 6.99 million! The efforts of the Kaohsiung Green Fruits Export Cooperative were most instrumental in this respect. The banana farmers prospered, and the prestige of Chairman Ngôo steadily increased.

There was a supervisors meeting that day, scheduled as it always was for every month. As Chairman Ngôo was listening to one of the briefs being given by one of the council members, he frowned and asked, "What's the case about? Why is our association getting a proposal from the Veterans Affairs Council?"

"Oh, it's not a proposal directly from them, but it was introduced to us through our own council member, Hung Hsi."

"The proposal matter is not at all clear. What is it that he actually wants?"

"I'm not quite sure. It's probably something to do with the placement of military veterans in our company."

"This doesn't have anything to do with our banana business. Don't put it at the top of the pile. Put it at the bottom."

"Yes, Mr. Chairman."

There were several proposals to work through at the board of supervisors meeting. All of them required time-consuming discussions before a resolution could be reached. Right up until the last proposal of the day, the chairman asked Hung Hsi, who had made the proposal, "I think everyone's pretty beat at this point, and our stomachs are all grumbling out of hunger. Let's save your proposal for the next meeting, shall we?"

"No. We can't. We have to work on this proposal right now."

"Is it truly that important? Well? Why don't we go take a break and adjourn for a bit and then go eat. With the power invested in me by the board of directors, I'll gather the directors and related managers into my office this afternoon to discuss it and make a resolution. Is that OK?"

At Tsín-suī's motion, everyone else roared in agreement.

After the meeting, they all headed over to a restaurant in Kaohsiung's First Building. It was famous for Chinese fare from Zhejiang and Jiangsu. During the meal, Hung Hsi tried many times to discuss the "important matter" with Tsín-suī but to no avail. He was an experienced executive. He thought about when Tsín-suī had first entered this world of decisions and policies, Hung was himself just a lowly supervisor. Later he would serve two terms on the board, and when he went up to run again for a third term, he came up against Tsín-suī. "When voting, this Ngôo A-Tsín-suī said he had secretly voted for me; but when we looked at the voting results, he was elected with an absolute majority with two-thirds of the vote."

"What was he thinking giving me his only vote? Was he trying to give an old-timer executive like me a bit of respect and save me some face? Or was he already aware of just how powerful he was and had plenty of confidence, enough to waste his vote on me? Or was he just trying to avoid looking greedy? Or maybe he was mocking me?" Hung Hsi saw how everyone was surrounding Chairman Ngôo, toasting each other until their faces glowed from the drink. There was envy deep down in Hung's heart—and a bit of admiration. He washed down a mouthful of beer in a toast, then thought, "This time, if I win, I probably won't be anything like him and won't be able to make our foreign sales thrive as they do now."

After the banquet had just about wrapped up, Hung walked straight up to Tsín-suī's office. Tsín-suī hadn't forgotten about it at all. Several minutes later, he was accompanying the general manager, Lee T'u-chen, and the Deputy Director, Tsai Kun-shan. There was the smell of alcohol on them. They hadn't even sat down before Tsín-suī cut straight to the point with Hung.

"Brother A-Hsi, I'm sorry, but your proposal has nothing to do with bananas, so I'm not going to handle the matter in the meeting."

"It has nothing to do with bananas or fruit produce. But it does have everything to do with the survival of our produce and export association."

"You're always going on about how important it is!"

"I'm nearing retirement age. This is the last thing I want to deal with."

"Thanks for all your concern."

"Do you know what department the Veterans Affairs Council is a part of? Do you know who the people are behind that council?"

"Of course I know. It's Chiang Ching-kuo."

"And knowing that alone is fine enough."

"Why do you think the Veterans Affairs Council wants to send veterans to our company? If they don't send any correspondence, then go through you to try to indirectly make their proposal to us?"

"This is something the former chairman, Chang Ah-Ming-suh, asked me to work on."

"Can Chairman Chang tell me this himself, in person?"

"He said he's no longer there. He said there was some friction between you two from before, so he asked me to make the proposal."

"Why is the Veterans Affairs Council only doing this through word of mouth? Let's just call up Chang Ah-Ming-suh and have a little chat. Do we need to work this out properly?"

"I wouldn't know, Chairman Wu. Maybe this human resource issue isn't something they want everyone to know publicly. Or maybe they'll send an official letter at some point. Nobody seems to have the flexibility to manage it—"

Tsín-suī suddenly thought of something critical and cut Hung Hsi short mid-sentence. He called over to Tsai Kun-shan, the deputy general manager, "Can you go over to the door and open it just a tad and see if that Ouyang agent is on the outside trying to eavesdrop on us?"

The director rose to his feet, and Hung Hsi called out, "There's no need. I told him to go before we began talking. I told someone to take him to a bar and have some fun."

"It's the middle of the day, and he's out at a bar to play around?"

"*Ai-yoh*! I didn't mean to dodge him like that. That wasn't my intention. What we're talking about today is something the Party core and the Investigation Bureau will already know about."

"Fine. Let's get straight to the point then. How many veterans do they want to plant in our company?"

"I heard they want us to take in two hundred."

"That many? What kind of work do they think they're going to be doing?"

"To begin with, we just have to get them started as odd-job workers." Hung Hsi hesitated for a second. "How haven't you seen what's going on? All of the national schools, elementary, junior and senior high schools, the police stations, in every organization, all of our odd-job workers are these military veterans."

"Where do we have space for that many new workers?"

"We've got such big collection depots. Recently, over on the west bank of the river in Kî-san, we've added a new one, and three new depots at

Malu-Sin, Malu-Bing, Malu-Tan, and on the east side, there are four new depots. Then there's also the produce collection depot on the docks where we could add a few more helping hands."

"If these people come, first, they don't speak the language. How are we going to communicate with them? Communication—"

"Language isn't the issue. It'll be hard for them at first, but everyone will just get used to it after a while."

"Second, we're doing well at the moment. There's lots of work to be done in the banana plantations of Pîn-tong and Ko-hiông, especially in the middle of planting season. So there will be lots of work for our local workers to earn extra money—"

"To be quite frank with you, the face of the Veterans Affairs Council is the face of Chiang Ching-kuo. Who's not going to bite the bullet for him? Chairman! We HAVE to. We can't refuse him. And we have to be proactive in inviting a few people out for a visit and make them feel proud of sponsoring us."

"Well, you're not wrong in thinking that! Thank you for reminding me, old friend." Tsín-suī glanced at the business manager, "At this stage, the one we can realistically rely on is still Hsu Pai-yuen. You haven't heard him speak about it, but the one behind him is Sung Mei-ling, Chiang Kai-shek's wife."

"Chairman Chang had reminded me of that. He said that Madame has taken over foreign trade, foreign relations, and the like; the prince, however, has seized control of military affairs and defense, information services, and so on and so forth. Those are the areas the Chiang family has carved up. He said to think of it as a kneecap. The prince is a bit more worth throwing your weight behind." Hung Hsi stopped for a moment to consider what he was saying before he continued, "Chairman! Please, whatever you do, do not think that having good relations with Hsu Pai-yuen is good enough. It will never be enough! It would be wise of you to put some consideration towards the Veterans Affairs Council."

"Ha ha! Thank Chang Ah-Ming-suh for his analysis... I'll think it over tonight..." Tsín-suī was about to continue when the telephone on his desk began to ring. While Tsín-suī was on the phone, Hung Hsi took the opportunity to tell Manager Lee and Vice Director Tsai, "If anyone brings up today's proposal or enquires about it, we must keep our story straight and tell them that the chairman is more than happy to accept and integrate the veterans into our association. He's currently working on the arrangements. Are we all clear on this?"

"Yes, I see."

"Got it. I see."

This evening, after Tsín-suī had finished work and got back home, he saw family members hurrying about busily in the cow pen. Tsín-suī put down his briefcase, threw off his dress shoes, and ran over to the paddock. Masa's stomach was bulging with what seemed to be serious flatulence. His belly was as round as a drum, and the bloating reached all the way to his back. "What did you give him to eat?" Tsín-suī yelled out frantically.

"Nothing. We haven't given him anything particular. When we were feeding him, we cut up a couple of the old sweet potatoes from the field is all," Giok-ìn replied with some unease in her voice.

"Ah! He must have eaten some *tshau-phan*g sweet potatoes. Must be that's why his stomach is so bloated."[42]

"Oh? What should we do?"

"Go quickly over to the creek side and cut several pieces of shell ginger and bring them back to me. It's the kind you use for steaming the giant *bah-tsang* dumplings. Go, quickly!"

Not too long after, with shell ginger in hand, she returned. Tsín-suī took them and gave them a shake. "I'll go and wash the dirt off of them first," Giok-ìn said with some urgency.

"There's no need. The more natural it is, the better," Tsín-suī said as he walked towards his bull. He began speaking with Masa, "Masa—please eat these shell ginger leaves. Be a good boy and chew on them for a bit. It isn't a flavor you like, I know. I just want you to chew on it. *Aiyee*. Chew. Go ahead. Chew." He gently packed one leaf into the bull's mouth. It was like watching a parent trying to entice their child into swallowing some bitter medicine. "Chew, chew, chew. *Aiyee*. Swallow the juices. That's right. Just swallow the juices. If you don't swallow the pulp that's OK, ah!"

Masa chewed once or twice, but then his jaws stopped moving. Tsín-suī reached out with one hand to massage Masa's face, slowly but softly patting him, from the top of the buffalo's face downwards, moving along the buffalo's cheeks towards its lower jaw, then in a soft voice, tried to encourage the bull, "Ah, you need to keep chewing. Keep chewing. Chew. That's right. Chew. Grind with your teeth. Masa, just chew a piece and swallow it."

---

42. When a sweet potato is dug up from a field and it's gone bad or has been infested with weevils, it's referred to as giving off a rotting odor; hence *tshau-phang*.

When Tsín-suī needed to give him the second piece, Masa gave his head a shake and groaned. Masa was obviously trying to say, "No. I don't want anymore."

Giok-ìn walked quickly over to the storehouse and brought out a piece of bamboo tubing that had been carved into a flat depressor. "I'll try to grind up the leaves. Maybe you can force him to drink it," she told her husband.

"Masa said he doesn't want anymore, so he doesn't need anymore. He's already swallowed one entire leaf. It's probably enough. Let's wait for a little. If nothing's happened with his belly, then we'll force him to swallow it," he replied as he headed into the house.

Ten minutes later, Giok-ìn came over to give some information. Beaming, she said, "It worked! It worked! I heard the buffalo making some farting and hissing noises. But, my dear husband, I have to ask you, why is our Masa coughing all of a sudden?"

"Masa doesn't have a cold. Why is he coughing? I think he's just trying to burp out the bad gas."

"Oh! But Masa's gas doesn't smell terrible. All I could pick up on was a grassy smell."

"Well, of course. Have you ever heard of a cow's urine or cow pies smelling bad?"

That evening before bed, Tsín-suī went alone back to the paddock and looked in. Masa was curled up with his legs tucked in, resting, but when he saw that his master had come to visit, he stood up. Tsín-suī asked, "Masa, are you feeling better?" Masa's massive eyes closed for a bit, and it seemed as if his eyes were moister than usual under the hazy moonlight. Tsín-suī had been well acquainted with this buffalo of his for close to a decade, and he clearly knew he was trying to say, "I'm doing fine, thanks to you."

Tsín-suī gently stroked Masa along his face and cheeks, then patted his horns. Masa lightly shook his head at this. He wasn't trying to get Tsín-suī to stop, but to say, "That feels nice. Keep giving me pets." There wasn't anyone else in the world who could understand Masa as Tsín-suī could.

Tsín-suī kept patting Masa and feeling around, and his hand moved to the top of Masa's neck, and he felt towards the vertebrae in the bull's neck. Masa's spinal bones were jutting, pushing up to his skin, as hard as iron. His hide around his back was sparsely covered with coarse hairs that stabbed at Tsín-suī's hands like needles, but they didn't hurt.

Tsín-suī kept moving along, and started to speak with his buffalo, "Masa, I've run into some trouble today. A very powerful person behind the Veterans Affairs Council wants to send us some old soldiers, but I don't want to take them. There's about two hundred of them. I have some vacancies, it's true, but those should go to my banana farmers so that our villagers can make a little extra money. As soon as they come, these extra benefits are going to disappear. I don't want that! Of course, it's not that I don't know I have to placate them. Heaven knows I've done as much legwork as I can. Last year, I knelt down on my knees, begging a man. That time, I was able to get down on my knees and grovel. I did it because if I could do it just once, I could bring all sorts of benefits to our farms. But today, when facing the Veterans Affairs issue, it's so difficult to make a decision. Masa, I'd ask you…is the woman more important than a child? To get to the point, does the empress have more power than the prince? Huh? Do you have my answer for me? I need to make a big gamble tomorrow. I'm going to be putting almost the entire farm up on that prince, but I don't want to gamble on this game. There's a lot of fear deep down inside. I heard Tsuān-tsong say that once he had spurned them, they punished him so severely that he didn't know whether he would live or die. I've got a huge conflict. Those veteran soldiers are also down on their luck and pitiable. I heard many of them were forced at gunpoint to join the military. It's a shame that these people must still have their own needs taken care of. Masa, what do you think is the best way to go?"

Tsín-suī went to bed with his heart filled with anxiety. He tossed and turned so much that he woke up his wife. The two of them then sat up and talked for what seemed like forever about what to do. Tsín-suī said, "OK. That's it then. I've decided." Finally, he drifted off to sleep as soon as his head hit the pillow. Now it was Giok-ìn's turn to toss and turn.

The next day, Tsín-suī called together the board with some solemnity and also notified Hung Hsi to come to the meeting. Before the meeting convened, Tsai Kun-shan whispered to Tsín-suī, "Do you think we should invite Commissioner Ouyang from the security room to attend this meeting?"

"Yes," Tsín-suī replied quickly.[43]

After everyone gathered in the room, Tsín-suī began with a proclamation. "This association wholeheartedly invites veterans and retiree soldiers and servicemen to come in and work. Please, all departments, all collection depots, wharf inspection zones raise your requirements

---

43. The Kaohsiung Green Fruits Export Cooperative Association originally set up a "security team room," but later changed it to secondary person's room, and then changed the name again to "security room." They were responsible for coordinating all internal and external "security" matters.

for workers. I invite the directors and managers to immediately send out the invitation to the Veterans Affairs Council after we've tabulated the statistics for placement."

Hung Hsi was sitting next to Tsín-suī and let out a sigh of relief. He, too, hadn't slept well the previous night. He spent the entire night in trepidation, worrying that this strong-headed latecomer chairman would refuse to let in the veterans. If Tsín-suī had done that, he would have destroyed the entire banana industry in one go. They would have said about Ngôo Tsín-suī, "Well, we don't know how he died, just that he did."

Tsai Kun-shan gave a quick sideways glance at Commissioner Ouyang as the latter left the room, returning to his own office to make a phone call.

21

The association representatives were all lining up trying to register. The meeting hall was already packed full of banana farmers, everyone's loud chatter creating a raucous din. Director Hung Hsi and Commissioner Ouyang were standing next to each other in the venue, chatting away.

"A couple days ago, Little Cheng took you over to the Hsin-Yi Chamber. Did you have fun?"

"Yeah, I went, but halfway through, I stopped and went back to the inspection station to take care of something."

"Oh, is that so? Why?"

"Well, for that place, the quality girls won't show up for work until the evening."

"Ha! You're too picky. Hmph. Well, did you leave Little Cheng there to keep having his own fun?"

"I did."

"Huh, this guy! You've already been transferred here to report on things. What will you do when you have to return back to the Investigation Bureau?" board member Hung Hsi asked bluntly.

"Oh, it's nothing. I'm just going back to the bureau to pay a visit to some old colleagues of mine."

As the two of them reached this point in the conversation, the meeting hall quieted down considerably and the MC began shouting, "The meeting is starting! The chairman is here."

But Hung Hsi still had things he wanted to talk about. "Yesterday, Chairman Wu was asking, do you think the Veterans Affairs Council will have any ideas for us?"

"No, I don't think so. They're very thankful to our association and to Chairman Wu."

"So then why has the Veterans Affairs Council only sent us just over thirty people so far out of all the people they had recommended?"

"Well, that's the thing. Aren't they already finished with constructing the cross-island highway and letting traffic through now? The news story was huge. You've probably heard that the Veterans Affairs Council has started opening up farm after farm up in the mountains. They're planting fruits, high-mountain vegetables, and the like. There's a lot of veterans who've been sent up into the hills for work."

"Oh, hmm, I see what you're saying."

"There's another factor. This is the world of you local Taiwanese. Everyone speaks Taiwanese here. There's a lot of veterans who are afraid they won't be able to speak with anyone and won't get used to it, and so they'd rather all go up to the mountains and do farming with others like themselves."

"Hmm, I see. But you've still helped us to communicate with the top guys. The salary and benefits are extremely lucrative here. You'll probably never find another outfit in the entire country as great as this one here. I heard the human resources unit is drafting another proposal—they're preparing to raise the workers' salaries again."

"Yeah? That's not bad at all." Ouyang's interest was piqued, "Hasn't the Association Representatives Meeting always been convened at a hotel or a giant banquet hall?"

"They're convening this almost at the last moment. They didn't have enough time for a formal arrangement with the usual place."

Just as they were saying this, they walked into the meeting hall one following the other. Today was a last-minute Association Representatives Meeting. The main item on the meeting agenda was celebration plans that had been drafted up by the board of directors. They wanted to get the approval of the entire organization. Hung Hsi quickly strode up to his seat up at the directors' table. Commissioner Ouyang sat among the crowd of workers down below the stage.

The meeting began, and Tsín-suī was very brief in his introduction, spending little time in quickly noting the agenda items. The relevant officials would explain them and then make a recitation of each drafted article. The planned proposal had already been discussed in the directors meetings, but Hung Hsi was striving hard to listen to the whole thing over again, trying to determine if there was any inappropriate wording.

The first thing he heard was the reasoning for the proposal. There was a "recognition and appreciation," following after the, "As a thanks to the government for their gracious support of our fruit farmers and to thank and commemorate the predecessors of this association and their continued success, and for the spirit of national patriotism and loyalty to this company by all its members and employees, the implementation of even more effort and hard work in the improvement of our fruits' quality and for vying for the goal of exporting more produce abroad, in which all senior and excellent representatives from the society, directors, supervisors, staff, and technicians, regardless of their current position, shall be honored for their merits. Among them, the first are 'those members who've contributed to the association and the banana farming industry'; the second are 'members and officials from the government and related organizations who have graciously given their support to this association.'"

After he'd recited the articles, Tsín-suī began asking those gathered, in a soft-spoken tone, "Does anyone have any thoughts or comments on this proposal?" Nobody gave a response from down in the audience. Tsín-suī then switched up his tone, "Is everyone in agreement about this proposal? Huh?"

A wave of "Yesses," and "Agreed" resounded throughout the hall. The council members began running a tally. Nearly everyone had given approval.

Next they took on the proposal. The directors and members began reading out the contents. Each person at the table had a copy. They were printed using a steel plate press, and the ink hadn't even dried yet. Ink smudged everyone's hands. The thirty representatives made joint proposals, each one of the proposals densely packed with details. They went into great detail about all of Tsín-suī's successes since he started serving his two terms. The content was rather plain and didn't include too much excessive praise. There were some new phrases that nobody had heard before. Hung Hsi was underlining things as he listened: "In only six or seven years, each farming community has grown from being poor hamlets where people barely subsisted to villages where people were self-sufficient, and then those self-sufficient farmers became wealthy... Chairman Ngôo has built a great big family by combining tens of thousands of banana farmers and those working in bamboo industries. He's the head of this family. Everyone, old and young, under his surpassing leadership has worked hard together, and they have all prospered. We've reached a high point..."

After the case was read to its end, they began to deal with concrete matters. Ha! Hong Hsi nearly shouted out, "One: Erect a statue of Ngôo Tsín-suī in front of the new association headquarters, immortalizing his contributions; and two: Award him with a gold or silver plaque, with strong commemorative value to recognize his hard work."

Tsín-suī patiently listened to the end of the proposal and then stood up and raised his voice. As if handing down a verdict, he spoke with iron-clad resolution, "Let's not discuss this proposal. Let's put it aside or just skip it altogether. Let's discuss the second proposal."

Just then, the audience instantly piped up, "Ah! Huh! Then what should we do?"

"We can't skip it!" Multiple voices in the venue rose up shouting this phrase, but Tsín-suī was a god to everyone here. Would they respect this god's wish or disobey his command? Several minutes passed by, then five or six hands shot up around the same time. Some of them were balled up in fists, expressing a strong desire to speak. Some were waving their hands in mid-air. They were meaning to say, "Come on! Speak quicker! Over here! I want to speak!"

Tsín-suī hesitated for about half a minute, then someone in the crowd couldn't stand waiting for the chairman's permission and called out in a loud voice, "There's a problem in the order. A problem with the agenda order. Please go back to the last proposal, Mr. Chairman. We want to discuss this proposal."

Others in the audience also called out, "Agreed!" and "I second that!" The voices of assent rose all around. Tsín-suī looked over and exchanged glances with Cheng Hsi-chüan, a very experienced board member sitting next to him.

Then Tsín-suī announced, "Fine. I will temporarily recuse myself and invite Director Cheng to stand in as the chair." He left after he spoke.

Director Cheng took his time, casually taking hold of the microphone, cleared his throat, then began, "Quiet please, everyone. The association rep who led the proposal has expressed that they wish to make a supplementary explanation of the reasons for this proposal, correct?"

A middle-aged man in a "floral shirt" came towards the podium. His shirt looked truly flowery, but on closer inspection, it appeared that the patterns were actually banana stains that had dried and just wouldn't come out in the wash. They were all over the front, back, and sleeves of his shirt. The blackish-brown and lighter brown drip stains were spread with remarkable uniformity, but you could still tell that the shirt had originally been white. About half of the men who had come to attend the meeting were wearing these "floral shirts." It gave the group of board members looking out from the stage a sense of familiarity and welcoming. Was it any wonder that all of the bar girls, restauranteurs, and jewelry store owners were desperate to please these banana farmers wearing their stained shirts.

The member's representative then began to speak, "Board members and representatives, good afternoon. My name is Tân U-lok-*hiann*. I'm from Pîn-tong. Why have we made this proposal? Our reason is clear in the wording of the proposal. We believe that nobody here will oppose it. What I'd like to add here today is the question of why we are proposing to give out giant gold plaques? We must give Chairman Ngôo a big award, but just giving a merit medal or an ordinary silver badge would be kind of inadequate. If we were to award him with a prize of a hundred thousand or eighty thousand New Taiwan dollars, then it would still be inadequate. And so—"[44]

Someone shot back from down in the first row, "A hundred thousand or eighty thousand! Why are you saying it wouldn't be enough?"

"You don't know it, but Chairman Ngôo is a very wealthy man. He encouraged everyone to increase banana production, but his own family have been working hard, as well. I've asked them myself. His family is planting a total of forty *kah* worth of banana fields—"

A wave of doubt rose from the audience. "Huh! That's a lot! Forty *kah* is massive!"

Tan U-lok, the representative who gave the proposal, said, "I'll add it up for you. You can harvest twenty thousand to twenty-two thousand bananas in one *kah* of land within one year, right? So, what's twenty thousand times forty? So...is our chairman a rich big shot? One hundred thousand? Eighty thousand? Is this amount really worth more than a drop in the bucket for Chairman Ngôo?"

The audience was unsettled now. Tan U-lok didn't let anyone begin arguing. He raised his voice, "So we need to think of how to create a giant statue and, at the same time, make a large gold plaque with characters engraved in it. It needs to be at least ten taels. Gold is our culture's most precious material for memorial objects, no?"

A wave of applause resounded throughout the room. Tan U-lok was quick to add, "I respectfully ask everyone for your support in this proposal," then made a bow and returned to his seat down in the audience. Afterwards, the discussion began. There were nine more speakers. They made much the same comments about Tsín-suī, but most of them proposed expanding the award amount. Several representatives gave their approval for the motion to create a golden award. The temporary chairman, Cheng Hsi-chüan, then passed the resolution as follows:

---

44. The golden years of Taiwanese banana exports to Japan was from the 1960s to the 1970s. A public bureaucrat's monthly salary at the time was between NT$750-1000 at the time, and they only got around NT$10,000 per year compared to banana farmers.

1. The motion has passed. The chairman of the supervisors as well as the managers are authorized to implement the motion.

2. Accompanying resolution: Recognition and appreciation is expanded to the association's directors and officers at all levels, as well as senior staff members of local offices. The expression of appreciation, which may at the discretion of the committee also include the presentation of an award, should take place during the celebratory meeting for the twentieth anniversary of the establishment of the association.

After handling the proposal, Cheng Hsi-chüan waved a hand and instructed a worker who had come forward, "Please go fetch the chairman."

The worker then asked, "I'm sorry, but where is the chairman?" He said this in Mandarin with a very thick mainlander accent, and his voice was loud and crisp. The entire room turned their eyes on him.

Cheng Hsi-chüan was taken aback for a second. Commissioner Ouyang had taken notice and quickly moved forward, telling the worker, "The chairman is in the break room behind this room. Go get him! Quick!"

Tsín-suī returned to his seat and first turned to Cheng Hsi-chüan, gave him a nod, and said, "Thank you." Then he took up the microphone, "I heard you all from behind the wall saying I was like a god. Truthfully, I'm not that amazing. I'm just an ordinary person doing ordinary things—"

"Don't be so humble!" someone called out from the audience.

"Listen, everyone, I've only done two things right to help everyone. The first one is getting our bananas sold to Japan for a great price. Trade had always been a monopoly held by the Taipei Green Fruits Trading Company up in Taipei, and they were making money hand over fist. We just represented our own banana farmers in asking for a share of the export quota, which means sharing the profits. This isn't something I did on my own. It was all of us here in this Cooperative Association. Everyone, so far, we've only earned about half of the profits and interest, and our hundred thousand farmers are making a good living. Later, when we implement the 'production and marketing unification' plan, the entire quota will belong to us—"

His speech was cut short by thunderous applause. Tsín-suī felt the radiant light of all those shining eyes casting their gaze upon him like fireballs. He felt a tremor in his heart so he paused.

"And the second thing?" Someone in the audience called to urge him.

"The second thing is that we've guarded the Japanese banana market. We've guarded it well and increased the size of the market. We used reasonable prices and appropriate quantity to control the market. We've guarded the position of Taiwanese bananas in control of the market. I didn't want the Japanese companies to start thinking about importing bananas from South America. I'm good friends with several Japanese company heads, and I have a good idea of what our Japanese counterparts want. That's just about all there is to it."

The audience quieted down. All those passionate hearts appeared before the eyes of each representative. Tsín-suī grew bolder. He continued, "We Taiwanese banana farmers should be proud! How did I manage to do business with the Japanese? Have you heard the tale before? It began with me setting a base price with the biggest Japanese firms, such as getting seven American dollars per basket. Then what we sent to other companies would increase one after the other. After we got the price up to its highest, these seven dollars would change to seven dollars and sixty cents. And then this price would be given back to our farmers as the lowest base price. This is called '*koo hâng tok tshī*' ('having a hold on the market'). You know, the Japanese call it an '*urite shijō*.'[45] Ultimately, these Japanese firms were willing to increase the price and buy our Taiwanese bananas. So, everyone, don't we Taiwanese banana farmers deserve to be proud?"

A clamor began down in the audience. Several representatives stood up and applauded. The board members sitting on both sides of Tsín-suī also stood up. Tsín-suī followed suit and began applauding as well. He took particular notice of Commissioner Ouyang, who was sitting to his front left and also applauding hard. This man spoke Taiwanese Hoklo with a Fujianese accent. His complexion was dark, and his hair all in a mess. If he had been wearing a "flower shirt" stained with banana juice like our own farmers, he still wouldn't have looked like a security officer sent from the top.

"OK, OK," Tsín-suī waved his hand at the audience. "I'm done prattling away. Let's continue on and take care of other proposals."

The meeting hadn't originally arranged for a press conference. There was just a journalists' box to the left of the stage where seven or eight reporters were seated, listening and scribbling on their notepads. After

---

45. *urite shijō* means a "seller's market." *koo hâng tok tshī* is the spoken equivalent phrase in Taiwanese Hoklo. It mainly comes from Taiwanese banana farmers but carries a Japanese linguistic twist. When the price is also reasonable, it leads to bananas being able to gain importation into Japan. Japanese trading firms only went to the Philippines for their cultivars after Tsín-suī's political demise.

the meeting ended, the group of journalists were allowed to go up to the chairman's office. Board members Cheng Hsi-chüan and Wu Ch'i-jui and supervisor Chiou Yun-yin also entered the room. Two or three workers were busy bringing in tea and dispensing cigarettes. An impromptu press conference, half conversational and half official business, thus began. Commissioner Ouyang came in uninvited, sitting with the reporters off to one side. Chairman Ngôo didn't want him to leave. It wasn't a good time to tell him clearly to get out.

Just at this moment, Tsín-suī unwittingly made the connection and noticed that everyone else was drinking oolong tea, but the veteran soldier workers had given Commissioner Ouyang a cup of jasmine tea.

One reporter began speaking, "Mr. Chairman, the representative meeting has passed it. They have passed a resolution to make a bronze statue of you. It would be best if you didn't wear Western-style clothing but wore a 'flower shirt' stained with banana milk."

This suggestion had a sublime power to it. Commissioner Ouyang noticed that several supervisors had smiles on their faces. The eyes of a newspaper journalist, Ms. Chen, lit up. It was like she had something playful to say. The journalist from the United Daily News, a Mr. Li, was sitting with his legs crossed. The *Central Daily News* journalist, Mr. Chung, had casually lit up a cigarette, but the chairman gave a short chuckle and, unconcerned about the social context, smiled sincerely, and then responded.

"Well, that was interesting! But you need to wait for the new building to be constructed before it's time to enter."

"Does the Cooperative Association already have this kind of plan and estimates?"

"How could we? They're the ones who have put out so many proposals."

"Mr. Chairman, with the assent of the entire organization, we want to express our thanks to those in the government and government organizations. Does our Cooperative Association have an implementation plan?"

"Not yet. I have to bring it up with the management department first and then send it to the board of directors for a discussion and a resolution."

"Will you send them something in gold as an expression of thanks?"

The manager, Lee T'u-chen, rushed into the room to give a status update. "Mr. Chairman, there's a horde of company representatives who still haven't left yet. You need to say something to them. Maybe you could take it upon yourself to say something that will have them going home happily, OK?"

"Sure. Let's go." Tsín-suī stood up, then continued, "I'll step out first for just a second. You keep chatting in here. Our supervisors already have a pretty good idea about our company matters."

After Tsín-suī stepped out, a journalist asked a question.

"Just now, during the meeting, Chairman Wu said that he had gone to Japan to consult on the Japanese market and that when Japanese firms were fixing a price, each one of their firms increased the price. I don't understand this point. If that's the case, are the Japanese companies really that stupid?"

"Hah!" Wu Ch'i-jui snorted. "There's a lot of different angles to this. The chairman never talks about it when we're in an open meeting. Do you know that Chairman Ngôo is also serving as the general manager of the National United Association? He holds all the distribution rights for foreign marketing of Taiwanese bananas. This is something that the Japanese firms know full well about. At the same time, the chairman is also extremely aware of the competition between Japanese companies, and all sorts of contradictions between them. At first, he used his distribution rights as bait and enticed one or two companies to buy in and work with him. How do they cooperate? Well, he first agreed to give one firm part of the quota and wanted them to offer a high price. Then, working with that Japanese company, he fostered a seller's market. After that, other Japanese competitors all decided to increase their prices, one by one. However, he couldn't let that Japanese company suffer any losses. The chairman guaranteed that they would make money, lots of money—"

"So how did he guarantee that?"

"Using subsidies through other official channels."

"What subsidies?"

"Oh, there's many different types. For example, our company can agree with that Japanese company to import fertilizer from the Japanese market."

"So Chairman Wu used his distribution powers to manipulate the Japanese market?"

Another board member, Cheng Hsi-chüan, responded, "It sounds wrong when you say 'manipulate.' The reality is that this is the matter of trade, and trade is like this."

Another board member, Wu Ch'i-jui, then added on with a self-satisfied tone, "As soon as bananas leave their plantations, they become a commodity. Chairman Wu has brought us a lot of income, that is, business. Trading is about making sure that these products fetch the highest price."

Board member Wu Ch'i-jui also revealed, "Chairman Ngôo has used these means. Other associations only see dollar signs. When they see that others are raking in far more money, then they all lean on their connections to actively seek cooperation with us. Chairman Ngôo is a god of wealth in the eyes of these Japanese firms. All he has to do is make an appearance in Japan, and the company presidents are bowing to him wherever he goes, bowing and shaking hands with him."

The journalists buried their heads in their notepads as they listened to Supervisor Chiou's additional words.

"There's a calligraphic piece with a motto placed under the glass cover of our chairman's office bureau. It says 'bait.' He told us he was inspired by this when he had been on a fishing trip once."

The journalists scrambled to their feet, crowding around the chairman's bureau to take a look. There truly was a motto in the upper right corner, written in formal calligraphic script, "If you want to succeed: bait, skill, patience, sacrifice."

After leaving the venue, the *Central Daily News* reporter, Mr. Chung, pulled board member Cheng Hsi-chüan aside and started pressing in a near-whisper, "One of our correspondents at the *Central Daily News* in Japan asked me to find out about a man, a Mr. Satō Kishin. Mr. Satō said he is a good friend of Chairman Ngôo's. You wouldn't happen to know what relationship or role this man plays with the Green Fruits Export Cooperative Association, would you?"

"He's a longtime Japanese friend of Chairman Ngôo's from the Japanese era. He married a Taiwanese woman and often comes to Taiwan for business purposes. He has absolutely no role in our cooperative. However, based on what I know, he is one of the people who has helped the chairman behind the scenes when it came to the Japanese firms."

"What about it? What does your correspondent in Japan want by asking after this man?" Hsi-chüan asked.

"This Satō-*san* moves between both the business and government world in Japan. Our correspondent in Japan would like to make use of his relationship with him and get to know him."

"Oh! Well, if that's the case...if Chairman Ngôo himself gives the word, it shouldn't be a problem. There's a true friendship between him and Mr. Satō."

"I'm not very well acquainted with Chairman Wu. I'm sorry, but could I bother you to put in a good word for me? It would be a great help to the *Central Daily News*."

"OK. I'll tell the chairman. If it's the Central Daily News, the chairman will certainly do his best to help you."

At the other end, next to the break room, reporter Chen was whispering with Supervisor Chiou Yun-yin using Mandarin, "I have a younger brother studying in Japan. He's graduating this year but wants to stay in Japan for work. I'll just tell you directly that he wants to enter our Kaohsiung Green Fruits Export Association Japan office."

"Oh. For this you should tell him to directly go to the Japan office manager, Hsu Te-lang."

"I don't know Hsu very well. I think he's probably also a Hakka from Bí-lông (Mei-nong), right?"

"Oh, Hsu is Hakka, that's true. But he's originally from Pîn-tong. As for whether his hometown is originally in Lāi-poo or Tik-tshân, I can't really say."

"Can you recommend me to him?"

"Quite frankly, I don't have any ins with him. He's one of Chairman Wu's most trustworthy core members. Ask the chairman to talk with him for a bit, and it will definitely happen."

"Well then, can I ask you to speak with him about the matter?"

"I can ask for you, but I'm not making you any promises."

The first floor of the building was jam-packed with people. Association representatives from all over were still making their way home when suddenly someone shouted, "Ah! Chairman Ngôo is coming!"

And Manager Lee T'u-chen, who was accompanying Tsín-suī down the stairs from the third floor, called out in a loud voice, "Chairman Ngôo is coming down specifically for an *ai-sat* with you."[46]

Tsín-suī's tall figure drifted about in the group of association representatives. Although completely surrounded, he was all smiles. Lee T'u-chen was at his side. He felt that Chairman Ngôo was like a conductor for some tumultuous orchestra. One moment, he would have his head down and arms spread, passionately engaging with people, then he would raise his head and it was impossible to tell if he was sighing or singing; yet another moment later, he grew silent, turning his head to listen to the representatives speaking. It was as if everyone were his old friends from hundreds of years back.

The busy orchestra conductor moved along, step by step, and the noise moved along with him. Finally, as he was being seen off out the front

---

46. *Ai-sat* was a common Taiwanese phrase originating from Japanese *aisatsu,* meaning to "greet," "pay a visit," or "exchange pleasantries."

door, some gave a simple handshake of farewell, others walked and talked, shoulder to shoulder out the building, walking several steps with him. The Great Hall in the First Building returned to tranquility.

Three representatives had waited until the majority of the attendees had left before they had the opportunity to get closer to Chairman Ngôo. Tsín-suī recognized two of the representatives as farmers from Nâ-pinn (Lin-pian). The other man was from Tiô-tsiu (Chao-chou).

"Which train did you take? Would you like me to call you a car to take you to the station?" Tsín-suī politely asked the trio.

"There's no need to call a car. Please, I don't want to bother you, Mr. Chairman." One of the members continued, "We'll stay here a bit longer. There's still another important matter that we need to discuss with you."

"What's the matter?"

"Mr. Chairman, were you aware that the government has already declared that next year it wants to select candidates for the Legislative Yuan?"

"Yes, I'm aware of that. What about it? Why did you want to bring this up?"

"Mr. Chairman, we think that you're the most suitable man for the job. All of these towns and counties south of Taichung have several tens of thousands of banana farmers, including their families, secondary industries, shipping companies, and so on. If you decided to run, I think you'd come out well on top of the entire field of candidates."

"Hah! I've never given any thought to this sort of matter." He looked very excited, and he said loudly, "How do you reckon that could happen? Do you really think it's going to be that simple?" After he asked these questions, he looked over at Commissioner Ouyang, standing just a short distance away, even though he wasn't directly facing Tsín-suī. He switched his tone, "Well, to be honest, I'm always going off in every direction and sometimes I have to travel to Japan for meetings. It wouldn't be that simple. When would I possibly have the time to run an election campaign?"

"You've got a good attitude about this, Mr. Chairman. For the rest, naturally, other people will help you. You'd still do pretty well."

After the three people had been accompanied out, Tsín-suī alone walked back to his office. He remained there for hours, pacing back and forth, but he didn't have the mental energy to manage the company's corporate affairs. A directors meeting was being held in two weeks' time. It was mainly being held to discuss the provisional decisions on proposals made by the firm representatives at the big meeting. The official worker units would have already hammered out their drafts and sent them to the meeting to be dealt with. Tsín-suī had requested that the committee members read out each line and character purposefully and slowly.

They read out the earlier remarks. "As a thanks to the government for their gracious support of our fruit farmers and to thank and commemorate the predecessors of this association and their continued success, and for the spirit of national patriotism and loyalty to this company by all its members and employees, the implementation of even more effort and hard work in the improvement of our fruits' quality and for vying for the goal of exporting more produce abroad, and to celebrate the twentieth anniversary of the founding of this association, we are planning on awarding workers, our excellent employers, those who've supported our Collective Association as well as the banana farming industry, and those organizational people who perform work related to this business."

"Stop!" Tsín-suī called out in one shout. "Here is fine. Is there a problem?" he asked the head director.

Nobody responded.

"OK, let's move to the second paragraph."

"We're agreeing on the purchase of gold and silver bars. They would weigh two taels, five taels, ten taels, fifteen taels, twenty taels, and thirty taels, etc. This would be handled by the general affairs department."

"Up to this point, does anyone have any ideas or suggestions?" Tsín-suī asked again.

"I do," Director Chen spoke. "Our management department's drafter might not understand the minting industry, gold bars, silver bars made of twenty taels or thirty taels. It's also quite a large quantity. The government nowadays has regulations and standards. We might not be able to even purchase that amount."

"Is that so? Why didn't I hear about this before?... Well, what's the best plan of action for this?" Tsín-suī asked.

"If we switch to goldware or silverware, there shouldn't be any problem."

"What kind of gold or silver items could we make?"

"Well, we can use gold or silver to make bowls, plates, or cups or something, for example."

"Oh, we could give out gold or silverware. That would have the same symbolism as sending out taels or bars of gold or silver, right? OK. Let's revise it then. Let's make it goldware or silverware. Any other comments or suggestions?"

Nobody responded.

"OK then. Let's continue reading the third paragraph."

"The internal awards shall be reviewed by each department and signed according to the level of merit and submitted for approval at each level.

"The list of external gifts shall be prepared by each department and represented by the chairman of the board of directors, supervisors, managers, department directors, and directors of local offices, according to the functions of the recipients and their contributions to the business of the association.

"All external gifts are made in the name of all banana farmers, not just on behalf of our association."

The councillors and staff had just finished reading off the sheet. Director Huang Tien-chiao raised his hand to offer a suggestion. "When growing up and studying Chinese characters under the Japanese, I never learned this '*kuì-zèng*' word before. Does it mean we're making an offering to ghosts or spirits?"

Several people in the meeting hall smiled.

Supervisor Chiou Yun-yin spoke half in Hakka, half in Hoklo, "Ah, did you see a ghost? I've more experience with reading Chinese than you. You have to read the pronunciation like this: *guì-zèng*, lah. It means you're sending a gift to a *guì-rén* (superior or one higher in stature)."

A person emerged from a corner over in the right side of the venue. "You're reading it as '*kuì-zèng*' or '*guì-zèng*.' Both pronunciations are wrong. The proper way to read it is '*guì-zèng*.' When you're kneeling and begging someone, you have to present a gift to them. That's what's meant by '*guì-zèng*.'"

"Alright, alright, settle down everyone. No need to *khue* (mock) anyone or anything. Quiet down!" Tsín-suī called out. The entire venue quieted down in an instant. He continued, "Director Huang, that's quite enough instigating people into arguments, wouldn't you say? What was your original idea you wanted to express?

"Well, Mr. Chairman, you can't use words such as *jiǎng-lì* or '*kuì-zèng*.' Since it's to memorialize and honor our association's accomplishments over the past twenty years, I think it's more appropriate to use the term '*jì-niàn-pǐn*' ('souvenir')."

"Oh! Well then, what's the difference?"

"Well, for those in the company, if you give yourself an 'award,' it doesn't look so good. If you 'send out an award,' some people might write it off as a kind of *hû-nnḡ-phà* (kissing up)—it doesn't look so good either. To be honest, everyone has already agreed to change the object to goldware and silverware. That ought to be a proper 'souvenir,' no?"

After Tsín-suī listened, he concurred in a loud voice, "That's a good idea. It's very circumspect! Does anyone disagree with the proposal?"

Nobody responded.

"OK then. I'd like to ask that the proposer immediately use today's discussion to write up a draft bill and then recite it for everyone to see what they think."

Several minutes later, the clerk began to read out the resolutions of the meeting. Tsín-suī closed his eyes and lowered his head as he listened carefully. He first pressed both his hands together as if in prayer and then held them in front of his forehead. He listened with deep concentration to every single sentence and word. Was there anything untoward or inappropriate that had been added? What will happen once this has been publicly implemented? What will our company's relationship be with the Party government up in Tài-pak? How will the world of journalism spin this story? He kept listening. He kept pondering. He thought of how this award proposal had originally been planned for him alone. Now it had been altered and expanded as a gift for people both inside and outside the firm. This ought to be something good. It was a fully collective decision. As he thought up to this point, he couldn't help but smile.

22

Commissioner Ouyang was about to get off work when he took a phone call from his former head at the inspection bureau. He was calling Ouyang to get him to come back to the bureau for a talk.

The old man no longer considered Ouyang his subordinate and spoke to him politely, as an old friend. They drank some tea and chatted for a while. After that, the bureau chief took Ouyang into the audio-visual room. "I have two recordings. They were picked up on the wire. Have a listen. I guarantee you'll find them interesting."

The bureau chief looked like an employee giving a briefing. He lightly touched the *on* button as he explained, "The first conversation was recorded in the news reporter's break room at the Executive Yuan. Several journalists were there discussing whether the golden bowls, fruit trays, and golden cups to be gifted by your Green Fruits Cooperative Association were newsworthy and should they write about it or not? Let me press the playback button and you can listen."

The tape went *ka-chhhhh* and the conversation came on.

"They say these are commemorative gifts for their twenty-year anniversary celebration. Tell me, what's so newsworthy about some memorabilia?"

"If you lead with that 'gold' character, damn it, it's a good story."

"Well you need to see how many taels they are. All I know is the items are two or three taels. Do you know if there's any heavier ones that are going to be gifted?"

"I heard the one being sent to Provincial Chairman Huang Chieh's office is thirty taels. The one for Executive Yuan Secretary Chiang Yen-shih is also thirty. There's several other golden fruit bowls that are thirty taels, but I don't know where they are being sent. If they are being sent to Vice Premier Chiang, would you write about it?"

"F*** it! You just write about it. Whether they print it or not is up to the higher-ups."

"But you need to get your facts clear before writing anything."

"F***! They sent them out with all that fanfare, saying that it was in the name of thanking the government for its benevolence and support. Why would they be afraid of what we write?"

"You're bullshitting me. What fanfare? It's not that over the top! Although it's true that they openly had an agenda to pay visits to the officials."

"Hey! We've been going back and forth over it all day. Are you going to write it or not?"

"I'll write it."

"I'm not writing that. You can write your shitty little exclusive. Just keep it limited to two columns."

"This is no shitty little exclusive. If there's twenty or thirty taels involved, I'm afraid it'll make the headlines."

"Stop fussing over it. Just wait a day or two! I'll check a couple places tomorrow, and we'll see."

"If they're sent to the ministry heads, the deputy ministers, and others at the top, are you willing to verify it? If you verify it, will the party reports and ministry reports print it?"

"If it's nothing more than some twenty-year anniversary celebration, and the Green Fruits Cooperative Association has been making lots of money and they want to thank the government for their support, giving out thirty- or twenty-tael gold—or whatever—is no big deal."

The tape made another crackly *ka-chhhhh* sound, and then there was silence. The chief switched out the tapes. "This one... This one's from the reporter's room at the Kaohsiung city government. You're definitely going to want to listen to this one. Let's start..."

"Our deputy director is coming down from Taipei for the interview with the Kaohsiung Green Fruits Export Cooperative Association's twentieth anniversary. Damn it! I've been co-opted on this, but I can't say anything."

"They're just subordinates of the deputy director. Our outlet is sending the director to do the interview in person."

"I'm going to ask the general editor to give it a look-over. It's just a civil group anniversary event. It's not a Double-Ten Day celebration. Why are we local correspondents being cut out?"

"So are the invitations being sent to Taipei or Kaohsiung?"

"We're going to send them to both."

"Do you know why? Everyone knows the Green Fruits Export Cooperative Association is generous. They're definitely flush with money. Otherwise, why would the bureau chiefs be so keen on accepting the invitations?"

"I asked already. The ones in Taipei have come down. They're all heading to the Huawang Hotel."

"Last time, the Green Fruits Cooperative Association just had a ceremony for the opening of a refrigerated plant, and they invited business journalists from Taipei to come down south for the story. The entire reporter group came down on a China Airlines flight and stayed in suites in the Huawang Hotel. I heard that they placed a 'spending allowance' on their pillows."

"How much did they gift them?"

"I never asked them. The Green Fruits Cooperative Association sent them. It wouldn't be a small amount at all."

"This time they probably will get gold cups or silver pans, right?"

"They had a 'small' bowl! The gold cups and bowls were sent to the head honcho officials."

The tape again went *ka-chhhhh*. Both tapes were finished.

"Well? What do you think?" the bureau chief asked.

"I think it's so complicated. Can I listen to it again?"

"Of course."

Commissioner Ouyang listened to the recordings again. "I'm sorry. The reporter wanted to know...who exactly those thirty-tael golden bowls were sent to. I'm not even sure myself."

"Don't blame yourself. Wu Chen-jui sent them in person when he was in Taipei. You wouldn't have heard about it down in Kaohsiung."

"So the bureau's on top of it?"

"Of course."

"So who did he send them to?"

"No harm in telling you. Yen Chia-chin, Chiang Ching-kuo, Chiang Yan-shih, Ku Cheng-wang, Hsu Pai-yuen, Huang Chieh, Tan Yu-tsuo, and others. The last one is a secret. I'll let you guess."[47]

Ouyang went silent but he obviously couldn't guess. "It's our own Wu Chen-jui. He gave himself an award," the bureau chief stated as he turned off the recorder and flicked off the lights to the interview studio.

---

47. During these years of service, Yen Chia-chin was the Premier of the ROC, Chiang Ching-kuo was the Vice-Premier, Chiang Yen-shih was the secretary of the Executive Yuan and the convenor for the committee on banana farming. Ku Cheng-wang was a famous anti-communist tv broadcaster on everyday television. Hsu Pai-yuen was the chairman of the foreign trade committee of the Executive Yuan. Huang Chai was the chairman for Taiwan Province, and Tan Yu-tsuo was the executive secretary of the Executive Yuan committee on banana farming.

"Oh, it didn't happen that way. The thing with the golden bowl was something where the association representatives all specifically wanted to gift the chairman an award, so they later expanded the gift recipients to include him."

"Oh, so that's what it is?"

"Oh, and there's one more thing. I haven't filed a report yet."

"Well I'm listening."

"Wu Chen-jui might be running for the Legislative Yuan. There were several representatives who were pushing him in that direction. He himself seemed pretty moved by the whole thing."

"Our bureau is already aware. Not only was he moved, he was moved enough to go have a consultation with Chiang Yen-shih."

"Did Chiang give his blessing?"

"Chiang Yen-shih has integrity and of course would voice his approval but advised Wu to go to the party and get involved in things."

"He hasn't openly expressed his intention to run. He's only discussed the matter privately with Tang Chuan-tsung (Tông Tsuān-tsong), Chen Hsing-tsun (Tân Hīng-tshun) and other friends."

"Oh, and what were the pair's thoughts?"

"We have no way of knowing yet."

The two men didn't speak as they made their way back to the sofa in the other room and continued having tea. They were silent for a long time before Ouyang asked, "Apart from listening to these recordings, what other directives do you have for me, Chief?"

"You're no longer a part of this department. What directives could I possibly give to you?"

Ouyang went silent again. He stayed like that for a while, then the bureau chief resumed speaking, "I've read all the reports you've sent back. You're pretty content with what you have there, yes?"

"It's fine."

"So they haven't excluded you?"

"They did at first, but after a while, I've become well enmeshed in their organization."

"Enmeshed? What do you mean?"

"How should I put it?" Ouyang paused to think for a bit, then continued, "I gradually got a sense of their kindness and goodwill, and they also sensed that I've gradually integrated into their entire organization. They've lowered their guard a bit and aren't as afraid."

"It's not an easy feat to do that?" the bureau chief asked.

"So how about Wu Chen-jui? I've heard he's like an emperor in the Cooperative Association and is a bit overbearing when running all his meetings, no?"

"He's not just seen as an emperor within the organization, but in the entire island's banana farming world, he's a god to them. Banana farmers all hold him in deep awe and affection. When he holds meetings, his words are usually taken as important, mainly due to his being extremely professional. Nobody knows this industry quite like he does."

The bureau chief didn't say anything, and both of them sank into a deep silence. It seemed as if they didn't have anything more to say, so Ouyang was about to get up and take his leave but then heard the bureau chief begin to remark, "Brother Ouyang...I want to enter your association. I don't care what position it is, but you can't let anyone know that I'm from the Investigation Bureau."

Ouyang's eyes grew wide and shifted back and forth. He was thinking deeply, "I'm already working there. Why isn't that enough? Are you worried about me?"

Then he heard the bureau chief emphasize a point, "Everyone in the organization already knows your background. I hope I can join and stay hidden."

"You won't be able to stay hidden," Ouyang quickly shot back.

"Why?"

"First, how would I be able to introduce you if it's coming from me, a mainlander with the surname Ouyang? How could you possibly stay hidden?"

"So then what do we do?"

"I could ask someone else. We could introduce another person and then have that person introduce you. But Mr. Bureau Chief..." Ouyang wasn't sure whether it was deliberate or not, but he stopped for a second, poured himself another cup of tea, and blew his nose into a handkerchief before continuing. "That's a world where people almost exclusively speak in Taiwanese. With your outsider's mainlander accent, your cover would be blown as soon as you opened your mouth."

"Well, damn it! We're in quite a bind here."

"Mr. Bureau Chief, are you trying to enter of your own accord or is someone else giving you the directive?"

"You can't ask me that question." The bureau chief stared deeply at Ouyang, then continued speaking, "The thought came to me on my own. I was drawn in by the royal treatment your association gives people."

"Understood."

"Argh. Let's put this aside for a bit. Damn it! I also wanted to ask you something. Does Wu Chen-jui have some romantic relationship going on with that Chen Hsing-tsun woman heading the Taipei Green Fruits Association?"

"I think so. Sometimes it seems like they aren't, and at other times, it seems like they are." Ouyang continued explaining, "From my limited knowledge, it's what some might call a 'twilight love' between a couple who are both older and have high stature. Love is what it truly is, but they present it as a friendship; love is the core, friendship is the application."

"Hah! You're couching it all in so much mysticism—and you say you have limited knowledge! Hah!" The bureau chief gave Ouyang a look, then with a crooked smile continued, "I want to know if the bastard's slept with her."

"I can't confirm that with you."

"She just gave up her position as director and was replaced by Chen Cha-mo (Tan Tsa-boo). Were you aware of that?"

"That was going to happen sooner or later. Their two sides have fought rather viciously for power over their company for some time. Chen Hsing-tsun had already gone over completely to Wu's side and lost her position. How could she go on trying to serve as the director of the board?"

23

Tsín-suī was in Kaohsiung for work one day when he received a phone call from the association secretary, Mr. Liu. "The Taipei United Association is requesting that you go up and convene a board of directors meeting. They want to take care of the Lawton Company case."

"Didn't we already settle this? Hsu Pai-yuen already gave his comments and critiques. Weren't you aware of that?"

"When? Where? How come I never heard of it? If that's the case, then why is Minister Lee Kuo-ting still concerned about it? Just now he was in a hurry to have me inform you about convening a meeting. They're asking if you can quickly decide to accept the contract with Lawton."

"What the hell is this all about!?"

"Chairman Ngôo—General Manager Ngôo—please don't be angry! Just take a trip up north and hold just one meeting. That's all! The Taipei United Association will send out a notice for the convening. I was directed to attend the meeting to explain things."

By the time Tsín-suī had rushed up to the Taipei United Association, everything regarding the meeting had already been taken care of. They were all just waiting for him to arrive to lead the discussion.

Just as the meeting began, the attending Secretary Liu asked to make a speech. Of course, Liu would be throwing his support behind Lawton. He mainly emphasized two points. The first was that using bamboo packaging was a traditional and backwards means of shipping. They had to make the switch to paper or cardboard cartons. The second point was that Lawton's electric cable collection method was representative of an efficient banana-harvesting method. The former was modernized, the latter was technologically advanced. "So we should invest everything in Lawton and evolve."

Tsín-suī maintained his calm as he listened to Secretary Liu finish his pitch, and then he saw Wu Chih-tsung raise his hand from the chairman's seat. "I just promoted you from deputy manager of the planning department to general manager. Maybe you're going to respond like I will and oppose Secretary Liu's motion and points," Tsín-suī thought. He then braced himself to respond to Liu.

Tsín-suī felt utterly stunned and betrayed when it turned out that Wu Chih-tsung threw all his support behind Lawton in agreement with Liu. He suddenly saw the light. "He's a patsy. He's one of those men from the Council for Economic Planning and Development and the Agricultural Revitalization Council. He was one of Chiang Yen-shih's men. Today's meeting seems to be about them trying to force me to accept the Lawton agreement," he thought.

Wu Chih-tsung finished his speech, and Tsín-suī went on a full counter-attack, but just as curiously, the secretary came in to report that Minister Lee Kuo-ting had made a phone call and was still on the line. He asked to speak with Tsín-suī. The telephone was on the right front corner of the chairman's bureau in the meeting room.

"Wei, Minister Lee, yes. This is Wu Chen-jui."

"Chairman Wu...uh, General Director Wu. I'm sorry to interrupt your meeting, but I'll try to keep what I have to say brief. Lawton's agreement would help to modernize our entire country. I hope that you all can come to an agreement today. You absolutely cannot reject their offer!"

Tsín-suī's command of Chinese had already advanced to the point that he could respond directly to the Minister. "We're right in the middle of discussing it, Minister Lee. Everything will be decided after a discussion with the board of directors. Would that be fine?"

"Excellent. I hope you have a successful meeting. I'll be waiting to hear from you."

Tsín-suī briskly returned to his seat. The atmosphere in the meeting room had stagnated to a dead halt. All of the attending members were silent. Nobody was whispering to each other either. What sort of weight did Lee Kuo-ting's personal phone call have? Maybe the Lawton assenters were thinking, "You're just one man, Ngôo Tsín-suī. If you ever hope to have a future in your banana kingdom again, are you really going to go head to head against Lee? Those opposed were apprehensive of the consequences. Chairman Ngôo is in a whole heap of trouble right now. What's the best way he can resist this pressure and refuse it?"

Tsín-suī opened his mouth to speak and went through all the points in opposition to Lawton. His tone seemed particularly resolute. Was it the phone call just a moment ago from Lee that had had just the opposite of the intended effect, making him more determined to fight this? Did his inner bull finally burst out of the corral and go on a rampage? He began his takedown of Lawton from the perspective of the acreage of Taiwan's banana farms, continued to present Lawton's proposal for a paper carton factory, then brought in the unfair and unreasonable memorandum with Lawton, dissecting each item one by one. If it had anything to do with bananas, Tsín-suí's forty to fifty years of accumulated experience, achievements, and prestige flowed forth effortlessly. He didn't need to use stern words or cutting remarks—just the air of his authority was enough. Even the attending officials from the Executive Yuan and its Council for Economic Planning and Development were listening in silence, nodding along to every point he made.

After he was finished speaking, Tsín-suí requested that all the directors vote against the matter, and in the end, that's exactly what he got. The Lawton Company's proposal was officially rejected.

The following day, Tsín-suí returned to Ko-hiông and put his office in order before returning to Pîn-tong. When he walked in through the door to the main building of his courtyard home, he found three men waiting for him in the living room. The trio looked very similar. They all had a kind of plump and round visage. At first glance, they all looked like brothers.

The first to come up and welcome Tsín-suí back home was Wu Ch'i-jui. He was a seasoned veteran director in the Kaohsiung Green Fruits Export Cooperative Association. He'd known Tsín-suí for a long time and had a very good working relationship with him. "Mr. Chairman, these are my two younger relatives, Wu Ch'i-fu and Wu Ch'i-sheng. The two of them are twins. Chi-fu is a well-known ophthalmologist and a director of the Medical Association; Ch'i-sheng is also a doctor and the head of the Provincial Pingtung Hospital."

"*Giu-ngiong, giu-ngiong* (It's a pleasure to meet you)," Tsín-suí shook hands with his Hakka guests and started heaping praise on them. "The Wu family in Kî-*san* is a mighty clan. So many brothers and siblings, all of them having achieved great things in their own right. None of it an easy feat either."

"Don't be so kind. You yourself, Chairman Ngôo, have also done something nearly impossible. You've raised the fortunes of banana farmers for miles and miles around. Everyone in Kî-*san* admires you for all you've done to improve their lot."

"I'm older than both Ch'i-fu and Ch'i-sheng. I'm their older cousin and they're brothers," Wu Ch'i-jui tacked on.

Giok-ìn had already brought out a serving tray with a teapot and snacks of all sorts. The guests and host took their seats, and Wu Ch'i-jui was the first to broach the real conversation. "Ch'i-fu is part of the medical world. Everyone is pushing for him to run for the Legislative Yuan. I brought them here with me to ask for your blessing, Chairman Ngôo. I'd like to humbly ask for your support. If the green fruits industry backs the medical industry, then the Party headquarters are weighing his running."

Tsín-suī responded, saying, "Coming all the way here to ask for my blessing to support your A-Ke-sui-*hiann*, how could I not support him?" But deep down in his heart, he was in turmoil, "These people are so quick to hear about anything. Only the day before yesterday, I made my own thoughts on running to someone at the Kaohsiung Party Headquarters and these people suddenly appear from nowhere, right out of the woodwork."

"We're delighted to hear your words of support, Chairman Ngôo. Our Ch'i-fu-á stands a chance with your backing."

As Wu Ch'i-jui spoke the words, Ch'i-fu stood up, faced Tsín-suī and made a deep bow. "Thank you, Chairman Ngôo for your support."

After, Tsín-suī began to tell Ch'i-jui about the previous day's event, being asked to convene the meeting, how Lee Kuo-ting had made a personal call to Tsín-suī right in the middle to put pressure on him, and how, in the end, the committee ultimately rejected the resolution. Then he gave his guests a brief rundown on the contents of the Lawton proposal. Ch'i-fu listened very closely and interjected several times to ask for more clarification. After they'd finished listening to him, he stared at Tsín-suī and then, in Japanese, said, "Go-san, with your being a professional, I think that's the right path of action, I think you should keep holding on. You'll need to be brave if you want to keep fighting. This is a matter of integrity."

"Huh?" Tsín-suī couldn't comprehend Ch'i-fu for the moment.

Ch'i-fu said it once more, adding, "This is what my Japanese teacher often told us in class."

Tsín-suī felt that this Japanese phrase was very elegant and repeated it to himself almost in a whisper. He felt carefree at heart now. The four men began to talk about all manner of topics until they had completely lost track of time.

Several days afterwards, Tsín-suī caught word that in his capacity as the Executive Yuan's Foreign Trade Inspection Committee chairman, Hsu Pai-yuen was inviting over twenty specialists and scholars to form a Lawton Study Committee. Tsín-suī was selected as one of the committee members. He felt excited. At the time of the first meeting, the chairman for the banana farming focus group was the executive secretary, Tan Yu-tsuo. One after another, all of the specialists and scholars gave speeches on the matter. None of the attendees had expressed support for Lawton. Tsín-suī was the last person to speak, and he gave his opinions on the matter as if he were the ultimate arbiter.

After the meeting had finished, Tsín-suī went to the chairman's office. As soon as he saw Tsín-suī, Hsu Pai-yuen said, "Tsín-suī-*hiann*, the Lawton proposal, they all want it passed."

"Is it the Minister of Economics, Minister Lee? He's already barraged me with several calls."

"I asked him, but he said he never called you. I'm a bit puzzled by this matter."

Tsín-suī was also perplexed by this. Just who was this "they" that Hsu Pai-yuen was talking about? He didn't dare to venture asking.

At the second meeting, the chairman was Chiang Yen-shih. The planning department general manager, Wu Chih-tsung, was unexpectedly invited to attend, but he was the first one to give his speech. He was fully on board with the Lawton proposal. Chih-tsung was part of the upper leadership of the United Green Fruits Association, but at the directors meeting, he had just rejected the proposal and, moreover, he had loudly opposed the proposal in public. Tsín-suī grew more enraged, the longer he sat listening. He waited for this jackass to finish speaking and then immediately raised his hand, standing up at the same time. He was filled with a righteous fury; but the moment he cleared his throat and began speaking, he decided to use an even tone and to speak about the entire banana industry. From production all the way to marketing, Tsín-suī analyzed the entire industry in terms of all the conditions that contributed to its success.

He was absolutely certain in that moment that there was not a single other person in the entire country who knew more than he did about bananas and this entire industry, with such in-depth professional knowledge. He spoke at length about the Japanese and the complicated structures of Japanese companies and their clever relationship. As he spoke, he spied several famed professors nodding in agreement. They had all taken out notebooks and were writing down every single word. Tsín-suī felt like he was on top of the world with the breadth of knowledge he possessed, his professional experience, and even his passion fed into it. It came flowing forth like a culvert flooded with torrential rain.

He switched topics and began to critique the seven articles that Lawton had put forth. He thought about the various kinds of pressure that the government had placed on him. Suddenly, he wanted to burst into tears, but he maintained his composure. He felt as if he were a criminal giving his "final testament before a firing squad." Yet, at the same time, he felt as if the hopes of hundreds of thousands of banana farmers had been placed on his shoulders. His speech only turned more impassioned as the minutes passed by. He wasn't sure where the eloquence came from, but he started switching effortlessly from Chinese to Taiwanese to Japanese, interweaving all of them into a wondrous linguistic mélange. He even threw in a couple sentences of Japanese-style English sentences and words for good measure.

As he was speaking, he noticed several of the attendees' facial expressions. Whenever he touched upon the paper carton factory or the Japanese benefits from the Japanese trading company joint venture business, he saw the foreign trade committee banana group specialist committee member, Wang Lan-ting, looking disdainful. He was the only person in the entire meeting to have such a scowl on his face. Perhaps he was that kind of mainlander who harbored hatred towards the Japanese. Tsín-suī ignored him and kept speaking.

It wasn't too long before he noticed that the committee chairman, Chiang Yen-shih, had quietly left his seat. He was going to use the restroom! No matter, Tsín-suī ignored him and kept on speaking. He didn't know why, but he felt as if everything was crystal clear at this moment. He felt that if he didn't say what he needed to, he'd never have the opportunity ever again.

After this, he kept on speaking quite a while longer. When he wrapped up his speech, the entire room erupted in loud applause. Chiang Yen-shih just so happened to return to his seat right at that moment and himself clapped as if entertained. Chiang then adjourned the meeting. He didn't bother giving concluding remarks about the Lawton proposal.

After they left the foreign trade inspection committee meeting, Secretary Shen, who had accompanied Tsín-suī, asked, "Do you want to ask General Manager Wu Chih-tsung to take a car together?"

"No thanks," Tsín-suī flatly replied.

Back on the road, Secretary Shen said, "Director Wu, you managed to speak for an entire hour and seven minutes straight! You spoke so incisively, like 'a whip cutting to the quick.' It was the most convincing speech about the banana industry I've ever heard."

"Firecrackers? What do you mean?"

"Oh, sorry, sir, not 'firecrackers'—a 'whip.' It's an old saying. I said, like 'a whip cutting to the quick.' It means each segment, each detail, was talked over carefully and to the fullest extent."

"Oh, I see now."

The following day, Chiang Yen-shih invited Tsín-suī out to the Ambassador Hotel for a meal. He also invited the head of the Joint Management Office. The Joint Management Office was a national cooperative management bureau. Tsín-suī knew right away that Chiang was intending to pressure him in any way he could. In the meeting room, Chiang kept appealing to the friendship that he and Tsín-suī had built over the last several years. He kept circling around and around trying gently to persuade Tsín-suī, pleading over and over for Tsín-suī to accept the Lawton proposal. Tsín-suī had always respected Chiang, but that day he drummed up the courage to contradict him. "Mr. Secretary, you're a gentleman of proper means. Things will be better for you if you please don't try to force the Lawton proposal through. The Examination Yuan is already looking at the true nature of the proposal."

"Which member of the Examination Yuan did the interview?"

"It was Tao Pai-chuan and two others."

"What did they ask you?"

"It came as a formal letter asking me to go. I was hampered by not understanding the Chinese that was written in the letter, so I had my secretary, Mr. Shen, to stand in as a proxy for me and give a simple reply to the matter."

"Oh, I see," he said with some annoyance.

Tsín-suī wasn't happy at dinner. The sentence in Japanese that Wu Ch'i-fu said had kept floating endlessly to the top of his mind. Tsín-suī was absolutely sure, deep down, that he could never accept the Lawton affair, and that it would just go away on its own if they let it.

As he was adjourning the meeting, Chiang Yen-shih whispered over to Tsín-suī, "If you're going to contend for the Party's nomination for the Legislative Yuan, you'd do best to make it smooth sailing for the Lawton Company. It would be a major boost for you."

Tsín-suī replied off-handedly, "If I don't get a nomination from the Party, that's fine too."

He returned to his office in Taipei. Right as he was in the middle of taking care of the official documents and reports stacked up on his desk, the United Association's director, Chang Chin-luo, rapped on the door to his office then entered. He was wearing his signature smile. It was the smile of someone fake, that of a people pleaser.

"Chairman—Director Wu, I have an important matter that I need to report to you." He had practiced speaking his Chinese, but it was a

Taiwanese Mandarin with a Hoklo tinge to it. Tsín-suī put down what he was doing, moved over to the couch beside the desk and then sat down, waiting for Chang Chin-luo to begin speaking.

"Mr. Chairman, I was just informed by a friend in the Labor Organization Committee to come over—"

"What unit is the Labor Organization Committee a part of?"

"It's the Labor Organization Committee of the Central Party."

"Oh, I see. So, what's the matter?"

"They asked me to convey a message: the Legislative Yuan elections are going to be held next year. There are four seats up for election next year, and one of them is a non-Party seat. The competition for that independent seat is going to be extremely fierce. All of the other contenders are heavyweights in their own right, such as Kuo Ta-p'ao and Kuo Kuo-chi; the Taitung County Magistrate, Huang Shun-hsing; and Tsai Lee-ing from over where you are in Pingtung. You're just a novice, Tsín-suī. You'll have to rely on the party for a nomination—"

"Why did they tell you to tell me this? It makes no sense!"

"The Party core hopes that you won't have any misgivings or disloyalty and if you decide to run, they want you to run as a party member. Your qualifications are good enough."

"I know that! I'm not necessarily running for election!" Tsín-suī continued, "I already have an acquaintance at the Kaohsiung association, Wu Ch'i-jui. His younger brother Wu Ch'i-fu is planning on running. It's best that I don't butt heads with them."[48]

"Oh, I see!"

---

48. The first election for the Legislative Yuan seat for a stand-in legislator was held in late 1969. Wu Ch'i-fu was elected with 510,000 votes, far ahead of Huang Tsung-kun who came in second place after garnering 317,000 votes. The third-place contender, coming in with 316,000 votes, was Liang-Hsu Chun-chu. Stand-in legislators were considered full legislators and didn't need to be re-elected. Starting in 1972, the number of legislators was increased, and their position changed to being elected for three-year terms.

24

The chairman was in the middle of taking a phone call that was placed from his office up north in Taipei. Because there was a heavy deluge falling that afternoon in Pîn-tong, Tsín-suī had to ask the caller to repeat themselves several times before he could understand what they were saying. "Mr. Chairman, something odd just happened..."

"What? You'll have to speak louder!"

"I don't dare speak too loudly." The conversation thus faltered until finally he turned the volume up and blurted out, "Chiang Yen-shih sent the golden bowl we awarded him back to us, right out of the blue."

"Did he say anything?"

"It was delivered by Chiang's secretary. They wouldn't say a word."

"Now that's quite strange! When we awarded him with it, he didn't refuse, and that was half a year ago already. Why is he returning it just now?"

"I don't know why. The secretary wouldn't give me any reason." The telephone went silent for a moment, then he asked Tsín-suī, "Mr. Chairman, if I may ask, what should I do with the golden bowl?"

"Put it in the office safe first, and take care that it's secured."

"Yes, sir, Mr. Chairman."

That evening, Tsín-suī had thought of making dinner arrangements with several of the other board members who he was close to and use the opportunity to discuss the peculiar occurrence, but he got a phone call from the chief of police for Kaohsiung County himself, asking him what time he was getting off work and when he would be getting home. He said he had a matter that required him to make an in-person visit. Tsín-suī would just have to find another day to plan dinner with his colleagues. He returned home straight away.

When he got on the road, the deluge pummeled his car. It pelted down on the roof of the car, making a huge din. All the while, the windshield wipers swung madly back and forth and rainwater gushed down the side windows like waterfalls. Sitting inside his car, Tsín-suī's heart was racing a mile a minute. It felt to him as if the raindrops were striking right at his chest.

No sooner had he stepped through the main door of his home than the police chief arrived right behind him. "Hmmm...was he already here, sitting in his car in the rain, hidden away from view, spying and waiting for me to come home before he showed his face?" Tsín-suī was filled with suspicion. He saw that the police chief was carrying a very heavy box, wrapped in a big red bag, like a parcel given to an acquaintance.

The heavy rain kept on falling without letup. It didn't seem like it would stop any time soon, either.

When Giȯk-ìn saw that her husband had a guest who'd come out all this way in such dreadful weather, she quickly grabbed a hand towel and invited their guest to wipe their hands and face. But the police chief, who spoke Mandarin with the retroflexed accent of a Northern Chinese, said, "It's fine. Don't worry. Thank you. Thank you. Well, now that I think about it, could I trouble you to pour me some hot tea?"

After Giȯk-ìn had left the room, the police officer didn't sit down but faced Tsín-suī and said, matter-of-factly, "The provincial chairman, Huang Chieh, wanted me to come. He said he wanted this thing of yours sent back to you."

Tsín-suī was utterly baffled. Of course, the packaging had looked remarkably familiar. The contents were a thirty-tael golden pan. It was the one he had hand-delivered to Huang Chieh's office. The official's office was extremely stylish. When Huang accepted the gifted golden plate, four or five subordinates came over and marveled at the gift. Tsín-suī remembered that, at the time, he had used stilted Mandarin to repeat the words he had memorized, "This is a small token that I am presenting on behalf of all banana farmers. It's not worthy of your respect. Thank you, Provincial Chairman, for your many years of benevolent governance and for blessing our farmers with your support."

At the time, amid the applause of the gathered crowd, Huang Chieh placed the golden plate in a very prominent place in his office, along with the gifts sent from others. He had a calm smile on his face.

It was a publicly given gift. At the time, he was absolutely thrilled. Why would Huang send out this police bureau chief to return the gift after all this time?

Giȯk-ìn came out of the kitchen carrying a pot of tea. She saw her husband just standing in the living room, as if in a trance, but their guest had clearly already left. The police chief had hurried all this way in all this heavy rain and then hurried back again. What strange reason could explain the policeman's bizarre behavior? Tsín-suī held his hand out for the pot of tea and drank by himself, explaining to his wife everything the police chief had told him. He also took the opportunity to tell the story about how Chiang Yen-shih had also sent back his bowl that afternoon.

"Why did it end up this way? We were sending them golden plates and bowls as thanks. Didn't we already ask the people up at the top for permission?"

"We did! The top government officials accepted the initial proposal. Only afterwards did our board of directors decide to go ahead with the proposal."

"It's nothing, *lah*! We didn't do anything wrong. Don't give it another thought! OK!" Giŏk-ìn took another look at the gift box on the table, then asked, "So, what are we going to do with it now?"

"Let's just put it in the bedroom for now. I'll take it with me to the office tomorrow."

Neither husband nor wife brought up the subject again. The rain still poured on.

That evening, at about eleven o'clock, Tsín-suī was still sitting alone on the sofa, thinking things over. Outside the window, the fat raindrops continued to fall straight down like so many strands of wire. In the gaps between the lines of rain, a haze of water vapor floated about like smoke or fog. Tsín-suī had been born and raised in southern Taiwan, and he had watched the rain his whole life, but today was the first time that he noticed the mist concealed between the torrents of rain. The streams of rain were powerful, while the mist was light and delicate. It was as if steel wire and the cotton batten were entwining in midair.

His daughter, Bí-ài, who next week would take her TOEFL English proficiency test, was still in her room diligently intoning English. When she came out and saw her father sitting on his couch, staring blankly, she asked him, "*A-Pa*, why haven't you gone to bed yet? You and *A-Bú* both look so troubled today. What's going on?"

"This rain's falling so hard, and it's been going on for such a long time. I'm worried that the river waters will rise, and it'll flood, into our village and fields... If there's a big flood..."

"There won't be, *A-Pa*. There won't be any flood. It's also not the first time it's rained as bad as this. Don't waste your time worrying about it. Go to bed!"

"It's January. We need the weather to be cold and dry now in Pîn-tong. Why are we suddenly being hit with a massive wall of rain?"

"The celestial lord wishes it to rain, so what are we to do? He wants it to fall, so he lets it fall. No use wracking your head over it, lah!"

Not long after, Tsín-suī headed back to his bedroom, but Giok-ìn took her pillow and headed to their daughter's room. "*A-Bú*, why are you sleeping in my room?" Bí-ài asked her mother.

"I'm going to let your father sleep by himself. I'm worried he'll be yelling, 'I'm afraid! I'm afraid!' all night long."

"There's definitely something on *A-Pa*'s mind, but he won't tell me."

25

Several days later, Tsín-suī led an entourage to Japan for routine trade talks. The objective of their talks were the Japanese banana import organizations. In January, they would negotiate the volume and prices of imported bananas for March. Afterwards, the talks would be moved to Taiwan in March, where they would negotiate the price and volume of bananas imports from April to July. The negotiations worked like this every year. For all the green fruit cooperative associations and for the banana farmers as a whole, it was like negotiating life or death.

The negotiations required everyone to spend a lot of mental energy for several days in a row. It was extremely taxing, and the attendees had to have resolute attitudes and a lot of emotional fortitude. Tsín-suī as the Chairman, however, was obviously vexed and mentally exhausted. His eyes were inflamed and swollen. He had nearly tripped on the first step at the staircase in his entourage's hotel. All of the attending supervisors and managers saw this.

"Mr. Chairman, what's the matter? Are you well? Are you OK?"

"What do you think? Does it look like I'm fine?"

How could he say this? On further prodding by his subordinates, he finally revealed with utter dejection, "Over the last few days, the golden bowls and pans we gifted to the officials have been sent back for some unknown reason. It can't bode well."

His entourage exchanged their opinions about this and grew dispirited as well. That evening's pre-meeting was hastily concluded, and they even dispensed with the final simulated attack. As Tsín-suī watched his team's interactions, he was startled. As a leader, how could he let this happen? If it kept on like this, they could return home in defeat! If they didn't negotiate a good price, then they weren't protecting banana farmers' livelihoods. How many families would lose their means of survival and their hopes and dreams? Thinking about it, he came to a realization and called everyone to gather in the room.

As the group started performing the *kamasō* (recess exercises)[49] from their Japanese era schooling days, some of the group cheerily followed along with the exercises. When they finished, Tsín-suī was out of breath, but he raised the tone of his voice and said, "Not long ago I went to see our old board member, A-Tsòng. As I was about to leave, he encouraged me, saying, 'A-Suī-á, don't be afraid. As long as you do the right thing and keep plowing along on your course, then that's fine. Just keep moving forward like an ox, tilling your own furrow.'"

"Everyone, I'm feeling very out of sorts and not myself today. In fact, I have quite a conundrum to deal with that's racking my mind, and I'm completely terrified. However, when I thought about A-Tsòng, I didn't feel so afraid. Let's try to regain our enthusiasm, shall we?"

"Yes, Mr. Chairman. Let's energize ourselves. Let's all get more enthusiastic!"

After the Taiwanese team had recovered their fighting spirit, the negotiation process went smoothly, from the Taiwanese point of view. During the noon meeting on the second day, the Taipei Association office placed an international call and requested to speak with Tsín-suī. In the past, these sorts of phone calls were common and nothing out of the ordinary. Tsín-suī left his seat to take the call. What he heard was that dreadful news that he had feared: "Mr. Chairman, the *Central Daily News* put out an article in the paper today. They wrote that when Lee Kuo-ting was giving a speech at the Central Premier's Memorial Ceremony, he openly criticized us."

"What did they write exactly? Read off the page for me."

"It's just a few short lines. They say, 'Japan's market for Taiwan's bananas being held hostage by a minority. They get a kickback on all domestic bamboo baskets and so are unwilling to use paper cartons.' That's what the article said. The Central Premier's Memorial Week was presided over by Chiang Kai-shek himself."

"Are the headlines in large font?"

"They're neither big nor small. But they placed the story right in the very center of the page, so it really catches your attention."

"Oh, I see now. Well, if you have any new information, don't hesitate to call me immediately."

"Yes, sir."

---

49. Elementary and middle schools during Taiwan's Japanese colonial era would all converge on the exercise grounds of the school after the second class period. They would follow along with broadcast music and exercise for ten minutes. After they were finished, they would go to their third period class. This was called a "*kamasō*" or "intra-class recreation."

Tsín-suī placed the receiver back on the hook, took several deep breaths, and slowly stepped towards the nearby window. The sky outside was half overcast. There were mounds of snow next to the roads. Dirt was mixed in with it, creating an unsightly slush of browns and grays. Occasionally, he could hear the coarse cawing of crows. "Damn it! Lee Kuo-ting is trying to 'fix' me, isn't he? Is he beginning his campaign of revenge? What would be my best tack in facing this?" He was deeply concerned, but he remembered that the meeting was still ongoing and he didn't know how far they had gotten. There's no need to be afraid of Lee for the moment. As A-Tsòng told him, "Just keep moving forward like an ox, tilling your own furrow."

Tsín-suī took a deep breath and then headed back to the meeting room. He clearly felt the energy in both his legs draining from him. Despite this, he kept reminding himself that he had to have a calm and confident demeanor when he reentered the negotiations. He still had to keep his own mind sharp. He couldn't allow his rivals on the Japanese side or his own team members on the Taiwanese side see that he had some problem and that the matter was grave.

When Tsín-suī stepped into the meeting room, a Japanese representative was right in the middle of asking, "Who among you can promise that you will have six hundred and twenty thousand baskets in March? If you're not certain about your amount, then our price is going to be hard to guarantee."

"Shibata-*san*, it's difficult to give you a promise for our winter crop. How about this: How about our Taiwanese side promise to use the entire produced amount as the trade amount?" Tsín-suī sat down as he made his reply. He looked around the room once, checking to see whether anyone had seen that the tone of his reply was already carrying some uncertainty.

"I heard that the weather in southern Taiwan has been warm and that there's plentiful rainfall."

"This is true, and you've got great information sources, but it's just one or two days of rain. It wouldn't be that easy for the winter harvest to be as good as the summer harvest—"

"Fine then, we'll go with the chairman's suggestion as before!"

"Good, and the price?"

"Just as you were leaving the room to take your telephone call, Go-san, we had already discussed it. The price isn't changing this year, no?"

"Oh, or perhaps Go-*san* wishes to add something?"

Tsín-suī would usually be seated when speaking, but today he was standing. He made a deep bow to his Japanese business partners and then in a tone of voice more solemn than he had ever used, he said, "To all of our Japanese friends and colleagues here today, we've been working in the banana business for over a decade. Because of Taiwanese bananas, your business has risen very swiftly. We farmers have also received such great benefits because of your assistance. As a representative of Taiwanese banana farmers, I would like to take this opportunity to express my deepest feelings and sincerely thank you all. Thank you for expressing your love for Taiwanese bananas. From the bottom of my heart, I hope that this relationship never changes."

All the Japanese representatives listened to him with eyes wide in amazement. Why was Go-*san* speaking such heartfelt words at a time like this? Tsín-suī could also sense from their expressions that he had misspoken, and he hastened to explain, "I'm bringing all of this up quite randomly because I've suddenly remembered my twenties when I followed along in the footsteps of our research lab's technician, Mr. Nakamura Jirō. I began my career under his wing as one of his pupils, and I have been in this business all the way up until now. Just as bananas had a future after this Japanese technician, Mr. Nakamura, had decided to turn Taiwanese bananas into something Japanese would love to eat, and even though Japan's government has already left, the Japanese have never left the side of Taiwan's banana farmers. It is from this reality and experience that I want to express my humblest thanks and gratitude for the ties we share."

Shibata Isamu, the main negotiator for the Japanese side, laughed and said, "Our business association will think of a way to find this Nakamura Jirō-*san*. The next time you come back to Japan for a meeting, we'll take you to meet him."

"That would be excellent. I hope we'll still have this opportunity." As soon as the words were out of his mouth, Tsín-suī immediately realized that he had misspoken again. The faces of the Japanese were full of confusion, and anxiety was apparent on the faces of his subordinates.

The next day, the Japanese representatives wanted to take their Taiwanese counterparts to an *onsen* to soak in the hot springs and relax and then take them to a banquet. This was standard procedure. In turn, when the Japanese representatives visited Taiwan for negotiations, the Taiwanese would also treat them to special outings and banquets. Tsín-suī excused himself from participating, saying he wasn't feeling well. He stayed in his room in the hotel for a while and waited for a phone call.

Not long after the others had left for their day outing, a phone call came in from his friend, Tsuān-tsong. "I went to your home in Pîn-tong as soon as I could this morning, and that's when I found out you were already in Japan. What a godsend! I'm breathing a little easier now." Tsuān-tsong didn't wait for Tsín-suī to respond before he kept going, "I have to tell you A-Suī-á, these last two days, the entire front-page story has all been about you. It's all nonsense. I have the suspicion that someone is behind the scenes providing them with false information. It's like they're out on a mission to get you—"

"So, what's being reported now?"

"I'll read off a handful of the headlines for you: 'One Hand Darkening the Sky, 'Monopoly Manipulations of Banana Trade With Both Hands,' 'Taking all the Profit from Banana Farmers,' 'Long-term Exploiter of Banana Farmers, Banana King or Banana Maggot? 'Flattery, Flattery, Wu Chen-jui Gives Himself an Award,' 'Winning Awards While Workers Continue Toiling.'"

"F*** their mothers! Those shameless bastards! These insufferable motherf***ers!" Tsín-suī erupted after hearing the headline names. He couldn't stop himself from cursing.

"Wait a moment, Giȯk-ìn-á wishes to speak with you."

"A-Suī-á... Well... Do you see what's happened to you now?" As the sound of sobbing came through the phone, Tsín-suī's heart was badly shaken and he himself began to choke up.

The sound of sobbing now came through both ends of the line. A while later, Giȯk-ìn stopped and spoke again, "Tsuān-tsong-*hiann* says not to come back to Taiwan for a while. What do you think?"

"There's no reason not to! I didn't do anything wrong. What should I be afraid of? I'm at peace in my heart. I ought to go back and try to reason with them. The entire world says that President Chiang is extremely smart. Over the past ten or more years he's given me several awards and commendations. How could all of that be false if he isn't smart enough to see through all this nonsense? How could he not tell the difference between truth and fiction? I can't believe it."

His wife's sobs came through the receiver again. The phone was handed over to Tsuān-tsong. Tsín-suī repeated to Tsuān-tsong what he had told Giȯk-ìn. The more he repeated it, the more he seemed to be able to convince himself.

Tsuān-tsong finished listening and then remarked, "I think you're being far too naïve. They're a group of brigands and thieves, this government. I'm serious that you should stay away for a while—"

Right then, someone knocked on Tsín-suī's door. Tsín-suī hurriedly ended his phone call with Tsuān-tsong, then ran over to answer the door.

A Japanese man he wasn't familiar with was standing at the entrance. The man pulled out a business card. He was a manager from Hīng-tshun's trade company branch in Tokyo. He passed on a message from Hīng-tshun. "She told me to tell you to keep your head down and stay in Japan. Don't return to Taiwan. Ms. Tân's company has a spare apartment for you to reside at."

Tsín-suĭ was grateful and also a little vexed, "I've got nothing to hide. If I don't return to Taiwan, then that will definitely make me look guilty in everyone's eyes, no?" After he had shooed the Japanese manager away, he felt bewilderment and terror as never before. He walked out of his room. There were people coming and going from the lobby, so he walked out onto the street. Late January in Tokyo was a truly wintery season. The winter wind scraped at his face, so let it scrape! His ears were so cold that they stung with pain, so let them sting!

There would probably be greater pain in the future. Right at this moment, the reputation that he had built his whole life had been completely destroyed in the newspapers. What fresh hell would he face when he returned to Taiwan? Had he wandered unwittingly along the same road to ignominious death as Vice Speaker of the Legislature Ia̍p Tshiu-bo̍k? His body convulsed with shivers all of a sudden. The entire time, his mind was racing as he walked around aimlessly. He had just turned into an alley where there were relatively fewer cars or people, when the words of Yamamoto Minoru suddenly rose to the surface of his mind: "Tsín-suĭ, when I look at you, I can tell… You're going to do something great for your people, but you need to pay attention to the Chinese Nationalist government. The realm of China's government is fraught with darkness and danger."

This was something he had heard all the way back in 1945, just as the war had concluded. Yamamoto was director of inspections at the research lab in Pingtung where he had worked. He had invited Tsín-suĭ over to the Yamamoto household for a farewell dinner several days before the family was to be repatriated back to Japan. Minoru had said this to Tsín-suĭ as they were eating. He remembered that moment. The Yamamoto household was packing up all its household goods. The house was piled high with books. After dinner, Minoru pulled out two books as gifts for Tsín-suĭ. He wanted Tsín-suĭ to carefully read them. These two books were later lent to one of Tsín-suĭ's friends but were never returned, and he'd already long forgotten the book titles. He only remembered that the contents were about China's government.

All in all, it had already been twenty-four years, but he'd never stopped sharing correspondence with his former senior officer. For over ten years, while he had been enjoying great success, he had found time to go and visit Yamamoto twice. Both times, the two had talked late into the night. Tsín-suī suddenly wanted to go and see him again. He lived in Miyagi Prefecture, in the northeast countryside, close to the sea. It would take half a day to get there by train. Moved by this idea, Tsín-suī quickened his pace back to the hotel. He phoned Yamamoto, then wrote his coworkers a letter, telling them all about the developments in "public opinion" back in Taiwan over the past two days. He urged them all to go directly back to Taiwan after the meetings and business trip schedule was completed, to go to work as normal, and that he would pay some personal visits to friends and then return to face everything, come what may. At the end of the letter, he added, "You have never done anything illegal or that would harm our banana farmers. You know this better than anyone. In the end, heaven will vouch for our innocence."

Right as he was leaving, the telephone rang. It was from Mr. Yamamoto. "Go Shin-sui-*san*, bring all of your luggage over. Stay over at my place for a while. You shouldn't go back any time soon, do you understand?"

"I managed to meet up with Mr. Satō Kishin. He's extremely worried about your current situation. We're trying to figure out how best to help you deal with it all," he added.

"Oh, that's wonderful. Thank you so much," Tsín-suī replied.

26

February 27, 1969, in the afternoon. Two groups of about ten people each were waiting in the arrivals area at Taipei's Songshan Airport. All of them were in the leadership of the Green Fruits Export associations. The two groups seemed to be well acquainted with one another, but the Kaohsiung file and the United file were standing off on their own, not exchanging much banter at all. They all seemed to be in a serious mood; their eyes were focused on the faces of the passengers coming in from the customs clearance area.

They didn't have to wait long. Tsín-suī walked in through the doors. He was wearing a Western suit and tie, holding a briefcase in one hand and a heavy coat in the other, but there was nobody in tow. The two groups moved forward to greet him. Cheng Hsi-chüan, from the Kaohsiung group, took Tsín-suī's briefcase and coat. "Didn't I warn you not to come back! Why did you come back?" he reprimanded in a near whisper.

Tsín-suī didn't say anything in response. He was busy going down the line in between the columns, shaking hands one by one, all the while wearing an awkward smile on his face. Not many people among those gathered were conversing. Slowly, the group moved towards the main exit of the terminal. Tsín-suī, his towering stature, spied Hīng-tshun standing a short way away, looking at him. The two smiled at each other slightly and gave a little nod in acknowledgement. She didn't walk forward, and neither did Tsín-suī move towards her. He was corralled into the first car of their small motorcade. As he climbed into the car, Tsín-suī just managed to see Commissioner Ouyang standing off to the side, gazing at him. There were two men standing at his side. It was obvious the three had come as a small group.

When the whole entourage entered the main doors of the United Association office, loud applause resounded from all around. "Welcome back Mr. Chairman! Chairman Wu, welcome back!" Of all those in the group who had walked into the building, the ones whose waves of cheers and clapping echoed the loudest were those from the Kaohsiung firm.

"Everyone, please get back to your work! Let's all get back to work as usual, yes?" Tsín-suí shouted out over the din. Then he entered the general manager's office, alone...

He didn't think for a moment that there would be a familiar soul sitting on the couch waiting for him—it was Lin Shih-cheng. He was the current serving provincial commissioner, following a tenure as magistrate of Pingtung County. He was an old acquaintance from Tsín-suí's hometown. He was a year younger and had attended Takao Secondary along with Tsín-suí, and they had an almost familial relationship. Shih-cheng stood up and walked over to shake Tsín-suí's hand. He didn't bother making small talk or making pleasantries. Instead, his words were icy and imperious. He spoke in Taiwanese Mandarin, "Chairman Huang Chieh told me to come here and ask you to resign immediately. He wants you to resign from all of your positions."

"Fine. I'll do so when I go back to Ko-hiông tomorrow. I'll convene a provisional directors meeting and immediately tender my resignation," Tsín-suí replied.[50]

"Chairman Huang says you need to resign immediately, or else he can't forgive you," Shih-cheng added, sharp-tongued, like a dagger.

"Forgive me for what, exactly? Just what crime did I commit? *Honnh*!" Tsín-suí thought, a chill running through his heart. "Please calm down. I've served here for over a decade, after all. I can't just up and quit at the drop of a hat."

"They're demanding that you step down right now. You'd do well to quit immediately." Lin Shih-cheng quickly left the room after he dropped the bombshell on Tsín-suí.

"What the hell was all of that about with A-Shih-cheng? The gall! Hmmph! He's gone too far!" Tsín-suí was deeply incensed. He looked over the piles of official documents and correspondence that littered his office bureau. Previously, he would have taken no time to sit down and furiously go through each file, but today, he didn't even bother to sit down. He took his briefcase and headed to the train station to go back to Kaohsiung.

---

50. Ngôo Tsín-suí had to first resign from his position as Chairman of the Kaohsiung Green Fruits Export Association in order to resign from the United Association's General Managership.

Tsín-suī convened the provisional board of directors meeting four days later. After declaring the convening, he first thanked all of the general managers who had assisted him throughout the years and then told the entire room about the "order" from the provincial commissioner, Huang Chieh, as conveyed through Lin shih-cheng. After he'd broken the news, he declared, "Everyone, I have convened this meeting today to request that you approve the tendering of my resignation."

"Mr. Chairman, you've run the association so well. We can't possibly accept your resignation. If we do, then we'll all have to follow your lead and quit on the spot too."

"We're a civil organization, governed by private law. How can outsiders interfere with us so easily? Where's the reasoning in that?"

"The government—let me tell you all—the government only has a duty to guide civil organizations. It doesn't have the right to order the resignation of a chairman."

"The government might have the right to use the law to disband a civil organization or to call for the resignation of a chairman, but it must have a sufficient reason to do so. For example, we would have had to have done things that contravene national security, harm societal safety, or disrupt the financial order."

"That's right! Where have we ever done anything like that? All we've ever done is improve the economy, raise the foreign exchange holdings, and stabilize rural communities, right?"

"Mr. Chairman, does that Lin Shih-cheng represent the provincial government? Invite him to send a formal letter to our association. We can't just take them at their word, not least something said in passing. We need a written document."

"We're an organization that represents all banana farmers. The chairman of the board of directors is the leader of all our representatives. But like today, when all of our farmers go out to harvest each and every day of every year, they are happy and celebrating. How could our board possibly let you resign?"

"Mr. Chairman, if you wish to hand in your resignation, the entire board will have to resign first and then you can resign, right? We're all a team. If none of us directors resign, then you can't resign either."

There was a supervisory committee representative in the room, Chen Chiang-shan. He wasn't invited to the meeting but decided to attend it anyway. After he had heard everyone else speaking up, he put forth his own little speech, "Hello Chairman Wu. Thank you, Mr. Chairman, for agreeing to allow me to attend this meeting. Today, I'm representing myself to understand the situation in your esteemed association. Everyone, if civil organizations have done nothing illegal, they can stand up on their own and they'll survive. Moreover, there's still many issues that the Ministry of Economic Affairs is investigating. Nobody needs to worry for the moment. It doesn't mean anyone has to listen to the provincial chair."

When this supervisory member said he had received the chairman's permission to attend this meeting, Tsín-suǐ immediately felt extreme confusion. If anyone wanted to attend the supervisory committee meetings, the chairman would have been the first one to know about it before it ever happened, but this day, Tsín-suǐ was not in the right state of mind. He unwittingly let this Chen Chiang-shan into the meeting room. The way this man had suddenly expressed himself, all the directors suddenly felt more secure in themselves. Tsín-suǐ couldn't resign with everyone else in such high spirits. He was left saying, "Well, OK then. Let's end today's meeting here. We'll discuss the issue again tomorrow."

The next day, that same supervisory committee member graced them with his presence again, expressing the same argument to embolden everyone at the meeting, but Tsín-suǐ begged the directors again and again, and in the end, their resolution was: "April to July's ROC-Japan banana trade discussions have already been set to commence in Taipei in mid-March. Wu Chen-jui once more proposed resigning. This matter will be discussed once more at the next meeting."

Commissioner Ouyang was the first to hear about the contents of this supervisory committee meeting's resolution. He quickly telephoned back to the bureau. Once he had made his report, his superior directed him once more, "The media is aching to fix this Wu guy. I need to understand the public sentiment and reactions from the lowest rung of banana farmers. I'd like a detailed report in my hand very soon."

"Yes, sir." Ouyang then asked, "Oh, by the way, how come the newspapers have so much information on him? How is it that the bureau got so much dirt on him and is willing to release so much of it?"

"Some of our friends in the media have concocted it themselves; some of them 'set free' some of the notes from your regular reports into their news stories."

"Where was I so negative towards Wu Chen-jui in my reports?"

"You don't need to worry about that."

"What's more, there's an inspector by the name of Chen Chiang-shan who's been in attendance. He's already spoken up twice, encouraging the directors to ignore Huang Chieh's order. Do you know where the heck this guy came from? We've never heard of him before."

"Oh, that... Um..." The bureau chief was stopped in his tracks for a moment. He then started up again, "This is not something a person of my rank would know. Don't worry about it. What the bureau needs right now is for you to get that report on the public sentiment and the pulse of local banana farmers."

"Yes, sir. I'll be right on it, sir."

The next morning, all the front pages of the papers were filled with stories about how the Kaohsiung Association wouldn't permit Ngôo Tsín-suí to resign. All these reports were accompanied by opinion pieces criticizing him and pieces calling for him to be cashiered. The most scathing of the opinion pieces had the title "The Banana Maggot is Reluctant to Give Up His Post. Is this a Game to Him?" Tsín-suí only read half of it before shredding the rag, balling it, and throwing it into the trash can next to his desk. Officials who saw him doing this decided to switch the mid-March meeting from being held in Taiwan to one held in Japan. They were intent on having Tsín-suí be able to temporarily duck the bad press and lay low in Japan for a while. The Japanese companies were more than happy to help, but when an association worker was sent to prepare the paperwork to get Tsín-suí's travel papers in order, they discovered that he had been blacklisted from leaving the country.

Like a buffalo who had its hindquarters whipped incessantly, Tsín-suí dug in his heels and "kept tilling his furrows" as he headed north to Taipei. After he walked into the United Association offices, he noticed that the gigantic pile of papers that had been waiting on his desk had been moved. It had disappeared. Doubt started to creep into his mind. Wang Lan-ting, the special committee member from the Executive Yuan's working committee on banana trade, had stopped by Tsín-suí's office with a very troubled look painted across his face. Wu Chih-tsung, the manager of the internal planning department, had also come by. After a couple of cold pleasantries were exchanged, Tsín-suí asked the two visitors, "I'd like to try to see the chairman, Hsu Pai-yuen. Please help me organize a meeting with him!"

"The chairman is currently working at the Central Bank," Wang said. "He's very seldom made his way over to the Executive Yuan. I'll try to put you into contact with him."

Wu injected, "Mr. Chairman, all of those nonsensical rumors in the newspapers are doing massive damage. Just let me take care of the matters from above."

"Mr. Ngôo, ah! I tried to warn you earlier, but you know," Wang cautioned, "if you go to a banquet and only toast people but don't eat, you'll end up being forced to drink a cup as punishment."

Tsín-suī gave him an awkward smile in response, "Right. That's absolutely right."

They'd chatted for a bit to this point and then the secretary came in to pass along a note to the chairman. There was an important guest who had come to pay Tsín-suī a visit. Wang and Wu left the room, and in came Lin Shih-cheng.

As soon as he walked through the door, he asked, "Brother A-Suī-á, are you going to resign or not?"

"I can resign at any time. Give me a time and a date and I'll work to convince the board of directors."

"*Aiyah!*" Shih-cheng seemed to have been slammed into an impossible situation, and he was cursing and muttering under his breath. "The way you're doing things, how do you possibly expect me to tell Huang Chieh any of this?!"

Tsín-suī felt an intense coldness towards him; he threw caution to the wind and cursed, "F***! You of all people, Lim A-Tshioh-sing. Go give that '*Aiyah!*' bullshit to your father! I have to gain the consent of my directors before I can quit. How the hell do you not understand this?"

Shih-cheng responded in just a single sentence in Taiwanese, "I've been harangued by them to try to convince you."

***

Commissioner Ouyang hand-delivered his "Report on Banana Farmer Sentiments" to the bureau heads. His direct supervisor made a copy. Then the original was sent to the bureau headquarters in Taipei with a "confidential" security clearance stamped on the envelope and papers. Once it was sent out, the bureau chief took his sweet time opening the envelope and read it aloud.

> Item 1. Actual Statements of Real People
> February 26th, Pingtung County, Chu-tien Township, Chu-nan Village. Residence of one Chen Tsun-lin:

> "Nobody's going to save him? I was hoping those Japanese executives would come out and say something."

"Don't think about it. These mainlander types loathe the Japanese. If Japanese businesses come out in support of the chairman, it might have the opposite outcome from what we want."

February 27th, Pingtung County, Wantan Township, No. 3 Banana Collection Depot:

"I heard the younger Chiang was in some big struggle for power over the economy with Sung Mei-ling. Ngôo Tsín-suī was just caught up in their power struggle, and he's nothing more than a slab of meat sitting on a chopping block, ready to be carved up by those jackals."

"I heard pretty much the same thing somewhere else, but it's not just Chairman Ngôo on the chopping block, but all of us banana farmers."

February 28th, Kaohsiung County, Ch'i-shan District, Yuen-fu Village. Residence of one Wu Lai-chin:

"I think the golden days are now done for on the banana farms. Whenever Ngôo Tsín-suī falls, nobody will be able to get our Japanese exports back up to what they were with him at the helm."

"He won't necessarily fall. Chairman Ngôo is a god who's always been there to aid us. Deities can't fall!"

"Ngôo is a god, yes, but there's still a more powerful god out there. If lesser gods don't learn their place, they might end up being eaten by the greater gods."

February 28th. Ch'i-shan District. Kuang-fu No.1 Banana Collection Spot:

"They just keep raking him over the coals in the papers! It seems to me that they can't just go and arrest him. It's not the days of 228. They can't just arrest him and shoot him, can they?"

"What would you do if they executed him? Would you be willing to stick your neck out for him... For justice?"

"No."

March 1st. Kaohsiung County, Mei-nong Township. Residence of one Lung Tu-chung:

"The Americans want us to buy paper cartons from them. If we just bought from them, there wouldn't have been a problem. Why is Chairman Ngôo being so insistent? If it were me, I would have just let it go. I would have done it just to please them. We could have kept earning money from bananas all the while. Chairman Ngôo is just a ngang-liang-giang (stiff neck). And now look where it's gotten him."

"Our chairman's got the temperament a bull. The ox in him has come out. He's a bit stubborn!"

March 1st. Mei-nong Township. Kuang-hsing No. 3 Banana Collection Depot:

"How could the banana god transform into a banana maggot? What kind of profits or benefits has he siphoned off from us banana farmers? None, that's what! He's done nothing but help us earn massive piles of cash, hasn't he?"

"The papers are trying to turn us against him. If they're all trying to smear him, then you know he's a good guy. You know it and I know it!"

"Item 2. In Public Sentiment Summary No. 1, the local Taiwanese value righteousness and they value profit, but it's rare that they will protest over earning a profit. This humble servant believes there may be some locals who are dissatisfied but who aren't willing to speak out against the general consensus for fear of retribution..."

As the bureau chief read to this part of the report, he spoke, "Very fine work, Brother Ouyang. You've tried your best. I'll be waiting patiently for the next few General Summaries of Public Sentiment. I reckon that after Taipei evaluates this report of yours, it will hasten the case. You might want to prepare yourself first."

"Really? What should we do to prepare?"

"We need to prevent them from moving all their important documents to other locations and hiding them or burning them—"

"They won't. They absolutely won't. Not only do they feel no guilt at all, but they're even proud of their account books."

"What do you mean?"

"The first time, before, when the Control Yuan came to audit their books, they thought that this organization's accounting records were the most conservative and well-documented of all civil organizations around the island. They even gave the association an award for it."

"This is a bit different from how we would handle this."

"Is there anything else that needs preparing?"

"Personnel. Control over the whereabouts of all the managers and accountants."

"Yes, sir. That shouldn't be a problem."

***

Today was like any other for Commissioner Ouyang. In the midst of the chaos around him, he brewed himself a nice big mug of jasmine tea, slowly sipping and slowly musing, waiting for the next shoe to fall. Suddenly, a light switch flicked on in his mind. He put his mug down, pulled out his fountain pen, and then scribbled some characters furiously on some lined paper. "I'm so sorry! I can't do anything to help you now. Please don't worry. I'll work hard to exonerate you." After he finished writing this mysterious note, he folded it in half and put it in his right pocket, then he made a mental note that it was placed in his right pocket.

He then pulled out a new sheet of paper and began writing, "Chief, there's an account book in the lower-right drawer of the office bureau in Wu Chen-jui's office, recording the golden gifts that he personally handled." After he wrote this note, he folded it nice and crisply and slipped it into his left lapel pocket. He pressed down on it with his palm, also making a mental note that it was on the left side. Once he'd finished, he looked around the room. "These people, these hardworking, wonderful office workers."

He lowered his head and said a silent prayer to himself. He wasn't a follower of any religion. He wasn't sure who he should pray to, so he just lifted eyes to the ceiling and made his plea. "Wait a moment. I hope everyone won't be too shocked. I sincerely hope that Manager Lee and the vice managers aren't shaken up too badly. Let the damage be light. Just make sure their scare is the slightest, the lightest, almost none... almost none..."

There were a couple of items lying on the table waiting to be dealt with. They were related to the inspection reports on wharf security for Kaohsiung Harbor. They were already planned out several months in advance. There was also a draft proposal for rewards and punishments written up by one of the personnel commissioners, and also...

Ouyang picked up one of the files and began to work. Things needed to be completed properly, so he tidied up his own case files. This Green Fruits Export Cooperative would continue on, regardless of the fallout.

About half an hour later, an old soldier-worker friend came by his side and asked in a low voice, "Why are there suddenly so many police cars parked outside? There's some out back too."

Commissioner Ouyang stood up and muttered. "They're here... They're finally here... They..."

At the entrance, two of the association's officials came striding in, leading a company composed of central operatives. Behind them were the chief prosecutor, with whom Ouyang had already been acquainted. Then there were several officials that he didn't know from the local prosecutor's office.[51]

After they'd barged in through the main entrance, they seemed to look and act like some small fighting force on a battlefield doing a maneuver. The chief prosecutor barged straight into Lee T'u-chen's office. Ouyang's direct subordinates brought three people quickly towards the vice general manager, Tsai Kun-shan. Another official brought his men over near the desk of the head of general affairs, Luo Ching-yuen. The head of accounting, Yang Hsi-chih, wanted to rush away from his seat, but he was held down by the shoulders by two operatives who were only too happy to be rough and course with the accountant. Yang's face was now crimson with anxiety, scared nearly to death. He looked as afraid as a rooster who realizes that the butcher's blade was about to come down on his neck.

After the men who had barged their way in revealed their true identities, all the officials in the association were yelling and hollering, "Pull out all of your record books, and put them on the tables!"

Vice General-manager Tsai Kun-shan was all aflutter in a mix of shock and anger. He asked in a booming voice, "What are you doing? What crimes have we committed!?"

"Cut the chitchatting! Hurry up! The ledgers. On the table. Now! If you keep talking, I'm going to handcuff you immediately."

---

51. When this story took place, the police case was being carried out under the orders of the investigation bureau. The directive to prosecute the case was a later development.

Commissioner Ouyang looked in through the manager's office window. Everything in the office was being conducted much more politely. He knew that the prosecutor was good-natured in general. The man was previously an elementary school teacher from Tainan. Manager Lee was from Kî-san, just a stone's throw away from the city, so he could use a more local way of speaking with him to cozy up!

Among this group of trained operatives from the Investigation Bureau were Ouyang's own former bureau chief, and his good colleagues. Were they all bandits and thieves carrying out their task? Oh no, they just couldn't be. Ouyang had in the past done the same things these men were doing now. How could he see himself as some bandit, some rogue? He saw that the "work" was almost finished now. He then walked towards the bureau chief and fished out the note from his left lapel pocket and handed it over to the man. The bureau chief speed-read through the note, then said a quick thanks. The chief then walked briskly towards the chairman's office. Two operatives followed. During this break in the action, he fished out the other note from his right lapel pocket and placed it before Vice Manager Tsai Kun-shan. Tsai rushed through reading the note, then both men's eyes met. That face that had gone as white of a sheet had now regained some of its color. Tsai had the best private relationship with Ouyang over the years. Both of them often went out for leisure activities or went to the Tsai household for meals or would go to other people's banana farms to drink tea and chat. They had become true friends. Ouyang had prayed that heaven would bestow its protection over Tsai and everyone at the office that day.

It wasn't long before these efficient "legalized brigands" had wrapped up their operation. Sack after sack of documents of all sorts were heaved up onto a canvas-covered jeep truck. All the core managers and folks who ran the association, including Manager Lee and the vice manager, Tsai, were handcuffed and forced to climb up into the back. The investigators and operatives were in a hurry to leave, and Ouyang stepped forward. The bureau chief spoke with him first.

"Brother Ouyang, thank you for this. You've had a hard go at this operation." Then the large group of people and several cars sped off. The clouds of acrid dust and grime kicked up by the departing cars and jeep truck filled his nostrils and eyes. Ouyang slowly took shelter behind a wall where nobody was around and pulled out a handkerchief. He blew the dusty snot out of his nose and wiped around his eyes, then he struck hard at the wall with his fists until they were stinging from the pain.

He didn't dare return to the office now. Based on his feelings at the moment, he thought everyone remaining in the office would single him out or even stare him down with deep-set enmity for what he'd just orchestrated! Tsín-suī was up in Taipei when the Kaohsiung hornet's nest was kicked. The chairman himself had gone to Beitou to a small inn located at the end of a narrow alley to hide out for a while. He called Cheng Hsi-chüan, the provisional chairman for that month and the previous, Chang Yuen-chi, and told them to immediately discuss a counterstrategy. Another phone call later, and he told Tần Hīng-tshun of his whereabouts.

Hīng-tshun rushed over to Beitou as soon as she could. She peppered him with questions as soon as she saw him, "I heard the reports. What were the problems with the ledgers that were taken? I'm not worried about those. The Examination Bureau had already audited them months before. All the accounts and records are in order. The receipts are all legally compliant. They even gave us an award for how tight of a ship we run."

"Well thank goodness for that," Hīng-tshun lightly patted at her heart. Then she suggested they go out, "Let's get up and go out to find a place to eat dinner."

The pair had just sat down at their low table in a Japanese restaurant. The food hadn't even arrived yet, and Tsín-suī began a rant, "What kind of an outfit is the Investigation Bureau? *Honnh*! How can they just barge into the offices of a civilian organization like that and run off with all the documents! *Honnh*! *Baka yarō*!"

"They're quite something. Just as you happened to call me and I came to meet you, they've gripped everything within their claws now."

"Baka!"

"What are your plans now? How would you like to respond to them?"

"I would like to face them head on. I'm not afraid."

"You've not thought of running away? I could help you find a way."

"I can't. Not when all of my team members have been rounded up. How could I flee all alone after what's happened? I'd rather go in on my own."

"That wouldn't be a problem for them. They'll throw you right into prison." Hīng-tshun continued, "They can still charge you even if they can't find any evidence. What's more, the media is fully in their hands. They're calling for you to be executed. Regular folks are believing the garbage they're spewing."

"My character's already been assassinated! All of society already believes that I'm some terribly exploitative bastard who's borne down on all Taiwan's banana farmers. F***! The bastards!"

The two were talking as they ate, but all of a sudden, someone swept back the papered *shōji* sliding door that separated their private dining room. It was Chang Chin-luo, the general manager of the United Association, a colleague known long to both Tsín-suī and Hīng-tshun. He slipped his shoes off outside the sliding door track and stepped into the tatami-floored room, then sat down on an empty floor cushion at the table. Tsín-suī handed him a bowl and a set of chopsticks, asking him, "How did you know the two of us were here?"

"I just so happened to be here with a friend for dinner and saw you two on the way in."

Looking very suspicious, Hīng-tshun said, "We didn't come here together. How could you have run into both of us? This is a private Japanese restaurant too. People can't just waltz right in for food."

Chang Chin-luo didn't immediately respond. He stopped for a moment before continuing, "I came here with a Japanese friend for dinner."

Hīng-tshun lightly tapped Tsín-suī's wrist, saying, "I don't think the food here is getting any better. We ought to go somewhere else to eat. Come! Get up. Let's move."

"Ah! Haha!" Chang Chin-luo gave a quick response, "Where's the fire? Why are you in a rush? There's no need to go so fast... I'll tell you something... Quite frankly, I've been sent here on a mission."

"Are you a *sap-á* (rogue) from the Investigation Bureau?"

"No. I've come here at the behest of someone even bigger than the Investigation Bureau."

"The Ministry of Justice under the Executive Yuan?"[52]

"Wrong again. I'm from the Garrison Command."

Tsín-suī was in full shock now. Normally, this Chang Chin-luo was quite amicable and polite towards everyone. He was fond of flattery and was enthusiastic in his participation in every event, no matter how great or small. How could Tsín-suī not have thought that Chang would have been serving another master as a *jiàu-pê-á* (back scratcher). As he thought of this, Tsín-suī put on a straight face and asked Chang, "This case you've put up against my Green Fruits Association, it's currently under the Investigation Bureau's purview. Why is the Garrison Command suddenly butting its nose into this business?"

"The Investigation Bureau is managing it, that much is true, yes. But the Garrison Command is aiding it from the sideline."

---

52. The Executive Yuan's Ministry of Justice was the predecessor of the modern-day Ministry of Justice. The name was changed in July 1980.

"And what mission are you on?"

"I'd like to persuade you to come with me and surrender yourself."

Tsín-suī suddenly lost all control of his emotions, and with teeth gnashing, he spat out, "F*** your mother. What f***ing crime did I ever commit? What case would I possibly have to surrender for? F*** your mother!"

"Oh, I'm sorry. I'm so sorry! Chairman Wu Chen-jui, I'm truly sorry. What I had meant to say to you was that I wished that you would be proactive and face the authorities and explain everything to them."

Hīng-tshun placed her palm lightly on Tsín-suī's elbow, talking in a soft voice to him. "A-Suī-*hiann*, don't get angry." She then turned to Chang and asked him, "So you're wanting Chairman Ngôo to go to your Central Police Headquarters for an explanation, yes?"

"No. We're going to the Investigation Bureau. The case is being handled by the Investigation Bureau." Chang Chin-luo recomposed himself and spoke in his Taiwanese-accented Mandarin, "I can help you with the arrangement and take you directly to the Bureau. I can arrange an interview between you and the bureau chief himself."

"Weren't you just saying that you were not an employee of the Investigation Bureau?"

"I work with both of them. There's a lot of back and forth between the two."

The three of them suddenly went quiet. Hīng-tshun lowered her head to eat some more food. Chang lifted up a glass and drank a mouthful of green tea. Tsín-suī picked up a piece of sushi with his chopsticks and dropped it in the plate in front of Chang. "A-Loo-*hiann*, I'm so sorry to have cursed at you just now. It was very unbecoming of me. This whole situation is just filled with injustices and there's nowhere to take out my frustrations, and that's when I'd lost my temper."

"I understand. I know you're not the sort of person to wantonly curse at others."

"I was planning on going myself to explain in person, but I have to wait until the board of directors in Ko-hiông agrees to my resignation from the chairmanship. I've already notified two of the provisional directors, Cheng Hsi-chüan and Chang Yuen-ch'i, to hurry up here. The two of them are probably already on their way. I reckon they'll arrive here about midnight or perhaps very early tomorrow morning."

Neither Hīng-tshun nor Chang Chin-luo spoke. Tsín-suī took a sip of tea, then continued, "I think, in this way, A-Loo-*hiann*, that starting today, you can just stick at my side the whole time. You can see how I discuss the matter with the directors from Ko-hiông. You can wait for me to take care of things properly, and then you can accompany me to the Investigation Bureau and help me explain everything to the bureau chief."

"Would you like me to go with you to the inn and stay with you?"

"That's right. Anywhere I go, everything I do, everyone I talk to, everything I say, you'll be right at my side."

"There's no need for that!" Chin-luo continued, "I know you're determined to give an explanation. My mission has been achieved already. Your matters will be accounted for. When you go to the Investigation Bureau, just call my telephone number and I'll show up and accompany you."

"What I was intending to say is that with you at my side, they will be more lenient. They don't need to waste time trying to follow me and monitor everything I do."

"Oh, even with me accompanying you, they'll still be monitoring you. There're several agents who've been tasked with watching you. I'm just merely one of many."

"F***! How could they treat me as if I'm a despicable Communist bandit? I'm a contributing citizen of the country who's done so much for society. The balls on these motherf***ers!"

Hīng-tshun could see the fire raging up again in Tsín-suī, so she placed her hand over Tsín-suī's elbow again. Chin-luo was silent. He began eating something off his plate. The three of them went quiet for some time. Tsín-suī then opened up with a question, "I'd like to get your opinion, A-Loo-*hiann*. What about my family? Are they all safe or are you keeping them in your crosshairs too?"

"They're not under my watch, no. That would be the intelligence unit." Chin-luo then continued, after a pause, "I heard them say that Tông Tsuān-tsong and his wife have already returned to Pingtung to watch over your wife. Many people from Penghu have gone over to console her. Please rest assured, Mr. Chairman."

"I've already given them a phone call. I'm certain."

"She didn't say much. She just asked that you feel at ease and that would be enough for her sake."

The two provisional directors of the Kaohsiung firm arrived the next day. At the onset of the meeting between the three of them, they didn't utter a single word for several minutes. They just sat across from each other, awkwardly staring at each other. These three colleagues had committed over a decade of their lives to their association and farming, working alongside one another the whole time. It wasn't a matter of not wanting to speak, but just that they didn't know how to broach any of what had happened.

After a while, Tsín-suī was the first to sigh and blame himself, "It's all my fault. I've harmed so many people, thrown them to the wolves and put them into harm's way and terror. Especially Manager Lee T'u-chen-á and the other four who've been dragged away. I've done enough damage..." He hadn't finished speaking before tears began to flood from his eyes. Cheng and Chang were startled by the sight of their chairman's breakdown. This godlike figure whom they'd highly revered and attributed prestige was now weeping quite openly in front of them.

"Chairman, please don't be that way. Please don't be upset. You didn't do anything wrong. I feel you only did the best you could and you were just too successful. You were a tree whose branches stretched too far, and you snagged the wrong person's clothes," Cheng Hsi-chüan said.

"Chairman, there's no way to share your pain. I'm also feeling extremely despondent and pained," Chang Yuen-ch'i said. "Before I came here, I went over to your house to take a look. Everyone was doing fine at your house. There were some family friends over, as well. Everyone was together. Please don't feel worried for your family."

When Chang Yuen-ch'i brought up Tsín-suī's family, Tsín-suī, who had only just managed to recompose himself a second ago, began to convulse and the sobs rose again. He covered his face with both his hands. The sounds of his weeping escaped through the gaps between his fingers. Both Cheng and Chang's own eyes began to redden and moisten, and they blotted at their eyes frequently.

Tsín-suī quickly regained his composure and started in on the real matter facing them. "Both of you need to convene a board meeting and allow me to resign. The sooner the better. After I've resigned, I'll immediately go over to the Investigation Bureau and meet them head on. I want to see how they receive me. When the time comes, don't worry about me. They can take me out and execute me, or whatever they like."

"Mr. Chairman, can you just decide not to resign?"

"No. If you don't allow me to resign. The whole affair is going to get much uglier."

"Let's go back to Ko-hiông. Back there, we can split up the task and inform everyone. We still need some time."

"It would be fine to phone them from the hotel. They'll convene within two days. It won't take more than two days."

"Yes, Mr. Chairman."

"OK. Let's comply with them immediately."

Two days later, the Kaohsiung Green Fruits Export Cooperative Association board of directors sent out a press report. "First, we are permitting Chairman Wu Chen-jui to resign from his position and duties. Second, we have agreed unanimously to hire the as-of-now former chairman to serve as an honorary chairman. Third, the board of directors has agreed to give the as-of-now former chairman a severance payment of one million New Taiwan Dollars."

When the news became known, Tsín-suī was half-sitting, half-reclining on his side in his room at the inn over in Beitou. The radio kept replaying the same news story over and over again. "It's time now," he said to himself. He rose up from his bed, pulled open the blinds. It was raining. Rain in early March in Taipei is still winter rain. If it were in his hometown down south in Pîn-tong, it would be a spring rain already. The rain had already been pitter-pattering for several days now. It was maddening.

"Maybe I need to cheer up. After today, I don't know what changes my life will take. I'll still need to cheer up," he tried to encourage himself. After quickly combing his hair and washing his face, he did a quick session of his *kamasō* morning stretches. He then got dressed and telephoned that "back-scratcher" manager, Chang Chin-luo. Nobody answered. He kept dialing. Nobody was answering. It didn't matter. Off he went! He would go in alone then. Even if he were to die inside, he'd go in with his hard-headed attitude! He opened the door forcefully and was going straight to the inn's reception counter to pay his bill, when suddenly, Chang Chin-luo appeared out of nowhere, like a ghost, standing next to the counter. He had his signature smile on. He was the first to speak, "Ngôo Tsóng-á—Director—do you wish to go to the bureau today?"

"Yes. Let's go, but wait for a moment first. I'm going to settle the bill."

"There's no need. I can help you settle it."

"You can't. I've been here for several days already. I've made so many long-distance calls already."

"It's really not that much! It's such a trifling matter. Go. Let's go."

As they walked out of the inn, the winter chill seeped into both the men's bones. Chang Chin-luo pulled out an umbrella and passed it over to Tsín-suī, who pushed it away just then. "I don't need it. I'm not afraid of some rain," Tsín-suī refused the offer.

He stood by the road, waiting for the car Chang Chin-luo was driving to come around. Unbendingly, Tsín-suī let the raindrops wash over his face, hair, and clothing, sinking into everything and soaking it. Frigid raindrops were flowing into his shirt collar. He felt a rush of cold, making him shiver. It spread from his nape and collarbone throughout his entire body. His skin was now covered in goose bumps.

When they reached the central headquarters of the Investigation Bureau, Chang brought Tsín-suī to the office of the bureau chief, Shen Chih-chiou. He called out a simple explanation, "Chief, I've brought you Wu Chen-jui. My task is complete. You can take it from here. We'll talk another time." He then waved goodbye to Tsín-suī.

Tsín-suī then locked eyes with Chief Shen. He'd never met the man before. The first question he blurted out made Tsín-suī feel as if he was in a fantasy tale. "Mr. Wu, you asked Chang Chin-luo to bring you here to see me. To what do I owe the pleasure?"

"Men from your bureau have gone to my association in Kaohsiung, and they've absconded with my association's ledgers and taken several people away. I've come here specifically to explain some things to you."

"That's fine by me. Please, what sort of things do you wish to explain?"

"As for the work of the banana industry, I'm afraid that I have to ask you to collect a few related people, for example, the Executive Yuan's special committee on banana farming, and start a roundtable discussion. That way maybe you won't go around creating criminals out of thin air."

"Sure. We can talk about that. This way, please," Bureau Chief Shen made a gesture for Tsín-suī to come in, directing the latter into an old house in the compound. They entered in through a round moon gate. The inside was spacious. There were several smaller rooms comprising the main hall. The bureau chief politely asked Tsín-suī to sit for a moment in one of the rooms and then walked out.

About an hour had passed, and a new person entered the room. His gaze was sharp, and he had an uncouth manner of speaking, "Are you the banana maggot mentioned in the papers?"

Tsín-suī was a bit angered by this, but he thought it better not to argue with this person, and so responded, "That's correct. I am the very banana maggot. My name is Wu Chen-jui."

The other person bared his teeth as he grinned. Just as he'd entered like a phantom so, too, did he just as quickly dart out of the room.

What felt like ages passed, and yet another person came in. His countenance and figure seemed boorish and rough. It didn't seem like he was an official here to conduct a meeting. His eyes were wide, as if scrutinizing Tsín-suī. It was like he was inspecting some complex machine.

"Bureau Chief Shen asked me to wait here for a meeting, I'm not sure—" Tsín-suī began politely.

The other man interjected, berating Tsín-suī with his mainland slurs and insults, "You *Mah-la-ka-bi*, haven't you figured it out yet? This is an interrogation room."

As soon as the words penetrated his ears, Tsín-suī was incensed. That bastard, Shen, had led him right into an interrogation room. He was angered, but the ire dissipated quickly. What exactly was this place? How are you going to deal with this now, Tsín-suī? Are you going to be allowed to have a temper at all? He pondered to himself. While he was reflecting on it all, the other person disappeared like a ghost. Another long while passed. A central operative who seemed even more stern and even harsher than the last entered, and he was holding a sheet of paper. He took it and plopped it down heavily onto the tabletop. He lightly struck the table with a first, then began shouting at Tsín-suī, "Have a good look! What is this?"

Tsín-suī had already been scared by the loud, heavy thud of a hand striking. He lowered his gaze again and was terrified now. Damnit! He was surprised to see it was an arrest warrant. Tsín-suī was actually being arrested today.

The stranger glared at Tsín-suī with fearsome eyes, as if staring right through this "criminal's" heart to determine if Tsín-suī was either afraid or enraged. He paid attention to the chairman for quite some time and then finally pulled out a prepared piece of paper and pen and began to speak.

"They can't necessarily read my mind," Tsín-suī thought. "I'm neither afraid nor angry, regardless of what they think. I can see this thug is just toying with me. He's intentionally trying to frighten or anger me and make me lose my calm, make me all anxious beyond control and then pick up the broken pieces as if nothing happened. Well today, this is just a bit of life's unavoidable bad luck. I need to cheer up. I need to keep on plowing along and stick to my path. If I can calmly face it, I can get past it all."

The interrogation had begun. "How many ingots or cubes of gold did you purchase in total?"

"None. Not a single ingot or speck," Tsín-suī answered.

"You sent out so much of it, and you're saying you didn't do anything?"

"I'm telling you, they were all goldware purchased from metalsmiths. They're not gold ingots."

"How many did you buy in total?"

"About three hundred, more or less."

"What were you doing buying that many?"

"It was the twentieth anniversary of the founding of the Kaohsiung Green Fruits Export Cooperative Association. They were purchased as a thank you to all of those people and officials who had helped our association succeed over the years."

"Did you send them to public officials?"

"Yes. Ones currently serving and ones who are already retired. Those living, and posthumously for those who've passed away," he quickly added.

The investigator was a bit shocked by the attitude of this "criminal" sitting before him and his attitude of answering everything right away. His tone of voice gradually grew warmer and more amiable.

"Good. Very good. Please take a look at the written record. If there's no mistakes, then please stamp it with your thumb."

After Tsín-suí had complied and made a thumbprint in red upon the page, the interrogator asked, "So were all the pieces of goldware sent out, then?"

"There's a few that haven't been sent yet."

"And where have they been kept?"

"Some of them have been stored at the Kaohsiung and Taipei offices. Some of them are at the United Association. All of them have been locked up in the safes."

"Are you going to go with me and collect them?"

"We have a very strict schedule to stick to. The weight of the goldware we sent off was based on the person's rank or seniority of office. It wasn't something I chose to do on my own. In any case, I've already resigned. I'm not the chairman any longer."

The central operative member's face suddenly darkened, "Then we'll just have to go searching for them, won't we?"

Tsín-suí's face also darkened a few shades and he cursed to himself, "Just what the hell are you up to? You're nothing but thieves and bandits. You're nothing but a gangster government!" But what actually came out of his mouth was, "What are you planning on doing with them?"

"It will serve as part of our proof in your case."

"Proof? What do you need it to prove?" Tsín-suí asked coldly.

"That's information you're not privy to."

After using a special car to come back with the goldware from both associations' Taipei offices, Tsín-suí was still led back to the small chamber at the Investigation Bureau. Nobody came in to ask him anything. Two plainclothes officers were posted to the outside of the room. He sat inside with nothing to do. "Have I started my jail sentence yet?" Tsín-suí was lost in his thoughts. The winter rains of Taipei just kept pouring outside the room, and the color of the sky turned from light gray to purple darkness. His heart and mind grew heavy.

An old soldier without any expression on his face came by to deliver dinner. It was a bowl of rice with a cube of tofu, half a soy-braised hard-boiled egg, and some greens and other vegetables. Tsín-suī was born in a farming village. This fare was pretty typical, but he had no appetite for any of it at the moment. Darkness drew on outside very quickly, and the yellow light of the room's only lamp glowed dimly, casting slanted shadows from the table and the stool chairs. It also cast a shadow from the rattan chair over in a corner. That seemed to be where he would sleep tonight.

"No wonder several of my friends warned me not to return from Japan. Returning home has meant that I've walked gradually into a jail cell. If I had remained in Japan, I would be able to go out casually for some sushi, some fresh sashimi, piping hot miso soup, or some tempura. I could go outside my lodging anytime I pleased. I could go walk around the tiny residential lanes and see the faint lights shining out from inside wooden Japanese homes, imagining the people inside eating dinner or sipping on freshly brewed green tea."

Tsín-suī's favorite activity after the talks and dinners was to go out sauntering about in the neighborhood near his hotel. He savored these moments when he was by himself. He loved being in Japan. He loved the small alleyways and lanes in their cities. They'd already been modernized, but it was a restrained kind of advancement. It was no longer the traditional wooden alleyways of eras long past but a kind of tradition intentionally retained by the residents. Whenever he was in Japan, he used to ponder on the Japanese sections of town in the Pîn-tong and Tâi-pak of his youth as he walked around. The streets were kept pristine and quiet. They held a warm tranquility.

He paced the room several times. It was quite small. After three or four paces, he'd run into a wall. He banged his head against the wall, lightly thunking on it, then turned back. Then he'd do it all over again after three or four more paces. He kept doing this time after time. He thought as he paced the room, thinking that if he had still been in Japan, wouldn't all of the lies and nonsense in the newspapers have been validated? And wouldn't it be justified to call him a "criminal in fear and on the lam?"

"If I had remained in Japan and knew of the raid on the Ko-hiông Association and that my longtime-serving manager and vice managers were all thrown into jail, how would I have been able to continue eating? How would I be able to sleep at night? Compared with returning to Taiwan and sitting in detention, it might've even been more difficult. Perhaps one day I wouldn't have been able to live with myself at all.

"So I think returning was the right decision for me. This banana farmer case of mine isn't some grandiose case—it's not corruption, it's not forgery; it's not murder or arson. Nobody has been hurt. Lee Kuo-ting was angry, of course, but why would this result in a case? F*** their mothers! These awful Chinese officials!" Tsín-suī thought to himself that he was determined to go to Japan after things were settled and never return to Taiwan.

He decided then to eat all the "prison fare" off his plate. Then he'd sleep, peacefully sleep. He'd never felt evil at heart, so he'd just calmly face all this horrible luck.

Outside the door, two plainclothes officers kept walking up and down the hallway, but they occasionally poked their heads in to check on whether their "prisoner" was still in there.

Though he decided to get some shut eye, sleeping in an unfamiliar, frigid room on top of that rattan chair in the corner wasn't easy. First, he had to move himself into an upright position, but it wasn't much different from him just sitting. The corrugated ceiling loomed before his eyes, so he closed his eyelids. His thoughts flew back to Japan. Those countless times when he was in trade meetings, the expressions on the Japanese business owners' faces, all their spoken language and bodily gestures, scene after scene arose to the top of his mind. He thought of the lead chief executive, Shibata-san, who, on the eve of the first meeting, had formally invited Tsín-suī to a meet in a large *ryokan* to discuss the bigger issues and principles of their business dealings. The two were sitting on tatami, their legs under the *kotatsu* table's blankets to keep warm. Shibata's white socks were spotless and pristine; they had absolutely no stains on them.

At many of these talks, both the Japanese and Taiwanese representatives resembled high school students in a math class. Each and every topic was deliberated on till their heads were all spinning, but they made sure that the outcomes for both sides were always beneficial and that nobody was left feeling bitter. When the talks concluded, everyone had a smile on their face and was feeling at ease, happy.

Afterwards, they'd go out and tour around and enjoy the rest of their trip as an actual vacation. Tsín-suī now had to relax. He had to let his neck unwind, and then his collar, then his shoulders, then finally the rest of his body. He definitely had to get some rest. He would have to if he wanted to have all his wits about him when returning to Kaohsiung tomorrow, even though he had no clue where exactly he would end up when he reached the city. He had full faith that he would be assigned an honest and upstanding prosecutor or judge that would handle the case.

His thoughts then leapt to Thâu-tsîng-khe in Pîn-tong and to all the paddies where the rice had been harvested. Some of the fields would be flooded and tilled over again. Some would be left as dry fields to lie fallow for a bit, although the remaining dry, yellow rice stalks could still sprout tender, verdant shoots.

Uncle A-Huàn was right out in one of his fields calling out to Tsín-suī about a *bāng-kah*, but terrible screaming shouts, bellowing, and snapping sounds were coming from the field. Ah! It's A-Tsòng frantically whipping a buffalo. Was it Mari? How could A-Tsòng take her out? Why was he still whipping her, and with such cruelty? "*Wei*, A-Tsòng! You can't do that! Don't whip her!" Tsín-suī tensed up and was about to shout out, but no matter how hard he tried, no sound came out. What was going on? He kept looking to Uncle A-Huàn for help, but the old man just lifted up his cane and didn't shout out either. Tsín-suī could only stare at his younger neighbor as he kept whipping away. He thrashed so hard that the whip broke. A-Tsòng now appeared to be dressed like a Manchu soldier from China, and he was viciously punching Mari with his fists. After a couple blows, A-Tsòng transformed into a Japanese soldier and continued to beat the water buffalo over and over again. Tsín-suī strained to scream out to stop, but there was nothing he could do. Streams of blood could be clearly seen flowing from the buffalo's back. She wouldn't last much longer! Tsín-suī was in a panic now and a horrible pain was spreading in his chest. Finally, Mari slumped down to her knees and fell over on her side. To Tsín-suī's eyes, she looked like a mound of black earth that had collapsed. The fear turned to anger, and it flooded over like a swollen river, finally giving him the strength to shout out in a booming voice, "*Hsia*! (Stop!)" At the same time, he ran into the field and gave A-Tsòng a kick. Right as his foot landed, A-Tsòng transformed once again into a Chinese Nationalist soldier.

He had been sleeping, half-sitting, half-lying in the rattan chair, and he kicked hard at the wall. When he awoke, he realized in an instant that he had been dreaming, but his heart was still pounding. Mari's death from the beating was so vivid! What a sorrowful, merciless dream. He couldn't fall back asleep. He picked up the blanket that had fallen onto the floor and draped it over his shoulders, then started pacing again around his cramped cell.

The morning light hadn't yet broken, and the night air still felt icy. "Dreams are just absurd paintings concocted by our brains. There's no special meaning to them." Or so this was something Tsín-suī had read in a popular science publication when he was on a trip to Japan. He kept turning this sentence over and over in his mind to try to calm himself down, but this demonic dream just couldn't be dispelled. He kept pacing the small room as the pain welled up again in his chest.

It wasn't long before he sat back down in the rattan chair. It was dark out, and the only light was that of the moon and the stars, bringing along ghostly shadows. He wanted to go back to sleep, but the fear in him wouldn't allow him. He didn't dare. A long time passed, then the words, "I'm afraid! I'm afraid!" suddenly issued from his mouth over and over.

The next day, all the newspaper headlines read out, "Wu Chen-jui Surrenders to Investigation Bureau, to be Sent to Kaohsiung Prosecutor Today Following Interrogation."

The media also caught wind of which train Tsín-suī and the police escort would be taking to head down south.

A journalist for the *China Daily News* boarded the train in Tainan, carrying a camera. He started searching from the first cabin of the train, and when he reached the fourth cabin, he found a lanky, gaunt, and sophisticated-looking man, who seemed to be Ngôo Tsín-suī. However, the journalist wasn't sure. After all, the man in the seat was well-dressed, wearing a black Western suit and tie, a pair of glasses, and had a briefcase sitting next to him. A great coat that looked like it was down-filled was laid over his legs. If this man was truly the "banana maggot" that had been somehow exploiting all these banana farmers, wouldn't he have been cuffed in a pair of manacles and look menacing?[53]

The reporter plucked up his courage and walked up to Tsín-suī and spoke in a low voice, "Pardon me, but you wouldn't happen to be Mr. Wu Chen-jui, would you?"

"That's correct. My surname is Wu. I am Wu Chen-jui."

The interviewer was soft-spoken and the respondent full of confidence. All the passengers around them heard him say, "I am Wu Chen-jui," and nearly half the car cabin turned their heads in a flash to gaze at once towards this stranger.

"Oh, so that's what Ngôo Tsín-suī looks like! Sure enough, he's quite stylish. He's sure dressed up like a major figure, that's for certain."

---

53. Television sets were already in existence back in those days, but they weren't widespread in Taiwan. Despite Ngôo Tsín-suī's legal case being widely publicized in the media, most people had no idea what he looked like.

"I heard that the 'Golden Bowls Affair' was a setup."

"How is it a setup?"

"You've not talked with anyone out here. You should flip your newspaper right side up for once."

The bureau agent next to Tsín-suī clearly wanted to cut the reporter's interview short, but the journalist handed over a business card showing he was from the *China Daily News*. All his questions conformed to the government's policies. Finally, the man felt compelled to ask Tsín-suī, "Mr. Wu, I've heard that you have a personal fortune of fifty million dollars in the bank and have several millions stashed away in Japan, no?"

"That's nonsense. That's never been the case. All of my earnings have been in Taiwan this whole time. The Investigation Bureau already cleared up that fact a long time ago."

"There's a young man, almost like a younger brother to you, who runs a shoe repair shop next to the train station, is that right?"

"Yes, he's my fifth youngest brother. He was born a mute and he's disabled. My wife often gives him money to help him survive, but he's also striven hard to earn his own money. He's very spirited and strong-willed. Is there something wrong with that?"

"I heard that when you were being interrogated, you said it yourself that you could earn several thousands of dollars in a single minute. Is that true?"

"That's not at all true. I never said that. That was an intentional lie placed by the Investigation Bureau. They're trying to defame me," Tsín-suī said this loud and clear for everyone in the train car to hear. The Investigation Bureau agent quickly shooed the journalist away, half-guiding, half-shoving him down the aisle. Tsín-suī's interview had come to a halt.

As the train pulled into Kaohsiung Station, the plaza outside was buzzing with excitement. About twenty or thirty news reporters were standing guard at the entrances. The police escorts had experience with prying journalists giving interviews on the train and called ahead to make sure that there were two rows of police outside the station to create a human wall to keep the journalists from pushing closer. Tsín-suī was tall, though, wearing a Western suit, and his posture straight as an arrow. His hair was neat and tidy, and he had one arm around his thick coat and his briefcase in his other hand. He took great strides as he walked between the two columns of policemen. He had a demeanor about him, as if he weren't a criminal at all. He briefly scanned the crowd all around, and several journalists were clumped together at the outside wall, the flash from their cameras incessant. The flashes made a *kha-tsha* sound as they furiously clicked away. It was as if Tsín-suī had been transformed into a living Wang-ye (the Royal Lord), the popular Pîn-tong deity, out on an inspection of his domain.

Ahead and to the right, there were several familiar faces. They belonged to his coworkers and colleagues from the Kaohsiung Green Fruits Cooperative Association. Among them were several people he didn't know, who must have been random onlookers. Straight ahead of him was a large military-style jeep truck. An operative from the Investigation Bureau ordered him up. The two short columns of police swung over on their own motorcycles to act as an escort. The motorcycles and jeep roared to life. Tsín-suī lowered his head as he boarded the truck. It was right at that moment when he heard an, "A-Suī-á!" He turned his head to follow the call. It was Tsuān-tsong-*hi-ann*. He and his wife had come to the train station.

Tsín-suī took another look and his heart caught in his throat—it was Giok-ìn. She was covering her mouth with her hands. She appeared to be weeping, hot tears running down her face. Their daughter, Bí-ài, and sons Ting-phang, Tîng-kong, and Tîng-hō were there too. There were policemen on all sides of their mother. *Aiyee*! Tsín-suī let out a loud sigh. He wanted to cry then. The composure and calmness that he had steeled up in himself utterly collapsed and drifted away in the blink of an eye. It was right then that an agent gave him a shove and pushed him into the back of the military jeep, then yelled at the driver, "Go!"

Six policemen's motorcycles had divided into two lines of three on each side, leading the way. The jeep picked up speed and jolted off. Tsín-suī turned his head back and watched. His wife Giok-ìn and their children and both Tsuān-tsong and his wife remained standing back there as the dust flew up. "What were they possibly thinking now? Were they placing all the blame at my feet? Could they understand this framing and miscarriage of justice? Would they loathe me as a husband and a father? Was I too consumed with investing everything in farming and bananas and neglected to take care of you all back at home? I'm so sorry!"

His family members slowly disappeared into the distance behind the car. He then realized that there were also six police motorcycles split into two lines of three following behind the jeep. "Just what kind of parade is this? Did they come to meet me as this 'Banana King?' Am I truly that important? Wasn't it only just a day ago that they called me a 'banana maggot?' Why are they making such a grandiose spectacle of sending me to prison? Maybe you feel guilty, and you're afraid someone will waylay you and spring me free in mid-journey?"

The motorcade went along quickly, but then the jeep slowed down gradually. He lowered his head just slightly and saw the large characters on the sign on top of the gate of this unknown destination. It read "Kaohsiung District Court Detention Center." The motorcade pushed its way in from beneath those large characters.

27

That evening, two shadows appeared in the deep ravine behind a five-storied apartment building in Beitou near the mountains outside of Taipei. The moonlight shone through the clouds from time to time, illuminating the figures. It looked as if they were the shadows of two men. One moment, they were crawling along; the next moment, they stood up and, with their heads down, moved closer to the building, step by step.

There were heavyset men in plain clothes patrolling on all sides of the building, all holding flashlights that sent yellowish cones in the darkness every now and then. Not far off, a cigarette lighter clicked and then sprang to light. In the few seconds that it took the men to take turns lighting up their cigarettes, it illuminated a group of policemen wearing official caps and uniforms. There were occasional chirping sounds coming from all around, but nobody could discern whether they were being made by insects or birds.

The shadows of the two men arrived below a giant downspout at the side of the building. They laid flat on their stomachs and watched. Not long after, when the patrolmen weren't around, they leapt up and, one after the other, deftly scaled the waterspout like monkeys, moving very quickly, as if their lives depended on it. When they reached the third floor, the one up above seemed to tire and stopped. Even worse, he began to slide down slowly, but the guy below him held him there. The two of them rested for about half a minute before finding the strength to keep climbing upwards. They resembled sloths, slowly grasping the waterspout one hand and one foot after the other as they continued upwards, inch by inch.

It was a real challenge to get up to the roof. There was a small five-inch-wide overhang. The two of them carefully stood up on it. Fortunately, the eaves were stable, though they were a bit slick. They were still able to move, their hands gripping the sashes of the window frames between the rooms.

The pair inched their way horizontally towards the left. The one in front gave a heads-up to his friend behind him, "Take your time. There's no need to rush. Don't get your footing wrong. Make sure you have a good foothold." He knew that if they fell, they'd fall into a deep pit and be seriously injured. Then he'd ruin his father's entire plan, among other things.

They slowly moved sideways, past three apartments, until they reached room 306, as their father had instructed. They'd been here to their father's place many times before, but the windows seemed to have been locked from the inside. They would have to break the glass. There would be noise for certain, and they'd no doubt alarm the policemen down below. What were they to do? He was just a good student, a bookworm honestly. He'd never been a thief before. The other man who came with him had more nerve. He struck the edge of the window glass hard and broke it.

There was a bit of a short *crunch*, and he stopped for a while, then struck the crack in the glass again. As he broke the glass pane, the other supported him. Once they were able to put an arm through, the one in front unlatched the window lock and they slid through the window, one after the other.

Once they got into the room, their hands and feet were trembling and felt like rubber, but they didn't dare rest even for a moment. They pulled out drawer after drawer from his father's writing desk, searching. They found everything. Oh, what a blessed moment it was! All of the documents were there! His father was saved!

This was Tsín-suī's third eldest child, Tîng-hō. He had just graduated from university and was preparing to leave the country and study abroad. He had received a note from a stranger. It was in his father's handwriting, smuggled out from prison. Everything was written out clearly. They had to get hold of these documents.

The other man was Tîng-hō's classmate, who was a loyal and supportive friend. He had cut his arm on the window glass and was bleeding.

The two of them had prepared large cloth sheets to tie up all the documents and secure them to their bodies as tightly as they could. Then they went back to the window and, shaking from the perilous situation they were in, crab-walked across the narrow ledge to the downspout and slowly slid their way down to the ground. Then they waited in the shrubs for their chance to make a break for it.

All their hopes of saving his father were resting on these documents. Ngôo Tîng-hō said a prayer as he fled.

Tsín-suī's second eldest son, Tîng-kong, was also in Taipei. He had run all over town, visiting all the high officials and important people who might have some sway to save his father, but everywhere he went, he ran into brick walls. He had even paid a visit to Chiang Ching-kuo, the son of Chiang Kai-shek, but all he received from the Secret Police chief was some words of consolation. Everything would rest with the court's decision.

In the dead of night, Tsín-suí's lawyer came knocking at Tîng-kong's door. He handed him a letter. When he opened it and read it, it was a letter written in his father's handwriting:

> Go as quickly as you can to our apartment in Beitou, number 306. Look in the drawers of the writing desk. All of the KMT Central Party members' donation solicitation letters are piled in there, including ones for donations from Japan to fight the Chinese Communists, as well as all the correspondence for donations to build the Sun Yat-sen Memorial Hall on Yangmingshan. All the receipts and awards are in there too. You need to hurry!

Tîng-kong quickly read through the letter. The lawyer explained it, "After enduring several days of no sleep and being interrogated multiple times by the Investigation Bureau, your father was threatened and cajoled into signing a confession written for him in advance. After he regained his senses a few days later, he was alarmed by the words 'misappropriation of foreign donations' in the confession. When he calculated it carefully, the amount 'misappropriated' was the sum of all of the donations from all of the years the associations gave money."

"Is that a major offense?"

"Yes. He could get ten years to life for it."

"I've been to the apartment in Beitou before. I'm going there now."

"How are you going to go there right now, in the middle of the night?" the lawyer asked.

"I'm guessing there's going to be a lot of policemen and inspectors in the area. You need to be careful at all costs," the lawyer added.

Tîng-kong was frantically pacing back and forth in the room. Not long after, his face tightened up and he told the lawyer resolutely, "It's not right. I absolutely have to go. I'm going now."

He put on a jacket and was putting on his shoes, when there was a knock on the door. It was his younger brother and a friend. The two of them looked absolutely exhausted and ill at ease. After they closed the door behind them, the pair took off the bundles wrapped to their bodies. The bundles contained all the letters and award certificates their father had collected.

Tîng-kong hugged his younger brother, and both of them began to weep.

After a while, the lawyer asked Ngôo Tîng-hō, "How did you know to go fetch these documents in particular?"

"There was some stranger who came looking for me. He shoved a paper into my hands."

"Let me see the paper."

Tîng-hō pulled the sheet out. It was the exact same as the one in the lawyer's hand. "Your father originally wrote two of them. He managed to smuggle one of them to me from prison through a warden. Do you know who the other person was that was asked?"

"It had to be one of dad's close friends, or else—" Ngôo Tîng-kong agreed.

"The stranger never said anything in particular to me. All he said was that his surname was Ouyang," Tîng-hō said.

"Ouyang?... I've never heard our father say he had any friends with the family name Ouyang," Ngôo Tîng-kong thought aloud, cocking his head slightly to the side.

At this same moment, in the middle of the night, with nobody around, Commissioner Ouyang slipped silently into the administrator's duty room at the Kaohsiung District Court Detention Center. A section chief and another warden knew that this man was a central figure in the Investigation Bureau. They were careful to mind what they said around him.

"I heard that there were several Japanese who came today to meet with the accused. Do you have any impression of this meeting? Is it the same people as before from last week?"

"They're all different. The ones who came today were very special though. They seemed to have high social positions."

The section chief passed around a guest book used to record the visitors' names, and Commissioner Ouyang saw three Japanese names listed— Takahashi, Shibata Isamu, and Nakano Eiji. He silently mouthed the names, then spoke, "Takahashi. He's the one. We still haven't figured out which company he's from."

"They were all wearing formal Japanese kimonos!" the section chief added.

"Do you know why they're wearing Japanese clothing?"

"We have a colleague who can understand Japanese. He said that when he wore Japanese clothing to a meeting it was to show great respect."

"Respect for what?"

"Respect to Wu Chen-jui."

"And who gave that explanation?"

"Our colleague who can understand Japanese asked them." The section chief continued, "That Wu Chen-jui is truly unlike the others. Oftentimes, a man of such renown as he would be downcast and crestfallen when they're put in prison, and lose any of their original demeanor, and be bullied and pulled apart by the old jailbirds; but he isn't like that. He stands up straight with a strong stature and does everything with dignity and grace. When they're venting their frustrations, all the accused still respect him very much."

"Oh, is that so!" Ouyang took out a fountain pen and began writing, his head bent over his notepad. "Anything else?" he asked after he finished.

"Wu Chen-jui only had two outbursts. The first time, he was with talking with his cellmates, Tsai Kun-shan and Luo Ch'ing-yuan. I'm not sure what they were talking about, but Chen-jui was suddenly agitated, and shouted out 'F***' in a very loud voice. He raised his voice even louder, yelling, 'You've all been locked up for those damned little anniversary gifts. None of those bastards who took the thirty tael goldware had anything happen to them!' And then he began swearing in Taiwanese. After he was finished swearing, he broke down and began to cry. He said—"

"Did he really cry? You saw it with your own eyes?"

"Yes, I saw it myself. It was shocking. I'm still hesitant to talk about it because I'm worried an 'accident' will happen. He clenched his fist and was punching himself in the head, and then he started beating himself in the chest. He was using so much force to harm himself. He was distraughtly crying out, 'It was all me. It was all my stubbornness like an ox. I ruined this good core team. All these good officials have been rounded up and are rotting in jail right now. It was me who hurt them all. I've hurt so many people—'"

Ouyang cut him short. "OK! OK! I get it! What was the other incident?"

"It was the day the newspapers wrote that Hsu Pai-yuen was removed from office. Ngôo Tsín-suī was cursing in Taiwanese."[54]

"Who was he cursing?"

"He said, 'It was all a political struggle,' and cursed those 'stupid idiots,' saying they had 'shit for brains.'"

"OK. Thanks. I can't convey that to anyone. Let's go back to talking about those Japanese visitors who came to visit our prisoner."

---

54. The year of Tsin-sui's arrest (1969) the president of the Central Bank and the foreign trade inspection committee of the Executive Yuan, Hsu Pai-yuen was also arrested and removed from his position, being sentenced to four months and twenty-nine days in prison, having been rounded up as part of the "Insufficient Supervision of the Green Fruits Industry." The news story broke the next day.

"Oh! Right. The leader of the Japanese entourage told Wu Chen-jui, 'Please take care of your health. You can't let them ruin your health.' When he was leaving, he told Wu again, 'Your country's president is turning a blind eye to our petition to release you. We will get justice for you. Japan's need for bananas doesn't necessarily need to be imported from Taiwan.'"

"Oh! Is that so?!" Ouyang lowered his head again, continued writing and then stopped. "Last time, I had asked you…Tsai Kun-shan, who's sharing a cell with Wu Chen-jui, is a good friend of mine. Has he had any problems? Has he had enough to eat?"

"Yes. We've made sure to take special care of him. He also knows you're often making special efforts to look after him."

"Well, that's good. Thank you both." Ouyang fished out a couple sheets of paper from his coat pocket and continued, "I have a few bits of old info. The court will be able to use them. Please give these to him. Don't let anyone see."

"Yes. Yes. I'll get it right into his hands."

Ouyang didn't say anything more. He just stood up and left.

$$28$$

It was early 1971. Chiang Ching-kuo, the vice premier of the Executive Yuan, had directed his secretary, Chiang Yen-shih, to convene a cross-ministry meeting of all officials. They were to develop policies for the consideration of the ministry that targeted a retaliatory boycott by Japanese companies, which had led to the precipitous drop in banana prices and instability in the rural villages. The attendees were all officials from the General Green Fruits Export Association, its Kaohsiung branch, the Ministry of Economic Affairs, the International Trade Bureau, the Ministry of Foreign Affairs, the foreign trade association, and the Provincial Department of Agriculture and Forestry.[55]

The Green Fruits Cooperative Association representative was the first to speak, "For more than a year, the bananas have just been piling up on the roadside in villages all across the country, exposed to the wind and rain. Our once-bustling market is now as cold as ice—"

Chiang Yen-shih raised a hand and lightly waved. "In this respect, the relevant unit's 'Banana Farmers' Public Sentiments Report' is plain for all to see. We're aware. Thank you." Secretary Chiang had a rather cheerful look to his face and asked without specifying who, "Mr. Shibata Isamu from Japan—is there nobody here who's done business with this man? Especially since he's come twice to visit a prison. Is there anyone here who has come into contact with him?"

"We went to the dilapidated inn where he was staying to meet with him. All he did was keep asking us questions. They came here using the name of the Japanese Banana Importers Organization to petition President Chiang Kai-shek. He kept asking if we were going to get him a response.

---

55. After Tsín-suí's case blew up, the Green Fruits Cooperative Association organization changed roles. The Taipei organization became the overall organization. Each cooperative organization changed into a subsidiary.

He wouldn't respond otherwise. Other than talking about their petition, they had nothing else they were willing to discuss," a representative from the foreign trade association answered.

"How much of the price has reduced so far?"

"Well, originally, it was six dollars and forty cents American a basket. The price was fine. But now, they won't buy anything unless it is below six dollars. The more severe problem of them all is the quantity. They're not as willing as they were before to chase after the quantity."

"Are they really going to start importing from the Philippines? Can they do it that quickly?"

"Our own farmers sold saplings to the Japanese importers. The Japanese companies then went to Mindanao over in the Philippines and planted cultivars. Due to some problems with their planting techniques and the soil and water, they still need about two or three growing seasons to catch up. They're only selling a small amount. The Vietnamese are also getting into the market. I heard it was one of our own people who went there and started a plantation."

"I've heard that banana exporters from South America have already made their way to Japan."

"I'd like to ask everyone's opinion here. If Mr. Wu Chen-jui were to receive bail and walk out of prison, if we plead with him to take charge of the banana trade once more with Japan, do you think he would return? Do you think he could turn it all around?"

"I think it's a definite possibility. Why do I make this judgment? Because the gigantic Japanese companies have a stranglehold on the market, and they aren't changing. And then there's the issue of those people—"

"I'd raise up both hands to vote if I could just to bail him out, but to put him back in the driver's seat of the industry? How would we explain that turnabout to the country? The papers are writing daily that he had exploited the banana farmers for ages, that he was absconding with all sorts of business profits and fleecing everyone. They're saying he had millions in savings. If we call the 'banana maggot' back to run the show, turning that show around would be difficult, almost impossible."

"And then there's the problem of the legal cases against him. If he's convicted, how could we possibly turn that all around?"[56]

---

56. There were twenty-five people from both the production and official worlds along with Ngôo Tsin-sui who had been implicated in the case. In June 1969, they were prosecuted by the Kaohsiung District Prosecutor's Office. They were charged with "Breach of trust, embezzlement, forgery of documents, and obstruction of the National Mobilization Act."

"Do none of you truly understand that none of the folks out in the fields believe that he's a 'banana maggot'? The Japanese businesses aren't buying what the press is spinning either. They still remember Wu with fondness. There's simply no easy means to pass by this little curve in the road."

"OK, that's fine for now. I've been thinking about something. I'll give my bureau chief some appropriate suggestions," Chiang Yen-shih said.

"We're in the middle of discussing how to deal with the remaining bananas. Is there someone in attendance from the Ministry of Defense?"

"Here's a report on the matter, Mr. Secretary. All the bananas have been sent to the troops, so there's no representative from the Ministry of Defense in attendance today."

"And the outlying islands?"

"They're loading the ships right now."

The meeting room went silent. Chiang Yen-shih piped up again, "Think, everyone! Let's see if there's anything else we can do. Let's get some thoughts going and mull them over."

***

Tsín-suí's second eldest son, Tîng-kong, woke up early to answer the telephone. The man on the other end of the line was a legislator by the name of Shao Hua. "Tîng-kong, I need you to come over to my residence. I have something I need to tell you in person. Come alone." He didn't leave any time for Tîng-kong to respond before hanging up.

Shao Hua and another legislator, Chou Mu-wen, were giving advice to Tîng-kong behind the scenes—they were like pieces of driftwood floating in the vast ocean that he could cling to. Tîng-kong hurried to reach the Shao household on Taipei's Linsen North Road. Chou Mu-wen arrived at around the same time and told him right as he saw him, "Your father's going to get out of prison very soon. Some top men have already ordered Minister Wang Jen-yuen at the Ministry of Justice to pull some strings and let your father go. Minister Wang told me to tell you this."

"Oh? That's excellent!"

"There's just one catch though. After Mr. Wu Chen-jui is released from prison, he has to pull some sway with the Japanese businesses he

In the court of first instance in August of that same year, twenty-three of the twenty-five were handed guilty verdicts. Ngôo Tsin-sui was sentenced to eight years imprisonment. When the case was appealed, the court of second instance handed down the same sentence.

was working with before. He needs them to come to Taipei to convene a meeting on banana sales."

"I'll go to the detention center right away. I'll tell him the news."

"Good. We won't keep you waiting. Be safe on your way."

Right as he was about to leave, he turned around and asked, "Who is the 'top man'? Is it President Chiang Kai-shek?"

"It's his son, Vice Premier Chiang Ching-kuo."

"Oh!!! I see!!!"

After Tsín-suī was handed a sentence by the court of first instance in Kaohsiung, he appealed to the district court in Tainan and had already been sent to the detention center there. His son, Tîng-kong, had set out early in the morning from Taipei but didn't arrive until well into the evening, though it was a relative breeze getting through the prison's security to see his father. All he could talk about with his father was the good news about the bail, but he hadn't even touched upon the conditions for bail yet when his father let out a sharp laugh, "A-ha!"

"Well done. I'll have to go back quickly and tell the others the good news."

"*A-Pa*, slow down. It's only a guarantee for your release, alone—"

"What!?" Tsín-suī's expression changed and he shouted out sharply, "Only one person can be let out? What's the sense in that?"

"*A-Pa*, listen carefully. It was a directive from Chiang Ching-kuo—"

"You've gone soft in the head! You're so selfish, you know! Honnh! Think about it for a second. I'm the leader of an entire company, and all of my subordinates are locked up in here with me. The core managers, my good friends. All of them are still locked up alongside me. Only I was given a guarantee of release? Would I ever be able to take advantage of something like that? How would I ever be able to live with myself if I left here alone without all of my men? How would I ever face them again?"

The guest meeting room was located right next to the warden's room. All of the people in the warden's office could hear every word that father and son were exchanging, and they walked over to check on things. Tsín-suī saw the warden standing at the door and switched to speaking in Mandarin, his voice growing louder and louder, "Go back to Taipei and tell them clearly. If they want me out, my whole team and association are to be set free. Only after the last of my men have been set free first will I decide to walk out."

Tsín-suī walked back towards his cell, calling out over his shoulder to his son. He'd already stepped over the threshold when he turned his head back. "Your *A-Pa* is going to teach you a valuable lesson. This is the most basic sense of justice that a man could ever hope to possess. Do you understand me?" he called out in such a stern voice.

Tîng-kong's face went dark as he watched the warden come up to him to ask some questions. "You said your father had a guaranteed bail to leave, but we haven't received any notice. What's that all about?"

"It's the truth. It's absolutely true. Minister Wang Jen-yuen gave me the information. You'll probably receive an official notice from Taipei in about a day or two," Tîng-kong said as he walked away.

As his father was in a rage just then, the image of a man had flashed before his eyes—Tông Tsuān-tsong. Long ago, people had told him that his father had the stubborn nature of a bull. Uncle Tsuān-tsong was one of the few people who just might be able to convince his father to change his mind.

Tîng-kong made a call first to Taipei, calling both Shao and Chou to relay what his father had said. They weren't angry, but Chou asked, "With your father reacting like that, it's going to be rough sailing ahead. Don't worry. Minister Wang will help us to smooth things over. Go home first, and tell your mother not to worry!"

Tîng-kong went back to Pingtung for the night and stayed at the family home. After dinner, he sat back in his father's favorite rattan chair. He thought about his father's intense words and fierce expression as he cursed—that "justice" of his. He looked up to see the massive placard hanging up on the rafter beam cutting through the center of the room. On it was written "Leader of the World of Fruit" in four Chinese characters, as well as four other carved characters to the side, "Kind and Benevolent Friend of Farmers" and "A Man Worthy of Profound Celebration" carved on smaller placards. There was one that made a play on his father's name: "Revitalizer (Tsín) of Banana Farmers – Benevolent (Sui) Worker." The shadow of his father was everywhere in this ordinary-looking farmhouse. For such a revered, larger-than-life figure, he always thought of himself as very small and without consequence.

The next day, Tîng-kong took his mother with him to pick up Tsuān-tsong. When she saw his father, Giok-ìn wasn't moved at all. All she could say was, "Everyone just wishes you would come out. Just come out, that's all." Then her tears started from her face.

Tsuān-tsong then said, "A-Suī-á, A-Tîng-kong already told me all about what you said. I truly respect your thoughts on this, but...your family... your sons...are all hoping you will come home soon..."

The warden walked over to them then and said, "Everyone, we've received an official notice that Mr. Wu Chen-jui may be given bail to receive medical treatment. Please come immediately and complete the paperwork."

Tsín-suĭ's expression was nothing but pained though. "A-Ìn-á, I haven't really thought of our family these last few years. I've been fortunate to have had you to take care of everything at home, watch over the fields, watch over our sons and daughters."

Tîng-kong's mother was thinking how to reply, but Tsuān-tsong spoke before she could begin speaking. "A-Suĭ-á, I think this is a sign. You're the master planner here. You need to lift your head up and walk out. When you do that, things will start moving again. All of your subordinates on the inside, all of your team—they're going to be released one by one, too."

Tsín-suĭ sat down in silence, pursing his lips.

"Come on. Let's go back home," Giok-ìn added.

"Tsuān-tsong-*hiann*, thank you for caring about me all these years and helping me to take care of my family, but what I want are my principles and my way of being a decent human being. I'm sorry, but you're going to be disappointed in me. All of my men who were forced to follow me here—if not a single one of them gets released first, then I will have to refuse to be let go at all." As the last of the words left his lips, he rose up and obstinately walked back towards his cell. He was already looking aged, like that old buffalo on the farm, trudging slowly, step by step, but with resolution, back to his cow pen.

Tsín-suĭ kept up like this for two and a half more months. The detention center formally started the procedures for his bailed release. First released was General Manager Tsai Kun-shan from the Kaohsiung Green Fruits Association, then Yang Hsi-chih, one of the department chiefs, next Luo Ch'ing-yuen and others. Only after they were all released, one by one, did Tsín-suĭ finally express that he was willing to be let out of prison.

29

The news of Tsín-suī's release from prison had traveled first from the Ngôo household in Thâu-tsîng-khe. His family read the newspaper the next day—the headline wasn't very large, but nonetheless, the entire banana farming world was already abuzz with the news. Hīng-tshun was the first to arrive at the Ngôo residence, then Tsuān-tsong and his wife, and others, all to accompany Giŏk-ìn. The flock of guests sat around drinking tea and chatting. The household's hired farmhand, A-Liōng, came rushing into the sitting room of the central hall to ask haltingly, "I'd like to bring along Masa so he can be there when the *thâu-ke* (boss) comes back home."

Giŏk-ìn hesitated for a bit and Hīng-tshun was the first to reply, "That sounds wonderful! A-Tsín-suī will be overjoyed when he sees Masa."

The telephone rang just in time. It was from Tîng-kong. He was calling to tell them that he had accompanied his father out of the detention center, and they had already set out on their way back home.

When Giŏk-ìn and the family friends had started to file their way out of the house, they found the entire courtyard of the family residence filled with people, with hardly an inch to move. A-Liōng's reaction was swift. He shouted out, "Make a pathway out! We're going to lead the buffalo out at the head of everyone to await the chairman. This buffalo is the like the crown jewel of the family. Chairman Ngôo will be so pleased as soon as he sees his animal."

The gathered crowd began to move away from the middle of the courtyard and sure enough, A-Liōng led the old bull out to the road leading to the home. His pace was slow and lumbering, and the crowd cheered him forward. "*Lāu-khok-khok.* It's so old and decrepit. It looks like it's definitely seen better days. Are you sure this buffalo is Chairman Ngôo's 'greatest treasure,' his pride and joy?"

"You've probably never heard, but Chairman Ngôo cares a lot for buffalo and oxen! Ever since he was a small child, he used to be just like old

Uncle A-Huàn who lived nearby. The old man knew all sorts of veterinary knowledge about oxen and buffalo, could speak with them, and was good friends with them."

"Take a look! You can see it in the bull's eyes! His eyes are lit up excitedly towards the Ko-Phing Bridge. It's as if he truly senses his master is about to appear at any moment and return home."

A-Liōng led the bull by the nose up at the front of the procession leading out of the courtyard gate. Giȯk-ìn, Hīng-tshun, Tsuān-tsong, and his wife were all waiting nervously behind Masa. The whole road was lined with farmers and villagers calling out greetings happily. All of them had sweated through their clothes by the time they reached the big intersection along the country road. Hīng-tshun waited behind, watching from afar. There were throngs of people who had come out! Before long, the hordes would completely clog up the pathways in and around the whole village.

People were crowded around everywhere now. The odor of musty sweat permeated the air. Hīng-tshun felt lucky that she had worn a long old skirt and cloth shoes. She wasn't afraid of them getting dirtied and dusty or creased.

It was already past ten o'clock now. The sun was climbing higher into the southern Taiwan sky, blazing away brightly. Everyone squinted in the bright sunlight, sweat pouring down. Hīng-tshun fished out a pair of sunglasses from a small hand purse, donning them. They were oval-shaped, the same kind that famous movie stars were wearing on the silver screens, very suitable to her figure, only adding to her beauty and glamor. She immediately became a scenic attraction in her own right. Not a few people started to whisper as soon as they saw her in the crowd. Whispers spread out, one by one. Just who exactly was this fashionable beauty who had come to see Ngôo Tsín-suī?

The crowds didn't have to wait much longer before a black sedan drew nearer, then came to a complete halt. The first person to step out was Tîng-kong and then his father. The crowds rushed forward to greet their beloved chairman, cheering, "*Ah! Aiyah!* He's so thin! He's too thin! He looks like he's still got some fight in him! What a relief!"

Tsín-suī had a smile on his face, though there was just a hint of shyness and awkwardness. The smile disappeared very quickly though, and he seemed to begin to weep. The moment Giȯk-ìn and Hīng-tshun went to take him by the arms, Tsuān-tsong and his wife called out from one side of the crowd, "A-Suī-á!" By then, Tsín-suī's mouth quivered and he began to cry.

Throngs of villagers and farmers had circled the small group. He quickly regained some control over his emotions, steadying himself to everyone's greetings and "welcome homes." He noticed that A-Liōng had lead Masa forth. They moved up closer, and he could perceive the emotions in his buffalo's eyes and gently stroked Masa along his face and cheeks. "Masa is so aged now. Is it a good idea to have brought him out?"

Just as Tsín-suī asked the question, someone set off a rope of firecrackers not far away, and the sound ricocheted like machine-gun fire, *rat-a-tat.* The buffalo was startled and was beginning to bolt away. Tsín-suī rushed to try to lay his frame over Masa's head and pressed down along Masa's neck. He spoke the entire time into the bull's ears, trying to sooth the beast of burden.

Masa was suddenly calmed down. He had already taken a couple steps forward, but his front legs were now tense and locked. He still had a lot of energy pent up within though and forcibly pushed Tsín-suī back two steps. A-Liōng, Giok-ìn, and Hīng-tshun had been standing right behind Tsín-suī just then and helped him brace against the brunt of Masa's "charge" so they'd been knocked to the ground. After Tsín-suī had calmed down Masa, with relaxed arms and unsteady footing, he also fell down between the two ladies.

The old buffalo couldn't seem to handle all this scene and all four of his legs went limp, with his legs buckling and him falling to the ground. Fear filled the eyes of this massive buffalo.

One bull and four people fortunately all escaped without anyone being injured. A-Liōng was the first to leap up. He then helped Tsín-suī brush the dust off his buttocks and shoulders. After Hīng-tshun put herself back in order, she had a slight smile to her face, amused by the whole affair. It was like she'd been jolted back to life by the whole event. Even before the dust had settled, Giok-ìn began yelling, "Stop setting off the firecrackers! Pass the message on down to the people in the back. Don't set any more of them off again!"

Hīng-tshun then called out in a booming voice, "Chairman Ngôo is back now! Everyone, just settle down. Don't shout!"

Their instructions were passed along to the back, "Stop setting off the firecrackers! Chairman Ngôo is back now! Everyone, just settle down and be cheerful in silence."

"Chairman Ngôo is back home safe now. Everyone, you can rest. Just settle down and be happy in peace and quiet."

The admonishment spread from the head to the end of the village. "Just settle down and be happy in peace and quiet" filled the air.

****

That evening, six "guests" from the Ministry of Justice's investigation department arrived at the Pingtung train station. They included Major Ho of the Southern Police Department of the Kaohsiung Police Headquarters; Captain Gu, the head of the Pingtung County Military Police Investigation Team; Lieutenant Lin, the senior staff officer of the Kaohsiung City Military Police Investigation Team; the director of the Kaohsiung Station of the Investigation Bureau; and the chief and deputy chief of the Pingtung County Police Department. After each one of them had arrived at the station, they headed straight into a meeting room to have a talk. The director and deputy director of the Pingtung branch of the Bureau of Investigation were already waiting for the newcomers.

All of them were already well acquainted with one another, but they cut the chitchat short and got right down to business. They didn't even bother with courtesies and introductions.

But it wasn't as if they were all solemn and poker-faced either. They vaguely acknowledged each other by exchanging glances, or faint smiles, or little nods by way of greeting. This was probably just the kind of personal relations that they were accustomed to in their professional lives. When they got to the conference table, they all sat down quickly according to an order that they seemed very familiar with. Police Superintendent Ho took the chairman's position. The director of the Pingtung Investigations Bureau sat beside him, and the others arrayed themselves on either side.

Without any opening remarks, Major Ho, who was acting as the meeting chairman, got straight to the point. "What? How could you not know that there would be such a crowd of people who would flock out to his residence to welcome him back?"

"We knew in advance that the mayor and several city council representatives would pay a visit and welcome him back. We just didn't realize that the people would swell to the point that they clogged up all the roadways or that they would set off firecrackers," the director of Pingtung branch answered.

"Who organized them? How did they go about doing it?"

"We investigated, but nobody had intentionally organized anything. His son, Ting-kuang, had phoned back home, but the information very quickly spread throughout the entire village and neighboring locales. The news reporters also caught wind of it very quickly. I saw the newspapers."

"What kind of people went out to welcome him?"

About half the villagers from T'ao-ching-hsi. The local police dispatch station sent out a notice saying that they only saw familiar faces—they immediately recognized that they were banana farmers from the Pingtung countryside and the area of Ch'i-shan.

"So you didn't notice anyone particularly suspicious, did you?"

"No, we had our own people in the crowd. The police station sent out an officer to help. However, later on, there were a couple younger folks who pushed their way in—"

"Wait—were there any students?"

"Yes, they were all students. About ten of them. Our plainclothes officers went up and made inquiries. They were all the children of banana farmers. Their families all see Wu as a benefactor."

"Hmm! You need to pay particular attention to this. Be careful that it doesn't turn into a student movement. Do you know which universities they attend? Is there a way to get ahold of their names?"

"They're all still senior high school students. They bicycled all the way here from Kaohsiung. But they're still residents of Pingtung. They were all wearing their school uniforms."

"That'll be easy to take care of. Their names and student numbers are all sewn into their school uniforms."

"Unfortunately, our unit members forgot to write down their identities. However, the report says that they all came out of pure intentions. They had all sorts of reference books and stuff strapped down to the backs of their bicycles. They're all busy preparing for their university entrance exams."

"Of course they did. We'll have to remember to keep a look out for them."

"What was the atmosphere like at the scene?"

"It was lively, but everything progressed peacefully. The group was later in front of the Wu residence courtyard. All of them were milling about chitchatting."

"Were they cursing the government?"

"Not directly, no. In their own words, part of the farmers are doubtful about the 'farmer exploitation case' and they believe Wu Chen-jui has been framed. Many more were reminiscing about how the price of bananas had been so great and how their lives had been improved so much by their chairman."

"Our dispatch station's policemen heard a discussion between one or two groups of people. They said that it was a 'faction struggle in the palace' that had ensnared Wu. All of the banana farmers would follow him to their deaths, it seems."

"That has to be bullshit! What else of note was there?"

"Well, there was a small incident. It nearly blew up into a disaster. The Wu family had brought out the family buffalo. They had led it to the front of the crowd in the middle of the village as they waited for Wu to arrive. Wu walked straight to the old bull as soon as he stepped out of the car and kept patting its head and stroking its face. The old bull lowered its head and kept shaking its horns from side to side, calling and bellowing out in a low voice, *oo-oo-hoo-hoo*. But right then, someone started to set off fireworks and the old bull was startled and tried to run away, nearly trampling on people in front of it. Our agent was there and was sweating bullets. If the bull managed to run away in a rampage, it might have struck or gored a few people to death. Before anyone knew it, Wu and his family all stopped the bull by standing in front of it or holding it back by the neck. Wu seemed to be talking with it, and the bull just quieted down. After that, their field hand came forward to help—"

"OK, whatever. This doesn't have anything to do with our task at hand. Was there any sort of 'It seems slow when I describe it, but it happened so quickly...'? Was there any recitation of stories or chant-fables, that sort of thing?"

There were a few snickers as Major Ho let the words leave his mouth, but they were only scattered. The others mostly just grinned along at the ridiculousness of it.

"Is it just an ordinary farmer's buffalo?"

"Yes. It's just an ordinary Taiwanese water buffalo."

"There was also a minor incident that was reported in Kaohsiung. It came from one of our informants. After Wu left the detention center in Tainan, his son accompanied him to buy a pair of leather shoes from a shop not too far from the Kaohsiung train station. The store owner recognized Wu immediately and shouted, 'Oh! It's Chairman Ngôo! I'm honored to be able to do some business with you today! Just pick out any pair you'd like, and they're on the house, free of charge.' Wu Ting-kuang couldn't just take the shoes for free, so he kept pushing the shop owner to take some payment and they settled on half-price."

"Oh, I see. Anything else?"

The meeting room grew very quiet. Police Major Ho then stood up. "Well then, I guess today's meeting will conclude here. Everyone, keep doing your best. I have to return to the station to write a summary report for my superior. Thank you, everyone."

After the meeting dispersed, Major Ho walked to the doorway, looked back, then raised one more thing, "As for the newspapers and radio stations, please get the county and city police departments to take care of the public relations. Don't let the news get out of hand."

"Oh. Don't worry about that. They'll do it on their own accord now. It wouldn't look good on the government otherwise. They'll proactively—"

"Maybe we ought to pay them a visit just to give them a friendly reminder..."[57]

---

57. When Ngôo Tsín-suī was released from prison, the 228 massacre had happened over twenty years earlier. Large-scale popular movements like the Chiao-tou protest, the Chungli Incident, and Tangwai Movement, that arose successively were still seven or eight years away. Thus, for the huge intelligence and governance system of the Republic of China, this was an "idle period," where there were almost no cases to prosecute and it was easy to make trouble out of nothing.

30

The following day, the former general director of the Kaohsiung Green Fruits Export Cooperative Association, its director, and vice manager had gathered at the house of Ngôo Tsín-suí in the small village of Thâu-tsîng-khe on the outskirts of Pîn-tong City. The guests brought a gigantic wok piled to the brim with soy-braised pork knuckles and vermicelli noodles. Some of the guests naturally brought up the subject of the former manager, Lee T'u-chen. Tsín-suí knew he was the first of the twenty-five of him and his men to have been released on medical leave. The second year after he had been released from prison, he had died a bitter man. But he hadn't known about the cruel fate that had befallen the Lee family. "When Manager Lee was in the clink, his oldest son, Lee Yuen-chi, had tried in vain, traveling between the south and Taipei, to get his father out, and unfortunately met his end in a car accident. It was another gigantic blow to Manager Lee."

Tsín-suí couldn't keep eating and put his bowl and chopsticks down. His face turned pallid, and he lowered his gaze, chin tucking in, and he gripped his chest. It looked as if he was severely ill and something bad was about to happen.

"Mr. Chairman, are you feeling well?"

"Are you well, Mr. Chairman?"

"It's nothing. Don't worry. I'm just feeling uneasy in my mind. It just hurts a little in my chest," Tsín-suí replied.

The whole group lost their appetite. One of the older directors, Tân Tik-hù, began in a soft voice, "Mr. Chairman,...were you tortured when you were imprisoned?"

Tsín-suí was silent for a moment, then said, "Mentally and emotionally, yes. It's much more horrendous than physical torture."

Tân Tik-hù then turned to Ngôo Tîng-kong, "You ought to go find a good hospital to do a full body checkup on your father. The kind you can stay in overnight. You really should."

"Yes! I certainly will."

Tsín-suī then added, "Since I'm out on medical release, the court has ordered me to go to a hospital, so even if I'm not sick, I ought to be admitted."

Tîng-kong helped his father to arrange a full-body checkup at Hong-En Hospital up north in Taipei, but it would be a full week before they would get the results back. They didn't lack for visitors, either. Representatives for banana farmers from all over had come up to pay their respects and wish him well, one after another. The Ngôo family was awfully busy.

The second day that Tsín-suī had been admitted to Hong-En, his two appointed lawyers showed up. They were there to deliver Tsín-suī a summons from the high court. Tsai Sung, one of the two suits, had told Tsín-suī, "The day you were released, there were too many people there to greet you at your home. And they set off too many firecrackers. This is definitely going to cause you more headaches."

"But I didn't tell those people to come out and meet with me. How could there be anything against me at this point?"

"I'm not so certain why myself, to be honest."

"You can do whatever you please, but if you're back in prison, there's nothing we can do!"

The day Tsín-suī was discharged from the hospital, Hīng-tshun had come by to him pick up, and they ran into Tsuān-tsong and his wife, who had come to pay a visit too. The four old friends made some quick pleasantries and settled on going to a nearby restaurant. As they were leaving the hospital, they left the discharge procedures and payment to Tsín-suī's son, Tîng-kong.

As they walked towards the main doors of the hospital, they saw Chang Chin-luo waiting by the doorway. Tsín-suī shyly made a polite greeting. "I've been sent to collect Chairman Ngôo. I'm here to treat him to a nice banquet," Chang said. The four friends hesitated at first, but Tsín-suī decided to not refuse him.

After all of them had settled into the car, Chang couldn't wait to explain things, speaking in Hoklo-accented Chinese, "Chairman Wu, even though I've helped the intelligence bureau with some of their affairs, I've never harmed anyone. I've never done anything to hurt you."

Tsín-suī hadn't even opened his mouth to respond yet, and Chang kept firing off, "I'm afraid you're going to misunderstand me."

"You've gone through an awful lot of effort just to pick up Wu Chen-jui here. What other special assignment are you up to?" Hīng-tshun said in perfect Mandarin.

"Oh," Chang responded in a sigh, hesitating to respond. But the car had just arrived at the front doors to a restaurant. He seized his chance to evade the question by getting out of the car first and then took care of arranging a table for five.

After the group had sat down, course after course of dishes had come to the table in a continuous stream. There was a bottle of imported whiskey placed at the center of the table. Chang Chin-luo seemed to have forgotten the question that Hīng-tshun had asked as they arrived at the restaurant. Excitedly, he turned towards Tsuān-tsong, eagerly trying to chat.

Tsín-suī and Hīng-tshun gave each other looks, and he mouthed a sentence to her, "It doesn't matter! Right now, it doesn't matter. They can't do anything anymore!"

At that second, Chang Chin-luo's ears seemed to have picked up on Tsín-suī's words, as if stumbling upon a great secret. Right then, he wheeled around and called out in a booming voice, "Oh, what's this? It looks our honorable couple have made a trip north to visit Chen Cheng's grave!"

"What's so strange about it? It's been several years. We've all come up here."

"The man's already been long buried in the ground. He's no longer with us. What's the benefit of you visiting?" Chang snipped back.

Chang then strove hard to think, then replied, "Ah! Now I see. Chen Cheng's eldest prince son looks as if he still has a future with the government."

Tsín-suī, his face having grown stern, replied, "*Honnh*! Look at you! Looking about everywhere, searching only for what benefits you can squeeze out of everyone, yeah?"

Chang rushed to explain, "It's not necessarily like that—"

"People need to know what grace is! When Chen Cheng was alive, he helped our Tông Îng with a big favor." The look on Tsuān-tsong's face was not one of amusement.

Hīng-tshun spoke out to try to calm things down, "Tsuān-tsong-*hiann*, you all used Taiwanese food to make your offerings, no?"

"Ah, yes, we did. It was a Taiwanese offering. What other kind of offering was I to make?"

"Oh! Well, that's very good. Chen Cheng's been getting his fill of his native Jiang-zhe cuisine at his graveside. If you're sending your Taiwanese goods, I guess it's fine to give him something different."

"Haha!"

"Ha! Even more, you've brought a bit of Penghu flavor with you, as well."

"After a good official is laid to rest, he still has offerings made to him," Tsín-suī remarked, as if giving the closing statement.

"He wasn't necessarily a good official, *lah*. He was a powerless official. Worthless and now accepting of any offerings, sure. When he was in power, when he was still with us, he had his fill of bronze, and iron, and silver."

Hīng-tshun turned to face Chang. "Mr. Chang, are you going to report my words I've said here today to the Investigation Bureau?"

"No, no, no. As I said, I won't harm anyone."

"Well, good then. So you still haven't told us why you showed up out of nowhere. What new mission exactly did the Investigation Bureau hand off to you?"

"I came out of my own interest, Ms. Chen." Chang picked up a whiskey tumbler in both hands and made towards Tsín-suī with a slight nod and a tip of his glass, beginning to toast him. "I'd like to ask you, Mr. Chairman, do you believe there's still a chance to sell Taiwanese bananas in the Japanese market?"

Tsín-suī somewhat absentmindedly picked up a tumbler from the table and had only wet his lips a little, but when he heard Chang's words, his eyes lit up, and he immediately shrank back, replying, "I'm not sure if you're aware, but I haven't been in the business for the past three years. I'm afraid it's no longer the same anymore. That market…(sigh), I had tried my hardest for twenty years to cultivate it, trying my best to tie up all the knots to make a strong, impervious kind of net. I think that this net has already been destroyed at this point by others, and the farmers in the Philippines and in South America have already taken over what's left of what we used to have."

"There's also Vietnamese bananas," Chang replied.

"How did you find out about that?" Hīng-tshun asked.

"I went there myself to set up a plantation."

"And how many hectares is the land?" Tsín-suī asked, clearly intrigued.

"Right now, it's only just over twenty *kah*. I've come here today to ask you to reconsider your retirement and to help me open up the Japanese market. I hope to expand my plantation to three hundred *kah*." Chang switched over to speaking with Tsín-suī in Taiwanese from Mandarin.

"You're asking me to destroy the net I made?"

"Don't think of it like that. If you come out, then you can use your connections to set things up. In helping me, I can help you in return. What do you say?"

All of them went silent. Chang then spoke again, "I've heard it all very clearly. Those Japanese businessmen were indignant about the treatment you received. If you'd like to make a name for yourself once more, I would be more than happy to help you, to help you retaliate...to show the government the error of its ways."

Tsín-suī poured himself a glass of whiskey, filling the tumbler up to the very rim. He threw it all back in one gulp and then fixed both eyes calmly on the tumbler. Chang then diligently refilled the tumbler, but Tsín-suī made no reaction. There was no expression on his face. He didn't even bother to look back at Chang. Hīng-tshun and Tsuān-tsong watched the whole scene, sensing that he was filled with pure disdain and anger towards Chang. Chang filled his own tumbler and then pressed on, "Chairman Ngôo, if you would be willing to help me—if I sell my bananas on that three-hun-dred–*kah* plantation to Japan, then you could become the Banana King of Vietnam. I have all the faith in the world that you could do so."

What power and chutzpah were contained in those words! Everyone at the table saw the skill of Chang's direct attack. Tsín-suī remained stoic and silent as a mountain. He stared at the ice cubes slowly thawing away in his tumbler of whiskey. He just kept staring. Chang saw there was no expression or response in Tsín-suī's face. He imagined himself plunging the legendary sword of the Yellow Emperor straight into the depths of Tsín-suī's heart. Yet he pressed on with his blandishments, "Chairman Ngôo, in Taiwan, those terrible Chinese officials are mocking you, abusing you. They framed you. They oppressed you. This is an opportunity for you. You can show them what for. This can be your revenge, your enmity."

As Chang said the words, "They are mocking you, abusing you. They framed you. They oppressed you," Tsín-suī's face changed. Both his lips quivered violently, but after just four or five seconds, he regained control. He held the glass and then downed all his whiskey once more. After he drank he mocked himself, "When I was in the cage for those two plus years, I never touched alcohol, so—"

But Hīng-tshun cut him off and asked Chang, "Haven't you always been a runner for the National Police and the Investigation Bureau? A 'faithful Party member'? How could you possibly be asking such a thing?"

"That was then and this is now," he retorted.

Tsuān-tsong was sitting next to Tsín-suī and moved closer, almost whispering into his ear, "A-Suī-á, you need to think about this clearly. This is a road to attacking Taiwan's banana industry by using Vietnam's."

"I know," Tsín-suī replied, moving to pour himself another glass of whiskey.

Right now, scenes from the movies of Miyamoto Musashi, the famed two-sword–wielding Japanese warrior that he had seen so many times, floated into his mind. It was the final scene of the movie, the two expert swordsmen, Musashi and Sasaki Kojirō, were facing off against one another. On the left, ocean waves were crashing onto the shore, to the right, tall mountain peaks rose. There was no wind. The sky and everything in it were calm. The swordsmen dug the soles of their feet deep into the sand, and they glared at each other, all their concentration being prepared for the perfect moment to unleash their blades.

Tsín-suī's eyes moved from the whiskey tumbler to Chang's face, and he stared hard into Chang's eyes. He then heard Chang say, "I'll give everyone here a guarantee. If Chairman Ngôo gives his assent, then I'll help him to settle that prosecution matter privately."

"How are you going to settle it? Are you going to have him judged innocent?" Hīng-tshun rushed to ask.

"That wouldn't be possible. However, I can adjust the sentencing period with the supreme court. I can make it so that Chairman Ngôo's sentence has been fully served. So Chairman Ngôo wouldn't have to be returned to prison again. He could immediately go to Japan and serve as my company's general manager." Chang took a long sip from his glass, staring back at Tsín-suī.

Then he said something that he knew would shake everyone at the table, "The way I see it, if Chairman Ngôo is locked up again even for a day, just a single day, that would be upsetting the natural order of everything."

Tsín-suī remained motionless. He just sat where he was, coldly staring back at Chang. The two of them made eye contact briefly, then Chang added, "Chairman Ngôo, I've already considered this entire business from every single aspect and angle imaginable. Everything would be settled and right in heaven and on earth and in men's hearts. Everything would be secure."

Tsín-suī pushed aside the whiskey tumbler, seeming to search for a moment of weakness in the master swordsman's defense in order to strike, "A-Loo-*hiann*, you could calculate it a thousand or ten thousand times, but you're forgetting something."

"And what's that?"

"In the decade or two that I've rushed around every which way, the more I rushed, the stronger my spirit grew. And the reason for that, in my eyes and in my heart, has only ever been the banana plantations of Taiwan—every acre, every hectare of them—also the banana farmers and all those bamboo workers who made baskets. I always thought about them. I always thought of them, seeing their faces. No matter which plantation or small field I went to, or to whichever harvesting collection point, even youngsters forced by their parents to toil, all of them called me 'Chairman Ngôo' with a smile on their faces and in their eyes. The elderly—they took my hands and shook them and called me 'A-Suí-á,' in endearment." As Tsín-suī reached this point, both his lips began to violently shake. He didn't know whether it was the alcohol or whether he wished to cry, but he forced himself to keep going, "It was them. It was always for them. I have put the entirety of my life and spirit on the line for them. And so, A-Loo-*hiann*, I'll tell you something. If you wish for me to switch over to some Vietnamese plantation that you own, and for those farmers, then I'm sorry to disappoint you but that's where your dream will die, and this is where we see differently."

"A matter of emotions. Time will tell if that's truly how you feel," Chang immediately shot back.

Hīng-tshun wanted to give him a piece of her mind right then, but Tsín-suī leaned over to Tsuān-tsong and yelled, "My head is spinning!"

Tsuān-tsong immediately lifted him up by the armpits, helping him to lean back in the chair as he fainted. Tsuān-tsong knew what Tsín-suī's drinking limits were since their days of youth about the town. He knew that those glasses weren't enough to actually make him drunk, but he saw that both of Tsín-suī's lips were forming an upward crescent as they spasmed. Tsuān-tsong also felt like weeping. The emotions of A-Suí-á's entire lifetime were expressed in the words he just spoke.

He heard Chang turn towards Hīng-tshun, enquiring about the banana trade in Japan. "A-Suí-á is drunk. I think we're done here today. I'm going to take him back to rest, *honnh*," Tsuān-tsong said.

After this incident, Tsín-suī remained in Taipei for a while and then finally returned to Pingtung. Giok-ìn was at home the whole time. Sometimes, she went off to the nearby Buddhist temple to meditate.

***

Several months had passed and one afternoon, when the sun hung large in the sky, the postman delivered a registered letter. Giok-ìn took it in her hands. It was a letter from the court. She couldn't stop herself from tearing open the edge. She ripped it open and took a quick look then called out to her husband over by the cow pen. "The final judgment has arrived in the post. Two and a half years."

Tsín-suī hurriedly rushed out. Their field hand, A-Liōng, was following close behind, wanting to take a closer look. Both husband and wife had their heads down calculating, "So how many days had you already been detained for? More than eight hundred, right?"

"I counted eight hundred and thirty-three."

"They handed down a sentence of two and a half years. How many days is that? A-Liōng, quick, go grab an abacus from inside!"

By the time A-Liōng brought the abacus, husband and wife had already figured it out. Tsín-suī would have to return behind bars for another ninety days.

Giȯk-ìn's hair had already gone white years ago. Her spine was already going crooked. She made a deep sigh full of lament. She then muttered a few phrases of Buddhist scripture as she walked into the house. Tsín-suī just took a couple steps over to under the awning eaves. The blazing sun was casting a shadow that fluctuated every now and then. A-Liōng moved a couple steps towards Tsín-suī and then asked him a question he hadn't yet gotten around to asking over by the paddock, "Do you want me to deal with Masa, boss?"

"Wait for me to come back, and then I'll see."

"Do you think he'll last that long?"

"I think so."

31

Very early that morning, Tsín-suī woke up from a deep slumber. His eyes were dry and his head felt foggy. He first lifted his head off his pillow to listen for a second. There were birds chirping and the sound of motorbikes. He could now say for sure that he was home in Thâu-tsîng-khe and not a prison cell. He slowly rose up from his bed. His wife wasn't at his side at this hour. She had probably gone to the Buddhist temple down the road for a morning dharma lesson. It was all quiet around the room. He slipped on a pair of sandals and walked outside. All he saw was his farmhand, A-Liōng, taking care of some things to do with the rice stalks.

"Where did my wife go off to?" he asked A-Liōng.

"Oh! She went out early to the temple."

"How early?"

"She got up and went out at about four this morning."

"She often stays the night at that Buddhist temple?"

"Yep, that's right. Since the whole thing with the Green Fruits Export Cooperative Association, bad news kept coming in all the time. Your wife said that the news articles were like sharp knife edges slicing at her insides. Every day it was a new cut. Fortunately, a monk let her go there whenever she wanted to for some solace and solitude."

"Oh! I see."

Pain began to creep into Tsín-suī's chest. He didn't do his usual calisthenics exercises but turned to go back in. His sons and daughters already had families and built lives for themselves, scattering off to far corners of the globe, one to America, one to Japan, one to Australia. Someday, Giok-ìn wouldn't be there anymore, and the house would feel even emptier than before. It was so quiet sometimes that someone could easily start to panic. Tsín-suī combed at his hair and washed his face, then called out to A-Liōng, giving him an order, "I don't have anything to do today. I want to take Masa out into the field for a bit of exercise."

"Boss, I think you know, Masa here is already very old. He can't do a lot of heavy work anymore."

"Don't worry. I'm just going to try to get him moving along is all." Tsín-suī then added nostalgically, "This buffalo's been around for so long, he's probably broken a world record."

"We have a banana farm that needs to be reestablished. Your nephew, Ngôo Sè-hiông, is going to come over with his 'iron ox' (tractor) this afternoon to do the work. An iron ox can make quick work of everything."

"Ngôo Sè-hiông...didn't he open up a small hotel in Tokyo?"

"The one over in Tokyo is his younger brother, Sè-tiat. Sè-hiông is his older brother. He's stayed here to grow bananas."

"Oh! Is that so?"

Several minutes later, Tsín-suī led Masa towards the banana field. A-Liōng had heaved a yoke up onto his shoulder and was holding a plowshare. The plow blade was facing downward, and he held a pair of reins in his other hand. He followed behind Tsín-suī. Tsín-suī and Masa, the man was too famous and the buffalo too old. Together they drew a lot of attention. "*Ai-yo*! What has Chairman Ngôo come back to do today? This buffalo can't do anything anymore!" A throng of neighbors and passersby came up to Tsín-suī along the road to the field.

He politely called out to them, master and worker endlessly trying to explain, "We're just going out to the field to see what he can do. We're just going out to have some fun!"

After the neighbors had finished peppering him with questions, they started to go their own ways, though some stayed with Tsín-suī, A-Liōng, and Masa, chatting for a while before heading their own separate ways too.

When they reached the banana field, Masa's old habits kicked in. Of his own accord, he went and stood at the edge of embankment where they would start to plow. Tsín-suī took the plow that A-Liōng handed him. He then put the yoke on Masa himself and attached the reins. He could sense Masa's spirits suddenly rising. Excitement and vigor were shining from the buffalo's eyes. The old animal seemed to be like an old soldier returning to an old battlefield, eager to get back into the thick of it. Tsín-suī felt much the same. It had already been more than twenty years since he had last touched a plow. Now, though, he was gripping the reins in his left hand and holding onto the plow with his right, giving it his best effort. Fortunately, he could hold the plow and could still apply pressure to it.

In a moment, he gave his ox driver's call and the buffalo began to move. The working of the plow all rested in his right hand, so he gripped tightly on the handle and pressed down hard, keeping the plow moving straight ahead. How deeply he wished to cut the furrow depended on how much strength he could put into the plowshare. Whether his furrows were straight or uneven also came down to him steering with his right hand. Twenty years ago, he was one of the best tillers in the area. Probably the only person in the area who could have done a better job than he did was old A-Tsòng, who had already long passed on. This little farming village of Thâu-tsîng-khe. Hah! You couldn't even call it a village anymore. Little Thâu-tsîng-khe was now a proper town with a street lined with shops, bustling and alive.

A single "*Yewwww*" came forth from Tsín-suī's throat. There was some phlegm in the old man's voice. Masa heard him and began his march. Tsín-suī could sense that the strength in his own right arm wasn't as it used to be. He could only make shallow furrows, too shallow to make the grade. He went on plowing the shallow furrow for about twenty meters and then noticed that Masa was straining to breathe, and he was having difficulty raising his feet. If they kept going, Masa would surely be too tired to continue, so Tsín-suī called out in a rising "*Uaaaaaa!*"

Masa stopped and stood still. "We can't do this. We can't abuse Masa like this!" Tsín-suī muttered to himself.

He walked up to Masa's shoulders and stretched out an arm to unlatch the harness and yoke, but Masa suddenly raised his head and made a two-syllabled *woo-hong*, in protest. He was trying to tell Tsín-suī, "I still want to pull the plow. I don't want to rest."

Tsín-suī could understand him, so talked aloud to himself, "Fine, have it your way. You're so stubborn. It isn't that I deliberately want to abuse you."

Then he returned behind the plow, gripped the handle, then shook the reins and shouted another yewww command. Masa struggled to push forward once more. This time, there was much more force behind Masa's pace. Tsín-suī worried that Masa was straining too much, so he slackened the reins and lightly drove the plowshare forward, not wanting to cut too deep a furrow. Masa seemed to have sensed his owner intentionally lightening the pull of the reins and the depth of the blade behind him, and once more called out woo-hong in protest, then he began to speed up.

"Haha! Well, now you're just showing off, aren't you, you old ox." Tsín-suī seemed to be over the moon with his old buffalo breaking the earth as if he were young again. He lifted his head and gazed off in the distance at the faraway Mount Tāi-bú, stout and towering above all else around. He lifted his gaze even higher and saw the sky, all one stretch of azure canvas. The scent of the earth and mud, mixed with the verdant grass, was an old, familiar smell flooding his nostrils. All the cells and tiny hairs on his body stood up, his senses being bombarded by the nature all around him. "Haha! I haven't been down in a field in over twenty years and now that I'm back in the dirt, it feels wonderful. I'm feeling completely elated and in my element," he mused idly.

These last few years, he was framed and had harbored much anger over having been forced into prison, and now he finally felt some of the pain crumbling away after all this time.

He was feeling elated and self-satisfied, when A-Liōng came up to bring him back down to earth. "Boss! Masa's too tired! He can't keep going."

Tsín-suī caught a glimpse of Masa, and immediately raised his wrists and called out, "*Uaaaaa!*" The buffalo stopped in his tracks. His nostrils were visibly heaving deeply and all too rapidly. Masa's entire frame was nearly trembling. Tsín-suī felt a deep pain within him and then went forward to take the yoke and harness off, but the buffalo once more raised his head, refused to concede to Tsín-suī. "*Ai-ya*! You big dummy! You've been toiling away for this family for your entire life. That's enough," Tsín-suī spoke as he walked closer to his buffalo. He lightly massaged Masa's head, starting from the base of his horns, then he flicked both Masa's ears thrice. Then Tsín-suī used the palms of his hands to lightly lift the yoke off. Masa obeyed this time and lowered his head, allowing A-Liōng to grab the yoke and harness from Tsín-suī.

Unexpectedly, as soon as the yoke was lifted away, the buffalo bent its front legs as if making a bow to someone. Then, as if dejected, Masa laid down completely, his nostrils expelling great blasts of air. Tsín-suī moved closer to Masa until he was practically standing over his buffalo. This small mountain suddenly crumbled over though, and Tsín-suī was unable to jump back in time. Half his body was now caught underneath Masa.

A-Liōng looked back with fright, but there wasn't anything he could do. He just kept asking Tsín-suī, "Boss, are you hurt? Are you OK?" stretching out both his arms, wanting to pull his boss out from under the buffalo, but then he thought better of Tsín-suī's age and realized that he might accidentally dislocate Tsín-suī's shoulders if he tried to drag him out from under Masa. How could he try to move the bull? A-Liōng thought for a bit, then told his boss, "Boss, just hold still for a while. I'm going to go run over to the neighbors and see if there's anyone who can give a hand and help lift Masa off of you."

"There's no need! A buffalo's stomach is quite soft. I'm able to pull my own legs out from underneath," Tsín-suī called back. "I just need to wait for Masa's breathing to stabilize and then I can do it,"

At this, he sat back and relaxed a bit, laying down for a rest. After a while, he massaged Masa's spine as if he were a masseuse, searching on both sides for any acupuncture points. He kept searching and kept pressing. Then he lightly whispered a command into Masa's ear, "Masa, I need you to use some strength in your front and rear right legs and straighten up. Lift yourself up slowly. Got it? OK, go!"

The old buffalo did as his owner commanded and slowly lifted himself up, but he could only lift himself up about half an inch. The lower half of Tsín-suī's body was set free, and he lightly shrank his feet into his chest, sitting up, pulling himself out from under Masa's weight.

When Masa sensed that his owner had made his escape, he stretched his legs and neck and raised his head like a child in the morning who still wanted to laze about in bed. He strained to flip himself over to stand up, but he was the image of powerless languidness. Tsín-suī went up once more, moved close to Masa, lightly massaging his horns and pinching his ears. He went again down along the buffalo's neck, petting Masa. Tsín-suī was mumbling to himself as he went along. A-Liōng couldn't hear what the boss was saying.

After this scene ended, A-Liōng took a deep breath and said something to flatter his boss, "Boss, I just thought of something. I heard you had once studied martial arts under Uncle A-Huàn."

"Now you know! I'm the only inheritor in the world of Uncle A-Huàn's knowledge."

"Well, that's certain. It's absolutely true. Everyone's said as much."

Just then, a string of *putt-putt* noises could be heard in the distance. They grew louder and louder. It was a tractor-cultivator that people called an "iron ox" moving along the road, drowning out their words.

TRANSLATOR'S NOTES

Banana King Ngôo Tsín-suī is the first work I've ever translated from Taiwanese Hoklo as were, to a lesser extent, the few Hakka and Japanese sentences or phrases that pepper the text here and there. I was initially approached about translating the novel during a major transition in my life in Taiwan, and I often went to a café after working hard at my day job to work on the first draft. What made the project worth taking on was that it felt like an honor, and I feel happy to have helped shed light on one of the lesser-known sagas of Taiwan's modern history and development during the martial-law era—and on a handful of unsung heroes.

Prior to reading the original work and parts of a background book about the Golden Bowl Affair, I had no idea who Ngôo Tsín-suī was. I am not alone in this experience. Hardly any Taiwanese people I've talked with—even those from Pingtung City—have any idea about him or his contributions to southern Taiwan and agriculture. I gave some thought to whether they're hesitant to speak about him (or the era in general) out of a sense of just wanting to forget the past and leave the pain of martial law behind or whether it's too ingrained into modern politics and seems taboo. At times, I've wondered whether it's just a matter of national history curriculums in Taiwan not going far enough in discussing the corruption of the martial law era or having people study their local history. At other times, I figured it could be boiled down to people not having any interest in history and just needing to deal with daily life.

Having a strong sense of justice, this book made my blood boil at certain parts and left me in a depressed stupor at others. Each time I sat down to write one more word, sentence, or paragraph, I felt as if I were on a mission to help vindicate these characters and give some voice to an era left behind. Writing about trauma, torture, and struggle is not easy, and researching the background stories of some of the victims and characters named in this novel was sometimes an eye-opening experience. Tsín-suī's friend, Ia̍p Tshiu-bok, in particular, was treated slightly better in the book than in real life, just looking back at some available records. (There is one gruesome corporal punishment that was left out, perhaps intentionally—he was basically castrated by knife in addition to having his nose and ears cut off and publicly executed by firing squad.)

Some of the background knowledge from researching real characters was a burden that couldn't be put to the page, yet something I used when it came to word choices in some areas. Translators sometimes have to jump into the author's mind, when reading through a text, and try to explore the author's psyche, not just the characters', through reading the original work. Then they attempt to replicate that in another language—not an easy feat and certainly thought-provoking, given the topic and heavy atmosphere in this novel. Being that the author was originally a journalist, I can imagine he went through many articles with a heavy heart when he was drafting his manuscript.

Character and place names, resources, and language approach

Being a translator of Taiwanese literature, I'm a firm believer in the importance of retaining and promoting as many aspects of Taiwan's culture as possible through linguistic variance, rather than using direct translation, or without culturally significant terminology that sets the work apart from something that could have been first written in English. Ironically, translations are not supposed to sound like, well... translations. Some might call it time wasted to invest so much in keeping Hoklo and Hakka a part of the translated result, but I consider it critical to understanding Taiwan's undercurrent of diverse cultures and history, after the nation has survived multiple colonial powers that forced their own cultures upon the land and its peoples, and where language helps to consolidate an identity.

When it came to character and place names, spelling conventions, and other tidbits, my aim from the outset was to use the most localized, natural naming scheme that I could—ones that these characters would have used themselves at the time. I changed character names depending on the origins of those speaking, following along with the timeline or based on the social situation (company meeting versus family life at home or when with friends). Doing so seemed better than forcing Mandarin names onto everything, which in some (ironic) sense would have been a reflection of the experience under the Kuomintang (KMT) party-state's language policy of the time. If the person was born and raised in Taiwan during the Japanese colonial era or earlier, I gave them either a Hoklo name or a Hakka name (some characters' identities were explicitly mentioned), as that would ostensibly be how they were addressed by family and peers. As for Japanese words and names, they are ones that I've found or put together through online searches or could reasonably be guessed or finagled with by searching dictionaries such as weblio.jp or jisho.org. Names can be notoriously difficult in Japanese-English translations, and this aspect added another puzzle while translating.

I also wanted to approach naming in a chronological way, following the real-world timeline by using the contemporary names to parallel real events, cultural and political changes, discrimination or trouble that characters faced due to their language use, and attitudes from different social circles.

For Chinese émigrés who migrated or fled from China to Taiwan between 1945 and 1949, I used Mandarin Chinese names to distinguish them from Taiwanese born during the Japanese colonial era or earlier, written using the Wade-Giles system or a modified version. Using Wade-Giles was a quick fix in situations where a real character was not a well-known historical figure or someone whose name may not have been anglicized. I also chose this transcription strategy to make it easier on the reader to pronounce names. This is also a work about Taiwan and Taiwanese, originally organized by a Taiwanese publisher and funded by a Taiwanese entity; to use China's Mandarin romanization system (Hanyu Pinyin) for names would have been downright inappropriate. It would have felt like a slap in the face, in light of the topics and themes brought up throughout the novel.

Using Hoklo and Hakka names was easier to incorporate in the earlier chapters, as Mandarin Chinese was virtually nonexistent as a language used in Taiwan until after 1945 when Nationalist (KMT) rule brought forced Mandarin-only education. Pre-1895 (before Taiwan was ceded to Japan), Mandarin was used in a very limited context, further limited to reading and writing in Classical Chinese (not the same as vernacular Mandarin), by exam-takers who were studying to become officials for the Qing Dynasty in China, where they would have been posted if they passed their exams. They would not have been allowed to serve in a posting in Taiwan.

Someone's manner of speech was also a consideration. The language in the original text is, to some extent, unrefined or unadorned and plain. There is also the issue of profanity. Some "creative" insults in use in Taiwan have their origins in Hoklo, and although I am not too keen on using harsh language myself, I tried to retain some of it in the translation under a principle of fidelity to the source text, to give the reader a fuller, more realistic view of life. *Banana King* is gritty in some areas and aspects, and I feel the tension brought about by use of profanity deserved to be available for the reader, if only to mark the extent of frustration exuded by some of the characters.

There were occasional terminology snags when translating the novel. My Hoklo teacher—much like our protagonist, Ngôo Tsín-suī, and the author of this work, Mr. Wang-tai Lee—was born to a farming family. She was an invaluable source when handling some idiomatic phrasings or older word choices. Having grown up in the countryside during martial law, she was also a great resource for explaining some cultural norms and the atmosphere from the 1960s and 1970s, such as having to make phone calls from the village head's home, as seen in Part 1 in the novel. Sadly, I have little experience with Hakka, apart from beginner-level textbooks. For any instance where I've transliterated Hakka, I used Sixian dialect spellings to the best extent where I could find online dictionaries and the like. As with Hoklo, I've preferred to use Ministry of Education–related (MOE-related) websites for these spellings. Although I've studied Hoklo using *Peh-oe-ji* (lit. vernacular) spelling, I used the Taiwanese government's *Tai-lo phing-im* (Taiwanese romanization phonetic spelling) system, as I think it's a little easier to read or pronounce.

At the time of translating the work in 2022, it was difficult to find definitions for certain Taiwanese terminology, requiring a lot of sifting through Chinese-language blogs and articles that occasionally went very in depth only to reveal a tiny snippet that could be used. Taiwan's MOE and others have put a lot of effort into expanding Hoklo (and Hakka) language use and research through smartphone dictionary apps, online dictionaries, the *Phah Taigi* app, and other keyboard software, but these resources were not as fleshed out at the time, so there is the possibility of error.

Vocabulary issues I faced mainly came from jargon or area-related choices, such as farm equipment or outdated names of things no longer commonplace. Some issues came from having to read through Mandarin-ized phonetic approximations of Hoklo words in the source text, which made word or phrase searches difficult at times, whereas using proper characters for Hoklo would have been a better choice. This presented a unique challenge, and I would have originally chalked it up to human error; however, the author cannot be blamed since Hoklo, Hakka, and other languages endemic to Taiwan were silenced in official spaces (e.g., schools, government) for over four decades. And languages other than Mandarin Chinese were often illegal to even transcribe. Although Hoklo-specific standardized characters are increasingly used in newer works, most of the writing in the source text was through a more Mandarin Chinese lens. Many Taiwanese have never encountered Hoklo-specific characters, and many have never used either of the two spelling systems incorporating Latin alphabet letters for Hoklo transcription, especially older non-Christian Taiwanese who might not have encountered such writing in a church setting with Bible translations.

Apart from Google searches for smaller place names, one of my great aids was iTaigi.tw. It was a challenge to find some names, as smaller locales aren't generally included. There were some pleasant surprises where I thought, "Surely, this place wouldn't be listed," whereas the opposite was true for larger towns.

When it came to whether to foreignize or localize, I tried to retain as much of the Taiwanese feel of this book as possible. Without going overboard with terms to stifle the reader, I tried to emplace Hoklo words or phrases where it made sense to keep the sentiment intact and to add short glosses or contextualized definitions in nearby sentences that blended in more naturally. In other places, I left the word unexplained, hoping the reader would pick it up through context.

Lastly, as for the editing process, I owe a huge debt to my translation reviewers in Taiwan and the American publisher and their associated editors and proofreaders for their efforts to make this novel to flow well and reach a wider audience. I feel a deep gratitude to them for all their hard work. I'd also like to express my deep gratitude to Mr. Wang-tai Lee and all others in Taiwan who were involved and helped to organize the translation project. Thank you to friends and family who helped me in other ways as I was working my way through multiple drafts and revisions. Thank you to the reader for your interest and for reading this novel (and for reading this far!).

GLOSSARY

A-	When used in front of a person's name, it usually means the speaker has a close relationship with the listener/person with A in front of their name. It can also be used to convey friendliness or soften speech.
-á	Much like the above word, it is used to convey affection or a close relationship. Can also imply smallness, cuteness, or a feeling of love. Usually used for referring to children (at the end of their name).
A-Huàn	the elderly neighbor and "ox-whisperer."
A-hiông	the shopkeeper in Mrs. Ong's ceramics shop.
A-hiann	brother. Also can be used to refer to an older male friend who you would treat like a family member; sometimes used to soften speech.
A-Bú	Mother, Mom, Ma.
âng-bîn-tshn̂g	A bed made from expensive rosewood or other dark wood, intended for a couple. It has connotations of marriage and was a rare item to have in a house in years past as usually only rich families could afford them. Some include pearl inlay, carvings, and other intricate woodwork.

A-só   sister-in-law.

bāng-kah   premonition, vision.

Bí-lông   Meinung township in Kaohsiung County, Kî-san/ Cishan.

hó-khang'   Rich, loaded, wealthy.

phôo-lān-pha   "To hold someone else's family jewels," a euphemism for doing their work or sucking up to someone else. Derogatory/vulgar.

Iûnn   a surname. (Mandarin: Yang)

Ko-hiông   Kaohsiung, the third-largest city in Taiwan and a major port city. Takao in Japanese.

Kî-san   Cishan, a township that is now a major Kaohsiung suburb.

la-jì-io   "radio" from Japanese.

Laʔk-tè-tshù   a Hakka town in Pingtung County.

Lîn-loʔk   the area next to Pingtung City where the banana research farm Tsín-suī first worked at was located.

lóo-laʔt   thank you.

Mî-tsioh-phuē   a cotton tarp/blanket for drying things in the sunlight.

nâ-tâu   pandanus bush / pandan bush.

Ngôo	a surname. (Mandarin: Wu)
Ông	a surname. (Mandarin: Wang)
oo-thóo-bái	*motorcycle, originally Japanese from autobike.*
pháinn-sè	sorry, excuse me, whoops.
Phênn-ôo	Penghu, referring to the Penghu Islands.
Phing-tông or occasionally Pîn-tong	Pingtung, used for either the county or the city.
Poah-pue	Moon(shaped) blocks used in temples for fortune-telling/divining.
Sit-lé	sorry, my apologies.
Tâi-pak	(Japanese) Taihoku. (Mandarin) Taipei.
Tāi-bú-suann	Mt. Dawu or Ta-wu, in southern Taiwan.
Tíng-bīn 頂面	superiors, master, those above.
Tông	A surname. (Mandarin: Tang)
Tông Îng	name of the steel plant in Kaohsiung. Tang-ying in Mandarin.
thài-thài	Mrs.
thâu-ke	boss.

Thâu-tsîng-khe / Thâu-tsîng-khe-á (Tou-Ch'ien-hsi)	The name of Tsín-suí's hometown. Literally means "at the head of the stream/river" and is not an uncommon name in many rural areas around Taiwan. The one mentioned in the novel is within Pingtung City's limits.
tuā-só	older brother's wife.

CHARACTER LIST

A-Liōng	a farmhand who helps Tsín-suī with tillage and other labor in his later years.
Giȯk-bí	Giȯk-ìn's younger sister.
Giȯk-ìn	Tsín-suī's wife, also called A-Ìn-á / Giȯk-ìn-á in an affectionate way.
Ia̍p Tshiu-bo̍k	Tsín-suī's childhood friend on the Pingtung city council and a 228 victim.
Iûnn Kim-hu	another famous banana farmer in southern Taiwan.
Kua Tsìn-hu	the Taiwanese opera director from Chapter 16.
Kueh It-tshing	the doctor and fellow 228 survivor from Chapter 8.
Lîm Kiàn-bûn	a city councilor in Pingtung during the 228 Uprisings who tries to make Tsín-suī take the fall for the violence.
Lôo Á-Tîng / Lôo Tîng	another "banana king" nicknamed "King-tsio-Tîng" or "Banana Tîng."

Ngôo Tsín-suī	our protagonist, nicknamed A-Suī-á, A-Tsín-suī or A-Suī.
Ngôo Tîng-hō	Tsín-suī's younger son.
Ngôo Tîng-kong	Tsín-suī's older son.
Ngôo Tshuo-Ing	Tsín-suī's father.
Ngôo Tsín-lîng	Tsín-suī's youngest brother.
Ngôo Tsín-bûn	Tsín-suī's brother.
Ngôo Tsín-bú	Tsín-suī's brother.
Ngôo Tîng-kong	Tsín-suī's son.
Ngôo Bí-siù	Tsín-suī's younger daughter.
Ngôo Bí-ài	Tsín-suī's older daughter.
Ngôo Sè-hiông 吳世雄	one of Tsín-suī's grandsons.
Ngôo Sè-tiat 吳世哲	one of Tsín-suī's grandsons.
Ông Gio̍k-ìn / A-Ìn-á	Tsín-suī's wife.
Ông thài-thài	Mrs. Ông; Tsín-suī's mother-in-law.
Ông Hōng-thiam	Gio̍k-in's older brother.

Ouyang	an antagonist in the story; a Garrison Command informant placed in the Kaohsiung Green Fruits Export Association in order to spy on employees. He helps mastermind the "Golden Bowl Affair."
Soo Tsòng-phik (A-Tsòng, A-Tsòng-á)	Tsín-suī's neighbor and colleague at the agricultural consortium.
Soo Tsìng-tik (Tsìng-tik-á)	Tsong-phik's son.
Tông Tsuān-tik-á	Tsuān-tsong's brother.
Tông Tsuān-tsong	Tsín-suī's main friend throughout the story, the son of a steel factory magnate who also survives 228 Uprisings, but whose family also falls from grace.
Tân Hīng-tshun	Director of a Taipei shipping consortium/ union and main female protagonist. One of Ngôo Tsín-suī's close friends and confidants throughout his trials and challenges.
Tân Tshâ-bóo	One of the other members of the Taipei agricultural association who develops a rivalry with Tsín-suī.
Tiunn a-thiam-hok / Tiunn Thiam-hok	A rich farmer who lives near Tsín-suī, befriended by the garrison command officer and a rival in the Kaohsiung fruits association.

ABOUT THE TRANSLATOR

Timothy Smith is originally from New Bern, North Carolina, in the southeastern United States. He earned a master's degree from the Graduate Institute of Translation and Interpretation at National Taiwan Normal University. His interests include cultural works and topics by Taiwanese Indigenous authors, Taiwanese Hokkien literature, and exploring different facets of Taiwan's multicultural society. He's an avid horror fan and loves goosebumps-inducing ghost stories and thrillers. Smith is also highly committed to telling stories and uncovering truths regarding Taiwan's authoritarian period and to helping international readers learn about Taiwan's human rights history, which is often neglected and intentionally obscured or sidelined. Apart from Mandarin and Taiwanese Hokkien, Smith also knows a decent amount of Japanese and is currently learning Hakka and Atayal. His translations have appeared in *Books from Taiwan* samples, *The Taipei Chinese PEN*, and other literary magazines and collections.

ABOUT THE AUTHOR

Wang-tai Lee is a seasoned journalist and author and was the most active writer in southern Taiwan for the *Taiwan Political Review* (政論雜誌) and other popular political commentary magazines of the '70s, '80s and '90s. In recent years, Lee has penned several novels, including *Gao Sai Zhe Yi Jia* (2018, Mirror Fiction), *Harima-maru* (2016, Yuanshen Press), and *Du Jiao Ren Wang Guo* (2015, Chun-Hui Books). He is the recipient of a literary award from the 6th HuaiEn Charity Foundation, in addition to both the 1st and 4th Taiwan Historical Novels Award conferred by the New Taiwan Peace Foundation, and he was shortlisted for the 2017 National Museum of Taiwan Literature Awards.